PRAISE FOR

THE DISAPPEARANCE
OF ASTRID BRICARD

"Splashy fashion-world fun with incisive observations about women's roles as muses and inspiration. Natasha Lester's most compelling novel yet!"　　　　—Kate Quinn, *New York Times* bestselling author

"Natasha Lester dazzles."
　　　　　　　　—Marie Benedict, *New York Times* bestselling author

"This spellbinding homage to fashion and feminism is a transporting, page-turning read. I could not put this book down!"
　　　　　　　　—Chanel Cleeton, *New York Times* bestselling author

"A delicious page-turner of love, family, war, and passion."
　　　　　　　　—JoAnn Ross, *New York Times* bestselling author

"No one does glamour, intrigue, and fashion the way Natasha Lester does."　　　　—Heather Webb, *USA Today* bestselling author

"An inspiring story of female vision and grit in the face of insurmountable odds. I absolutely loved it."
　　　　　　　　—Kerri Maher, *USA Today* bestselling author

"An immersive triumph—as sparkly as a silver Lurex mini-dress, as cool as Mick and Bianca, and as atmospheric as a seventies disco. Steamy love affairs, to-die-for clothes, and ballsy women make for a heady must-read."　　　　—Gill Paul, *USA Today* bestselling author

OTHER BOOKS BY NATASHA LESTER

The Paris Seamstress
The Paris Orphan
The Paris Secret
The Riviera House
The Three Lives of Alix St. Pierre

The Disappearance of Astrid Bricard

NATASHA LESTER

FOREVER

NEW YORK   BOSTON

Copyright © 2023 by Natasha Lester

Reading group guide copyright © 2024 by Natasha Lester and Hachette Book Group, Inc.

Cover design by Daniela Medina. Cover images © Alamy; Getty Images; Shutterstock. Cover copyright © 2024 by Hachette Book Group, Inc.

Forever
Hachette Book Group
1290 Avenue of the Americas, New York, NY 10104
read-forever.com
@readforeverpub

First published in Australia and New Zealand in 2023 by Hachette Australia (an imprint of Hachette Australia Pty Limited)

First trade paperback edition: July 2024

Forever is an imprint of Grand Central Publishing. The Forever name and logo are registered trademarks of Hachette Book Group, Inc.

The publisher is not responsible for websites (or their content) that are not owned by the publisher.

The Hachette Speakers Bureau provides a wide range of authors for speaking events. To find out more, go to hachettespeakersbureau.com or email HachetteSpeakers@hbgusa.com.

Forever books may be purchased in bulk for business, educational, or promotional use. For information, please contact your local bookseller or the Hachette Book Group Special Markets Department at special. markets@hbgusa.com.

Library of Congress Control Number: 2023036565

ISBNs: 9781538706961 (trade paperback), 9781538706978 (ebook)

Printed in the United States of America

CW

10 9 8 7 6 5 4 3 2

*For every woman who's ever had a man make her
into someone less than she truly is.*

*And to the Lesters, especially Dick Lester, who did rent a
chateau in the Loire Valley for his enormous family to celebrate
his eightieth birthday. I promise nobody in the fictional family
in this book is based on anyone I'm related to. You are all,
thankfully, much too equable and undramatic to be characters
in this book—and I mean that with love and gratitude.*

Astrid Bricard wasn't just a model. Nor was she just a designer, or just a celebrity. It's impossible to say what she was, just that—if a person could ever be said to represent an era, Astrid Bricard was the 1970s. She was a muse and a myth, and now she's the biggest fashion mystery of all time. What happened to Astrid Bricard? It's a question almost as famous as that silver dress Hawk Jones made for her.

—*Vogue*, "Fashion Legends" issue, 2010

PROLOGUE

In the same way that the Electric Circus nightclub in Manhattan is all about sensual overwhelm, so too is the Hall of Mirrors at the Palace of Versailles, Hawk thinks as he strides into the gallery beside four other men. The club's excess comes from bands like Velvet Underground playing so loudly the music feels like a secondary heartbeat, from the fire-eaters swallowing flames like candy, and from the light show flashing over canvas-draped walls that make you believe the room is leaning inward and, a minute later, that you're the one who's on a slant. But the extravagance here is of a different order, manifested in so many mirrors there's nowhere to hide. Hawk can see himself caught from all sides and reflected a thousand times beneath cathedral-like painted ceilings—the kind that make you feel guilty even when you've done nothing wrong.

For one disquieting second, Hawk wonders if this is what it will come down to—a belief that this kind of history makes French couture supreme, versus six American designers trying to show that a dress meant to writhe to the Rolling Stones is what fashion is now. He wants Astrid to saunter in right now and prove that very fact. But where is she?

He glances over at Bill Blass, dressed as always in tweed and tobacco. Beside him is Oscar de la Renta in dignified black, Stephen Burrows in naiveté, and Halston in self-admiration. Hawk knows better than to ask any of them if they've seen Astrid.

"*Allons-y!*" their French chaperone calls disdainfully, as if he'd rather be accompanying Yves Saint Laurent and the rest of the French team, who everyone believes will whip the Americans so completely that not just their clothes, but their skins will be left in ribbons.

To tell the truth, some days Hawk thinks that too.

As if to bolster Hawk's fears, Hubert de Givenchy—a man Hawk couldn't have named six years ago but who he's now chatted to several times—enters. He's elegant in suit and tie, so intrinsically the French couturier that even the lines on his face look to have been pleated with a seamstress's precision. Hawk almost tugs at the sleeves of his favorite gray sweater but he remembers that he's twenty-eight years old and has earned the right to be there—which maybe only proves how thin on the ground designers are in America.

He looks around again for Astrid before the Hall of Mirrors exposes his agitation. Against all odds, the Americans have to win tonight. Otherwise Hawk and Astrid will never be together—and that's not a thought he wants to even contemplate, let alone have reflected to the whole damn room.

Get it together.

He rubs his hand over the stubble on his jaw and reminds himself that Hawk Jones is the man *Life* called the premier fashion designer in all America.

"*Bonjour.*" Givenchy greets them with a handshake, always a gentleman. "Good luck for this evening."

Halston, who'd as soon be called a gentleman as Hawk would be called conservative, mutters, "Smug asshole," and Hawk sees relief cross Blass's and de la Renta's faces that Halston's expletive wasn't, for once, completely offensive.

And then the mirrors show Hawk some more sober reality. A team of American designers who are really a set of squabbling egos thrown together for a show that everyone from Princess Grace of Monaco to the Duchess of Windsor, as well as every newspaper and magazine across America and Europe, is attending. There they are at the Palace of Versailles about to do battle for their country's honor to be crowned fashion capital of the world, and the five of them are barely on speaking terms and it's seen as a win when Halston doesn't outright tell someone to fuck off.

And the whole of Hawk's happiness is riding on this.

The mirrors shift again. Now they reflect not just his terrified face, but a bundle on the floor near one of the statues. The bundle becomes, with a sudden, sharp twist of his heart, the delectable white column dress he'd seen Astrid making yesterday, a dress he'd believed would make everyone applaud her and acclaim her at last with the recognition she deserves.

Why the hell is the centerpiece of Astrid's collection lying sprawled on the floor of the Hall of Mirrors?

Hawk's feet move him forward. He's halfway across the vast glittering hall before anyone else notices the bundle.

He's three-quarters of the way across when he sees that a crimson sash of savage red now stains the silk.

His feet halt. His head turns away. But all around him, the mirrors double, triple and quadruple the violence of that dress and he swears now, loudly, the sound reverberating as if it might shatter every damn mirror before his fist does.

Because if the red staining Astrid's gown is blood, then he knows that means Astrid is dead or gone—and so too is he.

ACT ONE
THE LEGEND BEGINS...

ONE

ASTRID BRICARD AND HAWK JONES

NEW YORK CITY, JANUARY 1970

Astrid Bricard stands in front of a vitrine, face almost pressed to the glass, mouth, cheeks—even her freckles—curving into a smile that's been waiting to be freed her entire life. She might be twenty-four years old but real life has just started, and hugging the vitrine in the archives of the fashion school at Parsons School of Design would be the best way to celebrate. She leans in closer, bumping her nose against the pane that separates her from the dress.

Most people would see a 1950s dress designed by Claire McCardell. But Astrid sees a genius of fibers. The genesis of every piece of clothing is one single fiber. Not even thread—not yet. But fibers—cleaned and carded and combed, then wound and beamed and woven. A magic whose spells cast out cloths of damask and tweed, of crepon and lush velvet.

"You look like you're planning to put the devil into hell with that dress."

Astrid yelps. There's a man on the other side of the display with a smile on his lips as if he thinks he's delivered a not-half-bad pickup line. He has the kind of effortless good looks that make her think he was probably homecoming king once upon a time.

"I'm at least planning to put the originality into Manhattan with it, which that line never will," she retorts.

He laughs and he finally looks at the dress, rather than her. And she's oddly pleased when he focuses on the single most perfect element of its construction—the sash that crosses over one breast, loops around the back of the neck and then travels down the chest to tie at the side.

"I was thinking about wearing it," she says, her eyes fixed on the knotted sash. "If you tugged the bow just once, the whole thing would tumble to the floor. Maybe that would feel..." She pauses. The bow is both the dress's truss—the only thing holding it together—and its undoing. "It would feel powerful," she concludes.

This man couldn't possibly imagine how good that would feel for a woman—to truly be powerful. But it's what Astrid dreams of, and the smile that settles onto her face as she walks away is both her stay and her strength—but not her undoing.

* * *

"What are you wearing?" a tall girl made taller still by the height of her Afro demands of Astrid at the end of class that day.

Astrid looks down. "A blazer my dad was throwing out."

The girl snorts. "A man's blazer. Just a man's blazer. Nothing else."

"Well, I have underwear on but you'll have to take my word for that." Astrid grins and the girl cackles.

"I'm Velvet. Let's go eat. But first... Graham!" she hollers, and a man lopes over. "I found us another friend. This is—"

"Astrid," she says as they exit onto East 54th Street.

"Velvet and I met at night school a couple of years ago," Graham tells her. "Two people who hadn't finished high school and whose parents didn't want us to go to fashion school." He grins but Astrid knows that behind those words, there's a whole lot that isn't funny.

"My parents don't want me to be here either," she says as they turn into a diner.

"See? I knew she was one of us," Velvet says. "Outcasts unite."

The waitress comes over to take their order. Astrid and Graham give theirs but before Velvet can say anything, the woman turns away.

"I want the burger and fries too," Graham calls out. "And another soda."

"Thanks," Velvet says to Graham, smaller and less magnificent than she had been five seconds ago—before the waitress ignored her and then refused to look her in the face as she added the food to their tab.

Velvet lights a cigarette and exhales smoke. "You better get used to that or you should hang out with someone whiter," she tells Astrid.

And Astrid knows that even though she—a white girl from Long Island—sometimes feels like an outcast, she's braided into life whereas Velvet's holding on to its most frayed threads. But Velvet's stare makes it clear that if Astrid tries to apologize for something that, let's face it, she'll never be able to truly understand, Velvet will leave.

So Astrid nudges Graham. "I already am. He's as white as my confirmation dress."

"You mean you didn't wear a blazer for that?" Velvet says, a smile easing back onto her face.

The food arrives and Graham asks, "Why don't your parents want you to go to fashion school?"

Between mouthfuls of mac and cheese, Astrid explains. "My dad's a lawyer and he wants me to marry one of his junior partners."

Velvet and Graham grimace.

"Exactly. But..." She gestures at the blazer, at the sleek blond hair that sits in a bob just below her chin in opposition to the long locks that are everywhere right now, a style that's entirely and idiosyncratically her own. "I frighten lawyers. Being a fashion designer is the only thing I've ever wanted to do."

Her words are almost tripping over themselves to be told. She's not used to it—the junior partners her father invited for dinner were always the ones with the words. They'd take her for a drive after dinner and she'd direct them to the main street in spite of their urging to go somewhere quiet. She always jumped out at the traffic lights and went to a bar, which earned her a reputation. Never mind the junior partners who wanted to drive a girl to a quiet place to give their tongues an alternative exercise to talking—their reputations were unsullied. But Astrid of the odd clothes, late-evening bar habits and disinterest in lawyers was the one they gossiped about.

"It's the only thing I've ever wanted to do too," Velvet says, nodding fiercely.

"She should come and live with us," Graham says to Velvet, who laughs.

"She probably doesn't want a mattress on the floor of a tiny place in Chelsea."

"A mattress on the floor is about all I can afford," Astrid says almost pleadingly. "I can't keep commuting from my parents' place in Long Island. I need them to believe that wanting to be a fashion designer isn't something I'll grow out of, like when I was a kid who ate peanut butter on her hot dogs."

"Ewww!" Velvet shrieks.

Astrid grins. It's taken her twenty-four years of cajoling, culminating in a promise to her father to earn a ladylike liberal arts degree at Hofstra first. He hoped university would bore her into choosing marriage. Instead, she finished her degree. Which meant he had to stick to his side of the deal—that she could go to Parsons if she paid for it herself. She's spent the last six months working on a portfolio that won her a coveted scholarship and allowed her to start a year and a half into the course. And now she has two friends and a place to live.

Life is totally disco.

* * *

Hawk drops his rucksack by the door of the Park Avenue apartment, saunters into the kitchen and kisses his mother on the cheek.

She ruffles his hair.

"Hey," he mock-complains, taking a soda out of the fridge, still thinking about the girl from Parsons. He'd gone to the archives for inspiration—he needs to make something new for his shop, but everything he draws is less than he wants it to be. And he'd found her, wearing only a slim-fitting blazer and staring at a dress, lids half-closed, the curves of her body defined in a way that's now passé— the only girl in New York City who hasn't thrown away her bra. His hand had been suddenly desperate to draw a dress onto her body that made it look like she'd had her 1960s undergarments ravished off her.

He blinks, startled by the force of the memory. "I met a girl today," he says.

"So what's new, HJ?" his mother quips, then lifts an eyebrow. "Ah. She got the better of you. Or"—she smiles wistfully—"you've just experienced a *coup de foudre*."

"What if it's both?" he asks, serious in a way he's never been about his mother's badly pronounced French phrases and notions of love at first sight.

Meredith Jones sits on a stool, takes out a cigarette and says, "*Coup de foudre* also means lightning bolt. One flash of brilliance and then all you have is a dull gray sky. Maybe if you saw her again, that's all she'd be and you'd wonder what trick of the light made you think she was more."

But he doesn't want to imagine that a girl who thinks being unraveled from a dress gives her power could dull to gray upon a second meeting.

"I'll take Dad his dinner," he says.

He finds his dad in bed, a Babe Ruth biography propped in front of him. Hawk sets down the tray and picks up the baseball from the bedside table, throwing it laconically at the wall, which bears the marks of him having done this same thing for months now—catching the ball, tossing it back.

"Good?" he asks, gesturing at the book, the thud of the ball drowning out the slurping sound his father makes when he eats, a sound that embarrasses the hell out of him. Hence the ball, a trick Hawk had landed on by accident, and that had almost made him cry when his father had said, at the end of that first meal accompanied by the ball's percussion, "Thanks, son."

Hawk had had to run from the room because his father didn't need him crying over that *coup de foudre* of a different kind—a lightning bolt of a stroke that had hit nine months before, leaving a brain ruined by the tempest. Matthias's face drooped, his words were slurred, and he had to make a tremendous effort to hold anything in his right hand. The idea of him returning to being a lawyer who could command a bag of gold just by answering the phone seemed as remote to Hawk as his mother ever falling out of love with Matthias and taking up with a man who wasn't twenty years older and semi-infirm.

"Babe Ruth wasn't really an orphan," his father says carefully so that his tongue doesn't render the words incoherent. "He went to an industrial school for orphans, but only because he was so much trouble."

Hawk laughs. "Don't get any ideas."

"You're twenty-four, kid. You'll be moving out and leaving us before too long."

There's an empty space above his shop. It would be the perfect place to live. But if he did that, then his mom would be the only one left here to care for his dad.

Hawk puts the ball down, needing to get out of there—away from the shitty future he can foresee for the two people he loves most in the world. "Night, Dad."

In the kitchen, he catches his mother in an unguarded moment. Her hands are pressed to the countertop, a Tom Collins sweating in a glass between them. She's staring at the wedding ring on her left hand, maybe remembering the way she used to dance with her husband every night, in love in a way Hawk wants to be one day—but worries he'll never be good enough for.

"I'll stay in tonight," he says, even though he wants music and whiskey and to figure out, now that he's graduated college and opened a shop, how to achieve what he wants his own life to be—a span of years that will never be disrupted by lightning.

"No." His mother is firm. "I need to have a little cry, and I want to do it alone."

Fuck. He wraps his mother in his arms, kisses the top of her head and she pushes him away with the kind of smile that could break your heart.

* * *

At the end of the week, everyone in Astrid's class has to make a short presentation about someone from fashion history who wasn't a designer, but who influenced fashion. Velvet begins, gliding to the front as if the room is her runway. She holds up a magazine, back cover facing the class.

"This is *Vogue*," she says. She flips the magazine to the front. On the cover is a Black model.

"British *Vogue*," Velvet clarifies. "Meet Donyale Luna. She's American, but American *Vogue* has never put a Black girl on the cover. Needless to say, Donyale lives in London now. She's the first Black woman ever to grace the cover of *Vogue*. If that's not influencing fashion, I don't know what is. But will *Vogue* here ever be influenced by her?"

It's like Velvet's put a grenade in the middle of the room. Everyone's frozen, waiting for it to explode. People don't talk about these things so accusingly.

Astrid sticks her fingers in her mouth and whistles. "Go Donyale!"

The class startles into polite applause. Velvet takes her seat next to Astrid and says, "I bet she's the only person we see today who isn't white."

The next presentation by Candace Winters supports that theory. But that's not why Astrid feels sick when she sees the photocopied picture Candace holds.

"Christian Dior is the one designer who influenced fashion more than any other," Candace begins. "This is his muse, Mizza Bricard."

All of Astrid's joy curls up inside her like heated silk. She ought to have known someone would choose Mizza. Which means Astrid has to say it—everyone will find out soon enough. Even at conservative Hofstra it happened, although they weren't fashion people and didn't quite understand the implications. But here at fashion school, there won't be a single person who doesn't, and if Astrid reveals the fact rather than waits for it to be discovered, she might be able to control the fallout rather than looking like she has something to hide.

"Nobody knows where she came from," Candace continues. "She was either a dancer in a nude revue or a prostitute. She lived at the Ritz, never wore panties, but always wore fur coats—and not much else."

Astrid stands, cutting off the applause, and Candace glares. "Can I go next?" she asks the teacher.

He nods. "Let's hear from our Claire McCardell scholarship winner."

Great. Now more than a few students, who maybe didn't get the scholarship, are eyeing her.

Astrid tells herself to run at it like tequila minus the sunrise. "I'm Astrid Bricard," she says. "I'm adopted. My birth mother was…" It won't come out, those two words that have defined her life and will continue to define her unless she does something about it.

"My birth mother was Mizza Bricard," she says way too loudly.

The rustle sweeping around the room is one part shocked, and one part suspicious.

"You're the daughter of Christian Dior's muse?" Candace says, eyes narrowed, as if she thinks that's the only reason Astrid's standing there as the scholarship winner.

One of them, they were told yesterday, will leave Parsons and become a name designer. Five will serve name designers. The rest will be doing something else in five years. But of course Mizza Bricard's daughter can just stroll into the House of Dior and get herself a job in couture—she doesn't have to work at it.

But Astrid *does*. Harder than anyone. Because Mizza was just a stimulus. Astrid is determined to be the response.

"This," Candace says, tapping her finger on the photocopied page, "is your mother."

Astrid knows what Candace is doing. She's not clarifying the situation. She's making everyone look at the photo. While Mizza's been photographed by everyone from Avedon to Beaton, this is the image that encapsulates the famous muse. Mizza's wearing a fur coat, body leaning toward the camera. A long strand of pearls dives into her cleavage and the coat has slipped down her arm, baring the top of her breasts to the rim of her areola. She has a smile on her face that is most definitely come-hither.

Say the word *muse* and everyone thinks *scarlet woman*. Show a muse in fur, jewels and bared skin and everyone thinks *whore*. Or worse. Muses are the kind of women who don't even get paid for all the sex they put out there. Instead, they crave it.

Before Dior died, Mizza came to New York each year with him and she'd travel to Long Island to visit Astrid. Because Dior was more famous than the Statue of Liberty, and nobody could miss a woman who dressed like Mizza, her mother's friends would pop in on the same day Mizza appeared in a leopard-print coat and more jewels than a Tiffany window, utterly out of place in green-lawned suburbia, where everyone wore white gloves, hats, and one modest strand of pearls that never made acquaintance with one's cleavage. There, as in much of America, Bill Blass's style was the only style—*women should look terribly clean and healthy and fresh*, he's fond of saying.

Nobody would put *clean* and *Mizza* in the same sentence.

It's Astrid's mission to make sure her name and Mizza's are never used in the same sentence either.

At the end of class, Candace catches up to her. "So that's how you got the scholarship."

A group gathers behind Candace. Be it high school, Hofstra or Sunday school, one girl, whose power is derived from her cruelty— a girl who makes it her business to discover everyone's most vulnerable places so she can prod them often and publicly—makes Mizza into Astrid's scandal.

"The muse's daughter," Candace continues, each word tattooing the label deeper into Astrid's skin.

But Candace isn't the first, nor will she be the last, to say that. "Or the whore's daughter," Astrid says nonchalantly. She makes herself continue, even though maybe now she's being as mean as Candace. "I'm sorry you didn't get the scholarship."

The intake of breath is audible. And Astrid knows from the look on Candace's face that she was right. Astrid has something Candace wanted. And Candace will be nipping at her heels for the next eighteen months. Which means Astrid can't allow herself to be harassed at the one place she's fought so hard to get to.

"Being Mizza Bricard's daughter isn't like being the daughter of an astrophysicist," Astrid continues mildly. "At most, I inherited strong cheekbones. If that's my sole fortune, I'll have spent it in a couple of years. Luckily I don't rely on Mizza for anything and I make my own fortune."

She'd meant it to come out like bland fact. Spoken aloud, it sounds like a challenge. On one side, Astrid: Mizza Bricard's daughter, possessor of great cheekbones and—Astrid hopes—a hell of a lot more. On the other side: everyone who wants to make Astrid into the daughter of a seductress, aligned with Candace—most likely nobody's daughter, possessor of a more ruthless ambition than Astrid's own.

"We'll see about that," Candace says, as if yes, this is a challenge and it's one she intends to win.

But so does Astrid. There'll come a day when nobody will be able to call Astrid the muse's daughter ever again.

* * *

She's surprised when she hears Velvet yell, "Wait up!" and even more surprised when she turns to see both Velvet and Graham hurrying after her.

"So we really are the outcasts then," Velvet says as she links her arm through Astrid's.

For the first time that day, Astrid laughs. Because it seems as if, despite everything and unlike back in Long Island, she has two friends.

"We should go to a party," Graham says. "Let off some steam."

Which is how Astrid finds herself in a huge loft space on Broadway, the home of a friend of a friend of Graham's.

"You gotta pay two bucks," Graham tells her as they approach. "It's a rent party."

It takes a few moments for Astrid to figure out that a rent party means Graham's friend's friend opens up his loft for parties to help offset the rent. "Is there anything you can't sell in Manhattan?" she says.

"Just your morals." Graham winks. "You give those away for free." And he throws himself into the Dionysian beat of the dance floor.

Through a sound system the likes of which Astrid has never seen, the host is playing an eclectic but danceable selection of jazz and classical, soul and funk. Colored balloons bump against her arms and Velvet's as they groove, Astrid's floppy felt wide-brim hat long gone, white

tank top clinging to her skin from sweat. Eventually, Velvet beckons
to her and, breathless from the dancing and the smoke that makes it
impossible to see past her fingers, they move to the outer edges of the
room. They each grab a banana and a drink from the table that holds
none of the usual stimulants, only fruit, nuts and juice—it's BYO highs
and lows, Graham explained earlier—and collapse into a beanbag.

"That was just what I needed," Astrid says.

Velvet laughs. "The bananas or the balloons?"

Astrid laughs too, then elbows Velvet in the ribs. "Thanks."

"Anytime I can provide bananas to compensate for the bitches, just
lemme know."

Astrid remembers the challenge in Candace's eyes and her laughter
dies. She fights against the tears that are competing with the grass
haze to blur the room, trying to think of something other than herself
right now because, as far as acts of generosity go, Velvet's compassion
ought to earn her a halo.

"A girl who grew up as a lawyer's daughter in Long Island and
who got to finish high school and a liberal arts degree probably doesn't
have much to complain about to you," she says.

Velvet shrugs. "When you told Candace that you were going to
make your own fortune, I wanted to applaud. Because it's not fair but
it's fact—just like you don't want to be anything like your mother,
I don't want to be like mine. I have seven siblings and my mom did
her best, but by age fifteen, I was sitting at the dining table doing
alterations so we could make rent, rather than going to school. I'd
look at her across the table and I'd want to say, 'Make him use a fucking condom.' Feeding only three or even four kids might have meant
I could stay at school. I hated that she was so passive that I paid for my
dad's aversion to rubbers."

Astrid sips her juice, wishing it was a joint, which might ease the
tension in her jaw. Her words grind out. "And I hate that, as a muse,
my birth mother existed only to make a man great—that she had

no greatness of her own. Here we are with Betty Friedan saying the world depends on women's passive dependence and that femininity makes us a target and a victim of the sexual sell, and I see that photo of Mizza in my head, all sex and dependence, and I want to scream. Then there's my adoptive mom, who's exactly the woman in the kitchen Friedan's railing against."

Her fingers curl around her cup. "So I have both the mother who's the embodiment of the feminine mystique and the mother who uses her cleavage to inspire a man. And Betty also says that if we excise our femininity, we'll finally be powerful. I don't believe that."

She gestures at her white tank top, underneath which she isn't wearing a bra, like half the girls in the room. "Show your cleavage if you want. Stand naked at the front of a room wearing a temptress's smile. Screw around. But do it for yourself because it makes *you* feel good. Don't do it to make a man great. So it's not just that I don't want to be Mizza. It's that I want to take women's fashion, which is the epitome of this supposedly terrible thing called femininity, and I want to make clothes that are both beautiful *and* give women back their power—clothes that damn well never make them feel like their only job is to make a man more powerful."

The music shifts from effortless groove to something more anthemic, matching the urgency inside Astrid in this strange place where LSD blotters pass from hand to mouth as unabashedly as the private and ineloquent wishes that have just pulsed out of her like blood.

She tugs Velvet up and spins them both around to the crescendo of music and limbs and darkness. She tips her head back and feels it all on her face—the rhythm of the future.

"I'm not the muse's daughter," she says to Velvet. "And you're not the girl who wasn't allowed to finish high school. Let's both believe that, and we'll do all the rest too."

They spin and they spin until they're higher on belief and dreams than any of the day-trippers dropping acid in the corner.

TWO

BLYTHE BRICARD

PARIS, DECEMBER 2012

The taxi speeds into Paris from the airport, en route to taking Blythe and her kids to...*their doom*, she thinks wryly. When she'd received the invitation from her ex-husband Jake's parents to their fiftieth wedding anniversary celebration, her eyebrows had arched so high they'd just about waxed themselves. On the back, Jake's brother Ed had written, *Mom has cancer—late stage. This is the last chance we have to get everyone together. It's just three weeks—and in a French chateau. I'll make sure Jake isn't a total dick while we're there. Mom and Dad want to spend some time with Sebby and Eva. And they want to see you too.*

It was blackmail, but of course she'd agreed. What kind of person says no to the request of a dying woman she had once loved?

"One night in Paris and three weeks in a castle!" seven-year-old Eva says, bouncing up and down. "Will it have a moat?"

Blythe's laugh turns into a frown as Sebby coughs beside her. "Are you okay? I'll give you some more Ventolin at the hotel." She's already given him a healthy dose but her five-year-old's asthma is violent and unpredictable.

Then Eva squeals. "Look, Mommy! Isn't that Great-Grandma Mizza?"

Blythe's body tenses. They're outside the House of Dior. She'd read that Mizza Bricard was the inspiration for the latest collection and there she is, in leopard print, jewels and plunging necklines, all over the windows, an inscrutable little smile on her lips that suggests more than naked flesh ever could. Dior's designer said in an interview in *Vogue* last month that Mizza never wore any underwear, salacious gossip that's put the whole Bricard saga back in the headlines, which Blythe could do without.

"Yep, that's my granny," she says facetiously.

The taxi moves forward and Blythe relaxes.

The Hôtel Grand Powers blends so perfectly into the white stone and wrought-iron façades of the street—which is why Blythe likes it—that Eva stares, puzzled, having missed the unobtrusive black awning.

"This way, darling," Blythe says, taking Eva's and Sebby's hands as they slide out of the taxi.

"Blythe Bricard. Checking in for one night," she says to the receptionist, who stares for a second too long and Blythe knows she knows who she is.

Her suspicions are confirmed when the receptionist steps away to get the room key and whispers to another woman, who then levels a set of eyeballs Blythe's way.

Blythe sighs, pushes her sunglasses onto her head and shoves her hands in the pockets of the admittedly fabulous gold lamé Hawk Jones jumpsuit she'd worn in case the paps who haunt the airports were having a slow news day. And then she sees, open on the counter, a copy of *Paris Match*. There's Blythe at the premiere of *Atelier* last week, a film she'd designed the costumes for and which, along with the dress she'd worn that night, have reignited the buzz that follows her around like an earworm. Six months ago, while her name often came before her, it would have been fifty-fifty that she could pass through a hotel unnoticed. This month, it's more like a certainty she won't. She hustles the kids to the elevator before anyone points a phone her way.

Once in their room, Blythe tries not to think how much this one night is costing. Her kids deserve a night in a gorgeous Parisian hotel after everything they've been through the last couple of years. She's been saving every spare penny for months and, looking at Eva and Sebby's faces as they step onto the balcony and stare at the Eiffel Tower, she knows it's been worth it.

"Mommy, it's so pretty," Eva enthuses.

Yes it is, Blythe thinks, staring at black iron threaded onto a silvery sky that's threatening storms—except you don't have to be a weather forecaster to know the next couple of weeks will be nothing but tempestuous. Staying in a chateau with Jake, who she hasn't even spoken to in six months. Seeing his mom unwell. And the meeting Blythe is due at in just one hour.

Enjoy the moment, she tells herself. Her. The kids. Paris. That's a darn good trifecta.

She bobs down, wrapping her arms around them. Eva's fingers slip into her hair and Sebby takes out the old camera Blythe gave him and snaps a photo. He checks the screen and says, "It's a really good one."

Blythe blinks at the way their bodies are huddled together in the kind of closeness that makes your heart hurt. Their smiles outdo the tower behind them. She kisses his cheek. "It's the best."

But it's December and in the mid-thirties outside. Sebby's lungs are rebelling at the cold. She gives him another six puffs of Ventolin and says, "The babysitter will be here in half an hour. I won't be gone more than two hours."

Neither Eva nor Sebby slept well on the plane last night and they're both eyeing the big bed the same way they ordinarily gape at candy bars. So she tucks them in, turns on the TV, and touches up her makeup. When the sitter arrives, Blythe checks to make sure Seb's okay and asks the sitter to call if he gets worse. Then she leaves for the offices of Champlain Holdings, which are only a few doors down—a red-carpet length from the House of Dior and the photos of Blythe's grandmother. Across the road is LVMH, the group's main competitor in the fashion and luxury goods market besides Jake's business, which charged out of near bankruptcy more than a year ago and is now performing spectacularly well.

As she walks, she texts her friend Remy. *Remind me why you convinced me to say yes to this meeting?*

A reply pings instantly.

This is your moment, Blythe. Rather than being hot just because you're Astrid and Hawk's love child, you're hot right now because of your work. I know it's not exactly the kind of work you've always wanted to do but seize the day anyway. xx PS—It mightn't sound like it but I love you. PPS—Have you told Jake?

Right then, the sun drifts out, a sequin of gold softened by gauzy clouds. What if she just tilted her head up, let the sun fall on her face the way it's falling on the six stories of cream stone beside her and walked into this meeting like it might be something good, rather than expecting it to be another intrusion on a life already well trespassed? Remy's right. Costume designer isn't her first choice of occupation but if anyone else had their damn face in *Paris Match* they'd be toasting the gods of fortune.

You're right, she texts Remy. *I was being a spoiled brat but now I'm an optimistic bubble of champagne. PS—Have I told Jake I'm having a meeting with his biggest competitor? Mmmm, no, I haven't broached that subject yet.*

* * *

"You must get told this all the time, but you're somehow the exact replica of both Astrid and Hawk," is Nathaniel Champlain's greeting to Blythe. "And that is a great outfit," he adds, eyeing her jumpsuit over which she's thrown a coat refashioned from an ankle-length seventies leather trench.

She'd loved the wide lapels, but wanted it to hit at mid-thigh, so she'd attacked it with scissors and sewing machine. It's what she does when she's not making costumes for movies—resurrecting and refashioning damaged clothes from decades ago and turning them into something new and wearable. It barely pays the bills, and right now Blythe has the enviable problem of being overrun with orders she doesn't have time to make. But nor does she have the money to decline them, nor the money to turn her cottage industry into a business, which is what she most wants—what she's always wanted, in fact.

"Is it one of Hawk's?" he asks.

She nods, smiling as if she doesn't wear jumpsuits designed by her dad in order to quash the stories about her and Hawk never speaking. "The jacket's mine," she says.

She follows him to a boardroom with a magnificent view of ballgown-shaped Belle Époque domes. Nathaniel sits and turns a remote control over in his fingers. "I have a spectacular presentation," he says. "But I'm sure, now I've met you, that it won't work."

"What is it about me that says I don't like spectacular presentations?"

"It was a compliment."

He walks over to the window, leans against the sill, and it's just him and the Eiffel Tower filling her vision. He's good-looking, nearly ten years older than her, a tinge of gray feathering the edges of his brown hair, his jaw more square than Jake's and also more clean-shaven.

Without preamble he says, "I want Champlain Holdings to resurrect MIZZA. And I want you to be its creative director."

There's nothing he could have said that would have stunned her more. Nobody is resurrecting MIZZA, her mother Astrid's infamous clothing label.

"I get that you're reluctant—"

She cuts him off. "Reluctant is a massive understatement."

"Hear me out," he says. "Then you can congratulate yourself on having reached the decision logically rather than emotionally."

Patronizing sonofa—

Blythe gathers herself. She's faced off worse attacks than this. Being the granddaughter of Christian Dior's famous muse and the daughter of Hawthorne Jones and his legendary muse, Astrid, means she's nothing if not battle-hardened. But what the hell has she done to offend the gods so hugely that they're about to trap her in a chateau with her ex-husband for three weeks, and now they're forcing her to think about Astrid in front of a man she doesn't know?

She gives a wryly amused smile. "Fine. Dazzle me with your logic." She can't storm off. Women like her who don't play nice are savaged in headlines, chewed over on social media and spat out stripped of flesh.

"You're one hell of a talented designer, Blythe. The piece you made for Cate Blanchett to wear to the Oscars last year has just been bought from her by the Met for half a million dollars." He pushes over a magazine that's sitting in the middle of the table. "*Vogue*'s 'Fashion Who's Who' was published today. Take a look."

Her eyes follow his finger to the page.

Bricard, Mizza: widely considered to be the world's first fashion muse. Prior to inspiring Dior to greatness, Mizza was rumored to have been a courtesan, whose lovers furnished her with a spectacular jewelry collection. She had a fondness for leopard print, a passion that inspired at least one of the House of Dior's codes.

Bricard, Astrid: muse Mizza's daughter. Also a fashion muse, but to Hawk Jones and, notoriously, his lover for a time. Created her own label, MIZZA, in the 1970s, which is much sought after today by vintage fashionistas. Disappeared during the Battle of Versailles in 1973, presumed by some to have been murdered over a drug deal gone wrong, by others to have vanished after an altercation with Hawk's new inspiration, former college mate Candace Winters, whose blood was found mixed with Astrid's on the white silk dress Astrid left behind.

Bricard, Blythe: Hawk and Astrid's love child—daughter and granddaughter of a muse. Despite belonging to a fashionably fabled clan and showing flashes of brilliance in costume design and dressing celebrities, she hasn't lived up to expectations, although her sartorial style is much admired.

Below that are the three most famous photographs of the three women. First, the Louise Dahl-Wolfe shot of Mizza that's hanging in the Dior windows. Second, Astrid dancing on a podium at the Cheetah nightclub in 1970, wearing a minuscule silver lamé dress. Last is Blythe, hiding behind sunglasses, giving the finger to the press.

She hasn't absorbed the article's stinging assessment of her when Nathaniel flips through a few pages and points to another name.

Jones, Hawk (Hawthorne): Hugely successful creator of the Hawk Jones label, which is as modish today as when he launched the brand in the seventies. There are few designers who can lay claim to having presided over a fashion empire for decades the way he has. Even the loss of his muse, Astrid Bricard, couldn't stop him from ruling the sartorial world.

Blythe is tempted to toss the magazine at Nathaniel. Before she can, he says, "I heard that you've wanted to have your own label, recycling and remaking vintage pieces, ever since you left FIT. When was that?"

He keeps going, answering his own question. "Eleven years ago. I also heard that you and Jake Black had a deal after you finished grad school. He'd start up his business first, and then it'd be your turn to do the same. What happened to your turn? You make sensational costumes for movies—but only if they're shooting in New York, because you have to look after your kids. You spend your time between those flashes of brilliance making one-offs for suburban moms and minor celebrities to wear to charity balls. I don't believe it satisfies you at all."

There's a shocking prickle of tears in the corners of Blythe's eyes. *Please don't let me cry. Not here, not now.* Not over this legacy she'll never be rid of. She wants to accuse Nathaniel of misogyny—how many women have time to be satisfied? But she knows it isn't just time she lacks. Just like she knows that being creative director of MIZZA and resurrecting the legend of her mother won't make her happy.

What will?

"For two years in the seventies, MIZZA was everything," Nathaniel continues, relentless. "It's a cult brand, even though not a single thing has been made under that name for forty years. Hate it and fear it, if that's how you want to get through life. Or you could reign over it instead. With complete creative freedom, a hell of a lot of money and the backing of my company behind you."

He shrugs. "That's my pitch. When you want more details, give me a call."

He thinks surprising her with his idea and lecturing her about her life is a pitch? Everyone wants to tell Blythe how to live her life. *Be more like Astrid. Don't be like Astrid. Be like Hawk. Or Mizza. Or all goddamn three.*

When a photograph of your mother dancing in the shortest possible silver dress with half her ass showing has become a metonym for an entire decade—to publish an article or write a book about the 1970s and not include that shot of Astrid and Hawk is like trying to separate Neil Armstrong from the moon—then you grow up to be a certain kind of person. Everyone thinks your preferences must also be for nudity and exhibitionism and, of course, sex. It's a hell of a thing to have to grapple with as a child, as a teenager, as a woman, and now, as a mother. And if she'd thought it before, being Eva and Seb's mom has made her learn the truth of it—Blythe's only purpose in life is to be nothing and nobody. That's what she decided the first time four-year-old Eva came home from school in tears because one of the older kids told her she was descended from sluts, so she must be a slut too. Eva hadn't even known what a slut was, just that it was bad, and that dancing on a table while someone groped your ass made you one.

The only way to make everyone forget is to be unmemorable. Except Blythe's just designed the costumes for a movie everyone's raving about, and she stood on a red carpet in a gorgeous dress and let herself not just be photographed, but feel good about what she'd made. And now she regrets it for the damage it might do to her life's goal—that Eva won't spend the whole of high school, the whole of her life, trying to avoid boys and men and a voracious media who just want her to dance on a table minus her underwear.

She stands. "That wasn't a pitch. I know what you stand to get out of this. Money. Another brand in your stable. A publicity storm. But what do I get besides a title? Call me when you're ready to tell me exactly what you're offering."

He might go to the media and call her a bitch. That's what women who refuse to just roll over are usually called. But Blythe Bricard has never lain down and been the woman everyone wants her to be.

* * *

Blythe strides down to the Seine, needing to expunge the anger before she returns to her kids. She jams her earbuds in her ears, drenches her mind with Fleetwood Mac—an addiction to seventies music something that lives in her genes and one she can't renounce no matter how hard she tries. She's thinking about dresses—silk jersey and V-necklines, cashmere that molds to the skin like a lover's body. All the things she could make with a company like Champlain Holdings behind her. All the things she's been wanting to make since she had, as Nathaniel reminded her, left grad school and made a deal with Jake that neither of them had upheld.

She pulls out her earbuds and sets off for the hotel. She, Sebby and Eva have found an easy equilibrium these last few months, almost two years on from Blythe's divorce from Jake. She was the one who walked out back then, unsettling everything about their lives. Now she's her kids' only fixed point and they don't deserve for her to throw a MIZZA and Astrid bombshell into their peace and disrupt everything again.

As soon as she steps into the room, she can hear Sebby's lungs wheezing. "I told you to call me if he got worse," she snaps at the babysitter, who looks up from her phone as if she's only just remembered why she's there.

Blythe checks her watch. She can't give him another dose of steroids yet. She pumps more Ventolin into him, waits a few minutes and knows they won't be spending tonight in this plush bed. "Eva, darling, can you get your water bottle and some books? Grab my iPad too."

"Are we going to the hospital?" Eva asks quietly.

Blythe nods, packs Sebby's favorite plush puppy and a toothbrush, picks up her son and tries not to think the worst when she feels how hard his chest is working. The cab ride is interminable—Eva's serious eyes are fixed on her, and Sebby's breathing sounds more like screaming.

But they've been through this before, she reminds herself as the panic swirls. They'll be okay this time too.

She smiles reassuringly at Eva while she frantically considers who she can call to take care of her daughter. Back in New York, one of Eva's friends' moms would always help out. But in Paris, who? Jake should be here by now but...

The red and white *Urgences* sign comes into view at last.

They're ushered straight through and time passes in that way it does in hospitals in the evening when there's so much waiting in between frenetic periods of activity. When all you do is stare at your child, not wanting to miss even the slightest deterioration, as if by sheer strength of will you can make them better.

Eva sits in Blythe's lap pressing sticker dresses onto paper dolls until Blythe can't feel her legs anymore. One of the nurses keeps coming in to ask about Astrid and Hawk, telling Blythe that as a teenager, she had the photo of Astrid in the silver dress dancing with Hawk pinned to her wall.

"That time when they held hands walking onto the stage at that fashion awards thing, when they won't look at each other but you can just see how hard they're holding on—that's one of the most romantic things," the nurse gushes, and Blythe knows she's talking about the movie that came out in the eighties about the tragic love story of Astrid Bricard and Hawk Jones.

"It probably never happened like that," Blythe says and the nurse looks like Blythe just murdered a unicorn. Again there's that crushing sense that despite being stressed out and wanting to focus on her kid, she has to worry about being nice, otherwise the bitchy Blythe stories will start up again, no doubt accompanied by photos of Sebby alone the one time she leaves to use the bathroom.

When the doctors finally decide Seb should be okay with a bit more oxygen, meds and time, and that he'll most likely be fine by morning, Blythe calls Jake.

He doesn't answer. He never does.

"Okay," she says to Eva as she grapples with solutions. "You know I have to stay with Seb?"

Eva nods, her serious eyes back, fear there too.

"I will never leave you, darling," Blythe says almost too ferociously.

Eva buries her face in her mother's shoulder. Blythe strokes her hair, glad that Eva can't see she's almost losing the fight against her own tears, against the memory of a mother who did leave, a long time ago. She shoves it all back down into the dead place in her soul that Astrid left behind when she vanished in November 1973.

"What if I call Ed?" she says. "You could stay with him and Auntie Joy and your cousins? I bet they're in a super-fancy hotel."

"I liked our hotel," Eva says, and Blythe knows her daughter just wants to stay in her lap, Blythe's hands brushing over her hair. "But okay."

So Blythe calls her ex-brother-in-law. Saint that he is, Ed says he'll come get Eva and take her on the coach tomorrow that's ferrying all twenty-eight members of the family party to the Loire Valley.

"I'll rent a car and catch up with you," Blythe tells him.

There's a pause and she knows what he's thinking. "He didn't answer," she tells him.

Ed exhales a disappointed stream of air. Blythe just shrugs. She gave up being disappointed in Jake a long time ago. It's easier to expect him to let you down right up front.

Eva dispatched, Blythe spends an almost sleepless night by Sebby's side, drinking too much coffee and waking with a jolt anytime her eyes close for more than five minutes. By late morning, the doctors are happy. She calls Ed briefly and speaks to Eva, who says that Coco and Georgia, two of Ed's five kids, are teaching her a card game.

"I'm proud of you, darling," Blythe tells her and she can hear Eva's smile through the phone. *That's how easy it is to make your child happy, Astrid*, she thinks. One second and four words of praise. Parenting isn't so hard that you need to run away from it.

She hangs up and exhales. She's exhausted and starving and honestly feels like her legs might give way, but none of that matters because she got through another crazy juggle and everyone is okay. She scarfs a bag of potato chips so she doesn't pass out, and by the time she gets back to Seb, he's giggling at a movie on her iPad.

"Ready to go live in a castle?" she asks him.

"Yes!"

Once in the rental car, Sebby dozing in the back seat, it's tempting to let her mind wander back to her meeting with Nathaniel. But what last night proved was that she's stretched too thin already. Yes, she only takes on costume jobs when the movie is based in New York, like Nathaniel said—but she doesn't have a husband she can leave her kids with to go off to LA or Romania or New Zealand to run a wardrobe department. Jake's never had the kids for more than one night and he hasn't seen them at all for six months. He doesn't answer his phone because he couldn't even imagine there might be an emergency. She doesn't have a nanny because she can't afford one for a start, but also because she grew up without a mother and she won't let her kids be brought up by someone else. So she can't just go and be a creative director in a full-time job in Paris or wherever, because Eva and Sebby come first.

Just drive, she tells herself grimly. And definitely don't think about whatever hell she's driving into on the cusp of a three-week vacation with her ex-husband.

THREE

ASTRID BRICARD AND HAWK JONES

That day feels nothing at all like history when it begins. Astrid climbs off her mattress on the floor and grabs a man's white business shirt she'd found at a thrift store for fifty cents. She ties it around her waist like a sarong, the memory of the dress she'd seen in the archive last month weaving into her subconscious. The sleeves become the sash that she ties into a bow and which, when tugged, would make the whole thing tumble to the floor.

Velvet laughs. "Only you would think of doing that and would make it look so damn hot. And what is that T-shirt?"

"I bought it in the kids department," Astrid tells Velvet. It's a shade between turquoise and aquamarine, the color the afternoon sun would dye the water out at Gilgo when Astrid waited on her surfboard for a wave. "Nobody uses colors like this for adults' clothes. They should."

"*You* should," Velvet says as they take the subway to college, hungover enough to prefer the subterranean dark, but sober enough to be on time.

They've just taken their seats in the design studio when the man Astrid met in the archives walks in.

"Who's that?" she asks Velvet.

"I forget you weren't here last year," Velvet replies and Graham says, "That's Hawk Jones. A damn fine man."

"Hawk?" Astrid repeats.

"Somehow short for Hawthorne." Velvet shrugs. "I guess it was too much of a mouthful."

"Hawthorne." Astrid samples the word. It *is* a mouthful. A word that sits both on the top of your tongue and also in the deep recesses of your throat and she doesn't know why but the thought makes her flush. "He doesn't look like the fashion type."

Graham laughs. "No, he isn't the fashion type."

Astrid's been at Parsons long enough to understand something she rarely encountered in her lawyerly Long Island neighborhood. That fashion attracts everyone from conventionally married designers like Oscar de la Renta, to those who don't think about girls the way she's been told they should, like Graham.

While Hawk Jones confers with their teacher, Velvet tells her more. "He started out in advertising, then moved to photography and ended up in fashion by accident. One time, the dean dragged him to a Norman Norell workshop. So there's Hawk, who can't sew and who had no idea who Norell was"—Velvet rolls her eyes at this—"somehow draping silk into an outfit Norell declared was maybe better than anything *he* could make. He's good with his hands." Velvet winks. "Makes it hard to settle on one thing."

She says it like a warning but Astrid doesn't need one. Her future plans don't allow for men with predatory names to circle.

"He graduated last summer and opened his own boutique a few months ago," Graham adds. "It's not what you do—go out on your own without having served your apprenticeship with a name designer first. Half the girls here love him—he probably dated most of them in his time at Parsons. Everyone wants to know if he'll succeed. Some want him to fail for being arrogant enough to go against the accepted way of things. I hope he sticks it up their asses."

The instructor tells them Hawk is teaching the class that day, just like other alumni have occasionally come in for a morning. As Hawk takes over, Astrid assesses him. He has dark blond hair that's really too long, and wavy in a way that suggests it's probably in need of a wash. It falls over his brow and he reaches up to shove it out of the way, which only makes it tumble back down again, like it knows one half-hidden eye is the way to get every girl in the room to gift him her attention.

Astrid wants to laugh because even Velvet is staring. But so is she.

In the archives, he'd looked like the kind of guy who worked at nothing because the whole world yielded before him. But now he looks intent as he picks up a length of tricky silver lamé.

Everyone studies the fabric differently: Velvet with fierceness as if she doesn't want the contradictions of hard metal and liquid grace to get the better of her; Graham with consternation, like he'd been praying for the simplicity of denim. And Astrid feels a sudden thrill. Every fabric they've examined so far has been at odds with inspiration, like a butler in a three-piece suit on the dance floor at the Electric Circus. Whereas the lamé is the Top 40 hit she hadn't even known she craved.

It obeys every twist of Hawk's fingers as he drapes it over the mannequin beside him, leaving it long so it covers her legs. "Silver lamé doesn't need any encouragement to be flashy," he explains. "So you make the dress long, and suddenly it's more mood lighting than neon billboard."

Astrid narrows her eyes. It's like he took the drumbeat out of a rock song. You don't improve something by stripping it of its essence. If it's meant to throb, you let it.

She pushes herself up and walks to the front. "Or you make it so short that despite its tendency toward exhibitionism, the lamé isn't the first thing you see."

She re-pins the fabric so it barely skims the mannequin's ass. Now it's all about the woman, rather than what she's wearing.

Hawk's frown is of absorption rather than irritation—she hopes.

"Then it needs long sleeves for balance," he says, twisting the silver into two lengths that stop just above the wrist bones, which were, five minutes before, mere overlooked joinery. Now he's drawn attention to the delicate tapering of the arms in a way that's more erotic than a plunging neckline. "Actually, it should be even shorter." He makes another half inch disappear from the hem.

Astrid nearly smiles, but it's only almost perfect. She glances at Hawk, who's looking at her with the same not-quite smile. She slides her fingers through the lamé, listens to what the fibers are saying.

Disappear.

She tugs down the back of the dress, exposing the mannequin's shoulder blades—two exclamation points of confidence. "And a scooped-out back for power," she says, smiling at Hawk, at this reference to their previous meeting.

He laughs.

And everyone bursts into spontaneous applause at this dress that looks from the front like a lit match and becomes, by the time you circle to the back, a blazing fire. Astrid's whole body, her mind, even her heart, feel ripped. It was as if Hawk was in her head and she was in his, a feeling maybe everyone's chasing when they take up their LSD blotters at a rent party.

This dress is Astrid in textile form. And the whoops of her classmates tell her the dress is what they want to be too, or what they never dared imagine they could be. No one could wear this dress and not be the strongest thing in the room.

Her eyes catch Hawk's again. "Thanks," he says and it's so unexpected—gratitude rather than ego. How many teachers at Parsons would welcome a girl who's been there for all of a month striding up and telling them they'd made a dress too damn long?

And she wonders—how can she make this happen again? Or was it just one rare and unrepeatable moment of dazzlement?

Now Hawk's looking at her the same way he did in the archives, his eyes like pencils redrawing her bones. Even her ankles blush.

She turns away, retakes her seat. Because in her life right now, she needs only the outcome of what just happened, not the dazzlement. She hears someone whisper, "Of course you'd make something so microscopic it can hardly be called a dress. I guess it's in your genes."

Candace. Even though Astrid knows she should zip it, she says, "Were you hoping he'd get in *your* jeans?"

She feels Velvet stiffen and wishes she hadn't let Candace rile her. Meeting a bitch with bitchiness is like throwing a smoldering cigarette into a summer-dry forest.

"You know she dated him last year?" Velvet hisses. "And he did what he always does—let her down gently after just a couple of dates."

Which means Astrid didn't just toss out a cigarette, but a can of fuel.

Ignore Candace, she tells herself. Astrid's had years of practice at pretending to shrug off the taunts, and should be expert at it by now.

But what a thing to have had to develop a talent for.

* * *

After class, she and Velvet have just turned onto East 54th Street when they hear someone shout, "Hey!"

Astrid turns to find Hawk hurrying after them. She tries to look disinterested but can still feel, threading its silver through the air between them, the enchantment of their minds in unison.

"I don't know your name," Hawk says to her.

"Sure you do." Velvet grins.

"Sorry, Velvet," Hawk says in seemingly genuine apology for his single-minded focus on Astrid.

Perhaps it's his contrition that makes Velvet say, "This is Astrid. I guess in a school of only six hundred students, you were bound to find the one worth knowing. Catch you on the flip side." She unfurls a supple hand and glides away.

Now it's just Astrid and Hawk. He looks as though he was growing a beard and then gave up, leaving dark stubble over his cheeks that makes Astrid suddenly loathe the studied grooming of mustaches, and also clean-shaven skin. Hawk Jones is definitely an addiction she can't succumb to.

She starts to walk, thinking he'll move on to someone who's better at flirting—Candace, maybe—but he walks with her, asking, "Did you transfer from another college?" His tone is laden with a thousand questions, like an archeologist seeking to dust away the layers of Astrid. "What we just did, that was..."

He pauses as if considering adjectives, and Astrid can't help saying, "It was what that fabric was meant to do."

This is where he'll laugh and leave the crazy girl who thinks textiles have destinies. But he just says, "Yeah. It was." Then, "Do you want to come to dinner? Meet my parents?"

"Meet your parents?" she repeats. In Long Island, meeting parents was a planned event. "I don't think so." Which sounds like prevarication. "No," she says firmly.

"You think you won't like my parents?" He smiles, self-assured, and she almost reaches out a wistful hand to touch his abstract and lovely ease. Today in the classroom, it had made her own self-possession unfurl.

A thought chafes against her skull—how her mother's friends would laugh if they knew Astrid Bricard thought she lacked self-assurance. A girl who defies her parents' wishes to go to fashion school and who wears men's business shirts as skirts is not a person anyone thinks lacks self-belief. But seeing Hawk now, Astrid knows she can say all the right words to Velvet while lying in a beanbag with a rousing chorus backing her, but put her in a room alone with her thoughts and they circle back to one thing—her parents don't believe in her. All the people she grew up with don't believe in her. How the hell, in all that doubt, do you find the courage to not just say it, but to actually do it?

Whatever crosses her face makes Hawk say, "My mom always says a home-cooked meal makes you feel better. You look like you could do with feeling better."

"I have to maintain a ninety percent average to keep my scholarship and I'm working six nights a week to make rent. So I don't date," she says resolutely.

"My mom doesn't date either, so she'll be glad you just want to be friends."

Astrid laughs and he grins at her, which makes her say, "I'm serious," even though she's still laughing.

"I am too," he says.

They've been walking this whole time, weaving their way through pedestrians, working themselves into the fabric of the city, his arm occasionally bumping against hers. While she expected that a man who tried a one-liner on her about devils and dresses would take advantage of moments of forced proximity and let his arm linger, he never does. On Park Avenue, he stops outside an apartment building.

"I just..." he starts, and then she sees it—a flash of vulnerability beneath the ease, something he's learned to hide better than she has. "Today, with that silver dress...I figure there aren't too many people in the world you get to do that with. And you can never have too many friends. So if you want one more, come to dinner."

Because there is probably no one else who could hold one end of a length of silver lamé and she the other and magic would be the result, she says, "All right."

"Hey, Mom," Hawk calls when they enter the apartment. "I brought Astrid with me. I told you about her a while ago."

He's in front of her, so he can't see the searing flush of something that isn't embarrassment on her cheeks. He met her in an archive for

three minutes and he told his mother about her. His gray sweater
moves with the shape and swell of the muscles on his back as he tosses
his keys onto the hall stand and Astrid wishes she were charcoal wool
and could wrap herself around him.

* * *

Hawk's mom sweeps Astrid into the kitchen and pours her a soda
and Hawk sits on a stool, aware of the way Astrid looks today—not
as if she changes her costume to alter the way she feels, but as if she
changes her costume to recast who she is.

Today she's like a Janis Joplin song—fearless, unexpected. Whatever the hell thing she's wearing—like she just got out of a bed and
pulled her lover's shirt around her waist—makes her look completely
unlike the women at Parsons, who mostly wear bell-bottom jeans and
T-shirts. Her eyes are deep-set and appear brown on first glance but
change to green under the light, tapering away into the sultriest of
upturned corners. Her hair—cropped to fall around her chin, brushing her nape in the back—makes you look at her mouth, which is
slightly open, showing a hint of white teeth, and he has to turn away
because he knows he's staring.

Friends, he reminds himself. No man worth anything makes a
promise like that and breaks it within five minutes.

He jumps up, needing a distraction. "I'll take Dad's tray in to him."

Astrid's head tilts in inquiry. And he decides to show her what he's
never shown anyone—his most private grief. He indicates she should
follow him into the living room, where he can hear the sound of the
television, which means today is a good day and his dad is out of bed.

"Dad?" Hawk says. "This is Astrid."

"Pleased to meet you, Mr. Jones." Astrid holds out a hand Hawk
knows his father can't shake. As Matthias attempts to lift his arm,
Astrid reaches down, finds his hand and squeezes it.

It's then that Hawk knows he could fall in love with her. And also that he can't. Because the way she said it—*I don't date*—made it clear that with her, it was friends or nothing. Despite knowing her for just a couple of hours, *nothing* is unthinkable. So the only thing to do is to pretend that the quiet shock he just felt in his heart is nothing more than his blood changing rhythm, from a steady undemanding verse to a soul-stomping rock chorus.

He's quiet over dinner, listening to Meredith and Astrid talk, until near the end when Astrid asks him, "Can I see your store sometime?"

"Sure," he says. Then he adds self-deprecatingly, "I'm not exactly busy, so come anytime you want. I've been open three months and I know it takes time but—I think my clothes are good. Maybe that sounds arrogant but…" He frowns. "It's like the whole world thinks Bill Blass's style is the only style—that clean, healthy, fresh shit he goes on about. Who looks clean, healthy and fresh on the dance floor at the Electric Circus? I'm trying to make clothes that make women feel like that. Wild or free or…I don't know."

He smiles ruefully. "Maybe that's why I'm not busy—because I can't even explain what I'm doing. Just that it isn't what's being done."

He stops. He knew that setting himself up as a designer straight out of college wasn't going to be easy. No use complaining about something he chose to do.

Astrid smiles at him. "You've made me want to come and see it all the more. *It isn't what's being done*," she repeats. "I like that."

"Me too. And maybe…" He considers. "Maybe business is slow because I've only thought about the design and the clothes and not about what will make people come in the door."

His mother walks to the sideboard and pours out glasses of cognac. "Sounds like you two are onto something, so I'm going to leave you to it," she says, picking up plates and insisting Astrid stay put. "He needs more help than I do," she tells Astrid with a smile before she disappears.

"Your mom and dad are really nice people," Astrid says, almost as if she's surprised. "You're not what I expected."

He wants to ask what she'd expected and also what she thinks now but that's just vanity. Instead he says, "They're the best. Above the shop..." He pauses, not sure if he can say it without his voice cracking but the words press out. "There's a huge room above the shop I want to move into eventually but..." *That would make me a selfish asshole.*

He phrases it differently. "But that would leave my mom here alone with my dad. He's a saint, but it's just physically and mentally hard caring for him. I can't do it to her. Anyway," he says, to move on before he bawls like a baby, "come to the shop on Saturday. I'm going to the Cheetah with some friends, so come to the store and we can walk down together. Bring Velvet."

He adds that so she knows it's another non-date, hopes she can't hear the part of his mind that's thinking, *I just want to see you again.*

And maybe he got the tone right because she says softly, "That sounds like fun."

After that, there's a moment of silence, two cognac glasses between them and the memory of a silver dress, which is caught in Hawk's mind the way a photograph is trapped inside a camera—development is necessary to bring out exactly what the press of a finger has caught. It makes him blurt, "Can I measure you?"

He winces and sips the cognac, which is smoother than he is tonight, and tastes like Christmas—nuts roasting over flames, candied fruit, the soft leather of a well-loved chair. "That was weird. Sorry."

But she smiles. "I've never been asked to do that after dinner before. So, okay."

There's a tape measure in his room, one the dean gave him last year in despair at Hawk ever having any of the necessary tools. He wraps it around her waist, needing to get the numbers right because his seamstress will do the sewing—Hawk can draw and drape, working with fabric in his hands, but he can't sew even the most basic of hems.

He has to stand close to Astrid, his hands joined at a point near where her navel must be, her face upturned to his, not just the sound of her breath but the heat of it slipping past his neck. He tries not to think about that as he lets the tape unravel down her leg, placing his thumb near the top of her thigh, the white cotton of her skirt the only barrier between her skin and his. A flush slides over her jaw.

Jesus. He needs a cold shower.

Astrid offers him a quick and gorgeous smile. "I should go."

The door closes behind her and Hawk throws himself onto his bed, unable to think of anything except the inches of space Astrid now takes up in his world.

* * *

A half hour later, there's a knock on the door and his mom sticks her head in.

"I'm mortgaging the apartment tomorrow," she says prosaically, then tips half the Tom Collins down her throat.

Hawk jumps up. "What are you talking about? And why the hell am I wasting my time designing clothes hardly anyone's buying when I should be out earning any kind of money I can?"

Meredith smiles. "I'm using the mortgage to give you some business capital. So you can spend money on whatever it is that'll get people in the door, rather than always worrying about only spending what you have."

Hawk can't speak. This apartment is the place where his mother was carried over the threshold in the arms of her beloved, where the echoes of parties linger in rooms alongside the brilliance that was his mother and father, together. She'll never sell it, not for anyone. But she's mortgaging it for Hawk.

"And you're moving out," she says, still in that same crisp voice.

"No way."

"This is your time, kiddo. Be a grown-up later. There's always plenty of time—too much time—for that. Move into the apartment and turn your dreams into a city of women wearing wild and free clothes. And, Hawk?" Her tone changes to something almost frightened. "Don't fall in love with Astrid. She's a great girl but something tells me she'll break your heart."

Meredith's mouth twists on the words as if she knows the advice is futile—that the falling has already started and the only thing to do now is be ready with the safety net.

Hawk's reply is vehement. "She's not like that."

"Nobody ever means to be a heartbreaker, HJ."

His mother moves to close the door and so that their conversation doesn't end on that note—a version of the future he doesn't want—he calls out, "Thanks for the money." More words press out. "But what if I fail?"

"Don't." Meredith finishes her drink and walks away.

FOUR

BLYTHE BRICARD

MONTSOREAU, FRANCE

Blythe and the kids sit on a bed in a room that was probably the dungeon three hundred years ago. It's circular, built into the base of a turret. The bottom half is actually below ground level and it's colder inside than a text from Jake. Eva's breath is visible in the freezing air; Sebby is coughing uncontrollably. The chateau host, who's just left the room, was wearing a knitted hat, shearling coat and yeti boots. It's not as if Blythe thought a vacation with her ex-husband would be fun, but she was hoping not to be quite so close to abject misery within the first twenty minutes.

But they're in France on a holiday she isn't paying for, which means they just have to take the bad with hopefully—*please God*—some good.

"Maybe we'll steal that lady's yeti boots while she's asleep," Blythe jokes, trying to lift their spirits.

Eva shudders. "I bet they're full of lice. Except it's too cold for lice."

Blythe laughs. "We can do this. Put on thermals, beanies and mittens. There's an Auchan nearby—I'll go buy a space heater to keep us warm until the central heating kicks in. Maybe Coco can play with you until I get back." Ed's already told her Jake missed the bus that was chartered to bring everyone to the Loire Valley. *Of course he did.*

Thankfully, Coco agrees. When she arrives downstairs, Blythe wraps her in a hug. Coco was ten when Blythe met Jake and she's gone from a girl Blythe would take to the movies to give her time away from her four siblings, to a teenager who stayed with Blythe and Jake one summer, to the twenty-three-year-old woman she is now.

Eventually Coco says, "You know we'll both start crying if we don't let go."

Blythe sniffs and smiles and finally lets go. Then she leaves to buy the biggest space heater she can find to heat their dungeon, bathroom, sitting room and her own smaller bedroom. She's hurtling back to the chateau when Coco texts to say, *Dinner's running late. Can you grab some bread from the kitchen for the kids on your way up?*

It's nine o'clock. No one's slept much for the last two nights and now they haven't eaten either. Blythe doesn't care about herself, but her two cold, grumpy, tired kids are about to see their father for the first time in six months and they'll need food at least to get through that uncomfortable reunion.

She finds the kitchen and charms the chef with the halting French she learned at school. He gives her a tray of hot fries, fresh bread, French butter—every carbohydrate known to man and not one single fresh vegetable but she couldn't care less. She hurries back upstairs to the dining room, where her path to the kids is slowed by the process of greeting and kissing the cheeks of the twenty-odd ex-relatives gathered there, all of whom seem to have been lining their stomachs with champagne in the absence of food.

Over the shoulder of Herb, her former father-in-law, she sees Jake approach the kids. He ruffles Seb's hair and says, "Hey, buddy," before doing the same to Eva.

Blythe's heart curls up inside her. Why wasn't she five minutes earlier? Then she'd have been holding Eva while her dad patted her on the head like she was a puppy, despite it being the first time he's seen her in six months. Eva's eyes are shiny with tears.

Blythe marches over and deposits the tray on the table.

"That looks healthy," Jake says by way of greeting.

"Just like you gave up seeing the kids, I gave up feeding them fruit," she says brightly, breaking her rule not to be like this in front of Seb and Eva.

She slathers butter on the bread and passes it to her daughter.

Jake leans down, takes it from Eva and demolishes it, smiling cheekily. Eva's face crumples. As Blythe lunges forward to save the remaining bread for Sebby, she accidentally knocks a stray glass of champagne over Jake's shoes.

"Jesus, Blythe," he says, staring at his shoes. Always dressed to kill, he's wearing a white T-shirt and blue jacket, lighter than navy, darker than sapphire, a color that makes his blue eyes look—it's such a cliché, but in Jake's case it's always been an accurate cliché—piercing. Right now, they're piercing through her with annoyance.

"I don't think even Jesus is going to help us over the next three weeks," she growls.

She's rescued by Herb tapping his glass for silence. Jake stalks off. Blythe finds a chair, pulls Sebby onto her knee and drapes an arm around Eva, motioning for them to eat while Iris, Jake's mom, speaks.

"I just wanted to say there are no real rules for the next three weeks," Iris begins. "The chateau, while it might be as cold as one, isn't a prison. You're free to come and go as you please. And I'm sorry about the chill. By morning, I'll be in fine form to address the issue."

She says this last sentence obdurately but with exquisite politeness, and Blythe almost smiles at what the hosts will have to face. Iris's gray hair is freshly set, her nails manicured, her lipstick perfect, and the only thing Blythe can see that looks different is that her hands are thin, her rings sliding up and down, tinkling a discreet requiem.

"We're in charge of excursions." Ed takes over, sliding his hand into his wife Joy's. Despite having five kids, they've always been completely in love and Blythe hopes that never changes.

She finds herself forgetting the altercation with Jake and smiling instead at the visceral sense of love and camaraderie in the room.

"We're organizing something to do most days," continues Ed, who used to work at YouTube and now runs a research institute focused on developing strategies for an ethical internet, and who loves to manage everything and everyone. "Join in if you want to. David and Anton," Ed says, grinning at his brother and partner, "are in charge of food. There's a chef downstairs, but he arrived late, so just settle into the champagne. All hangovers, see Charlie and Frieda."

Yet another brother, Charlie, is a doctor for Médecins Sans Frontières, as is his wife. Blythe is pretty sure Eva and Sebby have only met them twice in their lives. Diana and Hugh, the two remaining siblings and their respective partners, are given other minor duties.

Then Iris takes back the reins by saying to the cousins, all of whom—except Eva and Sebby—are in their teens and twenties, "If I see any telephones at my dinner table, I'll throw them in the moat. I'm sure there is one beneath the mud. Cheers."

Everyone laughs, and as more champagne is poured, Iris summons Blythe and the kids over to the padded armchair from where she's directing the evening. "Thank you for coming," Iris says. "It wouldn't be the same without you and the children."

Her warmth makes Blythe succumb, as she's always done, to Iris's majesty, which is both terrifying and impressive. "It's good to see you," Blythe says, feeling her throat ache when Iris folds her into her arms. She's glad she came.

* * *

The kids are asleep and Blythe's about to collapse into bed when there's a knock on the suite door. Somehow she knows it's Jake. Her body will always sense when her kids are in a room, and she can't believe it but her body still senses Jake. Years ago, the sudden awareness of his proximity would make her head unconsciously tilt to the side in anticipation of the moment he would come up behind her and graze his lips along the curve of her neck.

It's only as she opens the door that she realizes her subconscious has tipped her head to the side. She straightens up so quickly she almost falls over. *Shit.*

Is it possible that her energy over the past couple of years has been so directed at helping Seb and Eva forget their father's indifference that she's forgotten to bury her own memories? She might not want to be married to Jake anymore, but they did have a past replete with love. Which means she needs to find a darned big shovel pronto because living in the same house as him without having laid their history to rest will only end in tears.

"You asked Ed to look after Eva."

Thankfully, Jake's such a jerk that giant chunks of the past have just buried themselves six feet under with no effort required. "And?"

"Mom just bailed me up for half an hour over the fact that Eva stayed with Ed last night. She wanted to know how far down your list of babysitters I am." He folds his arms across his chest.

Blythe is so tired she can hardly stand. She spent a sleepless night at the hospital, she's barely eaten and she can't do this right now. "Jake, I called you. You didn't pick up. And you're not on a list of sitters. You're their father."

She moves to close the door but he says, "Let's not play semantics. How many people would you ask before me?"

And rather than calmly reminding him that she *had* called him, everything erupts. "I would choose every single person in this chateau over you. And don't act like that makes me a bad person and I'm the reason you don't see your kids. You don't see them because you don't want to. The last time you laid eyes on either of them was six months ago for a total of one shitty hour, which Eva told me about." She holds up her fingers and counts off each of Jake's mind-boggling screw-ups.

"You took them to a wine bar, ordered yourself a wine but didn't order them anything. You answered three phone calls lasting a total of forty-five minutes of the hour you were there. You yelled at Sebby when he got bored and knocked your wine over. He wanted your attention, Jake. Doesn't that kill you a little? That your son was willing to make you yell at him just so you'd speak to him."

Don't let him hurt you, she wants to shout at herself. But it's too late for that.

"I asked Ed because he actually takes my calls. And because he made sure Coco and Georgia kept Eva busy so she arrived here happy rather than so angry she cried for a whole damn night."

Blythe swipes furiously at tears she doesn't want to cry in front of Jake, but she can't stop weeping—if divorcing him hadn't broken her heart, then hearing Eva that night after the wine bar visit had torn it to shreds.

* * *

After Jake's gone, she's too fired up to sleep, so she pulls out her phone and deals with her emails. There's one from the stylist of an actress who wants to wear one of Blythe's creations to the Oscars. A schedule of fittings that looks terrifyingly like a bullet journal made out with a Gantt chart is attached. Blythe only has to glance at it to know she could never make even half the meetings, which fall outside school hours. The next email is a job offer to be the costume designer on a new series for Netflix, which is apparently starting to make content. It's a nine-month contract—and it's filming in New York.

She exhales slowly, then checks her bank account. Staring at the numbers—which are smaller than she'd hoped—confirms one thing. If she keeps telling herself she's designing original gowns from damaged vintage pieces but is actually refusing half the work because she doesn't have time for it, then her bank balance will only get smaller.

To give her kids financial security, she needs to either accept the Netflix series, or accept Nathaniel's offer. By doing the first, she really will be saying goodbye to the dream she's held on to for more than a decade. By doing the second, she might be able to make her dream come true—but it will mean dancing with Astrid's ghost.

Nine months' work in New York isn't to be scoffed at. She opens the costume brief. The series is about aliens and the costumes are various iterations of space-age bikini and loincloth.

You don't want to be a costume designer, her heart calls, *especially when it means selling your soul.* But her brain yells, *You need the money.*

Then do MIZZA, the devil shouts.

She turns off her phone. She needs sleep. She'll figure it out in the morning.

* * *

They all sleep until midafternoon, then explore the castle. Their dungeon, which is slowly warming, is on the first floor, along with the kitchens. On the top floor are the bedrooms for the other twenty-five guests. On the floor in between are the living and dining rooms, and a library that Eva and Sebby stand in with their heads tipped back, staring at shelves that reach from floor to ceiling, and at a picture window with a glorious view of a lake. The smell of leather bindings and the majesty of so many books have them all saying, "Wow."

"Dinner!" Blythe hears David call and they hurry across the landing, so lured by the smell of food that Blythe doesn't notice Jake stalking up behind her.

"Blythe, can I speak to you?"

Ed offers her a sympathetic smile, David an exaggerated grimace, and even Jake's sister, Diana, turns her eyes from her newly minted second husband because Jake's tone is definitely not friendly.

But it's either go with him or make a scene, so Blythe follows him into the library, where he launches straight in. "What did you do when you were in Paris?"

"I met my lover at the George V Hotel," she says sarcastically and can't believe it when Jake actually laughs.

"No way you'd go there," he says. "Unless you wanted to break up with him. Aren't big-name luxury hotels only for people with no imagination and too much money?"

She almost laughs too—she'd told Jake that when they were at grad school, during one of her idealistic phases of trying to spend money only at locally owned, ethical businesses. But she's not used to laughing with Jake now.

"Although," he continues, "given you're sleeping in a freezing house with an ex-husband who, instead of letting you sleep after you've spent a night at the hospital, starts auditioning very badly to be a babysitter, I'm guessing a luxury hotel sounds like paradise."

She manages a wry smile because it *is* kind of funny. And they're having something like a conversation, which is good—she doesn't want the kids to see them fighting for three weeks.

"You know, after you told me you hated pretentious it-list hotels, I spent more time studying where to take you for our first weekend away than I did cramming for my exams," Jake says now, leaning against the wall. "I still remember the look on your face when we drove to the Hamptons and you thought we were staying there."

Her smile widens, recalling her disbelief at thinking he'd chosen the over-the-top Hamptons for a romantic weekend. From then on, in the way all couples develop their own shared vernacular, the phrase "I've been Hampton-ed" had become shorthand for suffering an epic disappointment.

"But we went to Shelter Island and it was perfect," he finishes.

For a brief moment there's only Jake's eyes, eyes she'd once loved so much that he only needed to look at her and she'd be grabbing his hand and leading him into a bedroom, eyes that are now a mix of too many feelings for her to interpret.

He turns and rests one hand on the bookshelves, shoulders rising and falling as if he's trying to get something under control.

And Blythe re-erects her defenses, which is just as well because he holds out his phone. "It's in the news."

The headline makes her drop into a chair: BLYTHE BRICARD IN TALKS WITH CHAMPLAIN HOLDINGS TO RESURRECT MIZZA.

Accompanying the article is a photograph of Blythe stepping onto Avenue Montaigne. Her eyes fix on another image at the bottom of the article: Astrid on the day she disappeared, wasted, rain-drenched and stumbling along a street. Blythe closes her eyes.

"Why would you go to him?" she hears Jake demand. "You know this is what I do."

Her eyes fly open. "I can't believe the only thing you can think of right now is your competitor," she cries. Of all the people in the world, Jake is the only one who knows that hiding behind the sunglasses and the word *MIZZA* is a lifetime of pain.

"Shit. I didn't mean..." He grimaces, and his next action—reaching out like he's going to touch her—makes her mouth fall open like its elastic just snapped.

"You always tell us not to argue, so you shouldn't either."

Jake almost falls over at the interjection. Eva's standing in the room with arms crossed, looking exactly like Jake last night. Sebby nods in furious agreement beside her.

And Jake says, shockingly, "You're right."

Then he does something Blythe hasn't seen him do for a long time. He crouches down in front of Eva and Sebby so he's at their level, not so far up and away at six feet five inches tall. "I don't know if you still cross your heart and hope to die or whether you're more into blood vows, but I'll do whatever you want so you know I won't argue with your mom again."

Blythe sees Eva on the edge of smiling at her father for the first time in months and she wants to drag that moment out of time so she can show Eva later and say, *Look! He loves you. He* does.

But Eva's unexecuted smile dies and Blythe is witness to the moment Jake realizes his daughter refuses to smile at him.

He unfurls and rubs the back of his neck, a gesture Blythe knows—because she loved him for thirteen years—means he's hurt too. It tells her he's more vulnerable to his children's mistrust than Blythe knew.

Then do something about it, she wants to say.

"Eva! Sebby!" Ed calls from across the landing. "Food's getting cold!"

Eva and Sebby run off and Blythe expects Jake to leave too but he moves back toward her. "I should have asked if you're okay." He gestures to the phone.

I'm not, she doesn't say.

But she finally admits it to herself—she wants to do what she didn't get a chance to do after grad school because otherwise she'll feel like a failure for the rest of her life. Except that what she needs to do for her kids is the exact opposite. Which means she has to say no to Nathaniel and take the costume design job for the Netflix series. It's finally time to forget dreams and focus on reality.

* * *

As soon as the kids are asleep, Blythe takes out her phone and reads the article properly.

Fashionistas rejoice. Word on the street is that the aloof but ultra-stylish Blythe Bricard will head up a reincarnated MIZZA with the money of Champlain Holdings behind her. While Blythe has some fashion credentials of her own, it's also her lineage that has the beau mode panting.

Blythe's mother Astrid Bricard met and fell in love with Hawthorne "Hawk" Jones at art school in 1970. Astrid soon dropped out of college but she inspired her lover to create the Hawk Jones fashion label, whose glory still blazes on, unlike Astrid and Hawk's love story, which ended in disaster. Two years later, Astrid surprised the world by re-emerging from exile and starting up MIZZA, coveted by every woman in the world over the short time of its existence—although there's much conjecture over whether she designed the clothes or Hawk did.

Whether she was a designer or not, Astrid was certainly famous. She's the subject of many books and films, which all converge on one point: the Fashion Battle of Versailles in 1973 when Astrid disappeared. Various theories exist—she was murdered by her drug dealer; she ran away from said dealer; she had an altercation with Hawk's new inspiration, former college mate Candace Winters; or she had an altercation with Hawk, who was by then her nemesis. The police closed the case, ruling she simply didn't want to be found. She's never been seen or heard from again, which is, of course, part of the legend.

There's a light tap on the door and Blythe finds Coco there, holding a bottle of champagne and two glasses. "I thought you might need this."

"You're officially my favorite niece. Come in."

"Bad news first," Coco says, making herself comfortable on Blythe's bed. "There are no hair dryers. The owner says the guests steal them. I told her they probably take them to use as heaters."

Blythe laughs. "We're all going to be wearing yeti boots soon, aren't we?"

"If you make them, they might be worth wearing."

"I'll find some flokati rugs at the markets to repurpose," Blythe jokes. "I actually made a sweater out of something similar during my awkward teenage years."

"No way were you an awkward teenager. You were born sartorially polished."

"I guarantee you I was the awkwardest. In fact, from the time I was thirteen, all I did was bury myself in books. The only time I went out was to visit thrift shops to buy clothes I'd remake into what I thought were darkly elegant and un-teenager-like pieces."

Just like she tries never to think of Astrid, Blythe tries not to think of the reasons why, as a thirteen-year-old, she'd shut herself off from the world—when that freaking movie was released that told Blythe too much that had been kept secret. Like why she lived with Meredith Jones. That her memories of sitting on the workbench in Hawk's shop, throwing fabric scraps into the air and giggling as they landed in his hair, were the exceptions to the rule of lying in her bed at night and not remembering Astrid, but remembering Hawk—the father who *had* known Blythe but who'd still chosen to leave.

Coco smiles and scrunches down like they're at a sleepover. So Blythe wriggles under the covers too and picks out the funny pieces of her past.

"The girls at school started copying what I wore because they thought I was testing prelaunch Hawk Jones ideas. So I traded my clothes with a girl who went to a school where they wore uniforms, and then I wore her uniform at my non-uniform school. Have I never told you this?"

Coco is killing herself laughing. "I think I'd remember! So when did you finally blossom? Didn't Dad once tell me you studied chemistry? It can't have been then."

It's impossible not to laugh at herself. "I did chemistry because it was about as far from fashion as you could get. But..." Blythe grimaces. "The Columbia campus was worse than high school. Boys in packs would snicker when I walked past and ask if I'd like to dance on tables with them because of that photo of Astrid. I won't tell you how I tackled that problem. Your dad would kill me."

"Remember, I'm twenty-three years old and don't live with my dad anymore."

Blythe still shakes her head.

Coco sloshes more champagne into their glasses. "Not leaving until you tell me."

Blythe recalls she's never won an argument with Coco. She rolls her eyes. "Okay. Well, I actually finished high school having hardly been kissed. But at Columbia, I don't know…Sex was everywhere, and I could see straightaway that I needed to make sure that whenever it happened for me, it was on my terms. Otherwise it would be just another thing for all the boys who loved making suggestive comments about whether I didn't wear panties like Astrid to joke about. I needed them to know that I was in charge of my body, not them. So I checked out every book about sex from the library and read them cover to cover. Not long after, I was at a party and there was a group of boys…you know, that group who mocks the loudest. Not dangerous, but cocky. After a round of the usual jibes about silver dresses, I looked the one I knew best in the eye and said, 'Do you think you're up to it?' And in his dorm that night, I demonstrated that if anyone on campus needed to be teased about sex, it shouldn't be me—it should be the brash eighteen-year-old boys who were definitely a disappointment. Soon, I didn't have to worry about overconfident boys anymore."

"Oh my God, that is the best!" Coco laughs, but stops when she sees Blythe's face. "I'm thinking the story doesn't have a happy ending."

Blythe waves a dismissive hand. "Someone spoke to the press. There was a stupid article about how I'd managed to outdo Astrid because I danced on tables balanced on my bed clad only in a silver thong." She rolls her eyes. "As if that's even possible."

"Was that when that photo was taken?" Coco asks quietly.

Blythe nods. There are photos of Blythe all over the internet, but one transcends them all—the first time Blythe got publicly mad with the paparazzi, who were shoving a new book about Astrid at her. When she saw the photographs of that day, everything changed.

They showed Blythe in a black mini dress and cowboy boots, over-sized seventies tortoiseshell sunglasses on her face, blond hair a mess of tousled waves, finger raised in the air in a screw-you gesture. She looked like the delinquent child of a rock star—except she'd been sober and had just come from an advanced chemistry exam.

The worst part was the photo they'd run alongside—of Astrid in 1973 outside the same apartment building, pushing a baby carriage. Astrid was wearing a black mini dress with tortoiseshell sunglasses, finger raised in the air too. That photo had always given Blythe night-mares because it was emblematic of Astrid and motherhood—it had once accompanied an article stating that Blythe was premature and had to receive specialist ICU care because of Astrid's drug habit. And while Blythe had always told herself she'd never be the kind of woman who abandoned her child, the parallels between her and her mother were obvious. Ignoring fashion was only making Blythe more like Astrid.

"It was," she says to Coco. "But it made me follow my heart and enroll at FIT. So I'm grateful for it."

Blythe had enrolled in textile design—different enough that no one could say she was copying her parents. She still hid behind sunglasses, but things were different once everyone got used to her. She made friends with people who loved fashion like she did. It filled her soul with something more than beating boys at their own game and being angry.

"I know I'm being nosy." Coco looks contemplative now. "I've been working at an ad agency as a copywriter, but I've had some freelance articles published about fashion. That's what I want to do. So I was thinking about starting a Fashion Studies MA."

"That's a great idea," Blythe says. "But... you might be better off talking to Jake. He's the only one managing global fashion right now." She shrugs, hating that postscript of a life where, as *Vogue* had so succinctly put it, she hasn't lived up to expectations.

She's reaching for her champagne when Coco suddenly says, "Don't you want to know what happened to her?"

Blythe knows exactly who *her* is. "I have no interest in what happened to Astrid."

Coco persists, going where no one's dared to go before. "Doesn't it make you—"

"It makes me rage, Coco," Blythe says furiously. But what is she raging at? Astrid leaving her? Hawk leaving her? The legacy of shame that made her think she had to learn about sex from a book just so she could prove herself impenetrable?

Or . . . the fact that Astrid is mostly remembered for a silver dress and a moment that wouldn't even register as nudity in today's Kardashian world, but in reality she was a brilliant designer. Or was she? Was MIZZA Hawk's, like the media say? Is that why MIZZA's so revered but Astrid is called almost everything but a designer?

Like she's reading her mind, Coco says, "Don't you ever want to reach into the internet and pull a woman out of the story she's been written into? I want to do that so often it makes me rage too."

What if Blythe *could* pull herself out of the story she's been written into? The one where she exists as the offspring of Hawk and Astrid, disappointing all expectations, but great fodder for online magazines needing pictures of people with clickbait appeal.

Coco kisses her cheek and stands. "I love you and I wasn't trying to pry."

"I know."

After Coco's gone, Blythe's phone pings with a message—from Nathaniel. *I was kind of an asshole.*

Only kind of an asshole? Blythe shoots back, the champagne having relaxed her way too much.

Haha. You wanted a plan. I have one. I can come to you if it's easier.

What if Nathaniel is offering Blythe a way to change her story? It's so tempting, that idea—that even if she can't change the story Mizza and Astrid have left her with, she can change the part where she's disappointing her own expectations of herself. If she did MIZZA, she'd have financial security and the chance to do what she's wanted since she left grad school. So maybe she should just talk to Nathaniel, and then try to figure out how to protect her kids and avoid the media attention after she hears what he has to say.

She watches her fingers type, *I'll come to Paris day after tomorrow. But don't get your hopes up.*

FIVE

ASTRID BRICARD AND HAWK JONES

Hawk stands outside his store, eyeing it critically. It's in a great location, just off Fifth Avenue, close to Henri Bendel's. It looks like any other store—which is maybe the problem. He wants it to be a unicorn amidst a string of horses.

He goes inside. There's a bare wide bench in the middle of the room with a few stools around it, covered in shades of lemon, lime and orange. Great clothes hang limply on racks. If this is a unicorn, it's barely breathing.

He moves over to the record player and lays down *Candles in the Rain*, remembers being at Woodstock last year and holding up a lighter against the rain, half a million others doing the same, song and unity the two things that were going to change the world. Now half his friends have been drafted for Vietnam and the act of holding up a flame and thinking it will make a difference seems as futile as putting a harpist on a stage next to Mick Jagger and expecting it to be heard.

Last December, he'd sat in his mother's living room with dozens of his friends watching the Vietnam draft, some of them outright weeping when their numbers were called in the first third, some of them rushing off to enroll in any college that would take them. He'd known that draft would change everything.

And it has. Spend a night at the Cheetah and you feel a wildness inside everyone, like they're trying to cram everything into now in case the future never arrives. They're all dancing the same way they want to fight against the world they've been given.

It reminds him of what he said to Astrid last night. He pulls a piece of paper out of his pocket and dials the number scribbled on it. "Hey," he says. "Hope I'm not disturbing you."

"Nope," Astrid says. "I was studying the principles of design and learning either that I'm unprincipled, or design shouldn't have principles."

He laughs, hoisting himself onto the workbench. "I was thinking . . . I don't know, a whole lot of stuff, and I guess I just wanted to say it aloud and see how it sounded. But not if you're studying."

"Please distract me from ever thinking I must always wear pants with my blazer."

He laughs again. "Okay." He tries to assemble his thoughts and what comes out is, "I was thinking that maybe the next few years won't revolve around the people who've always been in charge and the things they want. It'll be about what *we* want. And that maybe I'm trying to make clothes that give everyone a bit of fighting spirit to face all the shit going on in the world."

"So make sure your store feels like a place where you go in to buy clothes but walk out with a bit of fighting spirit too."

The song on Hawk's record player has reached its rousing bridge. The singer's voice almost cracks on the word *raise* and then again on *rain*, and he wants to punch the air because yes, that's exactly what he needs to do and he thinks that, far from breaking his heart, Astrid makes him feel like that one burning flame against the dark, forever raised.

He remembers the way she looked last night at his parents' apartment, how her false eyelashes had made her green eyes huge. His gaze falls onto the nearest stool, covered in green cotton drill.

Green eyes and green hips—and nothing in between.

It's an off-limits thought but he's going to think it for the next five minutes while he finds a roll of that same drill and draws chalk lines onto it that match Astrid's measurements. He asks his seamstress to make a hundred pairs of tiny green shorts. Then he hangs one pair in the window all by itself, sexy and bold and not needing anything to go with it. And, man, does it stand out from all the other stores.

Somehow, he sells eighty-two pairs of shorts in a day. And that night, with pieces of furniture his mother no longer needs, he moves into the apartment upstairs. The only part of the day that isn't perfect is when he farewells his dad.

Matthias nods at the baseball. "You should take that with you. I won't need it."

Hawk picks up the ball, remembering all the times when he was a kid and his dad would pitch the ball and Hawk would hit it into the outfield and his dad would run after it, throw it again. How boring it must have been for him. How magical it was for Hawk.

"Thanks," he manages to say before he kisses his dad on top of his head, hears his father's choked whisper, "Take care, son," and then walks away before he can't make himself leave.

* * *

When Astrid walks into Hawk's store on Saturday night, the whole place is buzzing. Vinyl is spinning, everyone has orange drinks in hand—Tequila Sunrises and Harvey Wallbangers—and people are dancing. The twisted ends of joints sit in ashtrays all around and there's a pair of green hotpants on a hanger she's desperate to try on.

Hawk's talking to a group of people, so she grabs the shorts. On her way to the fitting room, she picks up a black mid-thigh-length jacket too and when she emerges, she has on just the shorts and the jacket, which is open so a thin, vertical band of skin from her collarbone to her navel is visible. She puts her hands in the pockets and studies the outfit—and Hawk's reflection—in the mirror.

He looks like a rock star you want to feed chicken soup to in the hopes it tames him just enough—but now she knows he's not all front and no substance. He's talented. The black jacket, when buttoned, will look like a great dress. But unbuttoned, teamed with micro shorts and a hint of navel and breastbone, it looks…

"You look like an Avedon portrait." Hawk's leaning against a stool, watching her.

Across from him, she sees a familiar face. Candace is watching Astrid too, with what looks like envy. But no—her gaze goes deeper than simply wishing for what Astrid has. It comes from having her heart *set* on what Astrid has.

Velvet cuts across both Astrid's vision and that unsettling thought. "Your legs look longer than a flamingo's in those things." She turns to Hawk. "You're not doing too badly."

He laughs. "That's almost a compliment, Velvet." To Astrid he says, "I made something for you to wear, if you want."

She remembers the way he'd measured her the other night, how she'd had to stare at the football trophies on his shelf rather than think about the lick of heat as his thumb pressed against her thigh.

"If you wear whatever he made, then I can wear those." Velvet gestures to Astrid's shorts, grabs the parcel from Hawk and hustles them into the fitting rooms.

The package unfurls to reveal the silver dress Astrid and Hawk's minds made together in class. She slides it over her head and Velvet whistles.

"It was a damn fine dress when you two made it," Velvet tells her, "but now that you're wearing it, it's a fucking sensational dress."

Astrid smiles and lifts her arms to tidy her hair.

"What are you, five years old? You've got *Scooby-Doo* underpants on!" Velvet cackles.

"Shit." Astrid starts laughing. "They were on sale—they were all I could afford." But when she looks in the mirror, she sees that if she raises her arms above her head, Scooby and Daphne are definitely visible.

"There's nothing for it." She grins at Velvet and slips them off. "That'll make me keep my arms by my sides."

* * *

Astrid starts out walking with Velvet, but they run into Graham and she finds herself slowing until Hawk's at her side, this man who makes her feel like a bunch of musical notes tossed up in the air, searching for the right song.

"I moved into the apartment," he tells her. "My mom said she'd pick up my laundry every week and I was about to tell her no way when she said, 'Hawk, you and I both know you have no clue how to use a washing machine.' So I had to laugh and say okay." His smile fades and he says very quietly, "All this week, shitty as it is to say it, I've been more productive than ever. It's like having the store there below me..." He looks up at the billboards rather than her. "Not having to help my dad bathe himself each night has unlocked something in me I didn't even know was shut up."

"You know," she says, wanting to make him feel better for being human and thinking that's a weakness, "I ran away from home when I was seventeen. I'm..." She makes herself say it. "I'm adopted, so I hurt my parents in the worst way. When you're adopted, running away isn't seen as an act of teenage rebellion, but something deeper. As soon as I realized that, which took a few hours"—she gives a wry smile at the memory that her biggest act of defiance in her attempts to get her parents to agree to fashion school hadn't even lasted a day— "I went straight to my godmother so she could call them and smooth things over. I was terrified they mightn't want me back. But Alix— my godmother—said to me, 'Parents are very supple. You push them

and they bounce right back. Love is elastic, and unbreakable.' I liked
that."

"I like it too," Hawk says. Then he stares at her for a beat too long
and says, "Shit. It's you."

Which means he knows.

They're outside the club and she wants to walk straight into the
music and the darkness, but he says, "Wait. Please?"

Because he doesn't put out a hand to halt her, but leaves it wholly
up to her, she does stop beneath the neon *Cheetah* sign and the mar-
quee with Jimi Hendrix's name in red letters against the white lights.

"Before, at the shop—someone said Mizza Bricard's daughter was
at Parsons," he begins. "I didn't know who Norman Norell was two
years ago, but I remember Mizza was Christian Dior's muse. You
don't forget a name like that. Being her daughter—that must be…
tricky," he settles on.

Hawk takes up a position beside her and she wonders how they
must look—her in a very short dress that's making more than a few
sets of eyes roam covetously over the lamé, and him wearing contemplation on his face and a crumpled gray T-shirt and jeans, like
he hadn't given a single thought to how he looked before they left.
Which only makes him look all the better, she thinks ruefully.

"Maybe if Mizza had never visited Long Island, people out there
wouldn't have known much about her," she says quietly, trying to
explain. "But she did—six times—and as if the way she looked wasn't
enough to make people gossip, then they started asking their friends
in advertising about her, or their European cousins. And because gossip spreads fast out there, the teachers at school used to make me kneel
on the floor and they'd send me home every time my skirt didn't
brush the ground. They did the same to some other girls too, but they
mostly learned to wear longer skirts. I…"

She sighs. "I didn't. Before the prom, I had so many teachers ask
me what I was going to wear—like they were afraid I might borrow

one of Mizza's furs and wear it with nothing underneath. So I did go to homecoming in a fur I bought from a thrift shop and I got suspended from school. Like I said—I work six nights at the Corner Bistro. To get tonight off, I have to work all seven nights next week. I need to work like that because I have to stay at Parsons, then get an internship, then an apprenticeship with a name designer, so that then *I* can be a name designer. I've put everything into this. I'm living on a mattress on the floor, working every spare hour because I don't have a safety net. If I screw this up, I go back to Long Island and marry a lawyer and die inside, or I get a job as a secretary and live with knowing I wasn't good enough."

And all Hawk says is, "Mizza didn't want you back?"

He's known her only since the start of the year but he says it like he can't imagine anyone in the world not wanting Astrid back.

Right there on the corner of 53rd and Broadway, while Jimi Hendrix sings "Machine Gun" inside the club and the couple next to Astrid take a bump, wiping their noses once the powder's gone, she almost asks for one too. Then she'd feel nothing other than a chemical high. But that would never last as long as this pain does—the pain of the inelastic and very breakable love of a mother who didn't want you.

What she tries not to acknowledge is right there in front of her—the real reason she's doing this. It's not because she doesn't want to be the muse's daughter. It's not just because she wants to make clothes that give women the power they don't have in life. It's because she wasn't a good enough daughter to be kept.

And she wants to be good enough at something that Mizza will look at her and regret that she didn't want her.

Fuck. Nobody cries under the bright lights of Broadway at the glittering start of a Saturday night. But Astrid nearly does.

"I'm sorry," Hawk says.

As she looks at him, she knows he's the right song at the wrong time. She already regrets the moment when he walks into the club and makes out with a girl who'll gladly go home with him, one who isn't chasing after something so primal as a mother's love.

She blinks and pushes away from the wall. "Let's go inside."

A minute later, there's no space to think. So she leaves it all at the coat check and lets everything—the fur-covered bar, her dress, the way Hendrix's guitar almost saws your ears off as it crescendos into "All Along the Watchtower"—block out the world, allowing in only the pulse of music and bodies and light. There's no way to not fit in here because everyone has stepped out of themselves and into the music. She does too.

She sees Velvet spinning around, her arms outstretched as if she has quite literally shed her skin. Nearby, Graham dances freely in the arms of a man. Everything hidden is found in this room. It's Wonderland and Astrid is the wide-eyed wonderer.

Soon, she and Hawk are part of the chaos of bodies in front of the stage, dancing their limbs off. By the time "Purple Haze" plays and the lights of the club color the smoke violet and the crowd becomes two thousand people with one rocking voice, Astrid has forgotten Mizza entirely. Her eyes catch Hawk's and they share not just a grin, but the same, propulsive heartbeat.

After midnight, the band leaves the stage. Everyone is breathless and sweaty. The scent of weed overpowers the aroma of bodies. When yet another person walks by with LSD, Astrid asks Hawk, "Have you ever done acid?"

"Once," he says. "I hated it. Maybe I had a bad trip. A friend once said a good trip is like finding rapture at the end of the madness. I like my sanity too much to want to wade through bedlam to find the sunshine. But if you want to try it, I'll look out for you."

Astrid's had three or four drinks and Hawk only one or two, and there's something almost chivalrous about his restraint. But with her heart still pounding from the music, she says, "There's enough stimulation here without me needing to drop acid into the mix."

He grins. "Yep. I'm pretty much drunk and high on y——" He stops. *On you.* She knows that's what he was about to say.

"Hey, man!"

Someone slaps Hawk on the back. They both spin away from Hawk's truncated sentence and toward one of the group who'd walked down from the shop.

"This is Benji," Hawk tells her. "I met him at Parsons when I was doing photography. And this is Astrid," he says to Benji, who shoots her a grin.

"I haven't got the money shot I need yet," Benji complains to Hawk.

"Benji's here on spec for *Life*," Hawk explains, indicating the camera around Benji's neck.

"Yeah. Rich white people want to know all about the rise of the discotheque." Benji rolls his eyes. Then he looks at Astrid and says, "That dress. Silver under the lights. Lemme take a shot of you and Hawk."

And because the magic of music and dance is still cast like a spell around her, Astrid pulls Hawk onto one of the podiums on which girls in micro dresses frug energetically. Thousands of colored lights quiver on the ceiling and her arms fly above her head as the next song plays: "Let the Sunshine In." And it does—it's glittering through her feet, it's making her dress shimmer. She and Hawk share another addictive smile.

At first she doesn't know why Hawk moves toward her. Then she realizes, all in the space of a second, that one of the other dancers has crashed into him, propelling him forward and he's reaching out to stop himself falling. One of his hands lands on the back of her leg, the other a little higher, grazing the bare skin of her ass.

His touch is gone almost the same second it happens but it still makes fire burn through her like cognac.

They stare at one another, inhalations equally rough. And she knows she will never need LSD—the lingering heat of Hawk's hand on her skin is both the rapture and the madness of a trip.

There's no way she can kiss him. If she did, she'd never stop.

"I'm sorry," she says to Hawk. "It's cool if you want to dance with someone else."

She's the one who erected the barriers and, despite how much it would ache, she doesn't expect him to stay in this strange friendship, abiding by her crazy rules, when almost any other woman would be arching into his hands.

"I don't," he says, a wistful smile on his face. "I'll go get us some water."

SIX

BLYTHE BRICARD

Once she's in bed, Blythe's vow to be nothing and nobody circles like a nightmare. To stop herself from texting Nathaniel and saying she's changed her mind about their meeting, she thinks about the rest of the story she hadn't told Coco.

After Blythe finished her bachelor's degree, she worked for a couple of textile manufacturers, learning quickly that Bangladesh factories would break her heart. She sought out ethical producers in places like Peru and Chile, where they valued artisanal traditions—but paid her a pittance. It made her see that for her whole life she'd been making ethical fashion by recycling thrift store clothes into one-off pieces. She decided to make that her future, and enrolled in a master's in global fashion management.

On day one, as everyone introduced themselves, she heard gasps when she said her name, and felt the eyes of one person fixed on her—but they belonged to a man who was watching her as if what she said about recycling clothes into small-run, capsule collections was intriguing.

So she'd almost spoken just to him, to his incredible blue eyes that were like Peruvian mountain skies in June. At the end of class, while everyone was still whispering about her, he'd said, "I'm Jake. Do you want to get coffee?"

It was the first time in her life anyone had asked her out just for coffee. From that moment on, Jake wound around her heart like a silk robe she'd thought she'd never remove. But thirteen years on, she and Jake are divorced and Blythe has only a cottage business she runs out of her apartment. It's time to at least consider changing the second half of that sentence.

* * *

The next morning, Eva plonks herself by Coco's side at the mostly empty breakfast table as Ed asks Blythe, "What are you going to do about MIZZA? And didn't Nathaniel and Jake used to work together?"

Blythe nods. "They weren't adversaries, but I think they thrived on mutual competitiveness. And I haven't exactly decided, but I'm going to see Nathaniel tomorrow, which means I need a babysitter."

Sebby pipes up, "Can we ask Dad?"

Blythe recovers as quickly as she can with only a slightly strangled, "Sure!"

Once Ed's recovered too, he says, "I'll take you guys up to your dad's room and you can ask him. It's the best room, of course—the honeymoon suite, the only one on the very top floor. Your grandma couldn't manage the stairs, so she gave it to Jake."

Jake always gets the best of everything. Blythe assumes it's because he's the youngest. But she's glad of Ed's offer to take the kids up there because she doesn't want to visit Jake in a honeymoon suite and ask him for babysitting favors when he can't even get himself down to breakfast in time to eat with his kids.

They return with the surprising news that Jake's agreed to look after them. Blythe sees him only briefly midmorning on an excursion to the Château de Chenonceau. He spends maybe ten minutes there before he leaves. Coco's brother Nick—widely regarded as the naughty one—drops his phone in the moat, and their sister Emily has worn clothing completely inappropriate for the cold and moans the whole time.

They all return, pleased to discover the chateau has warmed enough to dispense with beanies and gloves. And dinner arrives on time, the kids falling on it happily.

One chair at the table is conspicuously empty.

"Where's Jake?" Blythe asks Joy, wanting to confirm he's still looking after the kids.

Joy darts a pained glance at her husband and Ed rescues his wife, saying, "He's on a date. With Marcelline Villiers."

"Oh," is Blythe's nonsensical response. Marcelline went to grad school with Jake and Blythe, is the marketing director at the House of Dior and recently dated Nathaniel. Of all the people in the world, could Jake not find someone without seven million connections to Blythe?

"Does that mean he's going to get married again?" Sebby asks glumly.

As if on cue, Iris turns to Blythe and says in a low voice, "There are some things about my son that I suspect he hasn't told you, but that I wish he would."

What the hell does that mean?

But Iris's attention is claimed by the hosts, who have questions about the arrangements for Iris's big party next week. So Blythe decides just to focus on her meeting with Nathaniel. She'll need all her wits to walk away from that with a deal that somehow lets her make the clothes she's always dreamed of, but with a level of protection for herself and the kids too.

* * *

Before Blythe goes to sleep, she texts Jake to confirm she'll bring the kids to the breakfast room at eight. He doesn't reply, but that's normal.

At eight, there's no sign of Jake. She catches Ed's eye and the look on his face makes her send the kids off to get some food.

"My dickhead brother didn't come home last night," Ed tells her.

Ed looks about as furious as Blythe's ever seen him and Blythe wishes she could be mad, rather than feeling her stomach concave with the knowledge of how hurt Eva and Sebby will be. She knows Ed will tell the kids if she asks him to. But no. That their father has let them down appallingly—by ditching them for his lover—is going to have to come from Blythe.

As soon as they return with their croissants, she squats down next to Sebby. "I'll stay. Jake's not here—"

"I *hate* him!" Eva flees. Sebby's body sags.

"You're going to Paris, Blythe." Ed's voice is firm. "Don't say no to Nathaniel because of Eva and Sebby. Seeing you over the last few days has made me and Joy realize how tough it's been. You don't get to drop the kids at their dad's and have a break. We want to help out more. So go get ready. I've got the kids."

Blythe leaves the room before Ed's compassion makes her cry.

She's only just got out her makeup when the suite door opens and she whirls around, thinking, *Thank God*. But it's Coco.

"I know you think you don't have time for this," Coco says. "But I'm about to confess something that's probably going to make you laugh, so at least you'll be amused while you do your makeup."

Blythe's fury at Jake dissolves in the face of Coco's persistent good humor. "Okay, tell me something funny. But I'm leaving in ten minutes."

"Got it. Remember how I stayed with you and Jake a few times? Well, I basically worshipped you after that. You were this super-cool aunt who was only fifteen years older than me and you took me to movies and let me borrow your clothes and...I'm still going to be your favorite niece after I've confessed all this, aren't I?"

Blythe laughs. "Yes."

Coco sits on the bed. "In my undergrad degree, we had to do a project researching a real person who wasn't traditionally seen as 'good' and make a presentation selling this person to the class. It was something to do with persuasive advertising and rehabilitating brands. Anyway, I chose Astrid—and this is the part where you'll laugh—because I wanted, like a young, romantic fool, to solve the mystery of Astrid for you."

"Coco." Blythe reaches out a hand for her niece. "That might be one of the nicest—but possibly most futile—things anyone's ever done for me. There's no mystery to solve. Astrid ran away. End of story."

"How can you say that!" Coco cries.

Blythe checks her watch, patience expired. "The police investigated. They closed the case. People are allowed to leave; it's not a crime. The media might love to throw around the question—is Astrid gone, missing, vanished or dead? But there is no mystery."

Because who would want to keep prodding the wound of being so unlovable that even your own mother would leave you?

But Coco is tenacious. "You know Nathaniel wants to resurrect MIZZA because it has an archive of sensational designs. Your mother created those designs. But how many people say, 'Astrid Bricard, fashion designer extraordinaire' when they write about her? I thought the other night when you said it made you rage, you meant it."

Coco presses a button on her phone and a voice like devoré, a fabric that takes its name from the French verb to devour, fills the room. Blythe can hear both the smoothness that got Hawk whatever he wanted in his youth, and the tones now burned away with whiskey, time, dope and cigarettes—whatever got him through the 1970s and out the other side.

"You want to rehabilitate Astrid? Well, let's start with the fact that she didn't have a drug dealer because she didn't do drugs. She got a little stoned maybe a dozen times in her life. Like that movie showed, *I* was the one with the drug problem." Hawk's voice pauses, then goes on. "And that photo at the Cheetah? We weren't even together then.

I don't know how many times I've told the media that. It was a crazy accident. Like the silver dress. Man, I hate that dress—at the same time as I love that dress. It brought us together. And it ripped us apart. Astrid's dress. It was always Astrid's dress."

There's the sound of Hawk clearing his throat. Blythe is frozen with shock.

More words spill from the phone. "How's Blythe? How's your aunt, I mean?"

Click. The recording shuts off.

"I think we can rule out that Astrid was driven away by her drug dealer," Coco says.

"Where did you get that?" is all Blythe can say.

"I interviewed him when I was eighteen. I never told you because I thought you'd be mad. Now I want you mad. Because if you're mad enough, you might do something about it."

SEVEN

ASTRID BRICARD & HAWK JONES

O ver the next month, Astrid goes to college during the day and
waitresses at night. She has dinner with her godmother, Alix
St. Pierre, on her night off. Alix runs *Élan*, a hugely successful wom-
en's magazine, and she's been behind Astrid's dreams since she was
a kid.

"You look happy," Alix tells her on one of those nights. "Like you've
found your place."

"I have." Astrid smiles. "And you know what? Maybe if it had
come easily, I wouldn't treasure it so much. When it's taken blood,
sweat and tears to get your one and only chance, there's no way you're
going to screw it up."

"Good," Alix says, smiling too.

On her way from college to work, Astrid also has a couple of quick
dinners with Hawk and his mom. The first time is a few days after
they danced together at the Cheetah and she's still got the rhythm
of that night, every second a drumbeat, pumping through her. She
meets him at the store and as she looks at the bare wooden bench and
the plain white walls she says, "You should drape white cloth over the
walls like at the Electric Circus. It'll make the space look bigger and
more intimate at the same time. And," she adds, seeing it in her mind,
"get a couple of your seamstresses to work here, at the bench. You

should work there too. Fashion design as performance art. Just like everyone goes to the Cheetah because it's not just a club, but because there's something to see in every corner."

Hawk's eyes sweep the room. "Far out." His hand lifts, then drops back to his side and she thinks maybe he was about to hug her. Instead he grins. "Thanks."

The next time she visits, the window is dressed with one large drawing: a woman with chin-length blond hair in a pair of tiny green shorts and a black jacket unbuttoned and with nothing underneath, just the way Astrid had worn it. The workbench is covered in fabric. Two seamstresses, Nancy and Fi, who Hawk told her were great with the sewing machines and overlockers but less so with the design work at Parsons, are busily working on what Astrid sees are the sinfully short silver lamé dresses. A group of customers are gathered at the other end of the bench—around Hawk.

She watches him listen politely to one of the women, his eyes dropping to the fabric and chalk on the table like he wants to make something, not chat. Another woman sashays out of the changing rooms, in the jacket from the window, letting it swing open and her breasts spill out. Hawk doesn't notice until she's practically poking his eyes out.

He's the kind of guy you could fall in love with, Astrid thinks, the same way you fall in love with a song—so it echoes inside you, making you shape your life around its beat. She stays in the doorway, keeping herself in that moment of just feeling everything—only feeling, not moving toward it or running from it.

He looks up and the smile that lights up his face is as sexy as hell.

She stands on the opposite side of the workbench, a safe distance between them. "The store looks great, Hawk."

"Thanks," he says. And his eyes don't drop, not once, to the fabric in front of him.

The following week, she sees an amazing L-shaped sofa in cognac-colored leather in a thrift store; Hawk, Benji and a few others carry it four blocks to the apartment and everyone sighs over it. The next time she visits, Hawk's papered one wall in solid amber so it looks like a permanent, glorious sunset. It's like the mood of that year, hot and hopeful—dazzling too. All the more so when Velvet races up to Astrid one morning before class, thrusting out a copy of *Life*. "Look!"

There on the cover is Astrid, legs ridiculously long, silver dress ridiculously short, dancing on a podium like she's been practicing for years for this moment. "Holy cow." *Life* must have taken Benji's photos.

But she's brought up short by a second picture—Astrid and Hawk dancing, taken the moment his hand disappeared under the hem of her skirt. Her back is to the camera, a glimpse of her ass on view. Hawk's face is visible but not hers, and somehow the image has caught and exposed everything they're trying not to feel for one another.

She sits on the floor, a thousand different emotions tussling inside her. A kind of thrill—she's on the cover of *Life*. Vulnerability—what if she's not the only one who can see what she feels, and maybe what Hawk feels too? Guilt—she shouldn't keep seeing him. But how do you separate the iron from the lodestone?

Velvet collapses next to her. "You're happy, aren't you?"

"Let me read it," is all Astrid says.

The article, which is about New York's discos and the explosion of youth and ideas and art and drugs that happen there nightly, also contains a couple of paragraphs about Hawk Jones, who's opened a store off Fifth Avenue and "is hotly predicted to be the Jimi Hendrix of fashion, rocking the likes of Oscar de la Renta and Bill Blass off their podiums. The crowd at the Cheetah aren't interested in prim suits for women who believe in waltzing," the article goes on. "The dresses Hawk Jones makes, like the silver lamé on the cover, are for girls who dance the same way they make love."

And farther down:

Astrid Bricard is another name to watch. Her pedigree alone dictates she be the hot blood that fuels every man's fantasy: she's the daughter of Mizza Bricard, the world's first fashion muse. Mizza was infamously shameless, didn't own any underwear, and was reputed to have had strings of lovers. Astrid seems to have inherited at least two of those traits from her mother.

Whatever momentary thrill she felt vanishes.

"Why aren't you screaming?" Velvet demands. "It might have taken nearly a hundred years to get a Black girl on the cover, but I don't even care about that right now because *you're* on the cover of *Life*."

"You mean the woman who doesn't own any underwear? What do you think Candace is going to do with that?"

"Fuck Candace." Velvet grins.

And Velvet's joy, her unconcern for anything except the fact that her friend is on a magazine cover, makes Astrid shake her head at herself, look at the cover again, and the sound that spills out of her now is a cross between *Oh my God* and a shriek. "That's me!"

"A name to watch," Velvet repeats, hugging her. Then she asks, serious now, "Are you in love with Hawk?"

Astrid returns to the photo of her and Hawk dancing together. It looks like infatuation—a grand passion so towering it can only burn itself out. But what sits inside her, folded up and tucked away where she can't feel it too often, is like a deep and lifelong ocean of passion, with islands of tenderness, warmth and intimacy awash in it too.

None of that is caught in the photograph.

Candace walks past and says, loud enough for Wall Street to hear, "How much money have you earned in Hawk's sheets? Enough to buy some panties?"

Everyone nearby laughs.

"Close the shades, Candace," Velvet snaps.

And then Astrid realizes what she's done—she's let herself be photographed for all to see. Like Mizza. Fear unspools inside her. It's like she was reaching for the moon and has just found a beaten-up tennis ball in her hand instead.

But...her eyes fall to the photo. She's dancing in a dress she loves. A dress that makes her feel powerful. She's not abusing anyone, hurting anyone. She's just a free, uninhibited woman.

Anger rushes in—anger at the world. Because, after first being drafted in 1923, the Equal Rights Amendment, asking for women to be recognized as equal to men, has been stuck in a judiciary committee for the past fifteen years because God forbid any woman ever have the nerve to think she has the same rights as a man. *Life* put Astrid on the front cover of their magazine because she's a young woman in a short dress and they're going to use that to sell some copies and decry her all at the same time.

Screw them. Screw Candace.

She strides into the classroom, head high.

Graham sits on one side, Velvet on the other. "You don't have to make yourselves into pariahs too," Astrid tells them.

"We're used to it," Velvet says.

The teacher calls the class to order, which silences the whispers but doesn't stop the stares. They want her to drop her head. To blush. For the first time, Astrid feels a flicker of kinship with Mizza. Was this why she posed so boldly in those photographs? Because she didn't want to accept the shame everyone wanted to drape her in?

The teacher tells them to draw something. To express themselves in one simple sketch. So Astrid does, remembering what she'd said to Velvet about wanting to design clothes that never made a woman feel passive or dependent. She draws what she wishes she was wearing right now. Something rash. Something bold.

Within a furious five minutes, on the paper in front of her is a dress that's like a flamenco dancer's—a deluge of delicate ruffles meant for the most scarlet of passions.

Everyone else is still sketching, erasing, frowning and casting sideways glances at Astrid. So she takes out silk organza in girlishly blushing pink and cuts long lengths, threads each with horsehair for stiffening, then attaches the shirring foot to one of the sewing machines, sets it to the gathering stitch, and ruffle after ruffle drops out. It's only when she scoops up her ruffles that she realizes everyone is staring at her.

"Today is just for drawing," the teacher says, judgment spilling from his eyes.

"We all know today is for gossiping," she says. "And my dress is more eloquent—and definitely more elegant—than some people's mouths."

She keeps going—mouth silent, dress fluent.

By the time class ends, she's pinned the dress together. She ducks behind a screen and slips it on. One ruffle stands up like a collar around her face, the neckline plunges down almost to her waist, and a bow cinches everything into pink flounces that cascade to mid-thigh in front and to the ground at the back. It's feminine. It's unafraid.

Graham whistles. "You look hot, babe."

Velvet expresses it better. "That dress is like innocence making out with sin."

The subsequent laughter shatters part of the wall the *Life* cover erected between Astrid and the rest of the class. And Astrid hopes her dress tells them she's at Parsons because she deserves to be and that there's no shame in being a woman free, stripped of the inhibitions society wants her to wear.

* * *

All that week Astrid tells herself she's not avoiding Hawk—that she's busy at Parsons and the bistro. The piece in *Life* made her see that now, more than ever, she can't let herself be distracted. Who she is and who her birth mother is means she needs to be twice as good as everyone else, otherwise those words—*Astrid seems to have inherited at least two of those traits from her mother*—will follow her, and the world will believe her skills are limited to flaunting herself and forgetting her underwear.

So she goes to the archives in the spare hour she has after class and before work and she studies dresses from decades ago, and she draws. But nothing looks right. It's like the door between inspiration and creation is shut but she needs to open it because . . .

"Your portfolio is the key to your future," the dean told them last week. "A strong portfolio will get you an internship over winter break. It will mean you're the one from your year group who becomes the name designer, or the lucky few who work for a name designer. A weak portfolio will mean you're in the majority who are taking up hems or waitressing in two years' time."

Graham had sighed. "So how come Hawk just went out and started a label?"

"Maybe Hawk's starting the change?" Astrid said stoutly. "Otherwise Parsons will just keep turning out people who design clothes like Bill Blass and Geoffrey Beene. I can't see you ever wearing a prim little Blass dress, Velvet."

Velvet shrugged. "Saying things need to change and thinking they will are two different things. But maybe Hawk'll do fine. He's a man after all."

Just like everyone else in fashion is a man: Blass, Halston, Beene, de la Renta.

Stop, she tells herself. Maybe it means there's a wide open space waiting for Astrid, as a female designer, to step into. The pink dress she made is a start. It's the kind of design that will get her an internship. But she needs others just as good, or better—needs to find inspiration and let it rush in.

But there's something else she has to do too. She calls in sick to the bistro on Friday night, which she never does, and takes the train out to her parents' place in Long Island, where they'll have been going bananas all week.

She knocks and braces for their anger. Beth, her mother, opens the door and calls out, "James! It's Astrid."

Her dad appears and they stand there, them inside, her outside. Her father clears his throat. "I called Alix," he says. "She said you're not taking drugs, you're working day and night, and the *Life* photos show a woman in her twenties dancing in a nightclub, which is apparently something most women your age do. Seems to me the photo shows a little more than that, but you can't argue with Alix."

Astrid shrugs. "I bet nobody around here's talking about anything else."

Beth says, very quietly, "They aren't—"

Her dad interrupts. "I didn't think you'd come out here. In fact, I thought we mightn't see you for a while."

Astrid turns away. She came because she knew they'd see the pictures, knew their friends would too. Staying away didn't change that, so she figured she might as well get her banishment over and done with. It hasn't taken long.

"Maybe you coming out here tells me Alix is right," she hears her dad say and she turns back slowly to face him. "I'm not happy about it," he continues. "But I'm happy to see you." He opens his arms and gives her one quick hug before he pushes her inside. "Come and eat. You're getting skinny."

That night, Beth watches Astrid when she thinks Astrid isn't looking, darting glances at the telephone every time it trills. James keeps bringing up Bill, a junior partner he'd invited for dinner earlier in the year, one who'd wanted to take Astrid somewhere quiet. She wants to tell her dad that Hawk has never suggested taking her anywhere quiet, but she knows the photographs tell a different story—a lie, actually. And she knows the subtext of her dad's conversation is love, so she accepts that instead of the words.

The next day before she returns to Manhattan, she hauls her surfboard out of the garage, borrows her mom's car, drives to Gilgo and throws herself into the water, where an offshore breeze is dealing out slow clean waves decorated with soft white foam. It takes a few waves to get her groove back, but soon she's sliding on water, her senses concentrated on the movement of swell beneath her feet, and she imagines silk the color of the sea rippling over a body. A dress with pieces cut out so you can glimpse skin here and there the same way you can see patches of light in the dark blue of the ocean.

At last. Inspiration. Designs she can add to her portfolio.

After a couple of hours, when the chill is almost too much, a figure appears and takes a seat on the sand. It's Hawk. The only way he could have found her is by going to her parents' house, speaking to her dad and borrowing his car to drive out here.

She's surprised he's still alive.

She hauls herself out of the water. When she's a few feet away, he stands, pulls off his sweater and hands it to her. And maybe if he hadn't done that, she would have just said *Hey* and they would have returned to Manhattan and nothing would have changed. But that one small action tells her he cares enough about her to have not only figured out where she's gone and to have faced her parents, but to offer her his sweater because he knows she's cold.

It makes her drop her board on the sand and keep walking, through the barriers she's erected—and still she doesn't stop. She tucks her head into his shoulder.

His arms are instantly around her, even though she's wearing a dripping wet bikini, sweater forgotten on the sand. She can feel the lean muscle of his torso beneath her hands, is acutely aware of the way his palm is pressed against the curve of her lower back, how her body is molded into his and his heart is racing. It's impossible not to lift her head up.

Three seconds of silence. Astrid and Hawk staring at one another on the beach and suddenly his lips are on hers and it isn't the messy kind of sophomoric kiss she's always had before. Hawk lets his mouth travel over hers in a sultry drift, so heady that all she wants is more.

"Hawk," she whispers.

"I know," he says huskily, tucking the nape of her neck into the crook of his elbow and holding her for another second before he lets go. "There's a paragraph about me in *Life* and the whole thing is about me. Whereas Mizza takes up half of yours. I can go out and open a shop and nobody cares who my mom is or what my history is. It's different for you. The article made me see that. The next time you're in *Life*, I want the whole paragraph—no, the whole damn article—to be about you. So"—he draws away reluctantly—"I won't do that again. Until you want to."

And because he actually believes she'll be in *Life* again, she tells him, "None of this is because I don't want to. But I feel like..." How to say it without sounding nuts? She needs to pour her energy and her creativity into making her future happen even if, right now, she wants to pour her entire self into Hawk. "I feel like if I kiss you again, I'll never stop. Which is probably the worst thing to say—"

He cuts her off, a flush coloring his cheeks. "Nope. It's just what I wanted to hear. I can wait. I have more than enough to do right now to keep me busy."

The way he says it, like he's half-buzzed on adrenaline and is trying to keep in some kind of incredible, ridiculous piece of news, makes her say, "What's going on?" Then she sees the shadows under his eyes. "When did you last sleep?"

"I don't even know." He grins. "Do you want to come and see?"

"See what?"

But he just says, "Race you back to the cars," and then he picks up her board and takes off across the sand. When they reach the parking lot, he touches his fingertips to hers for a too-short second before they return to her parents' house, get her things and take the train back to the city.

Inside the store, the racks hold only one pair of hotpants and two black coats. At the worktable, Fi and Nancy are sweating and looking at Hawk like he's pigeon shit on the sidewalk.

"You came back then," Nancy says sarcastically and Astrid realizes it's Saturday, that Hawk should have been in the shop and instead he's been chasing her out to Long Island.

"Where are all the clothes?" Astrid asks.

"We sold everything," Hawk says, like he can't quite believe it. "The *Life* article had Diana Vreeland in here—actually in the store—with an entourage almost too big to fit. Then everyone from *Vogue* told everyone else about the shop and it's been crammed with people every day. We had fifty silver dresses and they lasted two days. Fi and Nancy can't make the hotpants fast enough—as soon as we hang them up, we sell them. Now *Vogue*'s booked an exclusive shoot with Benji as the photographer, Henri Bendel wants to put me in the store, and I don't have a damn thing ready to be photographed by *Vogue* or to put in Henri Bendel because I don't even have enough to put in my own store."

He's pacing, and she can see he's riding so high it's a good thing his willpower is extreme—if he were prone to dropping acid or sinking tequila, he'd be a mess right now.

"I tried to draw a couple of things yesterday," he continues, "and Fi and Nancy tried to make them but they didn't work. I know that'll happen but I don't have time to draw failures. I need about a dozen more seamstresses, plus somewhere for them to work, and then there's all the money stuff I'm supposed to manage—except all I have is the money from my mom, which isn't enough to cover new capital expenses, plus the day-to-day stuff, so I can't afford the seamstresses and I'm in completely over my head."

"You sold everything?" she repeats, mouth stuck in a groove of speechless amazement while her mind is whooping for joy. "Hawk, that's out of sight."

And a brilliant idea forms.

"Come upstairs for a minute," she tells him, almost unable to wait until they're behind a closed door before she says, "Mizza sends me money every year with my birthday and Christmas cards. Guilt money. You can have it—"

Hawk's protest is vehement but she cuts him off, too excited to waste time on the tedium of manners. "I'll make it a loan if you want. Your dad will know someone who can help with the paperwork. Then you can use your mom's money to hire more staff and mine to rent space for a new workroom. It'll tide you over until more comes in. I don't want any interest. My only interest is in helping you make this happen. You sold nearly everything in a week, Hawk. That's *incredible*."

Her emphasis on the last word is as impassioned as his attempts at refusal.

At last he drops into a chair. "Shit. It *is* incredible." He shoves a hand through his hair, still-almost, but not quite, too-long rock-star hair that she suddenly wants to run her own hands through. "But you should use that money on yourself."

"Only in an extreme emergency will I ever use Mizza's money on me," she tells him. "I want you to have it."

His eyes are a mix of fierce and gentle. It would be so easy to tumble into another one of those slow kisses. Instead she says, "Take all of that energy downstairs and make something Hawk Jones with it. Sexy, but elegant and a little shameless too. Then go to sleep. I'll come back tomorrow with a check."

EIGHT

BLYTHE BRICARD

Blythe drives to Paris on autopilot, hearing Hawk's words bust wide open a couple of myths about Astrid. They weren't even together when the famous photograph that's meant to encapsulate their love affair was taken. So when did they get together? And Astrid wasn't on drugs, which annihilates one of the theories around her disappearance.

In playing that recording, Coco has undone Blythe's most tightly sewn seam and the questions are pouring in.

Firstly, why should she believe Hawk? She doesn't trust him—not after he all but left her to his mother to raise. Yes, Blythe had loved Meredith, but she'd died when Blythe was eighteen and in their every interaction was Blythe's tormenting mind, asking, *Would Astrid have hugged you then rather than scolded? Laughed rather than sighed? Would you have told her the things you don't tell Meredith, rather than hidden yourself behind sunglasses and books?*

She shakes her head. Focuses on Hawk. Maybe she doesn't trust him—but there's no reason for him to lie about the two facts in the recording.

Besides, all the other deplorable facts are indisputable: Astrid dropped out of design school after just a few months and became the woman famous for wearing Hawk Jones clothes and being the figurehead of the "youthquake." Then along came MIZZA. But how did a fashion school dropout best known for how great her ass looked when not quite covered in silver lamé create MIZZA? Was Astrid a brilliant designer who basically invented the idea of separates—stylish pieces women could wear to work and then out at night to play in— or did Hawk do that for her?

It's why Blythe's always believed Astrid left. Because all the lies caught up with her at Versailles and the truth came out—that Hawk was responsible for more of MIZZA than Astrid had let on. So she ran, caring more about not facing the music than her daughter. A dozen biographies, as well as the infamous movie, support that theory.

Halfway to Paris, Blythe's phone rings and she ignores it when she sees Jake's number. He's the last person she wants to speak to right now. When it rings again, she silences it.

The next time her phone vibrates, it's Ed.

"Are the kids okay?" she asks.

"It's Jake. I know you were relying on me and I screwed up. Again." He's speaking fast and in an un-Jake-like manner, as if he's rattled. "I know I disappointed the kids. I've apologized to Eva and she said to tell you she doesn't hate me anymore, but she doesn't like me much either. I don't blame her."

Blythe almost smiles at the idea of Eva giving Jake the tongue-lashing he deserves and wishes she could say, *I hereby relieve you of any responsibility for your children.* But she'll never say that because she grew up with an absent father.

"The last thing you asked me for was a divorce," Jake goes on. "As far as requests go, that was about as big as you can get. I haven't asked you for anything since then, but I'm asking for something now. Can you please put off your meeting with Nathaniel and meet me in Saumur?"

I haven't asked you for anything since then.

It's one of the things that most bothered her after their split. She'd had no idea when she asked him for a divorce that his business was dollars away from bankruptcy. Of course, he's far from bankrupt now—divorce has saved his career in a way it hasn't saved Blythe's. But it had taken her months to get over the fact that he hadn't trusted her—or loved her? Respected her?—enough to ask for help, or to tell her he was drowning.

Her mind's so scattered she's in no fit state to meet Nathaniel anyway. So for Eva and Sebby's sakes she agrees to meet Jake, and hates herself the whole way to Saumur.

* * *

The address Jake's given her is for the kind of romantic hotel you'd go to if you were proposing to someone. *I swear to God, Jake,* she thinks as she gets out of the car, *if I'm meeting you in the room you shared last night with Marcelline, then I will empty the contents of the minibar on your head.*

She squares her shoulders and adopts the Blythe Bricard posture—sunglasses on, stride easy, a woman who couldn't care less what people say about her. At the front desk, the receptionist does an all-too-familiar double take, then shows Blythe to a meeting room. Jake's there, beside a screen with the word *MIZZA* on it.

"What's this?" Blythe asks, jaw tight.

"It's an ambush, which I'm sorry about."

There's no sign of Marcelline. Jake looks a little tired, but he's hiding it well under his trademark stubble and signature blue—a T-shirt in a fabulously soft Prussian blue, which, if they were still married, she'd definitely be stealing.

It's either excessively hot in the room or the slideshow is making her sweat. She's wearing a coat over a strapless yellow top that was once a ballgown. She slides her coat off, feeling like a wilting sunflower beside a coolly undisturbed lake.

"You know resurrecting MIZZA is a great idea," Jake says. "If it wasn't, you'd have told Nathaniel to go to hell the second he mentioned it."

"I did, actually," she snaps, looking past the blue of his eyes and into the soul of a man who let his daughter down so unforgivably just a few hours ago.

He looks away and she's the cool and undisturbed one now.

But Jake is very good at boardroom presentations and controlling his emotions. He puts forward such a persuasive presentation about MIZZA that Blythe almost applauds for whoever will take this budget and strategy and make it a brand-new legend.

He concludes by saying, "Take out all the shit the last thirty-odd years have thrown at you and look at the spark this depends on. You. You were the most creatively talented person at grad school. I was the best at being the guy at the front of the room with the master plan and the silver tongue. Marcelline could have sold ski jackets to desert dwellers. Because we were studying global fashion management, there were plenty of people with the business smarts, but not as many with the creative flair. You got pregnant with Eva at the wrong time and had to put everything on hold. I want to give that chance back to you. I'll fund MIZZA. You'll have the backing of Blake Group behind you. But it'll be yours to run."

Blake Group. He'd called it that, back when it was just a dream, because it combined both Blythe and Jake and was almost the same as his surname. He'd been watching her unpick the seams of a moth-eaten 1950s Claire McCardell dress and had asked, "What happened to the brand? You said it was one of the most famous American sportswear labels of the 1950s."

"It vanished," she said. "Like Schiaparelli or Tina Leser. Not every label survives."

"What if someone resurrected them?" he said, starting to pace, at the beginning of an idea he wanted to chase. "They have all that goodwill. An archive of designs. So much unrealized potential."

"Maybe *you* should resurrect them."

He'd used all his contacts to find people to back him. He'd traveled the world, chasing down labels and micromanaging fledgling businesses, filling them with their classmates from FIT. It had gone well for a couple of years until he'd grown too fast, overcapitalized, and was almost bankrupt at the time of their separation. Then he'd sold off labels, honed the organization down to its leanest and brightest, and come to an arrangement to resurrect Claire McCardell and had a startling success on his hands within a year, which had allowed him to expand once again.

He'd done everything he'd dreamed of and Blythe had done nothing.

"This is what we agreed, Blythe," Jake says now. "It wasn't called MIZZA, but it's the same thing."

"Jake," Blythe says tiredly, "we also made a deal to be together until death do us part, yet here we are, alive and very separate."

His jaw twitches. "And whose—" He cuts himself off.

Was he about to say, *And whose fault is that?* It's lucky he cut himself off because Blythe sure as hell would have cut something off him. Their divorce was his fault.

They glare at one another across the table and Jake says stubbornly, "I owe you this. Remember?"

And yes, she does. After grad school, she'd taken on freelance work, mostly in costume design, as well as advisory roles for businesses trying to forge links with textile suppliers in South America. She'd also kept herself busy on her plans for her business—an ethical label of pieces made from recycled clothing. And Jake had held down a strategic planning job for a luxury conglomerate while he refined his business idea. Until crunch time had come. To move forward, they needed to quit their paid work and take the plunge into penury and self-belief.

"We can't both quit at the same time," she'd said. "We won't be able to pay the rent."

"Or eat." He grinned. Then sighed. "You're right. You quit. I'll wait."

"How about I deal with the elephant in the room?" she said a little sadly, because that elephant had been weighing on her for months, intractable.

He grimaced, then rested his forehead against hers, hand sliding over her cheek and into her hair. "Blythe..."

She reached up to kiss him. "Thank you for saying you'd wait. But you know if we do it that way, we won't be eating for a hell of a lot longer than if you go first."

Jake's business had an advantage for investors—he wanted to revive brands that already had a history. Blythe's business was *sustainable* and *ethical*, words that made investors think, *expensive*. There was also the fact that Jake was a man. They both knew men raised more money, more quickly, than women did.

"This way," she said to him, trying to smile, "I get to learn from your mistakes. And realistically, I'll get my business up and running in much the same amount of time as if I had gone first. I have to do a lot of educating about why ethical fashion is important, and I can start that now. So the groundwork will be there when it's my turn."

"The minute I'm making enough money that we can afford to eat, you're quitting. And I'll make sure I get to that point as fast as I can," Jake told her. "Deal?"

"Deal," she'd agreed.

But she'd unexpectedly become pregnant with Eva. After having suffered the heartbreak of an absent mother herself, she'd known she couldn't juggle a new business and a baby. So she put her plans on hold, intending to go back to them when Eva was one, but Jake was so busy then, his business demanding every hour, and he was mostly away and couldn't help care for Eva. The day the pregnancy test came back positive with Sebby, she locked her plans in a cupboard.

"I've been debating whether I should say this," Jake continues, interrupting her thoughts. "But Hawk Jones, your dad's label, is the one going strong today. Do you remember," he segues, "the night we had dinner with Alix and she told you she'd been waiting impatiently for years for a woman to rise up, but they kept slipping off the glass runway?"

Blythe nods, recalling the evening from several years ago with Alix St. Pierre, who'd been Astrid's godmother, and then Blythe's as well. Blythe had been so fired up after that—so angry at the gender imbalance in fashion. The workers were women; the famous designers and the executives were largely men.

"You told me you wanted to change that," Jake said. "And I believed you—not just that you wanted to, but that you would."

Is he daring her?

It's not the time to accept something stupid just so she doesn't look like a chicken.

But, shit. What a mess her life is. She's staying in an igloo with her ex-husband, she seriously contemplated making space-age loincloths, she's pretending she doesn't care what happened to her mother, she's telling Coco that the endless scrutiny of her life makes her rage—but why isn't she raging? If she ever thought her kids would grow up to be like her, she'd shake them.

An idea is starting to take shape but she needs a moment to let it come together. Jake wants something from her—like Nathaniel, Jake stands to win if Blythe takes on MIZZA. This isn't solely about him owing her; it's about him making money. Right now, the deal is very much in his favor—he gets a new brand, prestige and profit. Blythe gets a job. But Blythe wants something else.

She adopts his interrogative stance. "Why did you go out with Marcelline last night?"

"To grill her about Champlain. I wanted to know if he's changed. But I bet he went for the casual, you're-not-a-presentation-kind-of-gal approach, right?"

Blythe nods reluctantly.

"I disagree," Jake says firmly. "He knows MIZZA is interesting without you, but perfect with you. You deserve a presentation."

Like her kids deserve a father.

She walks over to the coffee machine and makes an espresso. While her back is facing him, she asks, "Were you ever going to look after Eva and Sebby today?"

When she turns around, his expression is troubled. "I *was*. I am. I know I fucked up. You finally put me on your list of babysitters and I let you down. I lost track of time putting this together and that's unacceptable—if I didn't have you as a fallback, I wouldn't have that luxury. I jumped in the car and thought I'd bring them here and they could wait while I did the presentation. Then I realized what a stupid idea that was. I tried to get the hotel to organize a babysitter and that took too long. So I rang you and..." He stops, for once in his life lost for words.

She will give him one *absolute* final chance to be a father.

"I have a proposition," she says, and she's the one daring him now. "Put all this energy into your kids, Jake. Create a plan to make Eva and Seb so happy that I never again have to hear Eva say that she hates you. I know what it's like to have a father who fulfills an obligation a few times a year and who you eventually never want to see because witnessing obligation rather than love hurts more than anything." Focusing solely on Eva and Sebby is the only thing that gets her through that sentence without faltering.

There's a dim warning in the back of her head that she's about to commit to restarting MIZZA, one way or the other. And that maybe a sense of anticipation is clawing its way out from underneath the fear.

Which makes her ask for the scariest thing of all. After what Coco played to her this morning, she's almost starting to believe there *is* a mystery to be solved.

"Your business has access to magazine and newspaper archives, right?" she asks him. "You have subscriptions for all that stuff?"

"Of course," he says, frowning, having no idea what she's angling for.

"I want you to give Coco log-in details for all of that. She's doing some research for me and she needs to trawl through archives neither she nor I have access to. So..." She tips the espresso down her throat. "Give Coco access to what she needs. And then you have three weeks at the chateau to execute a plan to be a father to our children. If you do, then I'll work with Blake Group on resurrecting MIZZA. If you don't, then I'll work with Nathaniel. And just to be clear, I mean eating breakfast with them. Putting them to bed. The little things, not just the boardroom presentations. And if you don't, then that's it. You walk away. I can't have you breaking their hearts once a year."

And there must be a blue moon in the sky right now because Jake says, "It's a deal."

NINE

ASTRID BRICARD & HAWK JONES

The following weekend, Astrid sits in Hawk's shop working on her portfolio, catching up on the classes she missed while meeting with one of Matthias's former partners to draw up the agreement to invest her money in Hawk. Matthias had grilled her for a long time—stipulating she be the first creditor to be paid off rather than Meredith if Hawk fails, which she'd tried to refuse, but he wouldn't arrange the contract unless she agreed. The result had been a check for Hawk, and Astrid losing ten percent of her marks for one class—she missed a surprise test, which they'd been warned about at the start of the semester. As a scholarship student, she has to maintain at least a ninety-percent average. Hence spending the day on her portfolio, which she'd meant to do in the library, but the mismatch between her brain and her pencil while she sat in the quiet was like a ballerina dancing *Swan Lake* at the Cheetah.

Now her pencil is moving freely. Hawk's store is buzzing. "Touch Me" by the Doors is playing, and the hotpants have been restocked and are flying out the door. At least a dozen customers have approached Astrid and told her how much they love the photo of her dancing with Hawk—which now hangs in the window, life-sized. She laughs and tells them she isn't with Hawk, but they exchange knowing glances as if there's an alternate universe out there where Hawk's hand doesn't stop when it slides over Astrid's ass.

It's a thought she doesn't let herself dwell on.

Indeed, she tries not to watch Hawk too much, but every time she catches his eye, she knows she's failing. Still, she has at least four or five great sketches, so sneaking semi-covert glances at Hawk and receiving a smile each time definitely seems to be working.

Maybe that makes Hawk her muse. She laughs.

"Whatever you've been smoking, I want some," Benji says as he takes a seat beside her.

Two girls interrupt, fervor in their eyes. "We want to buy a poster."

One of them points to the photograph in the window and says with breathless expectation, "And we want you both to sign it."

Benji grins. "Posters. Hawk should definitely do that."

The girls' disappointment is so acute Astrid ends up signing a piece of paper for them, which they take, along with two pairs of the green hotpants Astrid's wearing.

"It's like people have made up a whole story about me and Hawk," she says to Benji after the girls leave.

"Which is why—and Hawk told me not to say anything but it's gonna be my last shoot, so what the hell—*Vogue* wants you to be the model in the shoot next month."

"What do you mean it's your last shoot?"

Benji's voice is bitter. "Last month the government said anyone who got up to number one hundred and ninety-five in the Vietnam draft would be called up. I got number one hundred and ninety. I've been told to report for my physical."

"Five numbers," Astrid says, horrified. "If—"

"Ifs give me the shits." Benji grabs a cigarette out of a pack on the counter. "There are no what-ifs. Only what *is*. And what's happening is that I'm off to Vietnam. So you can either do me a solid and make my last shoot something to remember or you can send a man off to war with regrets. Hawk said he won't ask you, but we all know if you wear the clothes, it'll be a sensation. Besides, you told me you didn't want to have to pick up any more waitressing shifts because it would cut into time you need to spend at college—well, *Vogue*'ll pay you crazy money. You won't have to waitress for a fucking year."

"Benji." Hawk's voice behind them is sharp.

Benji grins unrepentantly. "Astrid, I'm telling you—you get money and a clear conscience. And you make me famous before I die in Vietnam."

He walks away, whistling like he hasn't just lit a match and tossed it on the floor between them.

Another woman buys a pair of lime-green hotpants. Her friend asks if Hawk will make any more silver dresses. When she's told no, she looks like she might cry.

"How many of these have you sold today?" Astrid asks him, pointing to her shorts.

"A lot," he admits.

"More than yesterday?"

"Hell yeah," Fi says, obviously eavesdropping on the entire conversation.

"Let's go upstairs," Hawk says, cutting her off, and Astrid is aware of how many eyes watch them leave.

"Everyone thinks we're sleeping together," she says once they're on the right side of a closed door.

"I know."

She starts laughing, unable to believe she's part of a world where people want to buy a poster of her, a world where what she wears matters. But she stops abruptly. "What draft number did you get?"

He rubs a hand over his jaw. "Number three hundred and sixty-four. I'm obscenely lucky."

Astonishing relief floods through her, followed by guilt that she's celebrating Hawk's luck when thousands of men fell on the wrong side of chance. Like Benji. What kind of person would say no to him right now?

Besides, he's right. If they get the energy of that night at the Cheetah into Hawk's first shoot in *Vogue*, the results will be epic.

"Let's do it," she says.

* * *

During the month before the photo shoot, Astrid rations her visits to the store. It's easy to fall under a spell when she's there—to live in the thrum and buzz of that sexy, alternate universe. Instead, she goes to classes, sees Alix each week for dinner and works on her portfolio. One night when she gets back late to the apartment after finishing her shift at the bistro, she finds a note from Velvet. *Call Hawk. Urgent.*

"Hey," he says when he answers. "I've missed you."

"Me too," she says truthfully.

"You might take that back when I tell you this," he says, trepidation in his voice. "Benji passed the physical. He's being shipped out. *Vogue*'s pulled the shoot forward to Friday. I got them to make it at seven in the morning so you can still get to class. But we'll just use a model if it doesn't work for you."

"I have an exam on Friday morning," she says. "At ten."

She considers. Surely it can't take three hours to shoot a few dresses? Benji snapped the shot of her in the silver dress in ten seconds. She can leave the shop at nine and be at Parsons in plenty of time. So she says okay.

When she arrives on Friday, Hawk's alone. He's wearing his usual uniform of jeans, gray sweater, bare feet and stubble, and the sharp heat of seeing him after a ten-day absence is something she isn't prepared for. She realizes she's staring, and that his eyes have turned the color of jet. She swallows and hoists herself up onto the workbench where she can study fabric, not him. But she can feel him walking toward her.

He stops right in front of her. There's a space between the edge of the workbench and his body, but it's only an inch or two, like the pause between the chorus and the bridge in a song—the moment of silence before everything changes.

"Hawk," she says, voice low, and now he's standing between her legs, palms braced on the counter on either side of her body. His lips hover in front of hers, as does the memory of the one time they kissed. His breath is hot on her skin, the anticipation of what comes next the hottest thing of all.

The jangle of the shop bell makes them both jump, caught by the *Vogue* team in what must look like a moment of ardor, even though nothing happened. Astrid's cheeks are burning; Hawk's are flushed too.

"Sorry to interrupt!" one of the women calls out gaily. "I need to steal Hawk from you for a moment, Astrid."

"I'll go get ready," she says, sliding off the workbench. "What do you want me to wear?"

But the editor hasn't decided, and it somehow takes an hour for her to confer with the hair and makeup people.

At eight o'clock Astrid says to Hawk, "Will they get started soon?"

"Benji's not here," he says, grimacing. "I'm gonna go drag him out of bed. I'll be quick."

Hawk returns half an hour later with Benji, who's too drunk to hold a camera. Hawk makes a pot of coffee and fetches a glass of water. The latter he tips over Benji's head.

"I'm gonna die over there," Benji says sullenly. "I dreamed it."

Hawk's eyes flicker to Astrid and he mouths, *Sorry*. But she wouldn't have him do anything else than walk Benji up and down outside in the cool air. Eventually they embrace the way men do, with a ferocious clap on the back that contains all the sentiment they can't express.

When Benji returns, he can hold a camera, but the look in his eyes is terrible. Astrid sees a reflection of it in the recesses of Hawk's.

"Are you okay?" she asks him.

"Yeah," Hawk says. "And I'll never be anything less than okay because I won't be sent to Vietnam, so I'd damn well better make something of that. All right," he calls to the *Vogue* team. "Astrid has to leave. Let's get started."

It's nine o' clock. She needs to go at half past nine at the absolute latest, which will still mean arriving at Parsons out of breath and harassed.

"What could Astrid possibly have to do that's more important than being here with you, Hawk," a junior editor purrs.

"She has an exam," he says, extracting his arm from the woman's grasp.

"I didn't know she was still in school."

Which makes twenty-four-year-old Astrid feel about five years old.

But it still takes twenty minutes for anything to happen. The *Vogue* girls argue over the styling. Benji isn't happy with the lights. Astrid waits in her underwear in the fitting room for the clothes.

"Come on," she hears Hawk say in exasperation.

"I suppose school is Astrid's fallback for when Hawk moves on," she hears the arm-clincher whisper. Then, more loudly, "Hawk, let's start with some of that fabulous sexual energy you have with Astrid. With her pedigree, she won't need much direction from Benji to know what to do."

That barb is like kneeling on the floor at school and having her skirt length measured. Parsons is her dream, not her fallback. She's here as a favor, not a life choice.

Astrid doesn't care that she's wearing only a pair of panties. She tugs open the curtain and strides across the store, hair flying loose behind her. "You want some sexual energy? A glimpse of what my heritage bequeathed me?" she snaps at the editor. "Well, here I am."

She comes to a standstill in front of Hawk, back turned to everyone, and looks over her shoulder at Benji. "Take the damn shot."

Then she hauls on her shorts, voice trembling with what she hopes sounds more like anger than tears. "Was that sexy enough for you? What a pity my panties aren't made by Hawk Jones. Although I guess you weren't expecting me to be wearing panties, not with my *pedigree*."

She's still tugging her sweater over her head as she steps through the door and starts to sprint, not even knowing whether a cab or her legs will be faster.

She arrives at ten minutes after ten. They won't let her in.

She's just failed her exam.

What the hell has she done? Had her head turned by *Vogue* shoots and money and all the things she never wanted. Because she hasn't just failed an exam. Not turning up today will mean losing her scholarship.

She slides to the ground, face buried in her hands. Rather than graduating next year, Astrid might never work in fashion at all. And she can't blame her parents or Mizza or her teachers or the world. The only person to blame is herself.

She wanted to be good enough. But a daughter who can't even keep a scholarship isn't something Mizza will regret. It's something she'll be glad she gave away.

TEN

MIZZA BRICARD

PARIS, 1917

Your face is a little too remarkable."

Mizza stared in painful confusion at her mother. Her father was being buried today. But her mother's eyes were dry and her attention was focused on Mizza's face, which was tear-streaked and red rather than remarkable.

The next day, sixteen-year-old Mizza was sent to a convent school, where she was fed prayers for breakfast, penitence for lunch, and expiation for dinner. It was a sin just to breathe. But no one could live without air.

It took three attempts—and three beatings—until finally she managed to run.

When she saw the front door of the familiar apartment in the 16th *arrondissement*, she smiled for the first time since her father's death. But inside, she discovered her mother had remarried. Her father had been not just buried, but replaced.

The man now occupying his study had taken down the beloved Klimts and Matisses and replaced them with oil paintings of women falling from grace. He said to her, one eye fixed on the image of a semi-naked sinner on her knees before a man, "You are how old?"

"She's a schoolgirl," her mother said tightly.

Mizza knew she'd be sent straight back to school. So she ran again, this time to the home of Ida Rubinstein, who'd been a friend of her father's, despite Ida being an infamous ballerina who'd scandalously danced *Salomé* nude.

"Oh, *chérie*," Ida said, folding her into her arms and touching a gentle finger to Mizza's cheek. "I think this is only the first time you'll discover that being beautiful can be more of a curse than a blessing."

Since the day of the funeral, Mizza had swallowed down the tears. Now they flooded out. Ida had called her *chérie*, like her father used to. But he would never do that again. Her mother had called her remarkable, with hatred in her voice. And now Ida was telling her the world was crueler than she'd known, but that she'd help Mizza through it.

That was six months ago and Mizza hadn't seen her mother since. It had taken a month not to cry over that at night. But she still sometimes wept for her father.

Not today. Today she stood in the bedroom Ida had given her and opened a box from the House of Doucet. Inside was a gown she fell in love with.

Ida appeared in the doorway, all dark hair and gracefulness, and smiled. "Will you wear it tonight?"

"It's from Monsieur Doucet himself." Mizza held out the note.

"Isn't that the second gown you've been gifted this week? You'll be more famous than I am soon." Ida smiled, as if nothing could have delighted her more. A far cry from most of the women with cruel eyes—like Mizza's mother—who ruled over Paris's salons, ready to cauterize anyone who so much as threatened the order of things.

"Enjoy it, *ma chérie*," Ida continued. "This time, your beauty is a blessing. But make sure you always understand what accepting a gift means. In this case, it's a trifle. With your face finishing off the dress, Doucet knows other women will rush to buy it. But in other cases..."

She paused. "I'm never sure if this is the kind of wisdom your father would have wanted me to pass on, but some people will see a ravishing and parentless sixteen-year-old and…" Ida's face became uncharacteristically somber and Mizza felt the buffeting of those words land deep inside her.

Parentless. Mizza had never considered herself an orphan until now. She sank onto the bed, remembering her father carrying her over to a Picasso sea on his office wall, showing her the one ripple in the water that lent the painting its majesty. Those ripples were like the folds of silk on the demimondaines' dresses at the races at Longchamps, which had fascinated Mizza and made her mother grab her hand and haul her away, insisting, "One must never look upon those women."

After living at Ida's for six months and learning more of the world, Mizza now understood what a demimondaine was. Women who'd accepted more than just gifts.

"Just make sure you're never ignorant of someone's intent, or unwilling to uphold your end of a deal," Ida finished in a gentle voice.

And for the first time, Mizza understood that life wasn't now. Life was what might happen in one year's time, or in two. She'd been brought up to marry, but parentless sixteen-year-olds who lived with shocking ballerinas were not marriageable in the way that a banker's daughter from the 16th *arrondissement* was.

Her gaze shifted to her reflection. Green eyes that curved up at the corners. Deep brown hair that could shine red in certain lights. Skin that was, she thought, her one true beauty.

"I think…" she said haltingly, "I think I needed to know that."

Ida kissed the top of her head. "I wish you didn't."

* * *

That night, artists, musicians and dancers, as well as the *emigrés* fleeing Russia—Ida's birthplace—crowded in. The salon was lit by only a few lamps. The brocade wallpapers were burgundy and gold, and curtains draped seductively in uncustomary places, beckoning you into their folds.

All around, women smoked cigarettes. They drank. Many of them, like Ida, wore garments that were more like costumes—gauzy, unexpected. Clothes that announced who the person wearing them was—or who they wanted to be. A coquette. An artiste. An innocent.

Two women stood in the center of the room surrounded by men— Coco Chanel, who'd just presented Paris with a couture collection unlike any other, and Jeanne Toussaint. Mizza had never spoken to them—they had a boldness that made society madams whisper behind their fans like they whispered about the demimondaines at Longchamps.

"Who gave Coco that bracelet?" Mizza heard one woman hiss to another.

"She's taken up with an Englishman," her friend murmured.

There was something about Coco and Jeanne that made Mizza study them more carefully. They exuded more than just seduction. Mizza remembered the way her mother had looked at her the day before she sent her off to convent school. That same fire had emanated from her. *Ambition*. Yes. That's what sparked from Coco and Jeanne.

What sparked from her? A lost and untethered quality, perhaps.

"Where's the girl Ida's taken in?" A voice came from nearby. "I heard she's quite a picture."

"But in the way of a *Madame X*, rather than the *Mona Lisa*," another voice said. "She'll end up a dancer like Ida or a demimondaine."

Mizza almost whirled around to challenge them. But, the truth was—and how had she not understood this before?—she was just like orphaned Coco. Like Jeanne, who'd run away from home when she was fifteen. The world was presenting Mizza, who couldn't dance, with one choice. To be the one with the bracelets who was the source of the *on dit* at a party.

"Which will you choose?" came a wry voice at her elbow.

Mizza turned to see Jeanne Toussaint beside her.

Jeanne shrugged. "It's not so bad."

"That's not a very persuasive recommendation," Mizza said equally wryly and Jeanne laughed.

"It's not," she agreed. "And I have a few years on you, so I should let you flounder, otherwise you might end up as my competition. Coco already hates you."

"I've never even spoken to Coco," Mizza protested.

"Cigarette?" Jeanne proffered an expensive-looking case and Mizza decided she might as well start smoking tonight, given everything else she was learning about the world.

She inhaled just enough that she wouldn't cough and said, "So are you going to tell me or let me flounder?"

Jeanne laughed again. "All right. If you decide to live the way Coco and I do, then choose the right man. Not the richest. Not the one with the most status. But the one who can unknowingly help you be something other than the demimondaine or the dancer. You need just one opportunity. I met Louis Cartier, the jeweler, not so long ago. Now I'm designing handbags for him. What you do at these parties is a stepping stone to a place where you don't have to rely on anyone. Trouble is, you've got to do a hell of a lot of relying first."

Mizza blinked. She couldn't cry at a party. But—*my God*. How did you live with yourself when you weren't a person, but an object? How did you endure years of being passed from hand to hand—well-cared-for hands if you were lucky, careless hands if you weren't. In five years, Mizza might be laughing in the center of the room beside Jeanne and Coco, still wearing a dress she hadn't paid for, searching for that elusive opportunity.

"Is that the only way?" she asked bleakly.

"Look around," Jeanne said. "Wife, dancer or demimondaine—that's the world. Runaways like us don't get proposed to—I think it would kill me anyway. I can't dance. So I'm just trying to make something out of the choice that's left to me."

"But how do you skip this step?"

"You think you can go straight from here with your beautiful face to what you want? Good luck." Jeanne stubbed out her cigarette.

And off she went, into the middle of the room, unashamed of her choices.

All Mizza knew was that she had to work out what opportunity she wanted, otherwise the world would work it out for her. Her eyes flew around the salon.

Over there was Picasso. In that corner stood Cocteau. Everywhere at Ida's parties was art and literature and intellect, knowledge Mizza was lucky to be exposed to. Which meant that if Mizza made this party her school, these people her teachers, then she might discover not only what opportunity she wanted to pursue, but she might even find a way to do it that wasn't the same as Coco and Jeanne's.

Wearing the confidence of a woman dressed in Doucet, Mizza stepped out of the shadows. She'd start with writer Colette, then speak to Ballets Russes' founder Diaghilev, finish with couturier Poiret. She would never let herself be the ravishing and parentless sixteen-year-old gossiped over in tales about who'd paid for her pearls—she'd be the one spoken of because of what she herself had done.

ELEVEN

MIZZA BRICARD

PARIS, 1917–1918

When the next dress arrived from Doucet, rather than smiling, Mizza frowned. There was too much lace. Last week she'd worn a dress by Vionnet and it had been sleek and simple. The unfussiness had somehow made it more about Mizza and less about the dress. And she'd liked that—the dress was the setting against which she could shine.

She took out her scissors and cut off most of the lace, letting the plunging V of the neckline down to the gently draped surplice be the thing that caught the eye because it let her be seen. That night, she had more attention than ever—enough to learn that it would take no effort at all for her to step onto the same path that Jeanne Toussaint and Coco Chanel had chosen.

She backed away into the shadows and collided with something. A man, breathtakingly tall and with eyes fixed on her.

"I'm Lev Narishkine," he said to her in a Russian accent and she knew he must be another *emigré* from the Russian civil war.

"I'm—" She went to introduce herself but he said, "The woman I'm going to marry."

She'd spoken to a dozen men that night and in the mouths of any of them, the words would have sounded like the lies she didn't want to hear. But this didn't.

Still, she said, "I'll give you five minutes to investigate my pedigree and you'll forget you said that."

He offered her a gentle smile. "When your home's been burned down, your family murdered, and you've traveled across Europe with only your life, one bag of clothes and the things that fit into your pockets, pedigrees seem like a very eighteenth-century custom."

And when your father has died and your mother's sent you away so you won't compete with her, and you're trying to start your life all over again, then yes—pedigrees did seem worthless.

"Come with me." She led the way out of the crowded salon and into the private sitting room and asked him to tell her more.

He told her about fleeing Russia, that his bag had held just two suits—that the things in his pockets were the family jewels. "My mother and father wouldn't leave," he said, turning a cigarette lighter contemplatively over in his hand, face shadowed. "They wanted to die in their homeland, together. But they wanted me to take our family's history, which they thought was preserved in the heirlooms that had been handed down over centuries. It's a romantic idea, but..." He paused, eyes two black pools of grief. "I think I would have preferred they'd left Russia, and the Bolsheviks had shot the pearls, not the other way around."

She reached out for his hand. Two orphans, adrift. But he'd lost his family through violence, Mizza through a stopped heart and a mother's selfish ambition. She still had her country. Ida. So much, in fact. "I'm sorry," she said.

His eyes caressed her face. "Would you like to dance?"

In his arms, dancing to the gramophone music that whorled in from the salon, she told him how she'd come to be with Ida. "In my mother's house, I left behind the person I would have become, like it was a dress I'd grown out of. Now I'm remaking myself. I'm a work in progress though," she finished with a smile.

"You're better than perfect," he murmured and she moved her head to nestle against his shoulder.

At the end of the night, he lifted her hand to his mouth, a brush of lip that barely touched her skin, but it worked its way right through her.

* * *

The next afternoon, Doucet sent a note asking her to come to the salon and to bring her gown with her. And she realized what she'd done. She'd cut up the work of a man who dressed much of Paris, thinking she knew better.

But you did, a voice whispered inside her, the same voice that kept replaying Lev's words, *You're better than perfect*.

Doucet would send her no more dresses. Other couturiers might withdraw their gifts too. She'd be left with only her wits and her old gowns and her apparently remarkable face to parlay with for the future she'd wanted. Couture had been her armor—men could scent desperation on a parentless woman in a dated gown. And rather than insist to Doucet that she'd improved the dress, it was her place to be silent while scolded.

She entered the salon, mind searching desperately for a way to fix this.

"Here she is," Monsieur Doucet said. Then he beamed, which made her stop short. Perhaps it was because the salon was so public. He'd take her into the workrooms away from his customers and excoriate her there.

"My new assistant is ready to help you with that, madame," he said to a lady dressed in the model of the gown Mizza had worn last night—the original, with all the lace. Then to Mizza, he said, "I believe you need scissors." And he gave her his own. A couturier's scissors were like their soul. And he put them in Mizza's hands.

* * *

She was the lowliest of Doucet's many assistant designers but he could have put her in a room beneath the basement and she would have felt higher than if she'd drunk a cellar of champagne. Having a job meant she had money—coins she'd earned out of fabric that wasn't a man's bedsheets. She hadn't just skipped over Jeanne's stepping stone, she'd soared over it.

Every day she went to the House of Doucet with a smile. She made the smallest of adjustments to the gowns, paring down the frills and lace so that the women looked as beautifully attenuated as Rodin sculptures, rather than as ornamented as boudoirs at the Palace of Versailles.

After some weeks, she began to say to Doucet things like "What if we used the motifs from Coptic linens in the next collection? Everyone wants something exotic right now." Or, "Can we use the lining of the dress to add another dimension, like the Merovingian queens used violet silk under their tunics?"

Doucet would often try her suggestions and, when he did, the garments would look just a little more exquisite. And Mizza was so thankful for the conversations she'd had at Ida's parties, which had filled her mind with knowledge and ideas she could translate into designs.

One night Ida said to her, "A woman fulfilled by the work of her own hands. My job is done."

And suddenly Mizza was crying in a way she hadn't cried since she arrived at Ida's, as if only now that she could bear it, all the pain was pouring out.

"Thank you," she said to Ida. "Most women would have let me stay a night or two, not forever."

Ida stroked her hair. "I hope you won't be here forever, *chérie*. That you'll have your own home one day, a place where some other woman might find both safety and herself, through you."

That only made Mizza's tears fall in still greater waves until eventually she hiccuped, "Look at me. Weeping all over you while I think about how good my life is."

Ida laid a hand on her cheek, a bittersweet shine in her own eyes. "No pain comes without joy, but no joy comes without pain either. Alas," she finished. "Now it's time to get ready."

Of course Mizza wore Doucet that night. She smiled at Jeanne, who smiled back; at Coco, who didn't; at everyone, because she'd never have to owe anyone for her life and her joy.

Then she saw Lev enter the room, and there wasn't a word to describe how the clasp of her eyes in his made her feel. Like a star, white-hot and sparkling, ready to hang herself up against his sky.

He walked toward her via the edges of the room, slowly, as if those moments of not being beside her, but wanting to be, were exceptional too. As if any second of time that had her in it was a treasure. And that was when she knew this was real. That a man who took the fastest route to your side didn't know what love was.

They escaped into the sitting room again where he pulled a ring out of his pocket, placing it on her upturned palm. He traced over the stone—a glittering shade of red.

"It's the nearest I can get to giving you my heart," he said.

Mizza's fingers closed around it, the same way they wanted to hold on to his heart.

* * *

A whirlwind courtship was a thing spoken of with amusement but with her and Lev it was like lightning—a fork of incandescence in the dark, suddenly gone.

"Don't fall in love, not now with the war on," Ida warned her that night when Lev had gone.

But Mizza couldn't prevent herself. And so they fell, unendingly, helplessly—agonizingly, as it turned out. They had six startling months of love before Lev joined a Russian legion fighting for France in the Great War.

"I have to," he told her, wrapping her in his arms in his bed, his fingers tracing her cheekbones, her hair, the path from her forehead to her lips.

"I know," was all she could say. War had taken his family, his home. He would defend his new home the same way he would defend her.

That night, he gave her all the jewels he'd carried from Russia—incomparable pearls like a strand of moons, sapphires as lavish as a midsummer sky.

"I won't need them out there." His tone was light but then he kissed her and said, "God, I love you. The only thing I'm scared about is losing you."

"That will never happen," she vowed.

But he shook his head. "Don't mourn me if anything happens. Think of me before you go to sleep at night and when you wake in the morning. But in between, live. Live, make beautiful dresses and be someone the world remembers. Don't bury yourself in grief over me if—"

"I would never forget you." She cut him off so fiercely it was almost like anger.

"Which means you can never forget yourself," he said, fiercer still.

Then he folded her in his arms, her mouth pressed against his chest so she couldn't protest that they had no need of this conversation because he was too fine to be given up to a war.

But wars take equally the fine and the flawed.

* * *

The year 1918 began. Mizza was seventeen, and she still walked to Doucet each morning with her smile overflowing her face. She was now the one Doucet called on most often to help him. Each day, she wrote to Lev and he wrote to her, letters that told her nothing about the fighting and the horror. Letters about his childhood. Letters about their future. Letters she cried over each night in bed because they were so beautiful—pain and joy.

One evening when she arrived home from work, Ida greeted her with a face broken apart by tears.

And Mizza knew.

Her legs buckled, but Ida held her up.

"No," she wept. "No."

At last Ida let her down onto the floor where Mizza lay her head on her arms on the seat of a chair, telegram clutched in her hand. Lev had died near Soissons in a battle with German infantry that killed almost all the soldiers in his legion.

All she had left of him were his pearls and sapphires, diamonds and rubies. She remembered what he'd said about his parents and she wanted to take every jewel out to the battlefield at Soissons, scatter the pearls on the ground and bring Lev back with her instead.

She stood up, eyes dry, throat parched with grief. The idea of him being left in a grave, far from her, unremarked and unsung when he was the most celebrated thing in her life was unbearable. Perhaps it made her mad, but she *was* mad—mad with a pain that had no joy in it at all.

"I'll be back when I can," she told Ida.

"Where are you going?" Ida demanded.

"To bring him home."

Whatever was in Mizza's tone made Ida the one crumpling now. She pressed one hand to her forehead, utterly still. For a dancer to not be moving—it was something Mizza had never seen before. Ida, motionless. It made her stop too.

At last Ida said, voice very low, "You're going to do this no matter what I say. So let me borrow a friend's car for you. Be careful, *chérie*. You're the one thing I cannot bear to lose. Which is why I understand what you're doing."

More tears. To be loved like this, and by a woman who wasn't even her mother, was a shocking pain to bear on top of the one she already couldn't endure. And so, with Ida's blessing, Mizza drove north to bring Lev's body home. She went at night, in the dark. She drove on the roads she'd been told were safe to the hospital where he'd died.

She was so very near Soissons when it happened.

A group of men suddenly on the road in front of her. She had to stop or else mow them down. It was impossible to tell what uniforms they wore until she was too close to flee. Germans.

She heard the car door screech as it was wrenched open. Laughter, base and low. Words spoken in German, a language she understood but could make no sense of. A hand dragging her chin into the moonlight. More laughter, brutish now. Her mind urged her limbs to hit, to thrash against everything, because she'd come for Lev's body and that was the only thing that mattered. The ruby ring on her left hand cut into a cheek and the blood fell onto her face, rank and vile.

No laughter now. Ropes circling her wrists. More blood—hers. Hands pressed against her throat, the sound of her screams so loud in her imaginings but barely penetrating the night. Then none of her senses functioned for an uncertain span of time.

Gradually, voices drifted against her ears. French voices. Something else was wrapped around her wrists now, soft like a cotton bandage. A bed beneath her body. Air in her lungs. The rustle of a nurse's uniform, words telling her she was in the military hospital, the one she'd been driving to, for Lev.

She curled her body inward, head on her knees, arms holding her shins, let her mind wander into the past, to the night she'd met Lev.

Days later, she returned to Paris with a wound snaking around her wrist, a wound that would harden into scar tissue—red, ugly, permanent.

TWELVE

MIZZA BRICARD

NEW YORK CITY, 1924

From the moment of Lev's death, Mizza closed her mind against the past. It was the only way to live—and she'd promised Lev she would. She understood now why he'd had her make that promise.

Each day held two beautiful moments—the seconds between consciousness and sleep when her mind remembered only the way he'd kissed her hand, rather than the fact he would never kiss her again. And the first moments of waking, when *God, I love you* echoed in her room like a voice rather than a memory. Every minute in between was agony, but it was an agony she'd learned to carry with her—a solid gold ball in the place where her heart had once been, heavy and beautiful.

Somehow six long years passed. Mizza now stood on the promenade bridge of the *SS France,* the so-called "Versailles of the Atlantic"—the first ship to have flaunted a monumental staircase, its walls accessorized with Boucher frescos and Aubusson tapestries, its rooms filled with an abundance of marble fountains and ironwork doors. But Mizza hardly cared for the luxuries—she just wanted to arrive.

Each day she surveyed the azure ocean, understanding why the Italians considered azure a primary color, and blue its inferior. This was a shade she'd never seen captured, not in a Van Gogh sky, or in the shimmering folds of Byzantium brocade. It reminded her of Lev—too brilliant to last. So she stood there, between worlds—France behind her, America before her—and let her eyes bathe in the beauty of untrappable color.

Her next designs would be azure too, in velvet and layers of chiffon. They would be the designs of a woman who, at just twenty-four years of age, had crossed an ocean, a fact she couldn't quite believe—most women never left their city, let alone their country—to meet with the largest garment maker in New York and sell him dozens of samples. Well, that was hope rather than fact, but it was a hope that made her hands, adorned with a Cartier ruby and Lev's ruby, hold tight to the rails of the bridge and whisper, "I'm doing it, Lev. I am."

As if in response, a sleek and beautiful gray creature broke through the surface of the water, curved its body over and then disappeared beneath the waves. A smile broke over her face.

"Madame!"

She took several seconds to turn around, reluctant to let go of that moment of just her, an aspiration, the ocean and Lev.

"Monsieur Charles," she said agreeably to the young man, an American she'd met at dinner the first night.

He and his friends were good-humored and helped make the time pass more quickly so she joined them for dinner. That night, they wanted to hear more about Ida Rubinstein and Paris—a bedtime story about people in another land who lived lives they could only grasp at for a few hours in the middle of the ocean, where the responsibilities of being like their fathers could be cast aside.

You don't understand how lucky you are, Mizza thought when she left at midnight alone, refusing one unsubtle offer of companionship. To be men—to be allowed responsibilities, to have ambition expected of you, to have a destiny within your control.

That was something she ached for as she took out her *croquis*—ink sketches of gowns and robes and dresses. She studied them for imperfections, for anything that might make this voyage a failure, which it couldn't be, not if Mizza was to finally be a designer in her own right, someone who kept her other promise to Lev—to be someone the world remembered. And someone who kept her promise to herself— to be the one spoken of because of what she herself had done.

* * *

Mizza stepped out onto Fifth Avenue in this staggeringly tall city inhabited by people either running from or chasing something, given how fast they moved. Paris was sultry, aloof and very proud; New York was breakneck, brash and maybe, Mizza thought with a shiver as she saw a man bowl over an elderly lady, a little heartless.

Armed with samples and a portfolio, she entered the head office of the Harry Angelo Company, where designs were purchased from the leading French couturiers, ready for wealthy New Yorkers to buy. Mizza was representing Doucet, showing designs that were mostly her own, sprinkled with a few drawings of his. But next year, after she'd spent this month making contact with potential American clients, she would come back representing no one other than herself.

Mr. Angelo, a thin, mustachioed man, sat in the salon cleaning his spectacles with a handkerchief. Mizza took out the five models she'd brought with her and said in perfect English, which she spoke as fluently as the German, Romanian and Russian languages, "Monsieur Doucet is delighted to show you our latest collection. We've taken the mood of the time—a longing for freedom, a wish for more—and added a touch of French elegance."

He came to stand at her side, eyes on her, not the sketches. "I'd like to see how these move," he said, indicating one of the models, a black lace floor-length coat with a ruffled red neckline that framed the face. It was one Mizza was particularly proud of.

"Put it on," he said.

Mizza laughed.

Mr. Angelo did not.

Mon Dieu. He was serious. "I'm a designer," she said, "not a mannequin."

"You're more…" He paused, no longer a benign man with dirty spectacles. "More alluring than any mannequin I've seen."

He held out the coat.

And Mizza felt so very stupid. She'd thought Doucet had sent her because he was preparing her to take the reins of one of his fashion businesses. But it was just because she was a woman with a pretty face.

Suddenly, all the jokes he made seemed like warnings: *when a man asks who your favorite florist is, tell them it's Cartier.*

Mr. Angelo thrust the coat closer.

Perhaps this was the price she had to pay for her ambition. Put on a coat and parade up and down a room. She could do that if it meant forging a connection with the most important garment maker in New York.

Just make sure you're never ignorant of someone's intent, or unwilling to uphold your end of a deal, Ida had told her.

Even as she took off her bolero, Mizza didn't fully understand Mr. Angelo's intent. Perhaps Jeanne would have. Did it make it better or worse that Mizza couldn't imagine what he wanted?

As she was about to put the coat on over her shirt and skirt, he said, "No. I want to see it without the rest beneath." And she understood that he intended to look and that his looking was not a passive act—it was a grasping, taking, stealing thing.

It was so hard to keep her eyes fixed on his face as she unbuttoned her shirt, as she slid out of her skirt, as she pulled the coat on over her underclothes. But she did. She made herself, cheeks burning red, eyes blazing too, watch him the same way he wanted to watch her—with contempt.

She'd thought she'd done what Jeanne had believed impossible. Gone straight from Ida's parties to what she wanted, skipping the step in between where she had to trade herself for opportunity. But she'd just delayed it by a few years and now it was time to pay.

She couldn't walk out. She was completely alone in New York. And if she returned to Paris without having sold any of Doucet's designs, he would fire her. Then Mizza would have to start all over again, at the very bottom, taking a couturier's sketches and rendering them into working drawings, before finally being permitted to design for whichever house would take her on after learning she'd been fired.

So, in an office on Fifth Avenue, she paraded up and down in a garment she'd been so proud of, a garment whose lace permitted Mr. Angelo to catch glimpses of the bare skin of her thighs above her stockings.

But she didn't have to show this man that the red on her cheeks was humiliation. She didn't have to let him rule over her. By not looking away, she kept that from him.

When she returned to Paris, she went to see Jeanne Toussaint, with whom she'd become good friends. When Jeanne opened the door, she looked at Mizza and said, "You've just had your heart broken again."

Mizza's words were thin. "You once told me to make sure I cultivated a man who would give me one opportunity. You said you'd met Louis Cartier not long before and you were designing handbags for him. *For* him. I went to New York thinking I was almost ready to design clothes for myself. But..."

Jeanne pulled her into a hug. "But fairytales where my name or yours hangs over an awning happen to one woman in a million," she finished. "Coco found a man who was happy to give her the money she needed and who didn't want to stamp his initials all over it. I think he was one of a kind, now extinct. But who knows what might have happened if he hadn't died?"

"But is that all there is?" Mizza cried, pushing herself away from Jeanne, wishing she could push herself away from this world.

"For now," Jeanne said haltingly, "yes. We just have to hold on until we can make things change."

THIRTEEN

MIZZA BRICARD

PARIS, 1937

In the studio at the House of Molyneux, Mizza—Captain Molyneux's assistant designer—adjusted the sapphire pinned to the center of her turban so it caught the light, winking with mischief.

"You're late," Molyneux said.

"I'm always late," Mizza replied with the hint of a smile. She picked up one of the illustrations lined up before him and said, "*Non. C'est affreux.*"

An *arpette* inhaled sharply at Mizza's declaration that the couturier's sketch was awful. Molyneux's scowl carved itself into trenches. "We need more day dresses," he said.

"But not these." Mizza dismissed the remaining *croquis* with a flick of her hand, the smile on her face suggesting she might even be enjoying Captain Molyneux's wrath. The *arpette* took ten steps backward, not wanting to be in the way of the explosion.

But the captain exhaled. "Something *is* missing," he assented.

And Mizza knew that whatever she made happen in this studio, provoking the captain just the right amount with boldness, gemstones, tardiness and a refusal to cow, had taken place once more. She'd said to Jeanne, "It's as if his dresses come from a kind of suppressed fury and he just needs someone to spark it off."

Jeanne had sighed and said, referring to Cartier, her lover, her boss, the man who'd married another woman who was better for his reputation than Jeanne, "That's how I feel about Louis."

Two women, trapped behind men whose names were known throughout Europe and across the seas. When Jeanne had said, *until we can make things change,* Mizza hadn't reckoned on a global depression, on the closing and collapsing of couture houses across Paris. She'd jumped from Doucet's House of Mirande, glad she wasn't sitting in a fledgling shop of her own in debt to a man at a time when money was scarce, watching her dream collapse. It wasn't yet time for her or Jeanne to make things change. But soon. She repeated that prayer every night.

"Monsieur," came the timid voice of another *arpette* who'd been sent on this errand to penetrate the studio by some less courageous soul downstairs. "There's a designer to see you with his sketches."

In came a man called Christian Dior. His sketches made Mizza nod with admiration. "You understand that sophistication is achieved with simplicity, monsieur," she said.

His face suffused with pleasure. She summoned over Molyneux, and let her hand rest on one *croquis* that would definitely solve their shortage of day dresses.

Molyneux tapped a finger against it. "I'll take this one."

When Mizza left that evening, she found Monsieur Dior waiting for her with a shy smile and a bouquet of flowers.

"I wanted to say thank you," he said.

"It was my pleasure," she told him. "It's hard for new designers. I can tell you which other couturiers you should try, if you like? Piguet would appreciate your vision. And I have some ideas about how to modify one of those sketches to suit Monsieur Lelong."

Mizza and Christian, or Tian as she came to call him, went out to dinner and then off to a party where they talked all night about art and music and fashion—kindred spirits. And Mizza had no idea that this one meeting would change her life in two ways—the first in a manner no one would ever know about, during the war coming for Europe. And the second after the war in a way that would be remembered forever.

ACT TWO

THE MUSE...

FOURTEEN

ASTRID BRICARD AND HAWK JONES

NEW YORK CITY, MAY 1970

It's ten in the evening after the *Vogue* shoot when Hawk pushes open the door to his apartment, the bouquet of flowers in his hand as wilted as his spirits. One lamp is on, and in its light he sees Astrid sitting on the concrete ledge of the arched window. He has to use all his willpower to stop from kneeling down in front of her and burying his head in her lap. He'd gone straight to Parsons after the *Vogue* team left but she wasn't there. He went to her apartment. Velvet told him Astrid hadn't been at the exam. He went to the bistro. Out to Long Island. To the beach. He'd been everywhere he could think of except his own place.

He walks toward her, leaving the sad flowers on the table. "I don't know if I should say this or if it only makes things more complicated but..." He rubs a ferocious hand through his hair. "I want to be the guy who makes you feel like you're sewn together with diamonds. Not the guy who screws everything up for you."

She swipes a hand over her cheek but he sees the tears anyway. He's never felt like such a prick. "The last thing I want is to be the guy who makes you cry."

A sad little smile flickers onto her face. "I'm only half-sorry I ruined the shoot."

"Man, she was a pain in the ass, wasn't she? I told her to leave. If she's ever in charge of *Vogue*, I'm history."

Astrid's voice is fierce. "I hope she'll never be in charge. I hope *she* has a fallback."

He doesn't smile at the joke. "What happened at Parsons?"

"I lost my scholarship. So—"

He interrupts, relieved beyond anything he'd done this yesterday. "Here." He pulls a check out of his pocket for half the money she loaned him. He doesn't have enough coming in to take so much out of the business, but nor does he feel right taking her money and her time and now her fucking scholarship. "Use it to pay for your tuition. I don't know why you never used it in the first place."

When she looks up at him, her eyes are still damp. "Using Mizza's money on myself is complicated. But I guess now I'll have to." She tucks her hair behind her ears. "I took my portfolio to the beach today and I drew. I don't know why, but I always draw best when I'm angry. It's like . . ."

She pauses, then her words come out in a rush. "No one can explain how art gets made, what magic trick turns out a New Look dress that the whole world wears. So the world attributes its genesis—only that, not the skill or the final accomplishment—to a woman with great cleavage and a come-to-bed smile. Art gets made when you feel something, sure, but it isn't always about sex."

Astrid shifts restlessly. "I don't know why I'm ranting at you. I'm furious at myself and I'm mad at Mizza. I get why my parents never wanted me to do this. Being connected to fashion makes people draw the parallel between me and Mizza even more sharply—like with the editor this morning. But damned if I'm going to quit. Succeeding at this is the only way to make people like her shut up."

Fire is just about igniting from the ends of her hair. And the words fall out of Hawk's mouth before he realizes he's saying them. "That just makes me love you even more."

Astrid looks like he's just said both the best and the worst thing in the world.

A buzz breaks in from the door below. "Who the fuck is that?" he growls. But he's grateful for the interruption, which might delay her telling him that she can't see him anymore, or some other heartbreak.

He lets in Benji, who's pulling contact sheets out of an envelope. "I should have bought a lightbox," Benji says. "Turn on the damn lights, Hawk."

"We called in another model this morning," Hawk explains to Astrid.

"But I told *Vogue* they have to use these."

Benji passes over a sheet of proofs—Hawk and Astrid standing together in a moment Hawk hadn't fully comprehended amongst the commotion. Astrid's naked back is to the camera, she's wearing just a pair of panties, and the expression on Hawk's face as he looks at her is of desperate, aching love.

He takes the next sheet from Benji—Astrid in her tiny shorts striding toward the door. It's a groin-stirring, magnificent photograph of a groin-stirring, magnificent woman.

"Fucking genius," Benji says.

The final shot is of Astrid silhouetted in the doorway, all legs and tousled hair, pulling her Hawk Jones sweater over her head, a sweater he knows is going to sell in the hundreds of thousands.

"Put on your dancing shoes," Benji says. "We're going to the Cheetah to celebrate. Might as well have one last night of getting high and getting laid."

Hawk glances at Astrid and the disturbance of their eyes meeting is physical. "You can get ready in the bedroom," he tells her. "I'll find something out here."

Astrid vanishes into his room and reappears five minutes later in the silver dress, which he'd kept at his apartment so Fi and Nancy could copy it.

He swallows. "We'll catch up," he tells Benji, who grins and clatters down the stairs.

Then it's just Hawk and Astrid, her in the doorway of his bedroom in the sexiest silver dress on the planet and him . . . too far away.

"You know," she says, "the only person I wanted to talk to today, to hold me and tell me it would be okay after I'd failed the exam, was you. Not Velvet. Not my mom. Not my godmother. And now, seeing your face in those shots . . ." Her voice is husky. "I want you to do a lot more than hold me."

His inhale is sharp and in his mind, he's already wrapped his arms around her and a lot more besides. But he makes himself stay where he is. "Are you sure?"

Her smile is beautiful. And her eyes . . . man. She's trailing them over his torso as if everything he's imagining, she is too.

"We both know *Vogue* is going to run that photo of us looking like we're about to fall back into a bed we've only just climbed out of. So"— she smiles, and her eyes are less *come-to-bed* than *who-needs-a-damn-bed*—"we might as well take a hit of that, rather than only feeling the frustration."

She crosses the room deliberately slowly and he can feel his eyes devouring every movement of her body under the lamé. He knows that the dress is all she's wearing. That if his hand slides the hem up less than an inch, he'll find Astrid's naked skin.

She stops in front of him and there's one second of searing heat before her lips are on his and one of his hands is in her hair and they're making out like he's never made out before. Indecently. Exquisitely.

He cups her chin, pulling her mouth closer, and she makes an impatient sound when he draws back a little because he's forgotten to breathe. The sheer desperation in that one whisper of his name almost finishes him off.

He leans his forehead against hers, their breathing equally rough, equally fast.

"Not like this," he murmurs. "Not in five minutes with Benji waiting downstairs."

"Your self-control is both admirable and annoying," she whispers.

"We need to go," he says. "My self-control is slipping fast."

Her hand in his, they take the stairs, finding Benji already buzzed on acid. At the Cheetah, the Stones are playing, Mick Jagger growling "Honky Tonk Women." The lights flash only across the ceiling, meaning it's almost completely dark on the dance floor, which isn't really a dance floor anymore, but a make-out floor.

They weave their way into its midst and dance, the music too loud for speech. When the movement of the crowd presses her body right up against his, he slides his hand under her dress, knowing no one can see.

Astrid whispers in his ear, "Hawk, I want you to touch me. Properly."

That's it. He has no more self-control.

He wants to think he helps her through the crowds but it's more likely they tumble through in a daze of lust. On the way back to his apartment, they stop in every secluded doorway and he does touch her, again and again, but never for long enough because footsteps approach every time.

He swears under his breath because his bed is so far away, and then with an effort that's truly herculean, he marches them onward until they're in his room and the dress is on the floor and she's finally and magnificently naked.

"Astrid, I know I should be, I don't know, gentle but... you're driving me wild and I just need a minute..."

"Hawk," she says, "if you're anything other than wild right now I'll never speak to you again."

They both laugh at how desperate they are, until they don't laugh anymore, and then they're both wild for a very long time.

* * *

Afterward, Hawk traces his fingertips over every inch of skin that he missed in the fast, hot rush of Astrid, watching her face—the way the green in her eyes drowns out the brown, the way her skin flushes, slowly at first and then everywhere.

"I love you," he says, drawing her against him, needing her to understand that it's not just the heat and the passion and the mania he wants but every other thing too. "I feel like I'm wearing you around my heart and I'm never taking you off."

He's made her cry again, tears trailing from the corners of her eyes and onto the pillow, and he kisses her to hide the fact that witnessing her tears is physically painful.

"I love you too," she says, and that hurts as well because he wants it to be like this forever and he's suddenly terrified that, one day, it might not be.

He never knew joy could hurt so much.

FIFTEEN

BLYTHE BRICARD

The day after Blythe's deal with Jake, the kids jump into her bed for morning cuddles at half past seven—a blissful sleep-in as far as she's concerned. They're laughing over a thankfully clean joke Eva learned from David, when there's a knock on the suite door.

"It's Jake," a voice calls.

"What's *he* doing here?" Eva hisses.

Footsteps cross to the kids' room, pause, then tread slowly back to Blythe's bedroom. Jake appears in the doorway, as polished as a storybook apple, whereas Blythe's hair is a matted mess and she must have sleep lines all over her face.

She jumps out of bed, straightens her pajamas and looks up to see Jake grinning.

"I prefer to be laughed at after eight in the morning," she says a little testily.

"I wasn't laughing at you. You're just—very you. I'd forgotten your aesthetic even stretches to your pajamas. Which are great, by the way. Perfect for MIZZA."

There's a teasing note in his voice and Blythe glances down at the scarlet men's kimono she's refashioned into a wrap-style top and shorts. They *are* great.

"Why are you here?" Eva interrupts.

"I'm in charge today," Jake replies. "I'm taking you out. I thought you might want time to work," he adds to Blythe.

Eva and Sebby exchange glances, and Blythe sees the pleading look in Sebby's eyes. Eva must see it too because she grumbles, "Fine."

"Let's go," Jake says, and he starts to usher them to the door of the suite.

"We're in our pajamas," Eva says as if Jake's an imbecile.

Jake glances at Blythe and she shuts her bedroom door, knowing he doesn't need the added pressure of her presence. Something like anticipation stirs at having a whole day to see if this MIZZA idea is just sequins, or if there's some solid boning to hold everything in place.

She's just finished breakfast with the late-risers when her phone rings.

"Darling, it's Iris. I'm a little shaky today. Would you mind coming up to see me?"

Blythe finds Iris in bed, a carefully folded stack of clothes beside her.

"It's funny," Iris says, one hand stroking the jersey on top of the pile, "I brought these with me when I could have given them to you in New York. But it didn't feel like the right place. After speaking to Jake last night, I'm glad I packed them."

"Jake told you?"

"It's a bad habit we have. When he was in college, he used to come to my room late at night after he'd returned from his misadventures. Sometimes he wouldn't say very much, but the day he met you, it was as if he'd never be able to stop talking."

Iris turns a desolate smile on Blythe—the smile of a woman aware of how much she stands to lose very soon. "Since we've been here, Jake's fallen into his old ways. While I did most of the talking the first few nights, last night he had a great deal to say. He told me about the deal he made with you."

Iris plunges her hand into the stack of clothes and extracts a sparklingly alive silver dress that's almost indecently short. "You know I'm only a little older than your mother would have been. I bought this infamous dress back in 1970 from Hawk's first store. Ed was about three and I'd just had David and I felt like a milking machine. I put this dress on and I felt like a woman."

Iris holds it against her body, frailty transfiguring to vibrancy. "When I look at this dress, I don't see myself as dying but as very much alive. It gives me back everything I'm about to lose. It's a very powerful legacy, Blythe. There's so much more to the story of this dress than your mother dancing on a podium."

Blythe's throat is so tight she can't reply. And then she's in Iris's arms and they're both crying, the dress caught in their embrace.

After a long moment, Iris says, "Jake is the one I most worry about after I'm gone. You can't love one child more than the others but there's always one raveled more tightly around your heart. I recognize..." Iris takes a deep and painful breath. "I recognize he's been a terrible father. But I want you to know what happened to him as a child. He had measles when he was nine. It developed into encephalitis— inflammation and swelling of the brain. For two weeks, we thought he was going to die. When it looked as if he'd turned a corner, the doctors told us that a quarter of children with encephalitis suffer neurological damage."

Blythe is wordless. Jake has never told her any of this.

"The encephalitis left Jake with speech muscle weakness, which caused him to have what's known as a neurogenic stutter. He also couldn't recognize faces, and had a limp. The kids at school tormented him for his speech and the fact he couldn't recall who they were. Ed took to beating them all up and got himself expelled."

So many things make sense now. Ed's protectiveness of Jake. The way the entire Black clan forgives Jake so readily.

"He..." Blythe's too stunned to finish a thought, let alone a sentence.

Iris picks up her story. "There was one particularly depressing morning at the hospital with a doctor who insisted we should just accept Jake's disabilities—it was 1980 and most people thought damage to the brain was permanent. And of course we loved Jake regardless. But Jake didn't accept that this was how his life would be. Things are different now, I suppose, but back then... The names he was called at school."

Another falter. It's as if Iris is girding herself for the next part, which can't possibly be any more heartbreaking than imagining Jake as a boy being teased remorselessly and Ed defending him. But it is, and Blythe listens with tears in her eyes, a hand pressed to her mouth, almost wishing she could hold on to Jake's hand too.

"After we came home from the hospital, Jake and Ed were watching television and somehow they saw a documentary about neuroplasticity, which wasn't widely understood at the time. The next day, Ed told me he and Jake were going to school, but they took the subway to see the doctor from the documentary. Can you imagine—a sixteen-year-old boy with his nine-year-old brother in tow, thinking he could afford a neurosurgeon. But the doctor agreed to help—on the condition that Ed throw all the energy he was using to beat people up into helping his brother, because what Jake would have to do would be the hardest work of his life.

"From that day," Iris tells her shakily, "Jake pushed himself almost to exhaustion, always with Ed by his side. Six years of hours of daily exercises before and after school. He was determined never to forget a face, never to trip over his words or his feet. And he succeeded. You can only occasionally notice a slur on his words if he's a little tired or a little drunk, or if he speaks too fast. His leg bothers him when he's tired too. The experience taught him a lot of good things but it also taught him a ruthless self-control that's very bad for him. He learned not to ask for help—that he must help himself. Whenever something goes wrong, he becomes that obstinate boy repeating sounds over and over, late into the night and alone—except for Ed, who was always there. So…"

Iris's voice thins and she exhales, almost out of strength. "He didn't tell you he was bankrupt because…I suppose he flew all over the world trying to put his business back together so he could show you Blake Group as a perfect entity, one without stutters and limps and memory loss. He wanted you to have perfect-Jake, not what he considered to be flawed-Jake, and in so doing, he gave you the latter. When you said you wanted a divorce, it floored him. He had no idea."

Blythe is still several steps back in the conversation picturing Jake, who *is* ruthlessly determined, trying to conquer the damage left by brain inflammation. She looks up at Iris, seated like a queen— magnificent still. But also wrong.

"It didn't floor him," Blythe says sadly. "He didn't love me, not then."

"He did," Iris insists. "He just didn't show it very well."

She places the clothes in Blythe's arms. "I hope these help you with MIZZA."

And thus Blythe is dismissed.

* * *

It floored him.

Blythe knows that's not true and, to be honest, she doesn't want to think about her end with Jake all over again. It hurt too much the first time. Thankfully, the door to her suite opens not long after she returns and Coco appears.

"You really want to do this?" Coco asks.

"I don't know," Blythe says honestly.

If she tries to find out about Astrid via Coco, then she has a layer of protection between herself and what's uncovered. She won't be the one staring at the screen and finding—nothing.

So, "I've organized access to media databases you might need," she tells Coco. "But if you realize you'd rather be out exploring France, you're welcome to go."

"Dad wants to see a cathedral. I told him I'm worshipping at the altar of Astrid, who, let's face it, was a bit of a goddess."

Coco's irreverent approach makes Blythe laugh. Coco isn't interested in gossip or glory. She wants things to be different, which Blythe has always wanted too, but Coco also wants them to be *right*, as if she believes the truth time has left them with is the one that was easiest to assemble—as if there's another account out there of lost facts that could be reconstructed if someone cared enough.

Coco sets up on the coffee table in the sitting room that connects Blythe's bedroom with the kids', while Blythe takes the sofa. But she isn't the kind of designer who sits down with paper and pencil. She needs a garment to inspire another garment, a beautiful ruin from some time past she can breathe new life into. Iris's stack will be a start, but her friend Remy has one of the best vintage collections in the world and probably a room full of ruins she doesn't have time to mend—and hopefully some of those are in the vacation house Remy owns on the French Riviera.

Are you in Saint-Jean-Cap-Ferrat yet? Blythe texts. *If Jake can get his shit together with the kids, I said I'd do MIZZA with Blake Group. Which means I need clothes. Anything you can't sell. I need...*

Blythe pauses, then makes herself write it. *I need to see if I have any talent left.*

Remy's reply is instantaneous. *I'll box up everything I have and send it to you.*

Let me know how much you want for it, Blythe types, wincing.

How the hell she'll pay Remy, she has no idea. Until she decides which way she's going—Jake or Nathaniel—she has to pay for everything herself. But with what money?

Because Jake was almost bankrupt when they divorced, she got no settlement. She'd had to, for the first time, dig into the account Hawk had set up for her as a baby. That's always felt like blood money—using it is like saying she accepts his indifference. She's now locked the funds up in trust for the kids so she can't access them again. And while Jake's been sending maintenance payments for more than a year now, Blythe only uses a scrupulous half for things that are one hundred percent kid-related, like Sebby's medical bills. Her own design work pays irregularly and doesn't leave her with a pot of thousands to purchase damaged but still-valuable couture from Remy.

She exhales noisily.

Coco looks up. "You sound like you could use a distraction." She smooths a hand over the brown pixie cut that makes her look like a dark-haired Twiggy, picks up a pen and writes on a sheet of paper:

Germaine Neustadtl
Germaine Biano
Madame Biano
Madame Biano-Bricard
Madame Bricard
Mizza Bricard

"What's that?" Blythe asks.

"Some of the names your dear grandmother used over her lifetime," Coco says triumphantly. "When I started looking into Astrid, I found something about Mizza that made me wonder if there was a pattern. And I know you're skeptical about all of this, so I figure that if I soften you up with Mizza first, you'll be more likely to believe what I found out about Astrid."

Blythe can't help laughing. "Are you sure you weren't an FBI agent in another life?"

"That would be very cool, but no. Those databases Jake gave us access to—they're the bomb. But I started out with a regular public database of birth, death and marriage records and that's how I found all of Mizza's names. If you know the names a person used, then you can find out things about them. And look—I found an article from a newspaper in 1928 talking about a black charmeuse wrap coat that was a hugely successful design for the House of Mirande."

Coco is pacing, speaking faster and faster. "The Queen of Spain bought that wrap. A queen, Blythe! And the article says it was designed by Madame Biano, 'the creator of all Mirande models.' Madame Biano was Mizza Bricard. Your grandmother was the head designer for the House of Mirande. She designed clothes for the Queen of Spain. Which makes her a lot more than a muse."

Mizza was a designer? For a queen? As much as Blythe can see the article Coco's pointing to on-screen, her skepticism isn't overcome. "One wrap doesn't change history, Coco. And what's the House of Mirande anyway?"

"A famous Parisian couture house in the 1920s and '30s, owned by Doucet. I get that it isn't evidence of much. But it's a story about Mizza that isn't on the record anywhere."

Coco pauses, contemplative now. "These days, we're so used to having access to everything. But you can't just go and read a newspaper article from the 1930s or the 1970s. They're all in paywalled archives or moldering in libraries. So it's like women from the past become the one most potent soundbite. Marilyn Monroe's a woman in a billowing white dress standing over a grate. Audrey Hepburn's a black dress outside Tiffany. How many people can name a Marilyn Monroe movie? She won awards for her acting ability, for God's sake. Those women are icons and we think we know everything about them because we know the one thing everyone else does. Which means it's not that Mizza and Astrid are mysteries who've done their best never to be solved—it's that nobody's bothered to try and solve them. So they live in the collective memory as a seductress in a leopard-print coat, and a siren in a silver dress. Is that what you want?"

Blythe remembers what *Vogue*'s "Fashion Who's Who" had said:

Mizza—"Christian Dior's muse." Astrid—"the muse's daughter." Blythe—"hasn't lived up to expectations."

"Okay," she says, "you've softened me up. Maybe there's more to Mizza than a predilection for swanning around in leopard-print coats without panties. But it'd be good to find more than one article."

"I'm already onto that," Coco says. "In the meantime, I'll tell you what I found out about Astrid."

What Coco's discovered about her grandmother is good news. Blythe feels a spark of hope that maybe she's about to hear something positive about her mother too.

"To summarize," Coco begins, "Astrid dropped out of Parsons after a few months to become Hawk's muse. She never graduated. And while she might have been a fashion muse, she spent a hell of a lot of time naked. She and Hawk were together, broke up, together, broke up, et cetera. He designed much of MIZZA until Versailles, when he got tired of always having to bail her out. They argued— everyone heard them. Then she shot herself up way too high, fell out with her drug dealer, or attacked Candace, Hawk's new paramour— or perhaps all three—and vanished before the show."

Nothing positive there. "Yep," Blythe says faux-cheerily, "that's my mom."

"Except what Hawk said rips a hole right through some of that. No drugs, no dealer. You want to find out what happened to someone, you start with the facts. It's a fact that Astrid started at Parsons in January 1970—her name is on the list of scholarship winners for that year. We know that at some point in 1970, she and Hawk got together because"— Coco holds up her phone, which shows a photo of Astrid sitting on top of a bar, Hawk kissing her bare stomach—"I don't think even he could call that an accident. Then Astrid went to Paris in April 1971 and they broke up. She came back to New York in 1972 and started MIZZA. All of that's indisputable. But you know what I can't find?"

Coco's expression makes Blythe brace herself.

"I can't find any evidence of Astrid and Hawk being together after she came back to New York in March 1972."

Blythe laughs. "There've been a lot of untruths leveled my way, but being an immaculate conception isn't one of them. They had to have been together because I'm very real. What about the Coty Awards—the late 1972 ceremony, not the early 1971 one. Everyone's always raving about how romantic they were there."

"There is a photo of them holding hands on stage," Coco concedes. "But you weren't conceived then because it's too early. You had to have been conceived in early 1973, but in all the millions of photos of Astrid and Hawk online, I can't find a single one showing them together in 1973. After you're born, there are photos of him leaving the hospital, a few of him leaving Astrid's apartment building, but nothing of the two of them until the flight to Versailles in November 1973, almost two months after you were born. Suddenly there are photos of them arriving at the airport together. One grainy shot of them kissing on the plane. Except Versailles was meant to be..."

"When everything fell apart," Blythe finishes for her.

"Exactly. So..." Coco frowns. "I don't know what all of that means. Were they ever together after they split up in 1971? You're the evidence that they were, at least once. But the lack of photos over the eighteen months from 1972 when they were supposed to have had another passionate, volatile affair..."

Coco shakes her head. "Maybe it supports the story—maybe Hawk was with Candace before Versailles but he turned his attentions to Astrid at Versailles and that's why she and Candace had a fight and Candace's blood ended up on her dress. Or maybe...maybe what we think we know isn't real," Coco says slowly. "To figure out what happened to Astrid Bricard, maybe we have to sift through as many stories as there are grains of sand on a beach to find the few glittering truths."

In all of the many photos of Astrid and Hawk online, I can't find a single one showing them together in 1973, Coco had said. There's something almost ominous about those words. They had to have been together in 1973—in love. Because if they weren't, that means Blythe was a mistake and that's why Hawk and Astrid both ended up all but leaving her.

Blythe wants to protest, *I'm happy with the story I already know.* But Coco seems determined to break that story apart, chapter by chapter.

"You know what got me onto my Astrid project at university?" she says now. "My friend's grandmother was on the board of a home for orphaned children in New York State in the 1970s. She knew you were my aunt and she told me that Astrid used to go out to the home once a month and make these amazing fabric murals with the kids. It wasn't for college credit. Nobody asked her to do it. She just did it."

"That's not true," Blythe says dismissively.

"She showed me a photograph." Coco's voice is gentle. "Of Astrid, sitting at a table, helping a group of kids who'd been left in a home make something beautiful. She doesn't look like the kind of woman who'd just up and leave her own child on a whim."

Blythe closes her eyes. Mizza was a designer in the 1920s and 1930s. Astrid maybe once cared about children. What if, in solving these mysteries, Blythe somehow finds Astrid? And what if she also finds a story that says she wasn't a thing worth abandoning—but that her mother once loved her. That would be a story worth finding.

"Tomorrow, I'll help you search," Blythe says.

SIXTEEN

ASTRID BRICARD AND HAWK JONES

In the aftermath of the *Vogue* shoot—Astrid on the cover wearing tiny shorts and pulling a sweater over her head—Hawk's business explodes. The atmosphere in his store is of excitement and creativity and passion and the future. It matches exactly the mood on the streets, a mood Diana Vreeland captures in the headline accompanying the photos—YOUTHQUAKE, as if Hawk and Astrid are a movement that will shock and shake the world to its core.

All around them, things are trembling. During summer break, Astrid moves in with Hawk and quits her job at the bistro—the money from *Vogue* means she doesn't need to waitress over the summer, nor use Mizza's money to pay for her tuition. Instead she throws herself into life, joining Hawk and thousands of others marching on the United Nations, demanding an end to the Vietnam War, carrying a sign with Benji's name on it. Then she and Velvet join Graham at the Christopher Street Liberation Day March. At the march's end in Central Park, there are men lying with their heads resting on their lovers' chests, women kissing their partners in broad daylight, and it's impossible not to believe that the whole world *is* changing and that Astrid is right in the midst of the change.

She returns to Hawk's shop, understanding still more why Hawk's been so successful. The Hawk Jones label is the mood in Central Park captured in a pair of hotpants. And she wonders, as she sits at the workbench, if she could learn more at the shop than she will at Parsons. Parsons is theory; Hawk Jones is fact.

"Nancy," she says. "Can I borrow your machine to make this?"

She opens her portfolio to a sketch of a long-sleeved dress with a flared skirt that borrows the beauty of the fifties and unfurls it in soft black corduroy so it can be lunched in with your parents or danced in at a nightclub.

Hawk grabs the roll of corduroy that had given Astrid the idea for the dress and says, "Let me pin it on you first."

Suddenly there she is, in the middle of the store, having fabric draped over her by Hawk, whose hands catch her waist, whose lips graze the side of her neck, and who she ends up kissing right there in front of all the customers.

"Who knew that wrapping you up in fabric would be as much fun as unwrapping you from it?" he murmurs.

Nancy makes the dress and it sells from Hawk's store by the thousands. It's such a buzz to see something she drew walking out on customer after customer. She knows it will make her portfolio one of the strongest in her year group—Parsons can't do anything other than give full marks to a dress that half of Manhattan owns.

When classes restart after summer, it seems juvenile to be learning how to design when she already has designed—for Hawk Jones, the man for whom Diana Vreeland invented a whole new word. It's even harder to concentrate when Hawk leaps on her the second she walks in the door one night and says, "Charles Revson—the Revlon guy— wants to license my name for a perfume! Look how much money he gave me."

Astrid stares at a check with too many zeros for her mind to compute. "Holy shit."

"He wants us to come to his party tomorrow night. You and me— going to a Revson party."

He looks so incredulous that she throws her arms around him and teases, "You're just a little bit famous, aren't you?"

Astrid cuts classes the next day to make something to wear. The theme of the party is "Legends." Everyone will don evening dresses, but Astrid makes a pair of white trousers in satin crepe. Then a white tank top that she turns inside out and, in the place where the label should be, she draws an oversized Hawk Jones label with scrollwork and fancy lettering, like a medieval manuscript about legendary deeds.

Hawk laughs when he sees it and it's the start of a night that's absurdly fun. There are as many five-kilo cans of caviar scattered around the Revson mansion as there are ashtrays, and Hawk and Astrid stare goggle-eyed.

"Maybe I'll spend my money on giant cans of caviar too," Hawk jokes, "although he'd probably like me to buy a suit first." He gestures to his Rolling Stones T-shirt and jeans, which stand out in a way that isn't all bad against the tuxedos and couture.

"You don't own a table big enough to serve five-kilo cans of caviar," Astrid says.

"I'll eat it off you instead."

A thousand cameras flash, catching the kiss that follows that declaration.

"Hawk, darling," a bejeweled woman interrupts. "Wherever can I get that?" She indicates Astrid's tank top. "I haven't seen it in the store."

Astrid's pretty sure the woman is socialite Babe Paley, which means Hawk is doing even better than she realized. "I'll cut classes tomorrow and help Fi and Nancy make the shirts," she tells him. "More people will come to the store if I'm there, wearing mine."

Hawk whispers, "I love you," and the cameras flash once more.

One hundred people sit down to dinner at a table almost bigger than Hawk's apartment. Afterward, Revson starts his fabled bingo game. Astrid comes second, and while the first prize is a set of Gucci luggage, the second is a toilet seat embedded with hundred-dollar bills.

Later that month, when she sees the pictures in *Vogue*, a close-up of her in the tank top, obviously not wearing a bra, pressing her lips to Hawk's neck, ridiculously expensive toilet seat under her arm, it's hard to believe it's Astrid Bricard. Her parents have been cool toward her since the feature in *Cosmopolitan* about the sexiest couples on the planet, highlighting Astrid and Hawk; since the picture in *Harper's Bazaar* of Astrid sitting on the fur-covered bar at the Cheetah in a crop top and low-cut harem pants, arms above her head, singing along to "Venus," Hawk leaning in to kiss the bare skin of her belly. They hate that she's fulfilled the prophecies of the Long Island mothers— that she's run wild.

And she has—but it's just that, for her, wild is not a pejorative term. Wild is like freedom, and whoever said freedom was a bad thing?

* * *

One rare night when they're at Hawk's apartment rather than out and Astrid's desperately trying to catch up on all the work she's missed— has she really cut that many classes?—the phone rings.

They're in bed, and Hawk almost doesn't answer it, but does in case it's something about business. It makes Astrid smile—that Hawk, the boy-man who tried to pick her up in an archive, now takes calls about his thriving business at nine o'clock at night.

He reappears in the doorway. "It's for you. It's Alix St. Pierre."

Astrid winces. She hasn't had dinner with her godmother in weeks. Alix has called Hawk's store a couple of times and left messages, which Astrid meant to return but...

She tugs the sheet around her body and climbs out of bed.

"I know you're alive because I see your photograph every day," Alix says, a hint of softness on her *r* sounds, a remnant of all her time spent in Europe. "But I wouldn't know it from your lack of skill at making telephone calls."

"I'm sorry," Astrid says. She tugs the phone as far as it'll go and sits on the sofa. Hawk pulls on boxer shorts and makes hot chocolate for her.

"I'm going to cut to the chase," Alix says. "I understand you're no longer in the scholarship program. That you haven't been for months. I was waiting for you to come and see me. But you haven't, so now I'm telling you to come and see me tomorrow. After class," she says with an emphasis, as if she knows Astrid has become as expert at cutting classes as she is at cutting patterns.

Shit.

* * *

In the office on Madison Avenue, Alix stands by the full-length window, her red-gold hair catching the sunlight. Instead of scolding her, Alix says, "I've missed you."

Astrid crumples into an armchair and wishes for toasted marshmallows, a blanket, sleep, and for all the coursework she's missed to suddenly pour into her head.

Alix sits opposite and says shrewdly, "I feel like I should let you nap first. I want to be sure you're listening. At least you don't look like you're coming down from anything."

Astrid shakes her head. "Most people would be surprised to hear this, but Hawk is my only high."

Alix's voice becomes very gentle, like the blanket and marshmallows Astrid craved. "I love you, Astrid. But don't forget what *you* want."

There's a prickling in Astrid's eyes and a tightening in her throat. Has she forgotten? Where's the drive and the passion she once had to make clothes that let women be female *and* powerful—clothes that made them believe that being the first of those words didn't mean they could never be the second? And she knows the answer. It's *so* much easier to love and have great sex and go to parties. But there's no power in love and sex and parties—not if you're a woman.

Alix crosses back to the window and with her back to Astrid says, "Did you know every woman I employ thinks I've made a mistake when I send her the paperwork about her salary? She thinks it's a mistake because it's the same as what a man would earn."

"I know the world treats men and women differently," Astrid says testily. "Isn't that why I'm here in Manhattan? To change that?"

"I don't know why you're here, not anymore. What I do know is that, once upon a time, two women named Chanel and Schiaparelli ruled the fashion world. There have been other women in fashion. Claire McCardell—but I doubt anyone outside the fashion world knows her now. And she wasn't a queen the way Coco and Elsa were. Now in Paris there's Yves Saint Laurent and Pierre Cardin and still the Houses of Dior and Givenchy. In America we have Bill Blass. Oscar de la Renta. Hawk Jones could join that list. But there has never been another Chanel. Can you see where I'm going with this?"

There has never been another Chanel. No woman has even come close. With a rush of shock, Astrid thinks—*does that mean there never will be?*

"I've been waiting very impatiently for years for a woman to rise up," Alix goes on. "Sometimes I think it's partly my fault—I was once Dior's publicist and had a hand in making him who he was. So I've tried my hardest to support every promising female fashion designer by covering her clothes in my magazine and introducing her to the right people. But they keep slipping off the glass runway. And some of them never try to get on it."

Alix stares owlishly at Astrid, then takes the chair beside her. "From the moment I returned from Paris with my mission from Mizza to be your godmother—you were eight then—you had the most evident sense of style. You were wearing a very short dress that your mother told me you'd cut the bottom off because it kept tangling in the jump rope—you'd presaged mini dresses by ten years. You were absolutely unlike every other eight-year-old on the planet. A couple of years later, you started to draw and you told me, here in this office, that you liked drawing people because they were never the same from one moment to the next, but somehow they were. I looked at your sketchbook and thought you were precociously gifted and I vowed I wouldn't let the world dilute that gift. That's what my speechmaking is about. Don't turn your talents to fashion if it isn't what you want. But don't be this."

She unfolds the picture of Astrid at Charles Revson's party with obscenely sized cans of caviar in the background, an obscenely decorated toilet seat under her arm, wearing a hand-ornamented tank top that now sells by the thousands from Hawk's shop. The headline reads, FROM HOMECOMING KING TO FASHION LEGEND: THE RISE AND RISE OF HAWK JONES. Astrid's name is littered throughout the article alongside the terms: *model, clotheshorse, femme fatale, bombshell.*

"He made shirts screen-printed with that design," Astrid says, pointing to the tank top, "and they're walking out the door."

"I bet they are."

"Hawk's not like what you read about," Astrid protests, thrusting herself out of the chair, furious that someone she trusts is uncharmed by Hawk. "He doesn't spend his life at nightclubs, and he isn't always lying around in bed with me. He works hard. His father is sick and Hawk visits him all the time and he's so gentle with him. You have no idea how gentle he can be. About the worst thing he does is stay out till dawn sometimes. You can't tell what someone's like from what you read about them."

"So this isn't true?" Alix's finger rests on the words: *model, clothes horse, femme fatale, bombshell.*

"I have to go." Astrid storms out.

On the street, she sees one woman wearing the Hawk Jones tank top, another wearing Hawk Jones jeans. He *is* a legend. And she's learning so much from him.

The trouble is, the things she's learning aren't the things Parsons examines her on. She almost fails her midterm exams. The only thing that saves her is her midterm portfolio. She shows it to Hawk once it's been graded and he pages through it, saying, "You're so fucking talented."

She doesn't tell him how close she came to failing. She doesn't tell anyone.

Instead, she sets her mind to proving to Alix that she's no mere bombshell. She's had a few months of fun but it isn't too late to get back on track.

She applies for the few remaining internships for the winter break—how has she missed all the deadlines?—but doesn't get any interviews. After three rejections, she looks around and realizes that the men in her class have the internships on Seventh Avenue. Donna Karan, the only woman from her class to have one, isn't paid for hers.

She takes another look at the sketches she sent off with her applications. There's the silver dress. The black corduroy dress. Her designs, selling like LSD tabs in a nightclub from Hawk's stores. Isn't she at least worth interviewing?

When the Bill Blass internship is advertised, she sends off the same sketches. But the name she writes on the application form isn't hers. She doesn't want to think that's the problem but...

She's called in for an interview. But she isn't allowed to pass through the doorway of Blass's office.

"My dear," he tuts. "I see why you lied about your name. No designer worth a damn is going to hire another man's muse."

Another man's muse.

Her heart punches her chest. She can't have spent so long getting herself to fashion school only to become both the muse's daughter—and the muse too.

"Screw you," she says, turning to leave.

Blass chuckles. "I know that's where your talents lie, and I'm not interested."

On the street, Astrid's steps slow. Two women walk past, both of them slowing when they see her, craning their necks, whispering to one another. "That's Astrid Bricard!"

People know who she is. But what do they know her for?

Don't be this, Alix had said.

What if it's too late?

SEVENTEEN

BLYTHE BRICARD

Late afternoon, Blythe's phone buzzes with a text from Jake. He hasn't texted her for at least a year. That he's texting her at all turns out to be less surprising than the message.

Eva tells me Georgia's her new best friend. So I've organized for the kids to have dinner and watch movies in Georgia's room when we get back. I'm planning to go for a run. I bet you haven't had a chance to run the whole time we've been here and I know you hate running alone in the dark. So come with me. J

Jake's taking their deal so seriously that instead of dumping the kids with her when he returns, he's organized for them to hang out with their cousins. And he's also figured out she's had no time to exercise. She's so shocked she has to sit down.

Her phone buzzes again with a picture of a hideously faux-medieval castle hotel that looks like it's had every French cliché thrown at it bar Breton stripes. It even has an inflatable Eiffel Tower out front. *So I took the kids here.*

Blythe bursts out laughing.

Another text arrives almost immediately. *You know I'm kidding, right? Maybe it's too soon to joke about my venue choices.*

She's about to text back a *lol* to demonstrate she didn't actually amputate her sense of humor when they got divorced, when yet another text pings.

It didn't go so well today. The comedy routine was me putting off telling you.

Blythe's stomach knots. Not long after, Eva storms in saying, too much like the teenagers upstairs, "If that was a fun day out, then kill me now."

Behind her, Sebby's dressed in a too-big coat and Jake's in shirtsleeves.

"Our father forgot to remind us to bring our coats," Eva continues. "He forgot Sebby's Ventolin, so we had to stop at a pharmacy. *And* he forgot to remind us to go to the bathroom . . ." She stops and Seb takes up the story.

"Eva had to go, but the toilet didn't have . . ." Sebby lowers his voice in deference to Eva's embarrassment. "A flush button."

Blythe has to press her lips together so she doesn't laugh. Jake looks totally bewildered.

"But we went to a castle with a real dungeon," Sebby adds more brightly.

"And Sebby ordered a burger the same size as his," Eva points accusingly at Jake, "and a hot chocolate, and he threw up. In the castle."

Jake looks about as mortified as it's possible to be.

"Okay," Blythe says, still trying desperately hard not to laugh. "You guys need some quiet time. Go get your books out. I'm going to talk to your dad."

Once the door's closed, Blythe sits on the bed and dissolves into laughter.

"What's going on?" Jake says. "I thought you'd march straight to Champlain's office and forbid me to take the kids out ever again."

She grins. "You took them to a castle with a dungeon, which sounds okay to me, and you fed them—obviously too much, but still. Age-appropriate destinations and food put you so far ahead of your last date that I don't know if everything is your fault this time."

"I forgot their stuff. There's so much I don't know." He exhales frustratedly. "Which is my fault." Then he leans against the door and says something that makes her gape. "I've told everyone at work that for the next three weeks, they should only get in touch if I'm going bankrupt again."

Wow. She can't remember Jake ever taking a real vacation. He really *is* trying. So she explains, because she wants this to work out for Eva and Sebby.

"When Eva was about four, she used an auto-flush toilet in the Paris airport that didn't sense her weight and kept flushing while she peed. She thought it was trying to suck her in. And Sebby's eyes are bigger than his stomach—if you let him order what he wants, he'll decorate the floor with it later. They have a million more weird quirks that you'll discover soon enough, if you're game."

He smiles wryly. "Looking forward to seeing what else goes on that list." He pushes away from the door. "Still up for a run before dinner? Let's say in an hour?"

"Sure." As she stands up to see him out, she adds, "Thanks for organizing the kids tonight."

"My pleasure," he says, voice softer now.

The space between them suddenly feels like two inches. She can smell the faint and fading scent of the aftershave he's always worn— pepper and sandalwood and clove, a scent that's teasing her nostrils, tempting her to step into that space where memory and ardor reside. How good it would be to feel a set of arms around her, to feel that fast ache, and that slow burn.

The door bursts open and Sebby bounds in, still wearing Jake's coat. Eva follows.

"We thought we should shower, since we need to be ready for Georgia by seven," she says loftily. "We're being *independent.*"

"I'll help," Jake says, turning quickly away.

Once the door's closed, Blythe collapses back onto the bed. It's the second time she's realized she's on dangerous ground living in the same house as Jake—that being furious with him for disappointing the kids isn't the same as not wanting him.

* * *

When Blythe puts her head into the kids' room, Sebby's sitting cross-legged on the floor with Jake, playing cards. Eva's pretending to read but she's watching her father. Blythe kisses her forehead, knowing that months of anger aren't going to be given up in a day.

Jake wriggles back against the wall and stretches his legs out as if he has nowhere he needs to be.

"Go get changed," Blythe says. "I'll meet you in the library."

"First, I want to talk about tomorrow. While Sebby was in the shower and you were busy reading…" He flicks a smile at Eva, who, knowing she's been busted, almost smiles back. "I found somewhere fun to go. So, can we try again? I made a list of everything I might forget." He folds notepaper into an airplane and tosses it to Eva.

Blythe forces herself not to slink over and check off the list against her own mental one.

Eva laughs. "You wrote down eyeballs."

Jake rolls his eyes crazily at her. "You told me today that I'd forget my eyeballs if they weren't stuck in my head, so I wanted to make sure that if my eyeball glue dries up and they fall out, I won't leave them behind."

"You won't be able to read the list without your eyeballs, Daddy," Eva giggles.

Blythe's eyes meet Jake's with a sad kind of joy. She can't remember the last time she heard Eva call Jake *Daddy*.

There's a knock on the door and Ed appears bearing a bouquet of lily-of-the-valley, like a fragrant cluster of fairy dresses. "These came for you, Blythe."

He stops when he sees Jake. "Did you guys have a good day?" he asks the kids casually, as if the answer doesn't matter much when of course it matters a great deal.

"I threw up in a castle," Sebby says brightly and Ed starts laughing.

Amidst the chatter, Blythe slips the card out of the bouquet.

You canceled our meeting yesterday and I'd like to reschedule. Nathaniel

"Who sent the flowers, Mommy?" Eva tugs at the note and it falls to the floor.

Jake bends down to retrieve it. He frowns, passes it to Blythe, then beckons to his brother. "Let's go."

* * *

Upstairs, Blythe can hear voices coming from the library. Of all the nights for everyone to be in there.

When she enters, the fire is blazing. And Jake is too.

"I don't care what your rules are," Jake is saying to the chateau owner. "We're not opening the window for ventilation. My mom is sick and she's already freezing from knocking on your door for an hour, wanting the fire lit. She chose this place because you advertised roaring fires. That," he says, pointing to the fire, "is what I call roaring."

Sensibly, the owner withdraws.

Iris holds out a hand for Jake. "Happily for me, the fire isn't the only thing that's roaring. Thank you, darling."

"We can always rely on Jake to not give a shit what anyone thinks of him and to defend Mom until his dying breath," Ed adds, grinning at his brother.

And the questions and contradictions spin around in Blythe's mind once more. Jake *is* ferociously protective of those he loves. Which is totally at odds with his behavior toward Eva and Sebby since he and Blythe divorced. A year ago, she hadn't cared that Jake was like a once-perfect pattern whose pieces had been recut into something lesser. But now her mind keeps trailing, like fingertips searching for flawed stitches, over the beautiful, complicated and aching seams of the life she and Jake had once shared.

"Ready?" Jake asks, rousing her.

"Where are you two going?" David asks with interest.

"You're going out?" Herb says, a strangely hopeful note in his voice.

"You two are going on a date?" Charlie's tone is rightly incredulous.

"We're going for a run," Jake says. And he manages to get them out the door and away from the questions.

"That was almost the same level of scrutiny as when I first met them," Blythe says as they walk down the steps.

"I don't think I can recommend the same treatment we used that night though." Jake darts a slightly wicked grin at her.

Blythe's skin flushes an extravagant red. The remedy they'd used after they left his parents' apartment the night she met the Black clan was to have sex in the elevator. "No you cannot," she says, flustered. Is he teasing her? Flirting with her? Rattling her?

Thankfully, he changes the subject. "Did you have time to work today?"

Blythe's laugh dies. "I spoke to your mom."

Jake is silent for a long moment. "She told me."

"Why didn't you ever say anything?" She stops. They're divorced. He doesn't owe her anything. She changes the subject. "I did do some work. I don't know if I should tell you though. What if I end up working with Nathaniel? You'd be my competition."

"Then you'd have lots of lily-of-the-valley to inspire you."

Blythe doesn't reply to that definitely argumentative statement.

"Sorry," he says. "That seems to be my most-used word when I'm with you."

"Not when we were married, it wasn't."

It's a low blow. But nobody can rile her like Jake can.

* * *

Blythe pushes herself, firstly to stop from turning to ice and secondly to ease her irritation. She knows that while she's running flat out, Jake's probably only in second gear. But her temper vanishes as he leads her into the vast grounds of the chateau and around the lake where the mist drifts up off the water and the silence is absolute.

And she prays, in this plein-air space of contemplation, that she can make it all work. That she can help the kids as they get to know their father again. That she can forget the memories about Jake that linger. That she can come up with a plan for MIZZA. And that she can find out what happened to Astrid. Each of those things might ordinarily take a year. She has two and a half weeks.

She feels herself speed up as they pass the twenty-minute mark, outrunning her doubts. Jake's always been more of a sprinter, she more of a stayer and, just like old times, their paces even out. They run past stables dressed in ivy, leafless tendrils wrapping around the limestone like fingers encircling a waist. The memory of a horse-and-carriage time still hovers in the air—everything around them is dark and ageless, their footfalls and the fog of their breath the only things that penetrate the night.

"It's beautiful," Blythe says and Jake smiles at her.

The tension they've carried with them dissipates.

He leads them down another path that ends at a tuffeau stone outbuilding. They stop, panting, walking circles to bring their breath back under control.

"Do you want to see inside?" Jake says. "The door isn't locked. I found it a couple of days ago." He smiles at her again and she wonders if maybe he's come this way deliberately.

So she follows him into what turns out to be the most exquisite secret theater. "Wow," she says, turning in a circle, taking in the tiny stage with a golden sun shining above it, the border of gold leaf at the proscenium arch, the trompe l'oeil stage panels. The walls are draped with tapestries in deep green, lapis and gold. Above, a chandelier hangs like a constellation, casting horoscopes of hope.

Jake walks over to the stage, taps a finger against the arch and says, "The team was stuck on the campaign for the second Claire McCardell collection. Feeling the strain, I guess. This place made me think of your old fashion magazines—the photos from one of the original Claire McCardell shoots with the model standing in an archway."

Resurrecting Claire McCardell the year before had been the thing that sent Blake Group from eager youngster and into the stratosphere. The first collection was a hit of the kind that hadn't been seen since Dior's iconic first showing, and she's heard much anticipation in the press ahead of the second collection, which must have put a ton of pressure on Jake to make sure his team cements the fledgling darling of the beau monde into legend. And suddenly she misses the way they'd always talked so well together about ideas and design.

"Go on," she tells him.

"Standing here, I had this idea to juxtapose shots of McCardell's original designs alongside our new pieces," he continues, a familiar passion uplighting his face. "I wanted to show how, like you've always said, trying to create a trend to fill up a future that doesn't exist yet is a poor second to using the richness of the decades that have gone before. Hope you don't mind me stealing your idea."

"You haven't stolen anything. You made something from my abstract musings. It's a great idea."

Her gaze travels over the blues and greens of the tapestries, the floor's golden lacquer, the bronze sun at the top of the arch, and her own uncertainties come out. "I need to find the me in MIZZA," she says. "Everyone's going to compare me to Hawk and Astrid. Hawk's aesthetic is monochrome—black, white, silver, gray. His cuts are sexy, whereas Astrid used the best shades on the color palette and kept her lines simpler. He designed for the woman who wanted to be a spectacle, but Astrid designed for the woman who already was a spectacle— she just needed to believe it. I want to do that."

"If you give that line to Champlain, I'm never speaking to you again."

She grins. "It was being here that made me think of it, so I'm kind of stealing from you now."

He laughs, such a Jake laugh. If his eyes were the exemplar of the piercing cliché, they also were the embodiment of eyes that danced. His did the tango when he laughed properly.

Which means it's time to leave.

She walks over to the door and they set off at a slow jog. After the camaraderie, she's completely unprepared for him to say, "Why did you ask me for a divorce? I figured you must have been seeing someone but, as far as I can tell, you weren't with anyone after we split and you aren't with anyone now so . . . I'm just trying to work it out."

He thought the reason she divorced him was because she was having an affair?

Her pace picks up. "The reason we got divorced is because you can't be bothered to figure out why we got divorced," she says flatly.

"As far as aphorisms go, that one's a little obtuse."

"No, *you're* obtuse." She's so mad she's on the verge of breaking their promise to Eva not to fight. So she takes a deep breath. "I wanted you to be a husband to me and a father to my kids and over at least the last year of our marriage, you were neither of those things. I deserved more." Her voice cracks, and her feet strike the ground harder, trying to leave all of it behind. "So did Eva and Sebby."

"Don't hold back, Blythe. I'm not going to yell or race off." He quirks a smile at her. "Do your worst."

"With an invitation like that, I don't know where to start."

The levity is quickly gone. The fact is, if he did a little soul-searching, he could figure it out himself, rather than her having to relive it just so he can understand.

She slows down and so does he, tempos matched but everything else about them out of rhythm. "I'd just had Eva by the time you'd hired your teams and bought your first couple of brands and Blake

Group was an actual business," she begins. "I wanted you to do it—it became my dream because we'd talked about it so much together."

"I could never have done it without you," Jake says, voice stripped of all the urbane detachment he's used since they separated. "Blake Group is as much yours as it is mine. You have no idea how much of you is in there—"

"But we forgot the practicalities," she breaks in. "At first you traveling all the time was exciting. You'd come home and…"

Her voice trails off; she can't go there. Doesn't want to remember what it was like when he dropped his suitcase by the door, his lips making that familiar promise against her neck, the unbearable wait for Eva to fall asleep, the bliss of having him back beside her. Her eyes brush past Jake's and he's looking at her the same way he used to—as if he's planning the path his fingertips will travel along her spine.

"We did have great moments, didn't we," he says uncertainly. "Sometimes I wonder if I imagined all those times when it was perfect."

"Sometimes it was perfect." Her voice is wistful as they pass the lake, so misted over you wouldn't even know water lay beneath the fog. "But it stopped being perfect around the time I found out I was pregnant with Sebby. I know now that the business was starting to falter, so you were in Europe almost every week. The year he turned two, you spent twelve weeks at home and forty weeks away. Maybe I could have got through that if, during those twelve weeks, you made me feel as if you missed me."

He tries to interrupt, but she doesn't let him. "You'd do things like…" She slows to a walk and concentrates ferociously on not crying. "Sebby had asthma and pneumonia, bad pneumonia, and maybe I minimized it on the phone because you were away, but you knew he was in the hospital for a week and I'm pretty sure Ed told you what was going on—that Sebby was cyanotic and they were giving him oxygen and about a million medications. One night was so bad I dreamed he was going to die. And I cried in Ed's arms, not yours."

Shit. Tears are streaming down her cheeks. She's going to end up sobbing the same way she'd sobbed that night on Ed's shoulder, loud and raw and wretched. She swipes at her face. "By the time you got back, Sebby was home recovering. You walked in and said, 'I'm exhausted. I'm going to sleep. Hope the kids can be quiet.' Not, *How's my son?* Or, *How are you?*"

She stops. Closes her eyes. She's done.

They've reached the back door. Blythe's about to go straight in when Jake clears his throat.

"Blythe..." He's silent for a long time, then he says, "I...I thought you hated me. I didn't realize I'd hurt you and the kids so much. I'm sorry. I'll apologize to them in the morning too."

She thinks she's strong enough not to cry anymore but then he says, "Fuck. I never thought I'd be talking to you about why we got divorced. I thought we'd be together forever. I...I loved you right up until the end, Blythe."

She almost wants to hold him, to wrap themselves and their pain in one another's arms. But she needs him to dig deeper so she can really trust him with Eva and Sebby's more tender hearts. So she says very quietly, "Loving someone and making them feel loved are two different things. It's easy to just love, but it takes effort to make another person believe in that love. I think...I think Eva and Sebby will vouch for that too."

She braces for argument. But Jake just nods and says, "Can I kiss them good night? I promise not to wake them."

"Of course," she says, throat aching. She watches him walk toward the kids' room, and she's almost sure his eyes are shining now too.

And maybe the soul-searching's just begun.

EIGHTEEN

ASTRID BRICARD AND HAWK JONES

Rather than going back to Hawk's apartment after her interview with Bill Blass, Astrid goes to see Velvet, who says, "Graham's at his boyfriend's place tonight. So stay here. There's somewhere we should go tomorrow."

Astrid didn't even know Graham had a serious boyfriend, hasn't seen Graham other than in passing for weeks. While her life has felt full of people and parties, it's shrunk to a stuck track of the *same* people and parties.

On the streets the next day there's a strange disturbance in the air. An uncontained energy radiates from Velvet too.

When they turn onto Fifth Avenue, instead of cars, Astrid sees women. So many women. Their chanting voices are oxygen and Astrid breathes them in as they cry out, "I'm not a Barbie Doll!" and "Don't iron while the strike is hot." At the head of the march is a banner reading *Women's Strike for Peace and Equality.* Everywhere there are smaller signs asking for *Abortion on Demand* or to *End the War. Equal Pay for Equal Jobs.* There are banners urging the Senate to pass the Equal Rights Amendment, making the obvious point that nearly fifty years is too long to wait for parity.

Not a single car can move in this part of the city. All that moves are the women, tens of thousands of them. They've brought Manhattan to a standstill.

"You used to believe in this stuff, Astrid," Velvet says. "Now you're just giving half of what makes you amazing to Hawk. Those fifty silver dresses—someone sold theirs to Veruschka for three thousand dollars. It wouldn't be the icon it is without you making that skirt so damn short and that back so damn low. Hawk's a great designer. A lot of stuff he makes up on the spot just by flipping a bolt of silk around you. But some of those pieces are yours too."

Astrid blinks, remembering the rent party where she'd danced with Velvet under a pink balloon and said, *Don't do it to make a man great*. It's never occurred to her that what she's doing for Hawk is work. It was love—except it's actually commerce.

"Let's just march," Velvet says.

They join hands and stand behind the women. And suddenly Astrid has a voice, a voice strong enough to stop every car in Manhattan, to make every male boss scratch his head at the absence of women in the office who might brew his coffee and take his phone calls. A voice strong enough to make her want to put her name on a goddamn dress, no matter what Bill Blass says.

Then Astrid spies a group from Parsons, Candace amongst them. It's a day to unite, so she drags Velvet over and finds herself calling for equality by Candace's side. Two women who want the same thing.

But Candace says, "I got the internship with Bill Blass."

Astrid knows her face reflects an emotion more petty than she wants to feel. Candace getting an internship is good news—now two women in their class have gained a foothold in fashion.

Then Candace leans into her ear and below the shouts of "Women Unite!" she says in an underbreath, "My dad's a drunk, out-of-work mechanic who beat up my mom until the day he disappeared. I was the girl everyone avoided because I came from a place worse than the wrong side of town. I fought for everything I have—literally, sometimes. And I'm here today because I'm so fucking glad that me getting an internship proves that a photo in *Vogue* and a famous name aren't worth more than my sweat. Watch out, Astrid Bricard. Maybe the Parsons scholarship was my trough, but the only way out of a trough is up. Maybe that scholarship was your peak—and it's all downhill from here."

Candace wants to make her weep. And Astrid almost does. Then a placard tumbles down the street, the words it carries—*Woman Power*—spin around, dented by every collision, cracked by marching feet. But still it flies.

Astrid pulls away from Candace and chases after the sign, wincing as it thwacks against a wall. At last she grabs it and the anger surges. Anger at herself, firstly. Then a larger, wider anger. She takes hold of Velvet's hand and they shout their wishes into the sky, hearing them rise and rise.

* * *

Astrid stays at Velvet's that night, holding on to the anger and the passion. Then she goes to college before class and studies her portfolio, realizes how many empty pages it holds. And she finally sees what she should have seen all along. To the world, she *is* a muse. Right now, it *is* all about sex—and Astrid is the one being screwed.

She goes to every class that day. And she stays after her classes are finished, takes out watercolor and brushes, strokes careful lines onto paper. Underneath each design she writes the words *Astrid Bricard*. Her name on a dress. She hasn't done this much work in weeks. An honest voice whispers that's why Candace got the internship. She earned it.

It's almost midnight when she returns to Hawk's apartment.

"Hey," he says tentatively, as if he knows something's wrong—they haven't spent this much time apart in months. "I missed you."

She leans into him because she's had to face some hard truths today that have left her bruised and not liking herself too much. She says quietly, "Remember the silver dress?"

"How could I forget it?" he says. "Seeing as how I just about ripped it off your body."

Another question unspools. "Would you have made the dress so short if I hadn't been there that day?"

He strokes her hair, wraps his arms more tightly around her. "God, that's terrifying. *If you hadn't been there that day.* Then you mightn't be here now."

No man could fake the tenderness and the fear in his voice. She knows Hawk loves her. And he can't answer her question because there is no answer. Her stepping to the front of the classroom and picking up the lamé destroyed all other possibilities.

Astrid was the one who volunteered to help Nancy make tank tops for Hawk's shop. Astrid watched delightedly as the corduroy dress sold to hundreds of happy customers. She willingly gave all that to Hawk because she had no idea what she was giving.

This isn't Hawk's fault. It's her own.

"I need to spend a lot more time studying, Hawk. Candace has an internship at Bill Blass and I'm hanging on by the merest thread. I didn't tell you because..." She shrugs. "You're a success and I'm almost failing. I love you, but being with you takes up so much time, just like I worried it would, back when I first met you. I don't regret this, and I don't want it to end, but I need to take back some of that time and energy and spend it on me."

He looks stricken. "I'm sorry. I've been a selfish asshole. You're the most talented woman at Parsons." Hawk's voice is fierce. "Like you believe in me, I believe in you."

Which is why a tear trickles down her cheek. Without Hawk, she wouldn't have so much joy, or the deepest kind of love. And without Hawk, she wouldn't be failing Parsons. Or maybe that's not true. Maybe Hawk has been her excuse. Not anymore.

"I'm going to make an end-of-year portfolio like Parsons has never seen," she tells him, her voice fierce now too. "Maybe I missed out on an internship. But that portfolio will make damn sure I get the job I've always wanted with a name designer when I graduate—and a couple of years after that, I'll finally be a name designer myself."

She can turn this around. There's still time before she graduates to be a success.

* * *

Later that night when Hawk is asleep, Astrid writes a letter to Mizza to explain what she hasn't yet told her. It's another way of proving her commitment—confessing her ambitions to Mizza Bricard.

Mizza's reply is one line long:

Chérie, why do you want to be a designer? Love, Mizza.

The brevity, the superiority Astrid senses in that one sentence, makes her pen one impulsive, angry line in response.

So I can erase your past from my present.

The minute she mails it, she regrets it. It was petty. But isn't it also the truth? And if it is—does that mean Astrid is basing her entire future on resentment?

It's a question that worries her over the next few months while she draws up her own study plan so she can learn all the things she needs to get better at, things Parsons doesn't spend enough time on. If she can perfectly master every possible skill then, while she might have missed out on step one of her plan, she won't miss out on step two— landing an apprenticeship with a name designer upon graduation.

First, Astrid makes a trade with Velvet to teach her some of the more complex hand-sewing techniques she's pretended she already knows. Hawk's had to trash so many ideas because what he could drape with his hands couldn't be made cheaply enough. But Astrid wants to know up front when something's impossible, so her portfolio isn't a repertoire of the unachievable. And Velvet is the best hand-sewer Astrid has ever seen. In return, Astrid shows Velvet how to improve her sketches.

Next, Astrid takes Alix out to dinner because she's worried that all the showmanship and spectacle have been used up by Hawk. Alix, who was once Dior's PR director, is certain to know a thing or two.

"Gimmicks are fine," Alix tells her. "Hawk making clothes on you in the shop is a gimmick. Just like when I traveled with Dior to America in 1947 and we staged a stunt where he measured exactly how close to the ankle his skirts fell because everyone was protesting against the extravagant length."

She smiles wryly. "Imagine that. Twenty-five years later and it's the opposite. Everyone's decrying how short Hawk Jones's hotpants are." She leans forward, fixing Astrid in her gaze. "That was a gimmick. Getting Rita Hayworth to wear a Dior gown to the Paris premiere of *Gilda* in 1947, and then dressing Hollywood stars—that was a strategy. A gimmick will get you noticed. A strategy will make sure everyone keeps noticing."

The following month, Astrid visits Hawk's dad to ask him about the business side of things. After he's explained the fundamentals of economics, he asks how Hawk's business is doing.

"Amazingly well," she says.

All she ever sees are customers entering the store and leaving with bags. The tank top with Astrid's Hawk Jones design on the back is still one of the most popular items—redone in black last month, in silver lamé this month—because it's the cheapest thing in the shop. With it, anyone can own a piece of Hawk Jones. But after talking to Matthias, she wonders if selling a lot of the cheapest thing is the best way to turn a profit.

"But what's he doing about investment? Expansion?" Matthias sighs. "I should ask him myself, but I worry he'll think I'm doubting him."

"And now I'm worried because I've never talked to him about that," Astrid says.

She kisses Matthias goodbye, thinking—are she and Hawk just about the good times, the fun of making and wearing and dancing? Where's their serious side, their depth? Are they just silver lamé, naked underneath?

That thought sits beside the question Mizza asked and that Astrid hasn't been able to forget as she takes the train up to Hastings-on-Hudson the following weekend, to an institution called the Graham Home for Children. This excursion has nothing to do with design or ambition, and everything to do with that fundamental kernel that sits inside everyone—their origin. Because if James and Beth, her parents, hadn't somehow made an arrangement with Mizza, then Astrid might have been a child in a home too.

She's brought with her all the leftover fabric scraps from Parsons and she puts them in the middle of a table surrounded by a dozen parentless children.

"I hate sewing," one of them says.

Everyone starts to complain about how boring it is and Astrid thinks she's lost them before she's even begun. "So what do you like doing?" she asks the girl.

"Swimming."

"I like surfing," Astrid says. "And where I surf, the water is..." She pulls dark blue denim from the pile. "Like this. And the foam is like this." Now she takes a handful of tulle, scrunches it and winds a length of lace through it so both the messy filigree of the spume and the texture of it are captured.

"The river here is like this." One of the boys grabs a piece of cotton the color of sand. "Boring."

"Oh yeah?" Astrid says. "What kind of ocean do you like?"

He cocks his head to the side and pulls out the longest piece of fabric and lets it roll off the edge of the table. "One that's endless."

His words make tears prickle in Astrid's eyes. She swallows hard. "How would you feel, swimming in that?"

Bit by bit, the kids start to make their own oceans. Astrid sews each one into a mural of an ever-changing expanse of water. The boy who wanted an endless ocean turns out to be expert at cutting and he helps the others populate their seas. The girl who likes swimming embroiders her name onto her ocean, and her stitches are tiny and lovely. Other parts of the mural are disorderly and bear no resemblance to water whatsoever—there's one aggressive strip of red near the middle that's painstakingly attached to all the rest by a boy who doesn't speak much, but who tends his little patch of crimson ocean like a pet he's never had.

On the train back to the city, Astrid takes out her portfolio. She studies not just her drawings, but the annotations, the fabric swatches and the explanations of the techniques she's used—French binding, underlining, couching and fulling—and she can see that it's almost done.

She made all of this. She, Astrid Bricard.

When she gets back to the apartment, she pulls out the pink dress she made in class last year and which she's never worn. She puts it on and Hawk halts when he sees her.

"Far out," he says. "It's beautiful, Astrid."

Tears dampen her eyes for the third time that day. She hears Mizza's voice, *Why do you want to be a designer?*

Because she's crying over a beautiful dress she made, one that expresses how she feels—just like a red strip of sea and a boy's endless ocean had expressed what he most wanted too.

She shows Mizza's letter to Hawk. "The answer to her question is: because I love it. That's it. So simple. But it's the best—the only— reason to do anything." She traces a finger over Mizza's ink flourishes. Is she, like adding a hidden corset to a dress, attaching subtext to a sentence that holds no other meaning?

"I wonder," she says hesitantly, "if Mizza asked me that question because she knew I needed to ask it of myself."

* * *

Fi and Nancy are squealing like teenagers and Hawk's grinning like he's higher than the Chrysler building. He closes the shop early and stands there, looking at the racks of clothes, at the photo hanging in the window of Astrid in her shorts stalking out the door, at the words *Hawk Jones* written on price tags and signs and tank tops. *Shit.* When word gets out, what will happen then?

He couldn't feel more like he's standing on the precipice of something big than if he were balanced on the edge of the Grand fucking Canyon.

At last he hears a key slip into the lock. He picks Astrid up the minute she walks in and twirls her around.

"Guess what?" he says when they're both dizzy and laughing. "Mick Jagger's girlfriend—you know, Bianca—was in here this morning."

How are these words even coming out of his mouth? How could someone so radically famous have been standing right here?

"No way," Astrid says, shocked into stillness.

"She bought a ton of stuff and…Far out." He sits on one of the stools because he can't believe what he's about to say.

Astrid sits next to him. "I can't tell if your news is good or bad."

He blurts it out. "She wants me to design her wedding dress."

"Holy shit, you're actually famous."

The smile on her face is gorgeous and it's impossible not to see that she's even more thrilled for him than he is for himself. And because she's the one person he can truly talk to, he says what's sitting deep in his gut. "What the fuck am I going to make?"

Astrid takes his hands in hers and says with so much sincerity he actually believes he can do this, "Something that sets the world on fire."

* * *

While Hawk works on ideas for a wedding dress for Bianca, Astrid sends out job applications. She finishes at Parsons in just over three months. Three months until step two of her plan, which is to get a job working with a name designer. She's caught up on everything she's missed and then some. Her portfolio is strong. She signs her name at the bottom of every application with a confidence she didn't have last year.

Her first rejection is from Bill Blass. She expects it, so it doesn't bother her. Velvet receives a rejection too and she just shrugs and says, "He gave the job to Candace. That man has no taste."

"So let's go celebrate that we don't have to work for a man who called me a muse," Astrid says.

They go to the Electric Circus, just the two of them, and dance like women who expect only good things from the world.

Her second rejection is from Halston. Velvet shows her the same letter.

"I thought I had a good chance there," Astrid says. "I feel like my aesthetic is similar."

"Our portfolios would scare a man like Halston," Velvet says resolutely. "We're too good and he won't want the competition."

Astrid is about to laugh at this very optimistic assessment when Graham interrupts them. "I got the job at Halston!"

She and Velvet relax only when it becomes apparent Graham didn't hear them. They hug him and take him out and Astrid tries to believe what Velvet said, which is easier with a Harvey Wallbanger in hand. But she's seen Velvet's portfolio and knows it's better than Graham's. It has more guts. And then she has to slip away to the bar to order another round, even though they haven't finished the first, because she's just had a thought that terrifies her.

What if the designers only want someone who's doing the same tried-and-true thing? What if no one except her wants to make clothes that give women back their power? What if she should never have made a portfolio of dresses she loved?

The second Harvey Wallbanger disappears too quickly and some freaking pap takes a photo of her knocking it back like she's already wasted.

The next day brings with it a headache and a rejection from Anne Klein.

"Don't tell me she's scared of us too," Astrid says to Velvet.

Needless to say, there's a fourth rejection and a fifth, and then Astrid stops counting.

NINETEEN

BLYTHE BRICARD

Jake's just left the suite after kissing the kids good night when Blythe hears Coco say, "Jake's gone, right?" and she almost falls over in shock. Coco's in her bedroom with a tray of food, a glass of champagne and a big piece of paper beside her.

"You eat and I'll talk," Coco tells her.

Blythe sits on the bed and picks up her plate. With Coco, it's easier just to obey.

"I've proven one of the things we talked about this morning," Coco says jubilantly. "Your grandmother was a pretty incredible woman. I found an article written by a professor at FIT. So I called the college, asked to speak to her, name-dropped you and *voilà*! We had quite the chat." Coco plucks a potato off Blythe's plate. "Yum."

"Where's yours?" Blythe asks, starving now after both the running and the blood-letting with Jake.

"I already ate," Coco says, stealing another potato. "But these are so good. Anyway: Mizza. It pisses me off that there are all these people writing books and articles—nonfiction, so everyone believes them—but they're missing ninety percent of the facts. And those facts might take some detective work but they're there, waiting to be found. Like how everyone says Dior used lily-of-the-valley in his collections because he grew up surrounded by flowers in Normandy. Untrue.

Mizza was the one who used lily-of-the-valley in Molyneux's spring 1938 collection. Then she used it at Dior. That's what the FIT professor showed me. She sent me pages from a few out-of-print memoirs about the 1930s that talk about Mizza—a woman so revered for her beauty that designers showered her with dresses. That Jeanne Toussaint, Cartier's famous jewelry designer, was such a good friend that she was a witness at Mizza's 1940s wedding to a husband Mizza stayed married to until her death. Mizza was married—twice actually. She seems to have made a bit of a mistake in the 1920s with a first short-lived marriage, but she wasn't a whore. And her jewels came from Jeanne because she knew that if Mizza wore them, other people would buy them. She was an influencer before the idea was invented. And then . . ." Coco pauses dramatically and Blythe can't help but lean forward.

Coco unfolds a piece of paper. "Something else I found in those newspaper archives. An article written by a London fashion writer in 1950. Guess what the headline is?"

"Mizza Wears Only a Fur Coat to Work Today?" Blythe says facetiously.

Coco reads aloud. " 'Dior's Assistant—A Woman of Chic. On the opening day of a new collection at Maison Christian Dior, you will find, seated at the back of the main salon, a charming, ultrasmart woman whose keen green eyes are focused on every detail of the passing models. She is a most important person on the Dior staff, second only to the great man himself. Madame Germaine Biano-Bricard, first assistant designer to Christian Dior. She works with him in the creation of every model.' "

"Give me that." Blythe grabs the paper. And yes, right there it says Mizza Bricard wasn't Dior's muse, but his assistant designer. *Second only to the great man himself.* "But . . ." she splutters.

"You want more than one article, right? How about a 1977 *Harpers & Queen* obituary for Mizza that says, and I quote, 'Many considered her to be a greater designer than Coco Chanel.' Have I convinced you now?"

Greater than Coco Chanel? Her grandmother?

"But," she repeats, still incoherent, "how could Dior let everyone slander her?"

"The professor said you have to remember Dior died in 1957 and that history is a patriarch with a thin spotlight of memory always trained on a man. Dior didn't know Mizza would be reduced in later years. And she *was* his muse. But she was a designer too. History forgot the second half because it's a man's name on the awning. History kept the first half because that's the way stories of male creators working with women are written."

"That means she was robbed of so much," Blythe says, tracing her finger over the photograph accompanying the article—a woman in a white cotton coverall with tousled hair, focused on re-pinning a dress. No fur. No plunging *décolleté*. And Blythe is seized with a yearning to know this woman. *How did you ignore*, she wants to ask her, *the version of you that existed everywhere except inside yourself?*

"Guess where the trail goes cold?" Coco says, sitting down beside her. "We know what Mizza did before the war—Doucet, Mirande, Molyneux. And we know that from 1946 she was at Dior. But what did she do *during* the war? Why can I find so many Mizza bread crumbs before the war and after the war, but nary a speck between 1940 and 1945?"

Blythe halts midway to finishing the last potato. "Are you asking me, or do you already have the answer?"

"Blythe, when was Astrid born?"

"May 1945."

"Which means she was conceived near the end of the German Occupation of Paris." Coco pauses, uncharacteristically cautious, and touches a hand to Blythe's back. "Do you know who Astrid's birth father was? There's no name on the birth certificate. And how did

Astrid end up in Long Island if she was born in Paris? Why wasn't she adopted out in France?"

Blythe stares at Coco. "I have no idea," she admits. "I guess I always thought Astrid's father was one of Mizza's many conquests. But if Mizza didn't actually have a swathe of conquests…"

"Like I said, the civil records show that Mizza Bricard married during the war and was still married to the same man in 1945. But her husband's name isn't on Astrid's birth certificate. Which means he wasn't the father. So who was? And is it somehow connected to why Mizza's a blank chapter during the war?"

Blythe frowns. "What are you saying?"

"Well…" Coco grimaces. "If you're going to run away from your life, it must be because of something big. I know it's a long shot, but what if it's to do with who Astrid's father was? And what if Astrid found out about it when she was at Versailles?"

* * *

They could postulate a thousand reasons why Astrid left and never guess the right one. Which doesn't change the fact that Coco's right— Blythe has no idea who Astrid's father was, and whether Astrid knew or not.

She looks through the documents Coco left, retracing all of her research, reading things about the grandmother she never knew.

Mizza did many extraordinary things, Coco's notes from her interview with the professor say. *History has forgotten them, and turned Mizza into something she wasn't.* Then a scribbled musing in the margin: *Just like Astrid was turned into something she wasn't?*

Blythe looks up and catches sight of herself in the mirror. What has she been turned into by these women?

The answer is there, staring back at her. Blythe has been made into a woman afraid.

Eva and Sebby are the loves of her life and that love has made her afraid to do anything that might hurt them. To do MIZZA, she needs to find the courage to let the media hurl all their words and photographs at her children and to trust that Eva and Sebby will, with her help, be resilient enough not just to survive it, but to keep hold of their spirit and their childhoods too.

Even though Blythe isn't sure right now where to find that courage, she knows she has to. She owes it to Mizza, to her children, to herself—and maybe to Astrid too.

She falls asleep with questions unspooling through her dreams— who was Astrid's father? Why did Astrid run? Were Astrid and Hawk ever together again after 1971? And if they weren't, is that why Hawk never felt any real ownership of child-Blythe?

But a man who's told so many lies will never tell her the truth about that.

* * *

After breakfast, Jake organizes the Blacks who are, like all families, a mix of temperaments: Charlie and Frieda are late for everything, David and Anton always early, Ed is happy to be bossed around by his little brother, his kids less so.

Eventually everyone's in a car. There's a sense of excitement and also a sense of doubt—it's fun to be heading out to a place unknown but, while Jake's an excellent manager, he's never been one to organize family outings. Blythe decides just to forget about Astrid and Hawk for the day and dress for the occasion in a red dress coat and fabulous black 1980s over-the-knee boots.

Jake takes the ring road around Saumur heading west, and says, "It's about a two-hour drive so I downloaded an audiobook for you guys. Actually, I downloaded three—I didn't know what you'd already read."

He passes his phone to Eva, who reads out, "*Charlotte's Web*—that one's nice. *The BFG* and *The Secret Garden*."

"What's a BFG?" Seb asks.

"It's a giant, so I guess that's it," Eva says, knowing her brother's fascination for mythical beings.

As the story of a friendly giant fills the car, Blythe risks a glance at Jake.

"You're impressed, aren't you?" he asks, grinning the way she used to love, but that had acutely annoyed her over the last two years. Now she doesn't mind it so much.

She laughs. Then the *whys* reassert themselves. Why didn't he do this six months ago? Two years ago?

"You look beautiful, Blythe," she hears Jake say.

The timbre of his words is tender and private, and every pore on her skin betrays her with a tiny quiver. Then an uproarious burst of laughter from the back makes them both jump and whatever had lingered in the moment is gone.

In Nantes, Jake pulls up at the Gare Maritime. He herds everyone onto the Navibus, which crosses the river toward Trentemoult, a little fishing village whose houses are more startling than a rainbow, painted in brilliant shades of ultramarine, cerise and sunflower yellow. On others, the shutters or ironwork are colored in hues equally striking—shocking pink, Dutch orange, emerald green.

"Wow," she says.

"Have I impressed you even more?" he asks with another grin.

She gives him a playful elbow and then it's as if the muscle memory in their bodies takes over while their minds are catching up. Jake reaches out as if he's going to draw her in and kiss the top of her head, and Blythe moves to tuck herself in at his side. The minute his hand brushes over the nape of her neck they both realize that, while that's what Blythe and Jake used to do, it isn't what they do now.

Blythe steps away. She can't look Jake in the eye. Thankfully, everyone's exclaiming over the colors.

"Daddy, this is so cool," Eva says, slipping her hand into Jake's.

Sebby takes his other hand and Blythe hangs back, letting Jake have the moment.

"That's the best thing I've seen in months," Ed says, smiling. Then he adds, "It was Jake's idea to invite you and the kids to France. He asked me to write the note because he thought if he wrote it, you'd throw it in the trash."

* * *

The sun comes out and takes the chill from the air. Eva and Sebby's shouts of, "Come and see this!" are a soundtrack of pure happiness.

Blythe walks with Iris, who winces even at their easy pace. She wants to urge Iris to save her energy for the days ahead but Iris says, "These are the days I want to expend my energy on. Days with my happy family."

They wind through the slenderest of streets—built so narrowly, Blythe reads to Iris from the brochure, because the houses were made to cluster together against the wind, their backs turned against the Loire and the weather, some with interconnected passages so the fishermen could move through the village even in flood. It's like threading through an embrace and Iris holds Blythe's arm tighter still.

"The fishermen painted the houses with whatever was left over from painting their boats," she tells Iris. "And over the last twenty years, the residents revived the tradition of adding color to the houses."

"I like that," Iris says decisively. "Taking something beautiful from the past and making it shine still more in the present. Like MIZZA, perhaps."

Blythe remembers reading Mizza Bricard's obituary in Coco's notes, which said that Mizza, the most elegant woman in the world, liked blocks of color—lilac, navy, a contrast of cream. Blythe pulls out her phone and snaps the color blocks in front of her now, wanting to capture the way every hue is more vivid because it's set beside other extraordinary shades. How theories of color don't matter here—that the rule-breaking renders even the unpainted houses in ivory and cream breathtaking.

She knows that if she uses this color and this excitement in the clothes she's making, then she *will* be able to show the world that MIZZA is unafraid. That the women who wear it are fearless. And that Blythe, while far from fearless, has the courage to stand on the shoulders of both her grandmother and mother and make something still better than they were able to.

Eventually, Blythe leads Iris into the brasserie the Blacks have taken over for lunch, and it's like a sign—the song growling into the room is by the Stones. "Woman in Silver," a song everyone has always said is about Astrid, who apparently once walked away from a Mick Jagger kiss. Coco, Ed and Jake each look like they're about to ask the manager to change the music but Blythe just shrugs and says, "You know what? It's actually a great song."

And it is. It's about a woman who seeks out the extreme edges of life rather than the boring in-between and, right now, Blythe wouldn't mind taking on a bit of that maxim for herself.

TWENTY

ASTRID BRICARD AND HAWK JONES

After the press finds out Hawk's making Bianca's wedding dress, one store isn't enough to sell everything people want to buy. He opens stores in LA, Chicago, Dallas, signs contracts agreeing to concessions in department stores around the country, spends so much time in meetings that he hasn't got any time to design the dress that brought him the attention in the first place. Then comes a free weekend when he can just hang out in his own store and do some work.

Astrid's sitting at Nancy's sewing machine frowning over fabric that's pulling and puckering. Hawk's trying to work on Bianca's dress, which should have been started weeks ago and isn't even drawn. He wishes he could ravel Astrid in silk jersey, knows he'd come up with something in about five minutes. But he also knows he can't make anything on her, even if he would never, ever see her as only a muse.

Between them on the workbench is a copy of *Vogue*, opened to the "Observations" page and a picture of Hawk, Astrid, Mick Jagger and Bianca at the one party they've been to in a month, a party Hawk still can't believe happened. He'd sat in a booth talking to Mick Jagger about football. Mick had draped an arm around Astrid and tried to smooch her on the cheek, pretending he only accidentally caught the corner of her mouth. Astrid had slipped her hand into Hawk's and asked if they could go home—hadn't given even a second's thought to choosing him over the biggest rock star on the planet. Every time he thinks he's as in love with Astrid as it's possible to be, he discovers that infinity is microscopic and his love for Astrid is the biggest thing in the entire universe.

The next song plays on the radio and Hawk grins at Astrid. It's the Stones, Mick Jagger singing "Woman in Silver." *She's like the trend you didn't get/Too cool until she's gone/And then you want her back.* The song is widely believed to be about Astrid because of a line in the chorus about a woman in silver dancing in the sky and on the sea, drawn to the edges, not the boring in-between.

And the lyrics are right, in a way. Astrid *is* way too cool for some people. He's seen men and women at parties stare at her but then step away if she comes near, like they don't want to catch her at the same time as they're completely in thrall to her. Others like Hawk, who totally get Astrid, just smile and think how lucky they are to have recognized the trend now rather than being the ones too late to catch on.

Astrid rolls her eyes at him. "That song is *not* about me. I met him for ten minutes."

"Ten minutes was enough for me to fall in love with you," he says. "You know that every time we play that song here, we sell about ten times more than normal." He leans his elbows on the workbench, knows he's teasing her, can't get enough of the way she's a little flustered. "One of my customers asked me if I was sharing you with Mick."

Now she's smiling too, and she mimics his pose, elbows on the bench, eyes fixed on him. "Did you tell her I've moved on from designers to rock-star millionaires?"

He takes her hand, runs his thumb slowly over her knuckles. "I said Astrid isn't like a T-shirt I own. I have no ability to share Astrid because Astrid is the one who decides what she wants. And that's how it should be."

"Did this customer then melt like butter at your feet?"

"No, but she did ask me to autograph her navel."

Astrid laughs and it's exactly the sound he was hoping for—an anthem he'd salute to every day if he could. "Are you going to tell me what's wrong?" he asks, now that she doesn't look so much like she wants to strangle the fabric in front of her.

She points to the silk jersey. "It looks nothing like my sketch."

"Try it on anyway," he tells her. "Nancy taught me that just because something doesn't look the way it does in your head, it doesn't mean it's a failure. Sometimes the fabric does what it's meant to."

"And that's why I come here to the shop, rather than college. I always leave with a trick I wouldn't have known but for you. I'd forgotten how I used to let the fabric tell me what it wanted to do." The frown resettles onto her face, deeper than before.

"What's really going on?"

She indicates her portfolio. "I've sent it everywhere, Hawk. My last hope, which was never even on my original list, was the Saks design department. I got the rejection yesterday. Neither Velvet nor I have anything resembling a job offer in fashion and we finish in less than three months. That makes me most likely to be in the ninety percent who are doing something other than fashion in five years' time."

"Hey," he says, coming around to her side of the workbench and drawing her in. He's seen some of Graham's portfolio. It's not as good as Astrid's. And he can't believe Candace's is better either.

When Astrid next speaks, her eyes are suspiciously shiny. "I thought that as long as my portfolio was strong enough, I'd get the job I wanted. What if I'm wrong?"

"You're not wrong. Screw all of them," he growls. "Do what I did. Open your own store. Make everything in your portfolio and I'll—"

"Can we not talk about it right now?" She cuts him off, voice more than a little forlorn. "Tell me how the wedding dress is going."

"It's not," he says, just as forlornly.

He opens her portfolio, wanting to show her the potential caught

in its pages, wanting not to think about his deadline in just one week
for Bianca.

He stops at a sketch of the white trousers Astrid wore to Revson's
party with the white tank top. She's since drawn a white tuxedo jacket
on top, borrowing from Yves Saint Laurent's Le Smoking. Something
about that jacket arrests him.

"What if it's not a dress?" he says slowly. "Why would Bianca wear
a wedding dress? She's marrying a rock star. What if she wore..." He
starts rifling through fabric and pulls out white silk satin. "A tuxedo
jacket—but with nothing underneath."

Astrid grins at him. "That might be one of the best ideas you've
ever had."

And he knows—*he knows*—Bianca will love this.

The dizzy rush of having finally broken through the creative slump
makes him take Astrid's hands and say, "I want to marry you, Astrid.
I want *you* to wear the white jacket with nothing underneath and I
want to imagine, through the entire ceremony, how you'll look when
I take it off you. But you're going to say no." He smiles wryly at this,
at the way he knows her so well he can understand her refusal, even
while it hurts just a little. "Because you want your turn. So I'll wait
until the day you walk into our apartment wearing a white tuxedo
jacket and I'll ask you again. Deal?"

And now she's really crying—and smiling too—as she steps into
his arms and says, "I love you so much, Hawk Jones."

* * *

Bianca Jagger's wedding suit does set the world on fire. Astrid hardly
sees Hawk over the next month, which leaves her with too much time
to panic over what she's going to do after graduation. She's sweated,
she truly has. But nobody wants her sweat.

Then Velvet comes to find her at college to say, "A Parsons alumnus just got nominated for a Coty Award," which are the most prestigious fashion awards in the country.

"Mmmm," Astrid says, not really listening.

"Hawk's been nominated for the Coty, Astrid."

Astrid hears her pencil drop onto the floor. "What?"

"Exactly," Velvet says, crossing her arms. "I could have sworn I saw a white tuxedo jacket in your portfolio."

All Astrid's hurt and anger rush out at Velvet. She pulls herself to her feet. "All Hawk did was look at a picture of a jacket I'd drawn and then connect a dot nobody else would have—from tuxedo jacket to wedding suit. I would never have thought of using it for bridal wear and that's the plain truth. Nor would you. Nobody but Hawk would. And Hawk isn't winning a Coty because of just one jacket."

"I guess that's true," Velvet says flatly before she walks away.

Astrid doesn't go after her.

Because it *is* the truth. An argument that sets out the black and the white. Except...black isn't a color. It's the absence of light. And white isn't a color either. It can't be printed; it can't be made. It's created when all light is reflected.

Right now, Astrid feels like both the black and the white. Lightless. Existing only as a reflection.

"Astrid?"

She startles. It's the dean, and what he says next is just what she needs to hear. "Your work this year has been a remarkable turnaround from losing your scholarship. Can you come to my office for a minute before class?"

Her heart leaps. This is it! The magical offer she's been waiting for. The dean is the one person who'll know where that final vacant position is that's meant for Astrid.

She smiles, feeling a happiness as pure as a Balenciaga pattern piece itself together inside her, especially when they're in his office and he adds, "Your portfolio is one of the strongest I've seen in my time at Parsons."

She wants to ask him why everyone has rejected her. But she's suddenly afraid.

Astrid Bricard, who wore a fur coat to her prom in defiance of her teachers' rules, who helped make a silver dress that people still talk about today, who orchestrated a photograph of that dress that helped launch not just a fashion brand, but a fashion designer, is afraid to speak. *God.*

"Despite that," the dean goes on, "I think it's going to be very hard for you. If I can be honest, I wish you'd never met Hawk. But perhaps then neither of you would be the geniuses you are." He sighs. "My job is to make sure my students leave here equipped for what they'll find outside these walls. I couldn't let you leave without warning you. I hope..." Another sigh. "I hope you'll forgive me one day."

It's that last sentence that does it. Why is the world so full of older men all telling a young woman she won't be able to do what she wants? How do women walk down the street beneath the weight of all the doubt everyone wants them to carry?

Why is powerlessness the only thing the world wants to gift them?

An anger like she'd felt during the women's march sweeps through her. And underneath it, the same desperate need to be more than what everyone wants to make her.

"I don't need a job," she says as she stands, head high, refusing to be cowed. "I'm giving myself the only job I want, at a label I'm going to design myself."

"I wish you all the best with that," the dean says, skepticism in his voice.

And Astrid walks away, off the campus she will never return to.

Hawk didn't serve a name designer first. He became one instead.

So will she.

TWENTY-ONE

BLYTHE BRICARD

The drive back to the chateau is full of laughter. Sebby, who can tell jokes for hours, regales Jake with his repertoire. They tumble into the chateau with smiles on their faces and Jake is turning to Blythe with a mischievous grin, looking so unbearably handsome that every muscle in her body contracts with the memory of Ed telling her that Jake had wanted her here. If the kids weren't there, and against her better judgment, she might just kiss him until she couldn't breathe. Something of that thought must show on her face because Jake's eyes travel in a slow circle over her mouth.

Then Coco barges in calling Blythe's name. "Asshole," she says, shoving her phone in Blythe's face and giving Eva a barely apologetic shrug for the language.

Blythe sees a *Business of Fashion* article announcing, CHAMPLAIN HOLDINGS NO LONGER INTERESTED IN MIZZA AND BLYTHE BRICARD. She reads on, even though she doesn't want to.

Talks between Champlain Holdings and Blythe Bricard over resurrecting her mother's legendary MIZZA label have broken down. Apparently, Bricard is staying in a French chateau with her ex-husband Jake Black, one of Champlain Holdings' biggest rivals. Bricard and Black divorced almost two years ago but, perhaps like her mother, Astrid, before her, who was drawn back to Hawk Jones time and again, the always à la mode Blythe is better at providing inspiration than committing to anything long-term. As well as raising concerns over her mercurial nature, Nathaniel Champlain noted that many more worthwhile opportunities existed for his business than gambling on an unproven talent to revive a short-lived brand with a murky past.

Fuck.

"Are you raging now?" Coco says.

Jake takes Coco's phone from Blythe and he swears too. Blythe plunges her hand into her bag for her own phone, brings up Nathaniel's number and dials.

"Blythe," he says, defensiveness in his voice.

"I swear to God, if I thought you were an asshole before, there isn't a word strong enough for what I think of you now," she says, stalking into the library. "Were you trying to crucify me?"

"Calm down," he says, and her hackles go up. *Calm down.* Wasn't that what a man always said right before he tried to gaslight a woman? "They've summarized and condensed what I said into sound bites. Those were not my exact words."

"I'm meant to believe you've come this far by thinking journalists only ever use exact words? What *exactly* you said doesn't matter—especially not when you say it about a woman. What matters is what you made it mean, and I think we can both agree you made it mean—as in cruel and damaging. Was I supposed to fall at your feet after you threw me a bouquet of flowers?"

Her voice is loud and she knows how this will be reported. Blythe goes crazy when a man walks away from her. Just like Astrid.

"Goodbye, Nathaniel," she says, hanging up before she ruins her reputation any further. Although how you can ruin rubble is anyone's guess.

Straightaway, her phone rings. Remy's number comes up and even though Blythe isn't in the mood, she takes the call.

"I need to tell you something," Remy says urgently. "Something I maybe should have told you when I first saw it but I wasn't sure if it would make things worse or better. But after what Nathaniel just said in that article, I think you need to know."

"Is it a recipe for performing voodoo on a man a couple of hundred miles away?" Blythe says, dropping into a chair.

"Maybe better. It's about what might lie beneath the supposedly murky past."

Remy's caught Blythe's full attention now.

"You know how I often access archival collections in museums? Well, I was at the Met six months ago trying to verify what I thought was a MIZZA piece. The conservator is a friend, and she wasn't supposed to show me what she was working on but because it was related to MIZZA, she did." Remy pauses. "She'd been asked to do some restoration work on the gown Astrid wore when Hawk won his first Coty Award in 1971."

"I didn't know they had that at the museum," Blythe says.

"They don't own it, but let me come back to that. What's important is that my friend had also been asked to do some restoration work on Astrid's Parsons portfolio."

"Astrid's Parsons portfolio?" Blythe repeats. "Astrid didn't have a portfolio. She dropped out after only a few months."

"She had a portfolio, Blythe. A portfolio that shows she was at Parsons until early 1971." Remy's voice is calm and quiet when what she's saying is explosive. All the more so when she adds, "In that portfolio is a sketch of the dress Hawk designed for Astrid to wear to the 1971 Coty Awards."

Why was a dress designed by Hawk in Astrid's portfolio, Blythe's sluggish mind is wondering until Remy goes on.

"Everyone says Hawk did a lot of the designs for MIZZA. Which maybe that portfolio proves—Astrid was passing off his work as her own even before MIZZA."

"Not making me feel any better right now, Remy."

"Except," Remy says, "what if it proves the opposite?"

Blythe stands, ribbons of trepidation coiling through her belly. "I don't know what you mean."

"Blythe, the designs in the portfolio are dated from 1970, well before she started MIZZA, well before anyone knew she was designing anything. By mid 1970, she was supposedly a college dropout who spent all her time at Hawk's shop being his muse. But the designs are fabulous. I compared them to Hawk's illustrations at the Met—he's a black ink guy, and his sketches are all about impression and movement. This portfolio is full of detailed watercolors, pastels."

Remy stops and Blythe knows the true bombshell is coming.

"Also in that portfolio is the silver dress," Remy says.

"*The* silver dress?"

"Yes."

"But Hawk designed that."

"Or so we all believe."

Blythe drops into a chair and searches on her phone for a picture of Astrid in the dress she wore to the Coty Awards in 1971. And now that Remy has turned the kaleidoscope and offered her a different view, all Blythe can see is the echo of the bloodied silk column of the dress from Versailles, the one Astrid designed and left behind. This is its genesis, right here.

And suddenly Hawk's words from Coco's interview—*it was always Astrid's dress*—words she'd disregarded, thinking he was referring to Astrid wearing the silver dress, take on a new meaning.

Did he mean Astrid designed that infamous dress?

Impossible.

She can feel her body curve inward, as though it's sinking under the weight of all the questions. Who was Astrid's father? Did it have something to do with why she ran? Why are there no photos of Hawk and Astrid together in 1973 when Blythe was conceived and Astrid was pregnant?

Then her head snaps up. "Who would have Astrid's Coty dress? And her portfolio? Why did the museum have them?"

"The museum had been asked to get them ready to be photographed for a new book about Astrid," Remy explains. "Which means someone is going to publish pictures of that portfolio, Blythe. But are they going to write about it using the same old story—or does this person, whoever they are, have something new to say?"

The hand of a ghost reaches into the room and Blythe feels it brush, terrifyingly, against her spine.

Who else but Astrid would have Astrid's portfolio and Astrid's dress?

It's like Astrid's coming back—from where? The dead, the past, the abyss?—to reclaim her story.

TWENTY-TWO

ASTRID BRICARD AND HAWK JONES

T he day after she walks out of Parsons, Astrid throws herself into two things—making plans for her own label and making a dress to wear to the Coty Awards. The day after the awards—after everyone's admired her dress—she'll announce her forthcoming launch. And the press, who loves taking her picture, will report on it. Women, who already pore over articles in *Cosmo* and *Vogue* about how to dress like Astrid, will want whatever she designs. She has a high profile. Mick Jagger once tried to kiss her at a party, for God's sake. Brands need the kind of visibility she already has. As an investment with potential, she won't say she's a no-brainer because she plans to demonstrate there are more than a few brains sitting atop her well-photographed body, but she will say she's a sure thing.

Her dress for the Cotys is the exemplar of her aesthetic. Simple in appearance but, technically, almost impossible to make. There are no fastenings whatsoever. Just two lengths of fabric and her sewing skills, which she didn't think would be enough. But in the end, they were.

She takes two lengths of fabric and instead of tying them around her neck in the easier-to-create and Halston-esque halter, she wraps them horizontally around her bust. The rest of the dress is cut to fall like a column that molds to the contours of her body as it drops to the floor. She's chosen silvery blue shantung and it shimmers against her bare shoulders, bare collarbones, bare neck. She leaves her hair loose and unfinished and wears no jewelry.

Hawk's mouth drops open when he sees her.

"Shall I twirl for you?" she asks with a grin.

"You'd better not," he murmurs. "Otherwise we'll never get to the surprise I planned."

"Surprise?"

"Come and see."

He says it shyly, as if he worries she mightn't like it, and then pulls her into a cab, smiling as she asks question after question, like a kid who wants to know what's inside the wrapping paper of an unexpected present. By the time they pull up outside the Cheetah, a strange place to be at six in the evening when it's not yet open, Astrid is literally on the edge of her seat.

Inside the club, it's almost dark except for white lights on the ceiling that pick out the words *I love you, Astrid*. Hawk draws her into his arms as a song plays—Bread's "Make It with You"—and they dance the way they always do, like two fibers ring-spun into the strongest yarn.

"Podium, or no podium tonight?" he whispers in her ear and she smiles and tries to tug him closer but there are no spaces left between their bodies.

"This is our moment before whatever happens tonight," he says quietly. "I'd be lying if I said I didn't want to win. But even if I lose, it'll be crazy, and I want to spend an hour with you celebrating that tomorrow you'll tell the world about your label and that maybe next year it'll be you nominated for this award."

"Hawk," is the only thing she can say. If tonight was a song, this moment would be the acoustically bare and too beautiful chorus that makes you weep. It's Hawk's night and he's tried to make it about her.

She tries to wipe her face. "I'm ruining your shirt."

"You can ruin me with love anytime," he says with a gentle smile.

"I love you," she tells him fiercely, urgently. "You don't know how much."

"I do," he tells her. "I fucking do."

It's hard to leave, and their bodies unpleat reluctantly from one another but their hands stay intertwined. Even when they get to Alice Tully Hall, they don't let go. The only time they separate is when Hawk steps onto the stage to accept his award. He won!

She's going to cry all over again. The only way to fit the happiness inside her is to let something out, so she cheers until her voice is gone. Then she listens to him thank her over and over again.

"This award is as much hers as it is mine," he says. "Astrid will be the one standing on this stage next year because she's a better designer than anyone I know."

Everyone applauds. And Astrid glows because of what Hawk said about her in front of people she hopes might soon be her peers.

They don't make it home until seven in the morning, and they don't go to sleep until ten because Hawk is all uncontained energy, directed at her.

Astrid wakes at midday, the sun stirring her, and she creeps downstairs to the studio, takes out white silk shantung and makes herself a tuxedo jacket.

She'll wear it that night. And she'll marry Hawk.

Then tomorrow, she'll launch her own clothing line. And maybe Mizza will see a photograph of designer Astrid Bricard in a newspaper and she'll pause for a moment. Even if she doesn't, Astrid knows, on the cusp of her future, that she *is* good enough.

* * *

The jacket is half-made when she leaves to get them some food. She grabs a few newspapers, wanting to see the coverage of Hawk's award win.

But she makes the mistake of reading them.

John Fairchild at *Women's Wear Daily*, who she'll need on her side if she wants the industry to take her seriously, writes:

> *Hawk's muse used his Coty Award win to get him to do her public-*
> *ity for her. Rumor has it she's not content with inspiring designers*
> *and rock stars—she's going to try to start her own label. Bricard's*
> *classmate at Parsons Candace Winters said, "You should see her*
> *portfolio. She filled it with Hawk Jones designs."*

For a moment, she thinks she's reading about someone else—a woman who flits from lover to lover and whim to whim. A trend in a T-shirt, a line in a song, worn or sung and then forgotten.

I think it's going to be very hard for you, the dean at Parsons said. *Another man's muse*, Bill Blass sneered. *Hawk's muse, Women's Wear Daily* declared.

Just like her mother begot Dior's dresses, so Astrid is merely a starting point for a man to rise up upon.

And the worst of it is, nobody—not John Fairchild or Bill Blass or Candace or Hawk—made this happen. She did.

Which means she's the only one who can change it.

She sags against the workbench. How can she make herself do it?

If last night was the beautiful acoustic chorus, this moment right now is when the singer's voice breaks.

* * *

Hawk wakes at around five in the afternoon and can't believe he's been asleep so long. God, he's tired. Running a business that keeps exploding in all directions is exhausting. He's in meetings half the time, meetings where he agrees to things that Jeff, his business manager, tells him he should agree to. He's vaguely aware he's hemorrhaging

money and he needs to sit down with Jeff and understand where the
Revson money has gone—because it *has* gone, apparently. How?

He rubs a hand over his face. He just won a Coty Award. He can
deal with the money shit tomorrow. Meantime, he should go see his
dad. And his mom. Celebrate with them. He should make love to
Astrid. That's all he should do today.

But she's not here.

He hauls himself to standing, head definitely on the wrong side of
delicate, finds a pair of pajama pants and walks into the main room.

Astrid is sitting in the arched window on the concrete sill. It's like
the day she missed her exam because of him.

Astrid doesn't sit in windows when she's happy.

* * *

Astrid feels her whole body stiffen in a way it never has when Hawk
walks into a room. It's the only defense mechanism she has and she
isn't sure it will be enough. She can't do this. Not now that she's seen
him, dressed only in a pair of pajama pants, torso lean, eyes blood-
shot with last night's celebrations. She wants to lead him back into the
bedroom, curl up with her back held against the front of his body, his
arm wrapped around her, feeling the way he can't ever be still with
her, how his fingertips are always moving, tracing her outlines.

She'd told herself not to cry but she's already broken her promise.

She opens her mouth but words don't come, so she points to one of
the newspapers.

Hawk picks it up and she knows he's reading the headline, THE
MASTER AND HIS MUSE, and the article about Hawk and Astrid.
A muse born of another muse. The blank canvas upon which he
creates. She remembers him saying to this journalist how incredible
Astrid was, how much of Astrid was in his work. But in black on
white it sounds all wrong.

The photograph accompanying the article is of Hawk and Astrid holding hands, and the caption reads, *Astrid Bricard wearing a Hawk Jones original.*

Hawk picks up the next newspaper. This one says:

Her job is to make him make beautiful things—and to make rock stars write killer songs—and at this Astrid Bricard excels, like her mother before her who inspired Dior to brilliance.

The accompanying picture is captioned with the words, *Astrid Bricard wearing a dress by Hawk Jones.*

When he looks back up, his eyes are redder than they were two minutes ago.

His gaze falls on the suitcase beside her. "Are we going somewhere?" Then, "I'll tell them you made the dress. I don't know why they thought I did."

"Nobody will believe you," she says flatly. "You didn't write those things and nor did I, but I'm going to pay for them. You're the master. The man. I love you, but..."

I love you, but. Are there four worse words in the world than those? Love has no buts. It is, or it isn't. Except right now, for her, it both is and isn't. If she loves Hawk, that means she can't love herself. If she chooses herself, then she can't love Hawk.

"If I stay here," she says, and she can hear the desolation in her voice, "I'll only ever be the muse. And maybe...maybe I'll start blaming you. I never want to do that—"

He tries to break in, but she presses on.

"I've lived in an alternate world the last couple of years," she says despairingly. "But in the actual world, women aren't paid the same as men. Women can't wear trousers into half the restaurants in Manhattan. Nobody will give Velvet a job. And nobody will ever see me as anything more than your lover if I stay. So I need..."

Her exhale is jagged—a broken needle, a torn hem. *Just say it*. Say it and go and then she can cry like she's never cried before.

But what if Hawk cries too? If he does, she'll never be able to leave.

She works hard to steady her voice. "I need to go away," she says quietly. "You'll probably hate me for it. Because I guess I'm saying that I'm more important than us. But if I don't think like that then I really will be nothing. And you..."

She really isn't sure she can make herself say this. But she forces the words out. "You should be with someone who loves you more than anything, the way I thought I did."

One tear falls, like a tiny sequin, onto Hawk's cheek. He reaches out a hand. She almost takes it.

She forces her fingers to grasp her suitcase instead. "If I touch you, Hawk," she says wistfully, "I'll never leave. And then I'll hate myself."

All that's left to do is to walk toward the door, where she stops very briefly. "I left my portfolio on the table. If you can send it to Parsons, maybe I'll graduate. Maybe not."

Then she leaves.

And the tears rain down.

* * *

Suddenly Astrid is no longer in the apartment. And Hawk's fixed in place, trying to understand. Where's she going? To Velvet's? To Long Island?

And when is she coming back?

You should be with someone who loves you more than anything.

Adrenaline kicks in. "Astrid," he calls. Then louder, "Astrid!"

He hurtles down the stairs. But she's not in the shop.

There's a cab outside. She's already climbing in and it's pulled away by the time he reaches the street. And the meaning of everything she just said finally penetrates.

She isn't coming back.

And he's left standing in the doorway staring after her, so utterly broken that he has to grip the frame to keep upright.

* * *

The following day, a photograph of this moment will run in the newspapers, taken by the paps waiting on the corner to immortalize him the day after victory. In the image, it will look as though he's getting rid of Astrid and she's running away, bereft. But he's the one who's bereft and she's the one who's done the heartbreaking—although, if he studies what she's said, he'll see that her heart is breaking too.

* * *

Hawk makes himself go back upstairs. On the table is Astrid's portfolio. His hand reaches out for it.

On the first page is the silver lamé dress. Then a white tank top with a drawing on the back. A white tuxedo jacket.

He closes the book. Too many memories lurk in its pages.

He pulls on a T-shirt and jeans. He can't stay here where the sunset wall is like Astrid, where he can smell her perfume, a ghost trailing him.

As he hurries back through the store, he sees a half-finished white tuxedo jacket waiting beside the sewing machine.

I'll wait until the day you walk into our apartment wearing a white tuxedo jacket and then I'll ask you again, he'd told her. How can it be that on the same day Astrid was planning to say yes to spending the rest of her life with him, she's gone?

The pain is savage. He might lie on the floor right here with her wedding jacket in his arms. But if the pain he's feeling now is savage, the pain of doing that would be catastrophic.

He steps outside. He'll go to the Cheetah and take whatever is offered so he can't feel any of this.

* * *

Beside tomorrow's photograph of a heartbreaking Hawk standing in a doorway and a heartbroken Astrid driving away, there'll be a photograph of Hawk dancing with Candace and the headline, HAWK JONES AMUSES HIMSELF WITH A NEW MUSE.

Astrid weeps when she sees it.

She doesn't know that, at home in bed alone, Hawk weeps too.

TWENTY-THREE

MIZZA BRICARD

PARIS, AUGUST 1939–1942

Mizza and Christian crossed the river at the Pont de la Concorde, then continued on to Rue Cabanis where Tian stopped at a gate guarding a cluster of buildings. Ivy softened the stone walls, and flowers burst like jaunty toque hats from manicured beds. But above the gate were the words *Centre Psychiatrique Sainte-Anne*.

"This is my secret," Tian said.

Since the day they met in 1937, they'd dined together several evenings a week. Mizza counted him with Jeanne as a person she trusted completely, so, when he'd appeared at her apartment asking in a troubled voice if he could show her something, she'd come without question.

Now, she slipped her hand into his and walked with him into the courtyard of a psychiatric hospital.

They ascended to the third floor and entered a long room with a black and white checkered floor, a row of beds along each wall.

"*Mon Dieu*," Tian said, crossing to a straitjacketed man. "My brother. Bernard."

"Your brother," Mizza repeated, feeling as if the walls were pressing in on her. She knew why Christian had brought her here now.

Nobody would admit to having a relative in the asylum, or the madhouse as most people called it, unless they had to. Only yesterday, she and Tian had discussed Hitler and his lust for something that went beyond land and territory—something almost too frightening to comprehend. And so, with the world falling to pieces around them, Tian must have decided he had to share this secret with someone.

Mizza's hand strayed to the scar around her wrist, which she covered with a scarf tied as a bracelet, always in leopard print. She felt suddenly as small as the physical space taken up by her body, inconsequential when it came to the things that mattered. Beauty, wit, the ability to converse about almost any artwork or book, opera or artifact, were useless frivolities when set beside the one expertise no human possessed—that of being able to keep alive and safe those you loved.

"It's coming again, isn't it?" Mizza said desolately. "War."

Tian nodded. "I'll be called to fight. I need someone to know Bernard is here."

There was such love in Christian's voice that Mizza said, "I won't just know that he's here. I'll visit him. *He* needs to know someone is here, for him."

Christian sat in the chair by the bed and buried his face in his hands.

Mizza rested her hand on his shoulder, then pulled out the book she always carried in her bag and began to read Bernard a story. He stared at the ceiling while Christian wept, and Mizza's voice wavered.

A few days later, Christian was conscripted.

This will make you my brother's keeper, he wrote to Mizza, *an obligation you can abandon anytime it becomes too much. The Nazis view the insane the same way they view men like me—as something to destroy. Don't be so loyal to me you end up hurting yourself.*

That same night, Captain Molyneux fled to England, accompanied by two other Englishmen who worked at the couture house—John Cavanagh and dearest Tommy, men who'd been not just colleagues, but friends too.

Now she was the one burying her face in her hands. For the last few years, she'd been making dresses and riding out the Depression and believing her time was coming. But it would never come, not now. Coco Chanel had closed her couture house. Vionnet too. The age of the female couturier was over after a too-brief flicker in time.

Mizza knew better than anyone that war broke and destroyed. It left behind only scars, and ruin.

* * *

The German Occupation of Paris was swift and shocking. One minute the French government marched out of the city, the next minute the German tanks and soldiers rolled in, the occupiers changing the clocks so that the now-silent church bells of Paris quivered expectantly at the same time as those in Berlin, awaiting the chance to chime.

Mizza watched it all from the window of her apartment, Jeanne's arm around her waist. Ida, being Jewish, had already fled the country. Cartier had gone too, like Molyneux. Through the window, the summer day was smeared with ash, just as the eyes of the women staring at buildings now owned by Adolf Hitler were smeared with tears.

"It's done," Mizza said despairingly as klaxons announced that Paris was now a German city.

"And we must survive and fight," Jeanne replied.

So, once curfew was over and they were allowed on the street, they wiped their tears away and marched through Paris, blinders on, not letting their eyes see the invasion of swastikas and *Heil Hitlers*, of boot polish and arrogance. They were Parisiennes, not German subjects, and their bearing would underscore that fact.

Jeanne reopened the Cartier store. Mizza asked couturier Cristóbal Balenciaga for a job.

He gave her an entire millinery studio.

"It would be an honor to have you, madame," he told her. "The wrap coat you created for the Queen of Spain... *Magnifico*."

A few days later, she stood on the threshold of her new domain feeling an impossible and despicable joy. How could she be happy when the art galleries were closed or showing only German-sanctioned art? When the newspapers told lies, the theaters peddled propaganda, the city of lights was dark? But this was survival. This was keeping her promise to Lev.

She stepped into the studio and the seamstresses stared. Around her neck, Mizza wore the seven-stranded pearl necklace from Lev. At her forehead, she'd pinned a sapphire Jeanne had given her. The sensible thing was to wear one piece of jewelry, to button her shirt up to her throat, to put her sapphire somewhere more ordinary—or else in a safe. But when walking past Nazis on the streets, who didn't want to be bejeweled and bold?

She laid out her sketches and the seamstresses crowded around, staring at hats that were so large they shaded the face entirely—but attracted the eye nonetheless.

"*Mon Dieu*," one of the seamstresses said. "They are fearless hats."

"Exactly," Mizza said. "Fearless hats for fearless women in a fearless city."

Silence followed. She'd just spoken treason. But nobody summoned a Nazi to punish her. The newspapers might say the people of Paris had welcomed the Germans, but the silence in the studio told Mizza their hearts hadn't.

She tapped her finger against her drawings. "Which would you like to work on?"

There was a clamor as the illustrations were tussled over, followed by a kind of sparkling quiet as the ponderings of the seamstresses flitted into the air, shimmered briefly and were then dismissed or unraveled.

Mizza started work on a calotte-shaped hat with a fountain of ostrich plumes. Then she made a circuit of the workroom. "Start again," she advised the first seamstress she came to, who was making a mediocrity of the sketch.

"That will have to go out with the trash too, *ma petite*," she advised the second, who looked as if she might cry and then said, resignedly, "You're right."

The seamstress who'd thought the hats fearless was the only one doing anything close to expert. To her, Mizza said, "*Pas mal.*" Not bad.

Balenciaga accompanied Mizza on her second circuit, observing the first seamstress making something that now looked like Mizza's sketch, the second taking more time to block the hat to achieve the right shape, and the third, perhaps wanting more than a *pas mal*, stiffening the paradisal so the hat was not just bold, but audacious. Mizza gave her a smile.

Balenciaga halted in front of a set of black bonnets Mizza had drawn, which were to be fashioned over a basketwork base to fit closely against the head.

"You're religious?" he asked.

"I attended a convent school. But now I have faith in art."

"They remind me of the Spanish nuns," the master said, indicating the hats. "Goya and Christ are my religion."

"It probably does Christ good to be held up to such high standards." She smiled and despite the blasphemy, Balenciaga laughed.

"Come to my studio," he said.

There, like in every other studio, were sketches. She leafed through them, seeing something very different from Doucet's or Molyneux's *croquis*. Here was drama. Tempestuousness. Passion. Severity. Things that shouldn't work together but did. So much black, but pale pink and scarlet too.

"Can you draw hats to go with these?" he asked, pushing three sketches over to her, *croquis* he'd drawn just then while she studied his illustrations.

The first was a red satin evening gown so imbued with Goya's portrait of a cardinal in red robes that it was like holding faith and belief— in what? France without Nazis, perhaps—in her hand. A black satin evening coat lined with white, so subtly evocative of a nun's gown that its wearer would be able to let any thought into her head and still appear perfectly innocent—a handy trick in a Nazi-occupied city.

From a black hat drawn by Mizza to the spine of a Balenciaga collection.

And so it began again. The prompting of greatness. The job of always being the one to ignite the spark.

Perhaps that was how wartime would pass by. Quietly, but with brilliance.

* * *

But in early 1941, the Nazis clattered into the studio to see Monsieur Balenciaga. They had no interest in quiet, or brilliance. They told the master that the couture industry would move to Berlin.

Paris couture in Berlin? *Never,* Mizza thought.

Indeed, the master laughed. "You might just as well take all the bulls to Berlin and try and train the bullfighters there," he told the officers.

Mizza restrained her smile but a ray of sunlight caught her sapphire and it twinkled in delight at Balenciaga's response.

"You!" A Nazi regarded Mizza. "You have brown hair and dark eyes. Gypsies and Jews have dark hair and dark eyes."

Mizza's insides coiled into ribbons. One firm tug and he could well start to unravel all her secrets.

"Madame Biano is an indispensable part of the atelier and you are insulting her," Balenciaga told the German, who narrowed his eyes at Mizza.

"Who is your husband? Who is Monsieur Biano?"

"My husband's name was Alexandre Bianu," she said, telling the truth. "He was Romanian. Romania is one of your allies."

All truth, hiding a lie. That Mizza had foolishly married a volatile man in the 1920s and divorced him more than ten years ago. He was in England now, working, she thought, on behalf of a group of exiled Romanians who opposed the Nazis. There were many other facts about her that the Nazis would take aim at—Mizza's mother was English, and the Nazis were at war with England. Mizza had mostly been raised by a Jewish woman. Mizza was caring for Christian's brother, and she'd heard the Nazis murdered the so-called mad. She couldn't allow that to happen.

So she smiled. "Rather than gypsy or Jew, Cleopatra is more usually the comparison gentlemen make."

It made the Nazi laugh. Mizza had never once been glad Lev was not there to see her, but in that moment she was.

"Come here," the Nazi ordered.

Which meant moving into the light where her profile was highlighted and the chestnut in her hair sparked red.

"It's lucky you have a husband," the Nazi said admiringly. "You're the kind of woman Paris is famous for."

Balenciaga scowled. The Nazi smiled. "We're moving the couture industry to Germany. You will enjoy Germany, madame," he told Mizza as he left.

* * *

Questions filled Mizza's head that night. The Nazis were planning to move an industry that was the soul of Paris to Germany and what was she doing? Surviving. But not fighting. Where had that girl gone, the one who'd set off into a war zone to bring back the body of her lover because it was the right thing to do?

She thought she'd had sleepless nights before but now she learned what sleeplessness was. A time to plunge deep inside oneself, beneath the lining and the boning and into the threads that moored a soul within a body. There she found, barely alive, a flicker of azure. It propelled her up and out of bed, made her write a letter to her former colleagues at Molyneux—John Cavanagh, Tommy, and Captain Molyneux himself.

Surely somebody in England would want to know about German plans to move profitable industries to Berlin, or about which hotels the Nazis occupied and which military branch occupied them. No army could fight without understanding its enemy and Mizza knew more about the Germans than the Allies did because she was in Paris and they were an ocean away.

She penned the letter in Romanian, the language that would be the most difficult for a Nazi to read offhand, asking how she could relay whatever information she could gather. Jeanne would help. She had wealthy Germans in her store all day and must overhear all manner of things.

A reply came. Her notes should be hidden in a book about Germanic art on the shelf in her sitting room and she should place a red geranium in her window box when she'd done so. In turn, someone would place a brandy glass on her coffee table if any communication was left for her. The supervisor of her apartment building, she was told, was helping the Allies too. He would make certain the notes were passed on.

You'll be risking your life if you do this, the first hidden note read. And that was when Mizza understood.

Swastikas and Nazi salutes were bad enough. But they could be blocked from eyes and ears. What lay beneath was a far more sinister menace, searching out those who mounted any kind of opposition. It was clear to her now why so much of Paris acquiesced to German food and radio, to rations and rules. Because they could sense that threat. The smart thing to do would be to make sure it never turned its head her way.

But her life right now was a small and frightened thing. Which meant she wouldn't, in fact, be risking her life—she would, at last, be living it.

TWENTY-FOUR

MIZZA BRICARD

I n between working for Balenciaga and doing whatever she could to help the Allies, Mizza visited Christian's brother every Saturday. One afternoon in late summer, she found him outside in the gardens, which meant it was a good day.

"Bernard!" she called and the smile on his face, such simple happiness when all around was ugliness, was worth everything.

She kissed his cheeks and for an hour in the gardens, Mizza could almost pretend there was no war, that the Nazi who'd studied her so intently at Balenciaga months ago hadn't been in the studio again yesterday, examining Balenciaga's records, trying to blackmail him into moving to Germany. She could almost pretend she didn't have clandestine notes from British intelligence officers hiding in her apartment.

All that shattered when she crossed the gardens to leave and heard a child crying. She followed the sobs, so familiar with the grounds after more than two years of visiting that she found the source moments before two young doctors from the asylum rounded the corner, eyes bright with fear.

"Madame!" one of them gasped. "This is nothing." He reached out a pleading hand for the girl, who shook her head and came, inexplicably, to Mizza's side.

She had brown hair and brown eyes, which meant nothing. Except there weren't usually children at Sainte-Anne, and the men were trying to shield her from view.

"I don't like it in there," the girl wailed, and the sound unknotted a corner of Mizza's heart.

She bent down and did what was likely the most foolish thing she'd ever done in her life. She took the ruby ring off her finger and pressed it into the girl's hand. "See how it sparkles," Mizza said. "It's like a light to keep the darkness away."

Jeanne had said those same words to Mizza six months after Lev had died, pressing the same jewel into her hand.

The girl quieted as she stared in fascination at the ruby.

"Why don't you go inside with monsieur." Mizza indicated the blond man. "I'm going to talk to his friend."

The girl leaned over to lift up the veil Mizza had added to her costume the day the Nazis visited Balenciaga, and the sudden removal of the filter brought it all rushing in. The rumors of three nights before when buses had driven into Paris and Jewish families were taken from their beds.

Trapped in this girl's eyes was every kind of pain.

Then she left, taking her desolate eyes with her.

Mizza regarded the man who'd remained behind, both of them like wary horses pawing the ground.

"That was a kind thing to do," he said.

"I wonder if you might be doing something kinder still."

His words came out in a rush. "She's Jewish, but if you bring the Nazis here, they won't find her. You'll look like a fool."

"I try never to be a fool," Mizza said quietly.

A sound made them jump—the other man returning and his sudden appearance made the one in front of Mizza drop a folder on the ground.

"*Zut!*" he muttered.

Mizza bent to help him and saw, amongst patient records, a detailed map of tunnels and doorways marked with skulls and bones. She shivered. "What is this?"

The young man blanched.

But his friend said, "I think a woman who's been visiting a man she isn't related to for years, when so many others never come at all, is probably not a Nazi-lover."

"I'm not," Mizza told them. "But you have only my word, just as I have only your word this isn't a trap."

"It makes everything we thought was trust look like a silly game, doesn't it?" he said. "This is a map of *les Carrières*. The quarries and tunnels beneath Paris."

A Jewish girl hidden in an asylum. A map of the thoroughfares that coiled like veins under Paris's skin.

Mizza hesitated for a long moment. How to measure how brave you are when the bravest act of your life has been to run into a war zone to find the body that once housed your true love?

"I'm in contact with people who might be able to help," she said.

* * *

"Madame."

Mizza had just reached her apartment when a Nazi stepped out of the shadows. The German from Balenciaga. He'd found out where she lived. Why?

She was grateful for the veil hiding the new secret she'd just added to all the others she carried. It was an immense effort not to let her hand stray to her wrist to twist the ends of the leopard-print scarf tied over her scar.

"You're divorced," the Nazi said, eyes fixed on her the same way Harry Angelo's eyes had been fixed on her in New York almost twenty years ago. He wanted her weak. He wanted her to give him power.

Never.

"You're the kind of woman Paris is famous for, and you don't have a husband. Where have you been on such a cold day?" he asked, tugging his coat around him.

"To visit a friend."

"Ah, a friend," he said, smiling. "Perhaps you should be careful who your friends are, *madame*."

Today she'd made a promise that would land her in prison at the very least if the Nazis found out what she was doing. And a Nazi had been waiting for her outside her home. She would need to be very careful from now on.

* * *

Instead of being careful, Mizza wrote a note for her Allied friends. Raoul—the man from the asylum—had told her the children had been led though the dark by a doctor earlier in the week when the Nazis came with buses to take their parents. Soon, they would be smuggled out of the city through the former stone quarries beneath Paris—if that was possible—but someone needed to collect them at the tunnels' end and take them to safety. She asked the Allies to put her in touch with people who could do that.

The following weekend, Mizza returned to Sainte-Anne and told Raoul it would be weeks before she heard anything. "While we wait, let me learn the route," she said.

Raoul gaped at her. "You can't go down there."

"Will that girl go willingly with you into the dark?"

The quarries were once a burial place for bones. It was inconceivable that a frightened child would walk silently past skeletons in the company of a man. And Mizza could not allow, ever again, a man like the Nazi who lurked outside her apartment to win, to take something precious from that small girl who had only Mizza's ruby ring to let a little light into her life.

Raoul sighed. "Come with me."

She followed him through the basement to a door hidden behind decades of detritus. "We were looking for a space for an air-raid shelter," he told her. "After I discovered where the door led, I knew I had to map it. I thought it might be important."

"It's lucky you did," she said gently.

The door opened. The dank smell of antiques and animals rushed out as Mizza stepped down into the underworld of her beautiful city. She knew, because she'd listened to every sort of intellect at Ida's parties, that Lutetian limestone had been excavated from beneath Paris to construct the buildings above. But after the emergence of sinkholes, the quarries were closed until a macabre use was found for them—that of housing the dead who, in the late eighteenth century, were overflowing from the Cimetière des Saints-Innocents and into Les Halles marketplace. By night, skeletons were moved from the cemetery and taken underground.

Now Mizza stood amongst them. Six million skeletons buried in snaking tunnels.

"The ossuaries are few and far between," Raoul said as they began to move. "Mostly it's just passages and chambers. The city appointed an Inspection Générale des Carrières to maintain the tunnels in 1777. As well as mapping and reinforcing the weaknesses in the tunnels to prevent sinkholes, the men built things from stone—staircases and galleries vaulted like the rooms in a palace. It can be quite..." He faltered as if he wondered at the madness of his sentiment. "Quite beautiful."

And Mizza, able to stand up straight as they passed from a low tunnel and under an archway that was cathedral-like in its grandeur, could only agree. The room they were in had been carved perfectly round, each wall patterned with delicate white. Long bones, she saw as her flashlight moved over them—a strange but, yes, beautiful kind of tapestry.

"How far do the tunnels stretch?" Mizza asked, feeling cold seep into her arms, her ears attune to the sound of water some distance away, and her nose detect decay and an odd kind of peace.

"Imagine the city of Paris turned upside down so that all the buildings above ground are now penetrating the earth."

"And you've mapped it all? *Incroyable*."

As they walked, Raoul pointed out the markings he'd made on walls and doors that would show her if she was going the right way. Skulls watched their progress. Occasionally the tunnels opened into rotundas, grottos, caverns. Here were ulnas, hipbones like butterfly wings, ribs white as tusks.

Mizza looked down and saw bones beneath her feet. "How far will the children have to walk?" she asked, to ward off the eeriness that had just settled upon her.

"It's two kilometers to the Porte d'Orléans. It would be best to get them at least that far from the city center. We'll try that the first time, and reconsider if it doesn't work."

The first time. Of course. Mizza should have known. There wouldn't just be one journey through hell. There would be many.

TWENTY-FIVE

MIZZA BRICARD

At last a letter appeared and a date was set for the children to be passed on to safety. Mizza waited in the basement at Sainte-Anne, not knowing who she'd be taking through the tunnels, whether it would work or whether it would fail. She knew only that this—the first time—would be one she remembered.

The sound of footsteps echoed outside. Her fingers reached for her pearls.

Raoul appeared with five children. She was to take five children into the dark and over bones and give them to strangers at the Porte d'Orléans.

She shook her head. "It's too many at once."

Then two men stepped into the room. "American pilots," Raoul said. "Their planes crash-landed nearby. They need to be taken to safety too."

To walk two kilometers in the cramped dark with seven people would take hours. Then Mizza had to return along the tunnels alone and get back to her apartment before curfew. *"On y va,"* she said.

But as they descended the stairs, the youngest, the girl she'd seen in the gardens, began to cry. The sound echoed, perhaps reaching up to a vent where it might be heard by a Nazi.

What did you do with a child who was frightened beyond belief? The same thing she did with Bernard Dior.

She held out a hand to the child. "I'll tell you a story."

She chose *Le Rameau d'Or*, a beautiful tale penned by the French-woman who invented fairytales. What a wonderful thing to invent, Mizza thought—a story to hide in.

The other four children walked behind, listening to the story too, and the men at the rear were silent, just as they'd been told. She didn't know their names. It was better if she knew as little as possible as then she could never betray them. That was what John and Tommy had counseled in their letters.

Soon, the ceiling lifted, and Mizza could stand up straight. Her back almost groaned with the pleasure of no longer being bent double. But the path narrowed and it was difficult to hold the child's hand. The girl faltered, staring horror-struck at the wallpaper of bones.

One of the men spoke. "I know a story too and I'm kind of scared, so can I tell mine? I can carry you at the same time." He stretched out his arms and mimed lifting the girl onto his hip.

The girl looked at Mizza, who nodded.

And even though Mizza was sure the girl didn't understand English, there was something about the soothing quality of the man's voice telling an English version of *Le Chat Botté* that made the bones recede, the image of a little white cat with resplendent red boots take their place. The story accompanied them through the darkness.

After an hour, just as the children began to yawn, Mizza bade them rest beneath a set of magnificent columns—one made entirely of knee bones, another of clavicles. She took out apples and passed them around.

The littlest girl's eyes drooped, her head resting on the pilot who'd told the story.

"You have a friend," Mizza said to him.

"Thank you for doing this," he replied.

The other man—a boy really—blurted out, "You're the most beau-tiful woman I've ever seen." His ears pinked, then his cheeks.

Mizza gave one, low, throaty chuckle. *"Merci."*

"You're like an angel," he went on in a whisper. "Really."

"I think you're an angel," one of the children whispered.

But this was the first time she'd done this. She could get everyone killed. Or lost. *Mon Dieu*, she had lives in her hands and she thought a fairytale would save them all from being turned into the bones that lay around them.

"We must move," she said, standing before she began to weep. *Help me, Lev*, she prayed. Silence. Mizza had never felt so alone.

The pilot picked up the little girl, who was soundly asleep.

"You have children of your own?" Mizza asked as they set off.

He shook his head. "There's a girl I want to marry when the war ends. But..." He hesitated. "Never mind."

He embraced the girl more tightly.

Mizza let him have his secret and she told another story as they walked.

Near the end, to prepare them for the shock of being handed over to a stranger, Mizza passed out the chocolate she and Jeanne had scoured Paris to find.

The children smiled at the unexpected treat and while they were eating, the pilot said in a low voice to Mizza, "The girl I'm going to marry—she can't have children. She had some kind of surgery when she was younger. It's not the kind of thing people talk about, so I don't know exactly..." He shook his head as if regretting his frankness and touched the girl's head. "What will happen to her?"

"I don't know," Mizza said. "We're not told more than we need to know, in case..."

The man nodded. "I hope they make it to wherever they're going."

"I hope you and your friend do too," Mizza said, turning back to look at the younger man, who said to her, fervently, "With a blessing from an angel like you, there's no way we won't."

At the same moment, the girl opened her eyes. They were in a section of the tunnel that was decorated with a heart made of bones. Her eyes widened, but with puzzlement rather than fear.

"Why is the heart white?" she whispered.

So Mizza told another story. "Some people have hearts that are white because they need to be so very strong. Most people have soft hearts, red hearts, but those are more easily damaged. You and your *maman* have white hearts, the only kind that is unbreakable."

The glimmer of a smile appeared on the girl's face. And soft-hearted Mizza hoped that, somewhere, somehow, the child's mother's heart would remain unbroken—and that she would stay alive for as long as she needed to for her daughter.

ACT THREE

THE LEGEND REBORN...

TWENTY-SIX

ASTRID BRICARD AND HAWK JONES

NEW YORK CITY, MARCH 1972

H ere it is." Candace drops a check onto Hawk's desk.
Sixteen million dollars. An obscene amount of money—
money to walk away from Hawk Jones. Money for his name to
continue—but without him. Money to see someone else—not Candace, he hopes—design clothes under the Hawk Jones name.

All he has to do is say yes to Candace, who has some kind of job
working for a business that owns a whole lot of brands, a business that
wants to own him.

"Face it, Hawk," she says caustically, "you have no other way to pay
back the creditors."

How do you sell your own name?

Who are you without your name?

He moves over to the cognac decanter and pours himself a finger—
two fingers, really—a well-worn habit. He stares at the liquid in the glass,
remembers the night he and Astrid drank cognac in his mom's apartment and he asked if he could measure her. It takes just two swallows for
the cognac to disappear. But alcohol isn't like a bump, the effects instantly
felt. He feels the same as he did a minute ago. Dead inside a living body.

"Hawk."

He turns around. Candace is there. That's why he's drinking

cognac at nine in the morning. How is he even awake at nine in the morning?

"Hawk," she says again and he realizes he's said nothing the whole time she's been there. But there isn't a word that fits this impossible circumstance.

He made a ton of money. Then he spent it all, and then some. He spent money the banks owned. Now they want it back—more dollars than there are beats in a disco.

"I worked my fingers to the bone on this," Candace says after she's waited too long for him to respond. "You walk away with enough money to pay your debts and never work again. Your mom gets to keep her apartment. It's a good deal, Hawk." Her voice has changed, almost like she's pleading with him.

It's her reputation on the line too—will she be able to pull off the biggest deal ever made in fashion? Or will she screw it all up, like he has?

He should never have opened discussions with her. But she kept calling until he was too tired to keep saying no. And the banks are pushing him to make a decision.

A decision? He has no choice.

He's in the gigantic office he now owns. It has mirrored walls, and a conversation pit lined with lime-green sofas where he's supposed to sit and throw ideas around with his team—he has a fucking team—a pit whose edges he doesn't dare walk near in case his balance isn't what it should be.

The radio announcer's voice breaks in. "...And now it's time for 'Woman in Silver.'"

Of course that song would play right now.

"She's not coming back, Hawk." Candace hasn't lost her knack for cruelty. Or accuracy.

He doesn't even bother to pretend the next drink he pours is a finger. It's a whole goddamn hand. Astrid's been gone nearly a year. She's in Paris, he knows from the press, has spent six months working at the House of Dior, and now she's at Givenchy.

He swallows more cognac and at last starts to feel benediction at the edges of his limbs. He picks up the check. Stares at the numbers. Stares at Candace.

"Is that a yes?" she says.

The phone rings. He only drops it once on the way up to his ear.

"Hawk." His mother's voice is barely audible. "Your father just had another stroke."

* * *

Hawk sits at his father's bedside listening to his mother weep. Matthias can't walk. He can't talk. He needs extensive rehabilitation and round-the-clock care. It will cost so much money. They need to mortgage his parents' apartment, but it's already mortgaged—to Hawk. And Astrid. He never paid his mother back and now he doesn't have the money to. And he still owes Astrid half the money she gave him—he never paid that back either, even after Revson gave him what seemed like stupid money.

How could he have sold so many clothes but lost so much money? Peaked and troughed all by age twenty-six?

Without cognac in reach and with his head aching from too many minutes of sobriety, he knows it's his fault. Alcohol and dope made everything in his stores look sexy. Now, strung out on the reality of an ill father, he can see that all the things he's made over the last year are repeats of what came before. They still sell like grass at Woodstock, but people want something new, and he isn't offering it.

Which leaves him with Candace.

How long will the Hawk Jones name last beyond his departure? The group Candace works for has just bought out Halston too. They won't want Halston and Hawk competing. It means they've decided to let Halston win, and Hawk lose.

He wants to cry, but tonight that's his mother's right, not his.

He squeezes his mom's shoulder and tells her he'll be back soon.

In his office, he seizes the cognac decanter. Then he takes out a sketchpad and draws Astrid wearing a dress. It's pink—a dress that looks like innocence making out with sin. He remembers every detail of it on Astrid's body that night in his apartment when she'd told him the one, simple reason she wanted to be a designer was because she loved it. Just like he used to love it—and her too.

He could have Nancy run it up tomorrow and it will sell, and sell, and sell.

He must have fallen asleep in his chair like some kind of filthy drunk because the phone wakes him. Piercing light tells him it's morning. He picks up the receiver and hears the rough, liquor-gravel of his voice. "Hello?"

"Hawk." The voice is melodious, a hint of a French accent. "We've somehow never met. Actually, that's deliberate on my part. I'm Alix St. Pierre. Astrid's godmother. I'd like you to come by my office in an hour. That ought to give you enough time to clean yourself up."

"How . . . ?" His voice trails away. It's not as if his party-hard life-style is a secret. He rubs a hand over his face and tries again "Why?"

"Just come, Hawk," she says pleasantly, but with steel.

* * *

He's on time to meet Alix. He doesn't dare not be. And all he takes is Tylenol, which barely cuts through the pain in his head.

In the office, a man sits behind the desk. Alix waves a hand at him, saying, "This is my husband, Anthony. He insisted on being here because he doesn't trust you. He wants to witness what we say."

Anthony quirks a smile at his wife as if to say, *That's true, but you didn't need to tell this loser that.*

And Hawk, despite having showered and shaved and worn a nice suit, does feel like a loser standing in this lovely office with a woman who started a magazine all by herself and has kept hold of it for decades.

"I'm guessing you didn't ask me here to abuse me," he says flatly.

Alix holds out a piece of paper. On it is written a much lesser sum of money than the check he already has from Candace.

"That should cover the mortgage on your mother's apartment," Alix says. "And get you out of the catastrophe you've wandered into. It's a four-strings-attached loan. One—I expect you to pay it back. Two—get rid of your business manager and employ someone you can trust. Three—design something. Four—cut back on all the licensing fripperies. That's where you're losing money. Who needs Hawk Jones hosiery, for God's sake? Your target market hardly wears a bra, let alone hosiery."

It's the rudest offer anyone has ever made him. But he sits in a chair instead of leaving. "You're Astrid's godmother," he says. "Astrid left me. So why would you give me money?"

The smile Alix throws to her husband is a beautiful thing. Anthony catches it and his own face becomes its mirror, and Hawk is witness to a moment of exquisite tenderness that hurts everything inside him.

"Astrid didn't leave you," Alix admonishes, sitting opposite him. "She left what she'd become. You happened to be a casualty of the process. I once did something very similar, so I've developed an interest in helping those who have to leave themselves behind to move on. And if you go out of business, Astrid will most likely be blamed. I don't want her to have any bad publicity right now."

None of that makes sense. Hawk watches her cast that smile at her husband again. Sees its reciprocation. And now Hawk pictures a dress, half black, half white. Two sides joining down the middle of a body. The pure light and its opposite.

He and Astrid.

Into his mind tumble a thousand pictures of Astrid and in each one, he draws a dress over her. If he stopped being angry at Astrid, he could design something radical.

Pride is a large thing to swallow. And it's no small thing to take money from Astrid's godmother. It hurts. He hates hurting. But he remembers the pink dress he drew last night, the one he actually thought for a minute he might sell, and he knows—he deserves to hurt.

"I accept," he tells Alix.

"Good. I'll send the papers over this afternoon. And tear up that other check. They would have torn *you* up, you know."

"I know," is all he says before he leaves.

* * *

"What did you do?" Meredith asks when Hawk takes her a check, terror in her voice as if she thinks he really did sell his soul.

"I made a good deal with someone I think I can trust."

His mother's lip trembles as she stares at Matthias, then she presses her knuckles to her mouth. "I need to stop just sitting around crying," she says.

"Me too." He wraps her in a hug and then he leaves and gets his shit together.

He tips the cognac down the sink. Tosses the disco biscuits in the trash. The next ten days are hell. When the headache has finally eased, his palms have stopped sweating and he sleeps through an entire night, he arranges carers for his dad, calls builders and organizes modifications to his parents' apartment. Then he sits by his father's bed and tells him everything, even though his father is asleep and can't hear him.

"Maybe it's a good thing I nearly lost it all," Hawk says. He's wearing black jeans, an old gray sweater, has one bare foot resting on the bed frame and, for the first time in months, isn't shifting restlessly. He isn't even aware of the nurses gazing at him.

"I thought I could wrap Astrid in silver lamé and it would magically become a beautiful dress. The press would photograph her wearing it and then everyone would want one. Because that's what happened. But I have almost no clue how that dress gets made. Or how much it costs to make it. Or how I got so far by letting everything happen around me. Maybe..."

He cuts himself off. He can't say it. But—if Astrid had stayed, would he have discovered any of this? Or would he have just kept making things for her to wear until suddenly that didn't work and he'd have been left staring at a ruin anyway—but having ruined her in the process too.

For the first time since Astrid left, he wants to call her. He wants...

Now he does shift uncomfortably in his chair. He wants to apologize. But she doesn't want to hear a single word from him, the man who made the press reduce her to the role of blank canvas.

He goes back to the office and works through a list he made with Alix. She wants to approve his choice of business manager—it's not that she insists, but she says in that clear and unchallengeable voice, "It's good to understand figures besides those on mannequins. But you don't have time to precisely manage everything and make art too. So, you need someone who'll teach you enough, but who you can leave the details to. I know two people who are suitable."

He interviews those people, not in the mirrored office but in the original store off Madison Avenue, sitting on one side of what used to be Nancy's workbench. He passes the candidates a set of accounts and asks, "What do you think?"

They quail at the size of the mess but he gives the job to the one who, after having quailed, says, "I can't make things worse. Which means there's unlimited potential."

That's the kind of optimism Hawk needs.

Over the next month, Hawk and his business manager and Alix shut down a dozen stores that were opened in a heady rush of overkill. They shut down one factory and concentrate on the original one on Seventh Avenue. They kill licensing deals.

"Pierre Cardin will put his name on toilet paper—Hawk Jones is godlike and doesn't require toilet paper," Alix says to him with a smile and he bursts into laughter.

Right then he wants so badly to call Astrid and say, *thank you*. He has no idea if she's involved in Alix's generosity and is too embarrassed to ask Alix, but he just wants to tell someone how good he finally feels to be doing, rather than drifting—and Astrid's the only person who'd understand.

"Thank you," he says to Alix. "I mean it. You saved me."

"I just threw you a life preserver. I'm not planning to get in there and help you swim. It would ruin my Hawk Jones dress for a start."

He knows she'll shake her head at him but he hugs her anyway.

The first time around, he spent more time celebrating than being grateful. This time around, he's going to get the balance right—gratitude first, because he wants the people he owes that to, to stick around. Whereas the fleeting moments you raise a glass to never last and aren't worth as much as he'd once thought.

When he walks back to his apartment, a place he spends very little time in because Astrid is in there everywhere—in the sunset color of the wall, sitting on the concrete ledge by the arched window, hanging in the wardrobe that still has some of her clothes in it—he passes a shopfront that's been empty for a while. It's in a location he's always thought would be a great space for another store.

The shop has been wrapped in chiffon in striking colors—emerald, sapphire and goldenrod. He tries to peer through the windows but they're covered on the inside in white paper. The chiffon dances in the breeze, casting shadows in yellow and green and blue on the pavement, colorful sequins that commuters step onto, smiling.

The colors remind him of Astrid. Or maybe it's just that everything reminds him of Astrid.

* * *

Astrid finally gives up on finding anything more than a ripple at the beach in Altea on Spain's east coast. She drags her surfboard in to where a woman sits in a white skirt and blouse, white hat obscuring her face, legs clad in stockings.

"Cristóbal was right," she says to Mizza, dropping onto the chair beside her. "There are no waves in Altea."

Cristóbal. She still can't believe she's on first-name terms with one of the world's greatest couturiers. Mizza and Balenciaga still call one another *madame* and *monsieur*, as people their age do in Europe, and Astrid's certain she's supposed to do the same, but years of discos and informality have made her tongue struggle with tradition. Cristóbal doesn't seem to mind.

She and Mizza are staying in the couturier's home for a week before Astrid returns to Manhattan for good. It's the last day and Mizza had wanted to see her surf. Such a simple wish, but it had made Astrid cry. Because people only want to watch you doing something they're completely uninterested in if they love you. And Mizza doesn't say anything but Astrid can tell she's ill, that having suffered from pulmonary embolisms over the last fifteen years has weakened her. Still, she's so beautiful, even at seventy years of age, that most people don't see the frailty behind the skin that has only the most strategically placed wrinkles.

Almost a year ago, Astrid stood on the doorstep of an apartment on the Rue Lamennais in Paris in a dry-eyed kind of shock. Anger had driven her there—anger at this woman at whose feet she could throw all the blame. But Mizza opened the door, touched a hand to her heart and said, "The world has been cruel to you."

And Astrid had found herself speechless.

In the silence, Mizza had shown Astrid into a bedroom, told her to sleep and said they would depart in the morning. Astrid hadn't woken for twelve hours. She ate the breakfast Mizza set out in the dining room, barely acknowledging Hubert, Mizza's husband, who kissed them both on the cheeks then left them alone together. Finally, Mizza drove them north and west to the town of Bayeux, where she led Astrid into a museum and told her to sit on a bench.

"Let your eyes rest on this." Mizza pointed to the *Bayeux Tapestry*.

Astrid tried to say she wasn't in the mood for history but—what was she in the mood for?

So she sat. Eventually her eyes had rested, her mind too, for several hours with Mizza by her side. They both looked at this piece of needlework that was never meant to be worn or photographed, revered or sold. And gradually Astrid began to see that each thread was like a word in a story of men conquering all. She shuddered.

Mizza picked up her hand. "There are six hundred and thirty-two men, two hundred horses and fifty-five dogs in this embroidery," she said. "It was painstakingly embroidered by women over many, many years. But do you know how many women it depicts?"

Astrid tried to see through the cluster of men and horses and dogs. She shook her head.

"Just six," was Mizza's crisp reply. "It's an embroidery about an epic battle, as is so much of art. But nobody will ever celebrate, in two hundred and thirty feet of linen and crewelwork, the bloodless, everyday battles of women just surviving. So, since 1918, I've tried to make clothes in which every filament and thread can be a woman's armor."

All Astrid could say, the first words she'd spoken were, "*Make* clothes?"

Mizza smiled. "That's a story for another day. Today's story is a tapestry commemorating men's heroic deeds. But who remembers the women responsible for the art those deeds have been captured in?"

Which meant the world was constantly, unceasingly cruel.

For the first time since leaving Hawk and Manhattan, Astrid cried. She cried on Mizza's shoulder as she grappled with how hurting herself and hurting Hawk could possibly lead to a happy ending. And all Mizza said when the weeping finally stopped was, "Which couturier would you like me to introduce you to? You've come to work?"

Her tone made it clear there was no option other than to concur.

So Astrid nodded robotically and threw out a name. "Yves Saint Laurent?" He designed for younger, more contemporary women...

Mizza gave one imperious, "No."

Astrid stared at her, speechless. Why had she come to Mizza's apartment? She'd thought only someone who didn't love her couldn't hurt her but it turned out Mizza could hurt her as skillfully as anyone.

"I'll only introduce you to someone who'll stretch you," Mizza continued. "Marc Bohan at Dior. And then Hubert de Givenchy."

And Astrid, who'd fought her adoptive parents almost all her life about her hopes and dreams, simply acquiesced. Which was lucky. Because it turned out Mizza was right.

Now, as the onshore breeze cools, Astrid smiles at Mizza, whose answering smile is smaller than it should be, enigmatic. Behind it are skeins of secrets Astrid has begun to unravel and it makes her blurt out words she's been holding in all week. "I'm scared."

"I know." Mizza takes Astrid's hand, the rings on her fingers setting off a multicolored light show, not even the sand and the salt getting in the way of Mizza's gemstone habit, which is a part of her the same way the scar on her wrist is—not adornment, but elemental. "You should be."

It makes Astrid laugh, Mizza's directness, never saying what Astrid wants to hear but always what she needs to hear. "I wasn't scared enough before."

Mizza sighs. "I wish I could say it hurts less when you're scared because you understand the potential for loss. But I don't think it does."

What happened? It's a question Astrid has never asked. Meeting people from Mizza's milieu over the last year has made Astrid understand they don't speak of the past, except to comment on the present's shortcomings in relation to those years. She tried, just once, to ask Mizza about her father but Mizza had looked so sad that Astrid ended the conversation, caring less about a man she didn't know than hurting the woman in front of her.

For Mizza and others like her, Astrid has discerned that the past is an extra shadow they wear, but never discuss. Just like people don't mention their underclothes—unless they're writing an article about Astrid. How many more articles will she have to endure when the world discovers she's had the temerity to return and set up a business named after her birth mother?

She'd considered naming the business after herself, but Astrid Bricard is a girl in a silver dress dancing with Hawk. Mizza is more nebulous—an idea rather than fact.

"I want you to succeed in being more and better than me," Mizza says suddenly. "I want you to do what I couldn't. Or perhaps do what I didn't—I don't know. Maybe they're the same. All I know is we can't have two generations of women who might have."

Astrid's grip on Mizza's hand tightens. The salt she can taste isn't from the spray or the wind. It's from being blessed by the last woman in the world she'd ever thought would bless her.

* * *

It's hard to say goodbye. To not know how many more times they might meet. To not know what she's going back to. To not know whether a blessing will make any difference or if Astrid will fail yet again.

On the terrace, Mizza and Cristóbal are dinking Perrier and watching the sun set. Astrid crosses over to Mizza, lifts her veil and kisses her cheek.

"*Bon courage,*" Mizza says. Then, "*Au revoir.*"

Until we see one another again. That's what *au revoir* means, not goodbye.

* * *

The next time Hawk walks past the empty shopfront, the chiffon has been replaced with new colors—violet, shocking pink, azure. And there's a sign above the door that reads *MIZZA*.

Hawk marches straight to Alix's office and doesn't wait to be announced. "She's back, isn't she?"

"You mean Astrid?"

He explodes. "No, I mean Marilyn damn Monroe. Of course I mean Astrid. That's her store, isn't it?"

Alix fixes him with those green eyes. "Yes."

He pushes himself away from the desk, paces one way, then the other. "So that's why you didn't want her getting any bad publicity now? You saved me to make things easier for her?" He tries not to raise his voice, isn't sure what he's saying. Is he mad or scared? He's definitely hyperventilating.

"Sit down," Alix orders him. "Have some water."

He sits and he sips. He breathes and he says, "I'm sorry. You're her godmother. I'm not going to make you a middleman for my screwed-up emotions."

Alix takes the chair opposite him and smiles. "Hawk, I didn't save you to make things easier for her. There's very little that will make things easier for her. I invested in you because I believed my money would be repaid quickly and it was. Going broke would have broken your heart. I knew Astrid was planning to come back and I wanted her to be able to focus on finally doing what she's always wanted to do—a heartbroken Hawk would have been a distraction. I want to think I've done the best thing for both of you, even though sometimes I worry it might also turn out to be the worst thing."

Her smile is very sad and Hawk leans forward, wary. "Worst in what way?"

"That depends on so many things, Hawk. On you. On Astrid." Alix stands and walks over to the window, speaks to the blue sky beyond rather than him. "And on the world."

TWENTY-SEVEN

BLYTHE BRICARD

After Blythe hangs up from Remy, her mind turns over a reel of images—Mizza, who designed Dior couture. And Astrid, who disappeared into a vapor of rumors about drug dealers and jealousy.

One of the images in her mind supports that story—Hawk and Astrid at a Charles Revson party, Astrid wearing a tank top with Hawk's name on the back, a style the brand updated often in the first few years and then abruptly stopped producing after Astrid disappeared. In the image, Astrid is holding on to both Hawk and a toilet seat embedded with hundred-dollar bills with the same kind of desperation—as if she can't let either of them slip through her fingers. She's laughing, looks drunk or wasted, and with her over-the-top toilet seat under her arm, she's the woman Blythe is ashamed to be related to.

But...

Blythe takes out her phone and pulls up the article about her own talent for providing inspiration rather than designing. None of it's true. What if Astrid *did* design the dress she wore to the Cotys? What if it's just that the falsehoods are too tantalizing to be disbelieved?

And she knows, with such certainty it makes her lean her elbows on her knees and stare at her reflection in the shining parquetry floor, that if she restarts MIZZA with Blake Group, the media will say: JAKE BLACK BREATHES NEW LIFE INTO MIZZA AND MAKES IT A SUCCESS.

Blythe's name will appear a couple of paragraphs down as the inspiration behind the idea, nothing more.

It will be his. Not hers. And Blythe will be the one walking away with tears on her face.

* * *

Blythe crosses to the dining room and Jake looks up straightaway, as if he's been waiting for her. She knows she's about to hurt him—again? Was he hurt by their divorce? Yes, she thinks he was. But she either hurts him again now, or she hurts herself.

She indicates that she wants to talk to him and they cross back to the library. Something about her expression has him dropping into a chair.

"You're not doing MIZZA with me," he says.

She stands in front of the fireplace and stares down into it. "I'm breaking my promise to you and the deal we made. I come from a long line of women who are crucified by the future for whom and what they supposedly love. Which means I cannot work with you. Ever." Her words are vehement.

How does she say this next part? She'll be making herself as vulnerable to Jake as she's ever been and she has no idea what he'll do with that.

She breathes out, tries to explain. "Even in our worst moments, we never had difficulty with..." She falters, feels her cheeks redden. But she has to be honest—she wants him to keep to his side of the deal even as she can't uphold hers. She wants Eva and Sebby to win for once.

"We never had trouble with sex," she says, voice a little too loud in her determination to have it done. "We were always attracted to one another. And I know you're not attracted to me now but I don't trust myself around you... Not seeing you made it easy to pretend I hated everything about you. But now..." She feels like Jake might be standing not far behind her and knows she cannot turn and look at him.

"I keep remembering the way you used to kiss my neck," she says resolutely. "But I need to be able to look at you and not think about that." She shakes her head. "So I'm doing MIZZA—but on my own. I have no idea how. But I am."

Words are all very well but she feels sick. Her financial issues won't vanish simply through the act of taking charge of her life. All she's doing is taking charge of dreams and wishes, whereas starting up MIZZA requires cold hard cash.

"Astrid is like a tragedy you want to turn back the pages of to the place it all went wrong," she says quietly. "I can't be the denouement of that story. I guess…" Her voice wobbles. "I guess it's up to you what you do about Eva and Sebby."

Blythe turns slowly to face Jake. She's never seen him look more gutted.

"Don't…" He starts, then stops, recovers and begins again. "Don't decide now. Keep working on MIZZA and decide at the end of the vacation. Maybe two more weeks of watching me muddle my way through fatherhood will cure you of ever thinking about me kissing your neck again." He reaches up and rubs the back of his own neck. "Then it won't matter if we work together. No matter what happens, I'll be Eva and Sebby's dad. And we'll just be colleagues."

It's so tempting. She makes herself shake her head. "We'll never just be colleagues, Jake."

It's time to finally and forever remove herself from Act Three of the Tragedy of the Muses Bricard.

* * *

Before Blythe can go into dinner, a dozen boxes of clothes arrive from Remy. She stares at them, frowning. This is her moment to act—to let whatever's inside inspire her to make something better from the damaged silk and torn hems and thready skeletons of once-glorious beings. Or it's the moment she can do what she usually does and think of all the obstacles, the biggest being she has no money and Nathaniel has effectively just told the world she's a talentless muse, just like her mother—which will make it nearly impossible to raise funds.

The boxes rest beside Iris's stack of clothes and the legendary silver dress. For the first time in her life, Blythe imagines how the famous image might make her feel if the person depicted wasn't related to her. If she wasn't the one standing on the sidelines wishing she had the courage to dance—but if she was the one who *did* dance. It would feel wild. Free. Fucking great.

"Dinner's on the table!" she hears Anton yell to the four corners of the chateau and she decides to take that feeling in to dinner, have a glass of champagne and get started on MIZZA properly in the morning.

The only empty seat is beside a new face—Cameron, one of Ed's friends who she's met a few times and who's in France for a few days. He kisses her cheek. "Blythe, you look incredible as always."

"Thanks." She joins the conversation between Ed and Cameron until Ed leaves to take an empty chair at the other end of the table that Blythe hadn't noticed. It's beside Jake, who's staring at his wineglass. Then his eyes lock with hers and she has a strange feeling the seat was meant for her. Except she isn't in primary school, and Jake's her ex-husband.

"I don't know if you know I got divorced last year," Cameron is saying. "I asked Ed if you were seeing anyone. He said you weren't, and I wondered if you'd like to go out for dinner tomorrow night?"

He smiles at her. He has a nice smile. He's a nice man. A friend of Ed's will be trustworthy and safe. But...

"I know dating's tricky after divorce," Cameron says, unfazed by her hesitation. "Think about it and text me in the morning."

"Okay," she says, just so she can stop talking about dating while Jake's at the other end of the table.

Thirteen years ago, she'd believed she'd never date anyone other than her husband. She remembers kissing him and kissing him and kissing him still harder when she'd realized that, knowing it didn't make sense—that if she had Jake for the rest of her life, she didn't need to make out with him like she'd never see him again.

"Hey," he'd said to her, obviously sensing some strange urgency.

"We can do this forever," she'd said, and most guys would have laughed and said something about being happy to make out forever but he'd said, "It isn't enough time," which was exactly what she'd thought—forever wasn't long enough to spend with Jake.

But they couldn't even manage fifteen years.

Cameron smiles his nice smile and stands up. "It was great seeing you, Blythe. Look forward to your text."

No sooner has Cameron left than Ed slips into the chair beside her. "Did he ask you out? And did you say yes?"

"No—"

Ed eyeballs her. "Blythe, Jake's been dating for at least a year. I'm ordering you to start dating too."

Blythe can't help laughing at the idea of Ed ordering anyone to do anything. "Isn't it bad form to go out on a date while I'm here?"

"Jake went out on a date the other night, remember?"

"He said it was for work…"

Ed snorts. "I'm sure he worked hard. You're not going on a date with Cameron because he'll be the next love of your life. He's a safe way to try dating, that's all. I'll tell Jake. Step back into the world, Blythe."

She reaches for her glass. Maybe Ed's right. One moment of tenderness doesn't mean Jake has any interest in whether Blythe dates. And it would be nice to experience intimacy again. She misses being embraced. Being wanted. Why not see if there's a space in her life for that?

She texts Cameron before she can talk herself out of it.

* * *

The next day, Blythe wakes with a start. It's eight in the morning. Where are the kids?

The door to Eva and Sebby's bedroom is closed. Inside, they're tugging on shoes and Jake's sitting on the bed, supervising.

"Daddy came to our room for snuggles," Sebby says cheerfully. "We played the quiet game while we got dressed and I won because Eva keeps asking questions."

Jake stands. "We're going to Mont-St.-Michel with everyone. We'll be out most of the day."

He's brusque, efficient, and he and the kids are gone five seconds later.

To block out an unsettling sense of disappointment at that cursory conversation, she puts on her favorite working playlist—the Stones, Diana Ross, Joni Mitchell. A box from Remy sits beside a blank notebook. Where to start? With the silk or the strategy?

She wants to pull out anything that has amazing color, like the buildings at Trentemoult. But she also needs to think about hiring staff to find clothes begging for reinvention. How to make enough one-offs from such a labor-intensive business to turn a profit. Not to mention conjuring up a strategy for diffusing the ideas behind the one-off pieces into a ready-to-wear line.

She makes herself sit for an hour and there's one idea she keeps coming back to. Her godmother, Alix St. Pierre, once told her that Dior's friends were the biggest public relations asset he had. Blythe has a lot of friends in the fashion world, and one hell of a reputation—people, the media especially, love talking about her. And if there's one compliment that's always directed her way, it's that she has that elusive *je ne sais quoi* when it comes to dressing herself. So—what if she spoke to some of her friends about what she's doing?

And what if she only spoke to the women?

She turns on her iPad and does a little research. She knows some of this stuff from Jake—investment in startup businesses is dominated by men. *Women own forty-two percent of businesses but receive just two*

244 NATASHA LESTER

percent of venture funding, she reads. Businesses run by men attract five times more funds then female-led businesses.

Rather than making her regret her decision not to work with Jake or Nathaniel, the facts set something inside her to burning.

She keeps reading. Women are less likely to ask for funding, but their businesses return almost twice as much to their investors. They receive less coverage in the media—she could probably buck that trend, she thinks wryly—so the prevailing belief is they're unsuccessful and less important. Women-owned businesses are better for the planet and thus better for the future. Women are often asked by investors how they'll be able to raise a family while running a business; men never are.

Blythe remembers walking into a venture capitalist's office with her plan for a capsule collection made from cast-off clothing when she was pregnant with Eva. Nobody could take their eyes off her stomach. She should have projected her PowerPoint presentation onto it.

They hadn't invested in her. It was the first time she'd put her plans in a drawer.

Fuck putting her plans in a drawer again.

One name keeps floating to the top of her mind. Before she can talk herself out of it, she picks up her phone and dials.

"Blythe." Marcelline Villiers's voice comes down the line. "Jake last week, you this week. What sins am I paying for?"

There's a smile in her voice and Blythe laughs. Marcelline and Blythe hadn't been good friends at grad school but had worked together on a few projects and, as Jake had said, Marcelline could sell ski jackets to desert dwellers. She's an expert marketer, and she has some family money from a business her great-grandparents started decades ago making the humble—and then almost unknown—zipper.

"The sin of being a woman," Blythe says.

"Now I'm intrigued."

So Blythe tells Marcelline that she needs investors for MIZZA.

"I was going to start off apologetically," she says, "and tell you I won't be offended if you say no but, actually, I will be offended. You've worked for Nathaniel and God knows how many other men. I know this is different and I'm asking for money. But wouldn't it be nice if the only jobs you could get out of grad school weren't at companies run by men? If I was a man, Nathaniel would never have said those things about me. And as a man, nobody would ever write things like that about him."

Now she's really swinging. Marcelline had dated Nathaniel. She might admire him more than Blythe does.

"And wouldn't it be nice if I'd thought about what to invest my money in," Marcelline says contemplatively, "rather than giving it to a financial adviser who, let's face it, most likely invests it with other men? But, Blythe, Nathaniel has effectively poisoned you with that article. I need to think about whether even my charms are enough of an antidote."

"But you will think about it?" Blythe persists, trying not to believe that *I'll think about it* is just a delay on the path to saying no.

"I will. Because you're right—if you were a man without a storied past, Nathaniel would have called you rather than letting the press do his dirty work. And, Blythe, your pitch needs work, but I can help you with that. *If* I decide to invest."

Blythe laughs. "Still as honest as ever, Marcelline."

"You bet. And let me give you some more honesty. It isn't always a bad thing to give the world the finger. So quit running from the Blythe in that photograph. And just in case you have any doubts whatsoever, I was not on a date with Jake. It was a business meeting. Dating Jake would be a complete waste of time for every woman in the world bar one," she finishes cryptically.

Blythe hangs up with the promise to meet Marcelline next week.

There are still a lot of gaps in Blythe's plans—how she can simultaneously sell a one-off to a customer and show the same one-off to buyers at a trade fair, for example. But without any one-offs, she can't do anything. So she might as well make something.

Before she can start, there's a knock at the door and the host passes Blythe a package. "This came for you."

Inside the envelope is a sheaf of photocopied pages. Illustrations in watercolor and pastel. Dresses. Gorgeous dresses.

It's a copy of Astrid's Parsons portfolio.

Where the hell did that come from?

She searches for a note, but there's nothing. Just pages of surprises.

Like Remy said, there's the silver dress. And an annotation: *designed by Astrid Bricard and Hawk Jones.* On the next page is a pink organza dress made from cascades of stiffened ruffles. It's dated May 1970 and it's fabulous. Then a white tuxedo jacket, like the one Hawk made for Bianca Jagger. The cult tank top with the Hawk Jones name screen-printed on the back.

This portfolio says the exact opposite of all the vicious rumors. Not that Hawk had designed MIZZA for Astrid. But that Astrid was a brilliant designer and that Blythe's father had—what?—stolen his designs from her?

On another page is a design titled—*Group Project 1970.* Underneath are the words: *designed by Astrid Bricard, Velvet Harrison and Graham Gee.*

Velvet Harrison. Blythe knows that name. Did a woman called Velvet visit her at Meredith's apartment a few times when Blythe was young? A tall woman with amazing hair that child-Blythe had wanted to scrunch her hands into. Velvet had let her, laughing. She was a model, maybe. She'd stopped visiting around the time Blythe turned seven.

Blythe takes out her phone, searches the internet—there she is. Velvet Harrison was the operations manager for MIZZA. After Astrid disappeared, she'd taken on the task of shutting down the business, returned to modeling for a few years and then...nothing. Another vanished woman.

But if Velvet and Astrid had been friends at Parsons, and if Velvet was Astrid's operations manager, then Blythe knows someone who must have known Velvet. She dials a number that's long been stored in her phone but almost never used. An assistant answers and gives an audibly shocked gasp when Blythe says her name.

"I don't want to speak to him," Blythe tells her. "But if Hawk knows how to get in touch with Velvet Harrison, then I need her number. You can text it to me. Please tell him not to call me."

She hangs up, half-wanting to hide her phone, scared that Hawk will take this as a sign of a chink in her armor and call despite what she'd said.

At age thirteen, when the movie about Hawk and Astrid had been released and everything between her and her dad had erupted so irretrievably, all she knew was that she didn't trust him and she couldn't let him break her heart again. Because she'd loved him—God, she'd loved him. Her dad, who'd let her sit on the workbench in the store off Madison Avenue and make a mess with cotton reels, the man who'd sometimes take her to Nantucket, Newport, the Outer Banks, where they'd spend a few days lying on beaches—mostly surf beaches, although Hawk didn't surf. He'd watch the surfers fight the waves, winning sometimes, losing often. It was only later, looking back, that she got the feeling he was searching for something but she had no idea what he hoped to find riding a wave into the shore.

But then from the time she was six until the time she was eight, Hawk became an intermittent thing, like the line of a song you think you know but whose rhythm only comes to you in snatches. She'd stay at Meredith's more often—*just for a night or two*, he'd say, but would come back two weeks later. He'd get a babysitter when she was with him and he'd be gone all night and sometimes not there in the morning either, and the sitter would feed her breakfast and get her to school. That was when the impromptu holidays stopped. When he didn't take her to the store anymore. When the unbridled joy she'd felt sitting on his shoulders at a Rolling Stones concert was a goodbye, rather than a return. It was the last thing they'd done together before he disappeared, like Astrid.

"Blythe?"

She jumps, so lost in the past she hadn't noticed Coco standing right in front of her. Wordlessly, she passes Coco the portfolio.

"Holy shit," Coco says.

"I know."

"And you know you could just ask Hawk about it."

Blythe flinches. "He's a liar." Her words are quiet but violent.

Coco is silent a moment, then says, "Remember when I was fifteen and I lived with you for the summer? I don't know if I ever thanked you properly for what you did for me back then. I was a long way from being myself when I got to your place in May but I was almost back to normal when I went home in September."

Blythe smiles. She'd loved having Coco, despite the circumstances. One of Coco's closest friends had taken her own life—a fifteen-year-old girl suddenly gone. Coco had been beside herself with guilt for not having known her friend was hurting. Ed and Joy had tried everything to coax her out of herself, terrified for their daughter, eventually acquiescing to Coco's request to stay somewhere else for a while. Blythe never told Coco that they called every day to check on their daughter.

"You got me to tell you one thing each morning about Rachael," Coco says, referring to her friend. "I started out giving you irritated pieces of nothing, like she had brown hair. But by the end, I was telling you all the good stuff I thought I wasn't allowed to remember because of how she died. We don't have time on this vacation for you to tell me one thing a day about Hawk. So you could just tell me all of it now."

Blythe's overwhelming urge is to run for the door. Her family is so good at running.

Coco waits. And Blythe's mouth opens.

"I know now," she begins haltingly, "that the reason he disappeared for near on a year when I was eight was because he was in rehab. I don't know why he was using the coke, pills and booze—because of Astrid disappearing maybe. But I know he had a fight with Matthias one morning—a loud, angry fight. That afternoon, Matthias had another stroke and . . . that's when he died."

Blythe pauses, her memory of her grandfather a hazy but gentle presence.

"That's also when Hawk completely vanished," Blythe goes on. "Went to rehab. And while I can forgive him for being an addict, there are two things I can't forgive him for."

Blythe closes her eyes, not sure she can say this aloud. But the words press out, too long trapped inside her. "I can't forgive him for not wanting me back after he got out of rehab. For leaving me with Meredith when he was better. No parent in their right mind would leave a kid whose mother had walked out on them when they were just a baby. But Hawk did."

Blythe wants to curl up in a ball. Before Coco can ask what the second thing is, she says, staring in a dry-eyed kind of grief at the wall, "I need a break. I can't . . ."

Coco wraps her in a torso-bruising hug. "I love you," she tells her. "Lots of people love you."

Just not the two who mattered most, Blythe's cruel inner voice reminds her. And as soon as Coco's gone, the memory of the thing that had finally broken her and Hawk apart rushes in.

Hawk had come to Meredith's to say goodbye—he was going on a two-week vacation because the much-hyped movie was coming out and he didn't want to be around.

"Just go and forget about it all," she'd heard Meredith tell him.

"I'll still go to meetings while I'm away," Hawk had told his mother.

Blythe had no idea what that meant until the movie exploded onto screens all over the country. That was when she'd first discovered her father's addiction. Not from him. In a freaking movie theater. *The Girl in the Silver Dress* it was called—demoting Astrid from Woman to Girl. Was there anything more horrific to a thirteen-year-old than seeing two people on a screen with her parents' names portrayed as two coked-up dope-heads screwing in a nightclub? And was there anything worse than returning to Meredith's apartment, thinking the movie was just a lie, but seeing Meredith's face and knowing she'd seen it too and then hearing her say, "He thought it was a secret. That people only knew he'd dabbled a bit, not that it would show—"

Blythe knew exactly what Meredith had cut herself off from saying—that it would show Hawk lying unconscious on a gurney, then having his stomach pumped at the hospital. He'd overdosed. Almost checked out. Had deliberately taken too much of something, not giving a shit how Blythe would feel if she lost her father too. How could she ever trust someone who cared so little for her?

He didn't call her from his vacation to see how she was. Instead, Blythe endured a schoolyard thrumming with innuendo, of boys thrusting their pelvises at her.

When Hawk finally returned, he walked into the apartment and said to her, "It's not what happened."

And she'd said, "You weren't an addict? You didn't nearly die?"

"I was and I did."

"So it *is* what happened. You just never told me. And now you want to lie about it. Don't call me anymore."

Only once in the intervening years, after Meredith's funeral when she'd found herself crying in his arms, realizing she had no one left, had he asked her to come and live with him again. She'd nearly done it, except she'd just started her chemistry degree and was battling another army of boys who wanted her to dance on tables for them. So she couldn't go and live with Hawk—that would be like inviting even more scrutiny into her life and she had enough to deal with. What had embedded itself in her when Hawk first disappeared was a belief that he should have known she wanted him—that he should have understood a child who'd lost her mother would never be able to forgive a father who vanished without a word too.

But now Blythe wonders—is she just as bad as Hawk? Abandoning her father for breaking her heart, just like he abandoned her. It was a tit for tat that had only hurt her all the more in the end.

Her phone pings, making her jump.

Blythe, here's Velvet's number. Hawk.

She can see he's typing another message, three little dots flashing on the screen. They flash and they flash and what eventually comes through is a message too short for it to have taken so long to write.

I hope you do MIZZA. I love you.

She knows she's going to cry. So she pushes her phone under her pillow, goes for a walk, and when she has herself back in hand, she dials Velvet's number.

The voice that answers is tired, old.

"It's . . . it's Blythe Bricard," Blythe says, "Astrid's daughter. Sorry—"

"Holy mother of God."

And Blythe blurts, "I'm trying to find out what happened to her."

Velvet's reply is instantaneous. "Then listen to this. Go look into the travesty that was Versailles—why the hell has so little been written about that event? Because it's a dirty little secret. A woman fucking disappeared. But everyone just points at pictures of Astrid in the rain that day and calls her crazy, a disaster running straight into a murder weapon. Like she deserved what happened to her. She didn't. And you . . ."

Velvet's fury is excoriating. "It's taken you this long to care about what happened to your mother? What kind of a daughter does that make you? She loved you, Blythe." Velvet's voice cracks, splitting Blythe's heart open. "She didn't want to go to Versailles. Because of you. She had to be persuaded by all of us because we thought we knew best. We didn't know shit. She should never have gone. Maybe she'd still be here now if she hadn't."

TWENTY-EIGHT

ASTRID BRICARD AND HAWK JONES

Hanging the *MIZZA* sign outside the shop makes the rumors swirl. John Fairchild at *Women's Wear Daily* is like a record stuck in the groove. HAWK JONES'S MUSE TURNS DRESSMAKER, he declares.

Astrid throws the article in the trash, then goes and sits on the stoop of a building in Chelsea. Two hours later, a young woman with a stubborn Afro and a long stride appears. She stops dead, drops her string bag on the ground and leaps on Astrid, almost knocking her over.

"I should hate you," Velvet sniffs into Astrid's shoulder. "Leaving like that. And now appearing just as suddenly. Come upstairs and tell me what the hell is going on."

In the old apartment they once shared, Astrid tells Velvet she went to France and stayed with Mizza, who told her to work at the Houses of Dior and Givenchy. "Mizza was right," she says. "Making things you'd never design yourself teaches you a hell of a lot. And making couture gowns so intricate only a few people are lucky enough to wear them teaches you everything. So now I'm an expert hand-sewer." She grins.

Velvet laughs. "If this tale doesn't end with you telling me you're about to start designing something for real, then I'll throw you out."

"We'd better make dinner," Astrid says. "Because it looks like I'm staying."

Velvet's shriek is the best sound Astrid's heard in a year.

They eat at the table where Velvet once taught Astrid the finer details of sewing and there, Astrid asks Velvet about her own metamorphosis.

Velvet shrugs. "I ain't no butterfly. I'm modeling."

Astrid is quiet, digesting this and the food.

"Say it." Velvet's dark eyes challenge her.

"Is it what you want to do?"

"It's what I'm allowed to do."

"But you make beautiful clothes."

"Beautiful *colored* clothes."

Astrid puts down her fork. "That's what they think?"

Velvet scowls. "Black models like me are a sign that we're not really a racist society. And between Stephen Burrows and Halston, I get enough work. But that's the only kind of work I'm gonna get. Did you forget Jackie Kennedy called Ann Lowe a colored designer when she was asked who designed her wedding dress? We don't get to put our names on pretty things."

Astrid stares at her plate, not knowing whether she should ask. Will it seem like charity? More good intentions hiding the fact that things don't change, or if they do, that change takes centuries, not years.

"You didn't come calling for red beans and rice," Velvet says sharply. "And you sure as hell won't survive long if you're not brave enough to tell me why you're here."

And Astrid feels very ashamed. Another white girl who doesn't know shit. "Do you want other work?" she says.

"What work?"

"Let me tell you what I'm doing first." Astrid pauses, tries to think of a way to pitch it, but then just tells the plain truth.

"In Paris, I realized I can't crawl around on a floor pinning hems while

I'm wearing a too-short Hawk Jones skirt. But if I walk into a department store or ladies boutique, all I can choose from are men's clothes, redacted. Stiff jackets with dead-boring knee-length skirts the same color as the jacket. A shift dress—again in the same color and fabric as the jacket. So imagine buying a jacket, and then choosing pants in a different color or a different fabric to wear with it. Navy paired with pink, say." Her hands fly as she speaks, like dancers in a club. "Imagine wearing that same pair of pants with a T-shirt on the weekend. No jacket at all. Imagine things you can work in and then, if you just swap one piece out, you can go to dinner in them too. I'm going to make clothes women *want* to go to work in, rather than clothes they *have* to go to work in."

She finally takes a breath and slows down. "I have designs. I have a name. I have a store. But nothing else. If you like the idea, you get to choose what you do."

Velvet gives Astrid one of her biggest grins. "Anything?"

Astrid laughs. "Oh God, what do you want?"

"Operations manager. You design it, I'll get it made."

"Really?" Astrid wants to whoop.

"What, you were hoping I'd settle for being your house model?"

Astrid shakes her head. "Operations manager is exactly what I wanted you to say."

* * *

Astrid unwraps MIZZA and sets "Woman in Silver" to play on the turntable.

"What?" she says in response to Velvet's raised eyebrow. "If a rock star's gonna write a song about you, you might as well use it."

Velvet grins.

And the breathless crowds pour in.

"It's not like Hawk's store at all," Astrid hears them say, again and again.

It's just what she was hoping for. She hasn't seen Hawk's new flagship but understands it's much like the old store—the anteroom to a nightclub, a space where famous people congregate at the big table and chat, where photography and music and theater combine. Where live models treat the store like a catwalk, and Hawk as their daemon. She tries very hard not to think about that.

Astrid's store, named after her birth mother, is the leopardess's den. There's a large fur-covered object—bed? Sofa? Chaise? Nobody seems quite sure—in the center of the room. There are antique armchairs and lamps, a fireplace with a mantel, luscious brocade paper on the walls. It's like the Parisian boudoir of a courtesan perhaps. Hanging on the walls are Astrid's drawings of the clothes so women can see what they look like in motion, not just on the hanger.

And then there are the clothes themselves. There are no micro shorts. Not much black or white. Instead, there is color.

Sapphire trousers. Dresses that are really just tank tops elongated to the ankle and slit to the thigh in a vivid spectrum of color. Unspeakably elegant navy fitted tops that wrap over just one shoulder. In the middle of the store is a large photograph of Astrid wearing a dress made from vertical lengths of pastel rainbow hues that plunge in a V to her waist. The photograph has been taken the second Astrid began to twirl so the lengths are just starting to lift, offering a sensual glimpse of her legs between the drift of aquamarine, pistachio, nymphaea and pearl. The physicality that has always been attributed to Astrid is still there, but its subtlety gives it power—woman power.

The photograph spins around atop a podium like the one from the infamous photograph at the Cheetah. It's pure theater, but what better way to get an audience?

"Look," a group of women say, pointing to the podium. And, "Look!" a gaggle of teenagers squeal over the shopping bags, made from iridescent silver. "Can I really wear that to work?" another lady says, eyeing the navy top with its subtle side-serve of skin.

Alix interviews Astrid on the leopard-print sofa while the customers swirl around.

She indicates the photos they'd taken the day before of Astrid wearing a pink gingham bikini top with the navy blue trousers, which suddenly don't seem as if they belong only in an office. In the next, Astrid's thrown a blazer over the tank dress and now she looks like she's ready to take charge of a meeting.

"Your idea is that women can wear everything together and in different combinations," Alix says. "A handful of pieces—a wardrobe of choices. Bathing suits with trousers. Evening dresses with...?"

"Nothing, of course," Astrid quips.

Alix laughs and all heads turn their way.

"Why go to work in something a man designed?" Astrid continues. "Something that's most likely uncomfortable and not suited to the work you do? Let's face it—how many men know what work we do? MIZZA is for the woman who feels young, but who also feels like working fashions are trying to make her invisible—or keep her where the men still think she belongs."

The last sentence is said in reference to a shoe advertisement currently running in *Playboy* of a naked woman lying on the floor, eyeing a shoe as if she'd do anything for it. The ad's headline reads: KEEP HER WHERE SHE BELONGS.

Astrid doesn't belong in the place she's been put—and damned if she's going to stay there.

No matter how scared she is.

* * *

The first photographs Hawk sees of Astrid reincarnated are sent to him by Alix—proof pages from the magazine. *I thought you'd want to be prepared,* she writes.

Astrid's hair is longer and wavier and a hell of a lot sexier. She's wearing a sapphire blazer and trousers, is barefoot, hands shoved in pockets, staring straight at the camera. He knows, because he knows her too well, that she's wearing nothing under the jacket and he has to sit down with how much of a gut punch that is.

He's still in love with her. *He's still in love with her.*

He stares at the photograph for a long time. Then he reads the article, arrested by one paragraph where Astrid talks about going to see the *Bayeux Tapestry* with Mizza Bricard, as if she and her birth mother had reconciled.

Mizza told me, as we stood in front of this complex work of thread and skill, that it depicts hundreds of men and dogs and horses but, despite being painstakingly embroidered by women, it shows only six. One's being hit by a priest. Two more are naked; one of them is being threatened by an ax, the other by a penis. If that's not a metaphor for the entire fashion industry, I don't know what is.

Christ. John Fairchild will never forgive her. Nor will designers like Halston.

She wants to make this fight about their egos—they want to pretend it's about her talent. Both are outsized. He wants to hope her talent is the biggest thing of all, but, shit—Fairchild recently said in the pages of his magazine that Jackie O is now Tacky O and that Gloria Vanderbilt was a matronly frump. He's banned designer Pauline Trigère from ever being mentioned by any of his journalists, and has just started up a new column devoted to gossip about who's doing the "boom-boom." That kind of ego is so huge it requires a fucking jumbo jet just to get around.

To top it off, Fairchild recently decreed that all women look awful in pants—and he said he'd never want his wife to be photographed because "a beautiful woman is something to be guarded like a flower and not publicly displayed to everybody." A photograph of Astrid in a magazine in a pair of pants isn't like poking the dragon—it's like holding a can of fuel in front of the dragon's mouth.

But look at him sitting there—another man who doubts her. Another man with a possibly outsized ego. Except it isn't that Hawk doubts her. It's that he's scared for her. But the pictures tell him she doesn't need—or doesn't want—his fear.

His favorite is of her in an Egyptian blue tank dress, head tipped back, eyes closed, body outlined beneath the jersey. Her arms are tanned and she's wearing a look on her face he's never seen before. *Relaxed*, he thinks. *At peace.*

And he knows she won't call him. And nor should he call her. He can't disturb that peace. The minute he goes to see her, the newspapers will talk about Hawk and Astrid, him first, her second—her paired with him, but lesser.

This is her chance to be Astrid—a woman remembered, rather than a woman forgotten. He owes her that.

Never in his life did he think he would just let her go.

His feet propel him toward the door, where escape beckons. But he stops, knowing too well that no hurt ever got better when treated with cognac and nightclubs. He sits back down and studies the clothes in the magazine and sees what she's done.

She hasn't gone after his customers, although there will be crossover. She's gone for the women who've had no choice but to go to work in ultra-conservative suits, looking the same as everyone else. MIZZA is like the nightclub's much cooler older sister, not a place you go just to buy a T-shirt. It's somewhere you go to build your wardrobe.

He crosses to the bar fridge, takes out a bottle of champagne, pours just one mouthful into a glass, holds it in the air and says, "Congratulations, Astrid."

She's just raised the bar damn high. And he needs to rise to meet it.

TWENTY-NINE

BLYTHE BRICARD

*S**he loved you.* Three words Blythe has been wanting to hear for her whole life, gifted to her by a stranger. But rather than making her happy, they make her weep. Because—*What kind of a daughter does that make you?* Velvet had asked.

Those words, and the anger propelling them, stick like pins into Blythe's conscience, leaving little holes where both pain and uncomfortable truths seep in. All this time, Blythe has believed—has lived her life propelled by the belief, in fact—that Astrid was bad. A bad mother. But Velvet has just turned it around and said that no, Blythe is the bad one because she didn't care enough.

Her hands cover her face but she can't hold back the tears. She wants to call Velvet again and say, just as fiercely, *I did care. I've always cared.*

Too much, perhaps. And in the wrong way.

God. Her elbows rest on her knees, fists pressed to her eyes, throat sewn tightly together with grief or pain or both. She tries to claw back into memory and time and see Astrid, feel her, but Blythe was only two months old when she left, so there's nothing. No sense of that love Velvet spoke of. Just a bleak, despairing emptiness.

Her elbow knocks against Astrid's portfolio. And as she looks at it now, that same question surfaces: *What happened to Astrid Bricard?*

But this time, it has a new meaning. Not *What happened to Astrid Bricard in the end?* Not *What fate did she meet?* The real question is: *What happened to Astrid Bricard from the time she came to Manhattan in 1970 until the day she disappeared?*

Blythe, and everyone else, has been focused on the one day she vanished. But maybe the story and the solution aren't to be found on that day. Maybe they're to be found in the almost four years preceding.

Mizza is dead. Astrid is gone. And Blythe is sitting in a room surrounded by boxes of dresses. Mizza and Astrid can't speak. But Blythe can, through these dresses. What would she have them speak of? The beauty of the world, or its spleen? The romance, or the loss? All of it, perhaps.

She picks up a box and carries it outside and over to the theater Jake showed her a few nights ago. Then she collects another. And another. She sets out all the handfuls of silk and wool and shimmering organza. This theater is now her workroom, the place where she'll create a show the fashion world will finally applaud.

* * *

Hours later, with clothes spread around her, able to see the patterns and potential, a collection begins to take shape around her idea of color and courage.

Then the doors to the theater open and Jake and the kids enter. Sebby's in Jake's arms, Eva's hand is tucked in her father's and Jake's laughing so hard he almost drops Sebby. The sound of his laughter weaves through Blythe like thread finding its loom.

"We found you," Jake says, putting Sebby down.

"We had the best day," Eva announces.

Then Sebby, who hasn't let go of his father's hand, says, "I love you, Daddy," and Blythe watches, her whole heart cracking, as Jake crouches down slowly and says to Seb, "I love you too, buddy."

A second later, Sebby, with a five-year-old's incapacity to understand the momentousness of what just happened, darts off to explore the stage. Before Jake can stand up, Eva flings her arms around her father and buries her head in his shoulder. Blythe hears her whisper, "I do too, Daddy."

As Jake hugs his daughter, he looks up at Blythe. She can feel how shiny her eyes are as she gives him a smile she hopes tells him how happy she is. And his own eyes are equally shiny as he mouths *Thanks* to her.

Then Eva scampers off to join Sebby and Jake unfurls from the floor.

"That dress looks beautiful on you," he says, even though his eyes have barely left Blythe's face long enough to take in the damaged and watermarked scarlet 1950s Balenciaga dress she's wearing. "Like you just need Prince Charming and a ball."

"I always thought Prince Charming was a bit dense. He dances with Cinderella all night but can't remember her face well enough to find her?"

"You're right," Jake says, leaning against the doorframe. "When you find your true love, they're impossible to forget."

His voice is low, and every inch of her feels the slow, progressive flushing of the skin his gaze travels over.

There's no way Ed has told him about her date with Cameron. The realization is like cold water and she steps back, sees the time and almost swears aloud.

Cameron will be there in half an hour.

* * *

Blythe stands in the shower, seeing the look on Jake's face from ten minutes ago. Right now, it's almost possible to believe that he's yearning too.

Or that she's delusional.

Maybe she should cancel the date? But why?

Despite every effort Jake has made with the kids lately, he still hasn't told her why he did a vanishing act in the last couple of years of their marriage, and why he continued to be absent from the kids thereafter. And—she realizes with a pang—he might never tell her. Which means she has to move on.

The alarm on her phone beeps, reminding her she has five minutes to get ready. For the first time in her life she wants to hold on to whatever she can of her mother, so from Remy's boxes she pulls out a MIZZA tank dress in Egyptian blue, a color made from malachite, limestone and fire—the luster, the sediment, and the flame.

She rounds up the kids but can't find her coat, which is probably upstairs. As they pass the library, she hears Jake's voice. Cameron will be here in about one minute, so she nudges the kids into the dining room and scoots back to find Jake and Ed with brandy glasses in hand.

Ed is saying, "Blythe's going out tonight."

And she blurts out, "Cameron asked me to dinner."

It's suddenly very hot in the room. And Jake looks like she just slapped him.

"You look great, Blythe," Ed says, and only then does she realize she's chosen one hell of a sexy dress. Her cleavage is definitely visible and the skirt is slit from ankle to thigh, and while she has no truck with people who say women should keep themselves covered, she doesn't want Jake to think she's worn the dress for Cameron.

Her coat is on the back of a chaise, but the fire is roaring. Ed and Jake are in rolled-up shirtsleeves. Putting her coat on will make it look like she's trying to hide.

Then Cameron's in the room, slipping an arm around her back, kissing her cheek and saying, close to her ear, "Wow."

"Have a great night," Ed says cheerily.

Jake glares at Cameron like he's an understudy who's stepped onto an already occupied stage. Blythe reminds herself that she and Jake have been divorced for nearly two years. But she sees Ed shoot Jake a warning glance.

"Let's go," Blythe says, grabbing her coat, hurrying out to the lobby and praying Cameron's not far behind.

When she turns to close the front door, Jake's standing in the foyer, watching her. He has one hand in his pocket and the other curled tightly around his now-empty brandy glass, and she has a sudden urge to have dinner with him instead, to savor his gaze on her across a table all night long.

The door closes.

* * *

It's well after eleven when Blythe arrives back at the chateau. Voices drift from the living room, so she goes into the library—which is silent—crosses to the fire, rests one hand on the mantelpiece and stares into the flames.

"How was your date?"

Jake is sitting in a chair in the corner, the wingback having hidden him from view.

She tells him the truth. "Probably not even as good as our worst date." Then she actually laughs, knowing only Jake will find this funny. "He did a Tripadvisor search and took me to a restaurant in Saumur with the highest rating. It was at..."

Jake winces as if he knows what she's going to say. "A big luxury hotel?" he guesses.

"Yep."

"Wow, I almost feel sorry for him." He grins, showing no contrition whatsoever.

"It was fine," she says. "He made an effort. But..." Her voice is a little like Jake's had been earlier when he'd seen her in the gown she was remaking—empty of something, but wanting it very much. "I kept thinking you and I would have driven to a town we hadn't explored yet and we'd have walked around until we found some place that felt right. The food would have been fabulous, the decor most likely fifty years out of date. And I would have been overdressed," she adds with a smile. "The restaurant tonight had five stars." Her smile falls away. "But the food was tasteless. I hardly ate."

Jake sets down his glass and crosses the room and she can't look away from this man she knows so much about—that she could make him go to pieces by pressing her mouth over the flat expanse of skin below his navel, that he could do the same to her by trailing his lips down the curve of her neck.

He stops in front of the fireplace and says, voice the right side of husky, "Blythe, you look gorgeous. Cameron probably told you that a million times, and if he didn't, he's a dick. Will you have a real dinner with me now? I'll get some food from the kitchen. I need you to trust me if I'm really going to be Eva and Sebby's dad. Which means I need to tell you some things."

And Blythe says, "Okay."

THIRTY

ASTRID BRICARD AND HAWK JONES

Hawk's always just put out pieces as and when inspiration strikes. But this time, he's going to create an entire collection and put on a show.

He takes his time, doesn't rush it. Pulls Fi and Nancy out of the factory and back into the store and sets them up at the workbench how they used to be. For one thing, they take up enough space that it stops almost all the customers from draping their bodies across the counter like entrees he has no interest in consuming, and for another, Nancy's tongue is sharper than his scissors and she can cut off at the knees any woman who still doesn't get that he's not interested.

"I'll be the bitch, you be their fantasy," she says to him. "And I promise not to shatter all their illusions by telling them I still have to remind you to put on your shoes." She looks askance at his bare feet. "How old are you?"

He laughs and it almost feels like old times, good times—the days when you're high on nothing but living.

But mixed in with that is a feeling he carries around like a pinstripe suit—uncomfortable and unfamiliar. As he sits in the store, wanting to design but staring at paper and fabric like he has no idea what to do with it, he starts to understand what it is. Nerves. He can't remember feeling nervous about anything in his life except Astrid, and he's sure as hell never felt nervous about designing. Then he remembers Bianca Jagger's wedding suit. He'd been nervous about that and the result had been the same—empty pages in his sketchbook and fabric still raveled around the roll.

"You're not used to trying," Nancy says, interrupting him.

"What?"

"Trying," she repeats. "You don't do it. You just pick up a piece of silk jersey and it falls out of your hands in the shape of a dress. You're all about easy—but now you want to make an effort. You don't know how. Whereas Astrid, she'd sit right here and she'd draw and redraw. She was an outrageously talented artist. I used to say that, didn't I?" she calls to Fi, who nods and says, "She did."

"Whereas I'm a startlingly untalented lazy jerk?" he says brusquely, thinking now would be a good time to send them both back to the factory.

Fi and Nancy laugh. Then Nancy says, "Sit down and don't get on your high horse."

He sits on one of the stools—of course he does. He's never won an argument with Nancy.

"Your effort takes place in your head when you don't even know it's happening," she tells him. "You can't stand here and scribble or rummage about in silk jersey until you've seen what you're gonna make in your head. So you've gotta go do whatever it is that gets the pictures in that too-handsome head of yours. That's why her clothes are technically better than yours," she adds, cutting *him* off at the knees now, and traitorous Fi nods at this assessment of Astrid's designs.

Nancy just grins at his dejection. "Her clothes are like that moment at the start of the night when everything hasn't yet happened—but it might. When you're standing there with only one drink inside you and another in your hand and all you feel is possibility—when you still know where both your shoes are. Your clothes are that moment hours later when your mascara's smudged and your lipstick too, and morning's still far enough away that you can have another drink and make out with a stranger because none of it matters—yet. She's spirit, and you're danger. So quit being what you think a designer should be and just go be dangerous."

"Wow," he says, smiling now, "who knew the way to make clothes was to suppress all my better instincts and let my worse ones take over."

Now it's Fi's turn to harass him. "Nobody ever got dangerous by swimming down to the bottom of the cognac vat. That's how you get stupid. No need to go back there."

He takes the reprimand on the chin. He hadn't known even his staff had thought he was drinking too much all those months ago. "Okay, how about I go find some dangerous ideas instead of some dangerous habits," he says to them.

He goes for a walk, his feet taking him to Parsons. Once there, he turns in to the archives where he first met Astrid, stopping in front of the Claire McCardell dress Astrid had said would make her feel powerful. There's a danger in power, he thinks now. The people who have it see those who want it as dangerous. And those who don't have it see the people who do as the true threat. Danger isn't always wildness—it's when you're vulnerable and everyone knows it.

And he remembers how, just last month, the Equal Rights Amendment had finally passed through the Senate and how, as a man, he's never once felt the need to wear something particular in order to feel powerful. He remembers how wistful Astrid had sounded that day.

Nancy doesn't know what's hit her when he races back to the shop and twenty designs pour out of him in a way they haven't for months. She stares at the pictures and then at him and says, shaking her head, "Ladies and gentlemen, he's back."

* * *

When the collection is finally something he's proud to put his name to, when it feels easy and dangerous and complex all at once, he hires five Black models and five white. He has placards made for them to carry. He doesn't spend too much money. He sends out invitations to everyone. Even Astrid.

He eschews a daytime showing and holds his at midnight, as much for the way it suits his brand as for the way it gets everyone talking. It takes place in the old store, where white silk still billows from the walls like it has since Astrid told him to hang it there.

By eleven at night, the crowd is thicker than at the Cheetah and everyone's having just as good a time. In the chairs nearest the runway, his loyal clients, as well as current and former magazine editors, congregate: Diana Vreeland, Bianca Jagger. Alix St. Pierre is there with her husband, Anthony, who still greets Hawk with a nod and suspicion, even as Alix smiles up at him and says, "Do you think you'll forgive Hawk anytime this century?"

Hawk laughs—nothing can get him down tonight, not even the knowledge that Astrid won't come. She won't want tonight to be about her and him. But his smile wavers as he realizes—this is how it will be from now on. Astrid is back in New York but she'll avoid him and he'll avoid her and it'll be as goddamn wretched as when she left him.

But he'll also get to watch her flourish. It will have to be enough, for now.

On the stroke of midnight, a guitar riff plays. A drum breaks in. Someone in the front row whoops, someone in the back row takes a toot. He hopes it's too dark for his mom to see all the dope out there but, really, she's always been tolerant of just about anything. Then "Long Cool Woman in a Black Dress" blasts through the speakers and the models start to dance backstage.

He sends out Pat Cleveland in a long article that's either a dress or a jacket or both. It's made from black sequins and done up with just one button halfway between the navel and the breastbone. The dress holds in it a memory of the black jacket Astrid once wore with tiny green shorts. The press recognizes the motif and begin snapping their cameras. The crowd goes wild.

Pat's bearing a sign that reads, *In memory of Benji*. It's the only time Hawk feels his eyes sting. Because Benji should be there taking the official photos, rather than lying in a coffin after being killed in Vietnam six months ago.

The show ends with Harry Nilsson singing "Without You." It's billed as a tribute to Benji, but as the models crowd the catwalk, dragging Hawk into their midst, singing at the tops of their voices in that epic, intoxicated way that has everyone else joining in too, he knows he chose it for the one woman missing from the room tonight.

* * *

The second interview Astrid gives is to John Fairchild from *Women's Wear Daily*. It might have started out as a trade journal but now with its book and theater reviews, social pages and gossip columns, as well as exclusive fashion reporting, the magazine reaches a hell of a lot of influential consumers. And the whole trade reads it. While Alix's article has worked wonders with the women who buy clothes, Fairchild can also work wonders with her peers.

The morning he's coming in, she arrives at work wearing pants and a jacket with a shirt underneath. Her hair is pulled back in a tidy ponytail.

"Where did Astrid go?" Velvet says when she sees her.

"Haha."

"I'm serious," Velvet says. "The whole world wants to turn me into something I'm not. Don't let Fairchild do it to you."

But Astrid still takes Fairchild up to her office, rather than talking to him on the leopard-print sofa.

He looks so unthreatening. Hair graying. Teeth slightly bucked. Not especially tall. Jowly. A regular, middle-aged man. Why is she so scared of him? He wrote one article, one time, back when it might have seemed to those who didn't know her that she was inspiring Hawk in some way. And he's written one acerbic headline in the lead-up to her starting her business. This is her chance to show him his barbs are misplaced and that she has what it takes to land herself on the "In" side of his famous "In and Out" column.

"Where would you like to start?" she asks once they're seated.

"Why don't you just talk," he says. "I'll interject if I need to."

So she tells him about her vision for helping women build their wardrobes from separate items that can be mixed together, and showing them they don't need to divide their clothes into separate countries—formal, work, weekend—whose borders never touch.

He doesn't interject once. He doesn't even mention Hawk, which is good because Astrid can barely think about Hawk without needing to wrap her arms around her torso to protect her still-broken heart from the fresh punch of grief. He doesn't mention Mizza Bricard either. He just listens and he even takes notes. She asks him several times if he has any questions but he just says, "No. Keep going." He smiles when he says it and his smile looks sincere.

Hope rather than fear takes up residence in her chest.

At the end, he smiles that same smile. She stands to shake his hand, like two colleagues—equals maybe.

And that's when he says, "It was all very fascinating, dearie. Shame I already wrote my piece."

He drops two typewritten pages on her desk.

And she drops into her chair.

Podiums and Lamé in the Kitchen and the Office? is the headline. It's followed by the words:

Perhaps men of a certain type won't mind it when their secretaries turn up to work dressed in silver lamé sans panties but it might cause a few problems when Mommy bends over in the kitchen to pick up little Johnny's toys off the floor.

She wants to shout after him that he's an asshole with a chip on his shoulder. She wants to call Mizza. She wants to call Alix. She wants to sit in Velvet's office while Velvet hurls profanities Fairchild's way. But if she does any of that, then they'll know Astrid isn't as strong as she needs to be. What if they start to doubt her too?

If only a few people believe in you, you have to do everything you can to make sure they keep believing. Otherwise you might end up not believing in yourself.

It's taken so much guts and grit to get herself back to New York. She's refashioned her self-belief thread by thread, from that very first day in France sitting before the *Bayeux Tapestry*, not wanting to be the woman forgotten.

But Fairchild's just unpicked some of the threads. Her first sob is so loud that she picks up a handful of silk jersey and presses it to her face, smothering the pain no one can ever know about.

THIRTY-ONE

BLYTHE BRICARD

B lythe sits in one of two chairs Jake's placed at right angles around a side table. *You're too far away,* he used to say if they arrived at a restaurant to find two chairs on opposite sides of the table. Then he'd reposition the chairs the way they are now and slide his hand into hers.

There's a rattle on the landing and Jake appears with a trolley so laden with food it's impossible to imagine they're going to eat even half of it. "I took everything the chefs gave me," he says as he hauls it inside.

The first platter holds thinly sliced charcuterie, saucisson, duck rillettes, olives, pâté, cornichons, and toasted slices of baguette. Blythe's stomach flips with pleasure.

"And champagne." Jake produces a bottle and two glasses. "I don't think I've had too much brandy that I can't have a glass with you."

"I'm scared to ask how much brandy you've had," she says as she loads her plate.

"Probably too much," he admits, smiling.

He's wearing a crisp white shirt with the sleeves rolled up to his forearms and the trousers that match the jacket she'd seen him in the first day here—a blue that's lighter than navy and darker than sapphire, a color that makes his eyes look sexier than anything.

It's very seductive—the thought of eating charcuterie and drinking champagne with the man who's the only person in the world who makes her breath catch every time he so much as smiles at her. But...

"Jake," she says as he slips into the seat beside her. "I know you said you wanted to tell me some things and I'm hoping they're the same as the things I want to know, but if you don't feel like being interrogated," she says, offering a small smile to show she's only half-joking, "then maybe you should take this back to the kitchen."

He pushes his champagne glass to the side. And in that gesture she knows he's ready at last to talk about what went wrong.

"Okay." She takes a gulp of her champagne. "I need to know *why* you stopped being around. It's not like I wanted me and the kids to be your sole focus. I wanted you to start Blake Group and make it a success and... I'm really proud of you. You've done everything you ever wanted."

"Not everything," he says, resting his hand on the table near hers. "There are so many important things I fucked up along the way."

Blythe concentrates on the *jambon cru*. She can't let expressions of regret and physical proximity leave this undone. So she says, voice as level as she can make it, "For the last two years of our marriage, you were like this fleeting, ephemeral thing. After I asked for a divorce, you vanished completely. You saw the kids once a week to start with, always at my apartment, just dropping in like you were a visitor. Then it was every fortnight. Then once a month. That became two months. Then three months passed and there was the disastrous wine bar visit. I see you with them now and I know you love them. So how could you stand being apart from them for so long? I can't reconcile what you did with the man I married, the father I thought you'd be."

The charcuterie looks like raw flesh. She pushes it away.

"You're right," Jake says slowly, staring at the fire, the flames leaping into the mirror of his eyes. He stretches his legs out, one hand in his pocket, like he's trying to make his body comfortable even while his thoughts are discomfiting.

The mantel clock ticks off at least thirty loud seconds before Jake says, "When we said our wedding vows—*for better or worse*—I thought the worst was you in bed for a week with the flu and me bringing you Tylenol and orange juice. I didn't understand that marriages ended because of all the small and terrible things—I thought marriages ended because of one huge catastrophe, like death or infidelity. When you asked me for a divorce, all I could think was that you must have been having an affair. I guess I knew, deep down, that I hadn't been around. And you're so darned stunning—why wouldn't some guy have swooped in? So I thought you'd made the catastrophe happen. But now I get that every time I picked up the phone for hours instead of eating dinner with you, or when I didn't see the kids for days because I was always at work—those were the worst things. I made you feel like I didn't love you, and I made the kids feel like that too. And that... that was the true catastrophe."

He leans his elbows on the table, propping his chin on his hands. The flames flicker in his eyes again, turning the blue to gold and the contemplation to something harder, like apprehension.

"But that just explains my attitude after we split. It doesn't explain why I let things get so bad. Part of it was because..." A pause.

"I've hated hospitals, since..." Jake takes a healthy swallow of champagne. "Since every doctor told me I was going to be a *stuttering, dumb cripple* for the rest of my life—and I'm not making that up; those were the words they used. So every time Sebby was sick... I let you deal with it."

It's then that Blythe hears the slightest hitch, the characteristic lull that everyone at grad school joked was Jake's annihilation pause—when whoever he was trying to convince of something would surrender beneath the blue eyes and the silence. He'd always laughed, called it his secret weapon, but Blythe suddenly comprehends that the pause is a remnant of his stutter. That maybe Jake's obsession with exercise is a leftover from the rigorous regimen of a nine-year-old boy trying to retrain his brain to lift his foot without stumbling. That his dismissal of an intermittent bodily gingerness as "back pain" was his way of disguising the trace of a limp that bothers him when he's tired.

"That time I was away," he goes on, "and Sebby was in the hospital with pneumonia, Ed called me. If words could kill, I'd be a dead man. He told me he'd never been more disappointed in me in his life. And that he thought..."

Jake's eyes are resolute on the fire. "That he thought you'd leave me and I would deserve it. He was right. I did deserve it. It was the same day the receivers met me in Paris and told me they'd declare bankruptcy in three months unless I did something drastic. You gave up a lot of stuff so I could work on Blake Group—we put my dreams ahead of yours. But there I was, sitting in a tiny hotel room because I couldn't afford the one I'd told you I was staying in, hearing that my business was just about bankrupt, that my kid was in a place I was most scared of in all the world, and that the person I loved more than, more than..."

His words trail off. "I don't even know what to say there. I loved you more than anything is such a cop-out. And it isn't enough either. I loved you more than the word *love* can even accommodate. There isn't a word for what I felt for you. But you're right—I thought just having the feeling was enough. That all I had to do was adore you and nothing could go wrong."

He finally looks at her. There's no point trying to hide the fact she's weeping, silent tears trickling down her face at hearing once-longed-for words come too late.

He takes hold of her hand, clasping it painfully hard. "I'm so fucking sorry. Iris said she told you I flew all over the world trying to put the business back together so I could show you Blake Group as a perfect entity, one without stutters and limps and memory loss. I guess that's true. That's what I did the year after Sebby spent that week in the hospital. But there was a whole year before that where I was trying to do the same. To make it up to you for having to shelve your dreams. To show you I was worth your sacrifice. Every phone call I didn't take, every hour I didn't spend in the office, meant I wasn't doing my best to get the business up and running as fast as possible so that the woman who was the most creatively talented person in our year at grad school could put her talents to use.

"You said the other day that loving someone and showing them you love them are two different things. I thought I *was* showing you I loved you by working so damn hard. And there's the irony—I was terrified of failing and ruining your chance to make your dream real and that's exactly what I made happen. I couldn't tell you I was going under because it would have been like saying to you, *No, I'm taking your turn too.*"

There's so much raw pain in Jake's voice. And Blythe finally understands how hard he'd worked while they were married—but at all the wrong things. She swipes despairingly at her cheeks.

His next words are spoken in a voice so low she has to lean forward to hear. "When Ed told me about Sebby, I've never been so fucking scared in my life. Scared asthma could turn into encephalitis and Sebby would have to go through what I did. I would actually kill someone before I let that happen. The day I got back from Europe..."

He rubs his free hand over the back of his neck, jaw set tight. "All I wanted to do was hold you. But if I was alone with you, I'd have to tell you I'd ruined your dream. I said I needed to nap but I hid in our room calling investors, refinancing loans, selling businesses I should never have bought. I wanted to fix everything right then because you'd had the worst week of your life and I couldn't be the one who ripped whatever was left of your heart to shreds by telling you we had no money and your turn was never going to come."

It's obvious from his expression that the very idea of saying that to her was physically painful to him. It makes Blythe think more about Jake's intentions over those last few years of their marriage, rather than his actions. She offers him a gentle smile to show she understands that, despite appearances, his heart had been in the right place.

Eventually, he resumes. "Sebby was two when we separated, and three and a half when we divorced, so I'd visit the kids at your place because I didn't know what to do with a toddler and a preschooler— I hadn't spent enough time with them to know. And all the while I was remembering something you once said to me—that you knew I'd be the world's best dad. I know you were thinking of Hawk when you said it. I wanted to be that so much—the very best—for them and for you. But Eva would look at me like I was some kind of criminal and Sebby would pick up her vibe. They'd talk and it would all be about you. Sebby would cry for you. Eva would tell me about all the great things she did with you and how boring it was with me. Then she'd cry too."

Blythe winces. "I didn't know that." And she can almost guess what he's going to say next. If he wanted to be the world's best dad, then there was no way he'd force his kids to do something that made them so upset.

He shrugs. "I should have persevered. I know now that Eva was testing me, but I really thought they hated spending time with me. I didn't want to compel them to see me and have a shitty time. Then Sebby got croup one night and asthma another, and both times I freaked out that it was something bad and he might need the hospital, so I took him straight back to you. All those things meant I saw them less and less, and then I took them to a wine bar because I was so nervous I needed a drink. The first thing Sebby said when we got there was, 'Mummy's going out too. Maybe we'll see her.' All I could think was how ashamed I'd be if you walked in."

He finishes in a very low voice, "I didn't see them again because I knew I'd fucked up, and that I'd caused my own failure. Being a failure at everything connected to you, when I'd learned as a kid that failure meant being a *dumb, stuttering cripple*, was something I didn't want to face. So I was a coward instead."

He leans back in his chair and, with that action, their hands separate.

* * *

Would she ever tell anyone she was a coward, Blythe wonders as her fingertips play restlessly with the stem of her champagne glass. No—ironically, she'd be too scared to admit it. Which makes her search deeper inside herself too.

"I was jealous of you," she confesses, "from the day I went to that meeting with the investor who stared at my stomach. When my dream died..." She finishes her champagne. "I think I died a little too. Maybe some of my anger was about me, not you. No marriage ever ends because of what one person did."

"I think you're being overly generous," Jake says.

But her mind is pairing Jake's words to memories, and the past is starting to look achingly like a road not taken that they could have traveled together. It hurts, his confession, but with agonizing regret rather than anger.

"Would it be okay if we just eat?" she says, not sure she can handle any more emotion right now.

"I skipped dinner in favor of brandy, so I'm starving." Jake pulls a dish off the trolley, removes the lid and the smell of leek and potato galette is heavenly. "Don't let Sebby anywhere near this. I don't think it'll look as good in reverse."

She laughs. "Hand it over."

The next dish is cheesy, warm gougères and the last bowl is filled with Lyonnaise salad, which is just as well with all the pastry and cheese they're about to consume.

"There's dessert too," Jake says.

"I'll fall asleep by the fire, too full to move."

He smiles. "I'll make sure the kids look for you up here when they're ready to crawl into someone's bed in the morning."

The relief of Jake being familiar with the kids' routine makes Blythe smile too. And she realizes she's enjoying herself. That she has one hundred percent forgiven him.

"How was Mont St. Michel today?" she asks.

He mock-groans. "A hit for about the first half hour, then the fog blew in and we couldn't see a thing. Ed took Mom back and left me with a herd of kids, who I managed not to lose in spite of the fact that Hugh's kid literally wanted to walk on top of the ramparts and I caught Nick trying to order a brandy—which was actually a damn good idea, because it was freezing. I don't know whether learning to be an uncle *and* a dad in one week was such a great idea. Eva and Sebby are the perfect kids. Thanks to you." He raises his glass in her direction.

"I guess that's why you needed the brandy tonight."

"Nope. The brandy was an attempt to forget Cameron touching your back and then you going out to dinner with him in a dress that makes you look so gorgeous I can hardly concentrate on what I'm saying. Which is probably because of the brandy. And I should switch to water." He pours himself a large glass while Blythe methodically slices her galette rather than look at him.

"How about we don't talk about Cameron or even the kids," she says. "Tell me about Claire McCardell. I've been dying to know more."

Jake turns his chair a little more toward her, stretches his legs out again and tells her about that one colossal success and how it changed his life. "Which means I have no chance of going bankrupt again," he concludes. "I keep putting money into that account but you hardly spend any of it. You didn't get a single penny when I moved out and you're raising two kids and fitting in whatever work you can but, Blythe, that money is yours. I wish you'd spend it."

"I do," she says a little abruptly. "On school fees."

"I just opened a whole separate account for their school fees. So that in the unlikely event I do go under again, that at least is covered until they graduate high school."

There's no way she could ever put enough money into an account to cover years of school fees. Her shoulders sag. "I just..."

"Don't want anything from me," he finishes softly. "But if you're happy and working on your dream—which is a chance I still owe you—doesn't that make everything better for the kids too? I'm way too involved in the day-to-day management of Blake Group—everyone says so. If I leave my managers to it, I can pick up the kids from school twice a week so you can work for a whole day. I don't have a kid-friendly apartment right now, but I'll get one. Until then, how about I come over in the morning on those two days and organize breakfast, get them to school?"

Blythe wants to say yes. But... "If people see you near me, won't there just be more articles about me being as fickle as Astrid? I can't afford that kind of attention."

"You're not one misstep away from being Astrid. I've known you for thirteen years and you've always been you. Perfectly you. Let the world see that, Blythe."

He offers her a smile that makes not just her breath catch, but her insides too.

Neither speaks, but it isn't silent in the room. The fire is a hot pulse in the background. And Jake's eyes blaze as they sweep over her jawline and down to her throat, where they pause before traveling lower, to the V of her neckline.

"You said there was dessert," she says a little shakily.

"Dessert," he repeats, downing his water. "Yes."

He places champagne-soaked pears and chocolate soufflé on the table and all Blythe can think of is the taste of Jake's skin on her tongue. Thankfully, the door opens and Joy and Ed enter, laughing, with brandies in hand.

"That looks amazing," Joy gasps when she sees the soufflé. "But we should leave them alone, shouldn't we," she whispers to Ed.

"To kill one another? Nope. Besides, I'm hungry." He sits in one of the chaises.

Blythe is so grateful for the chance to redirect her undisciplined mind that she jumps up from the table.

"Oh, that dress," Joy says. "Did you know I told Ed the night we first met you that if Jake didn't marry you, I would?" She subsides into a chair with a plate of soufflé, the brandy obviously doing some of the talking for her.

Ed grins. "Given we had five kids under the age of ten at the time, I wasn't sure whether to be angry or relieved."

Blythe laughs as she and Jake make their way to a sofa. It's small and antique and means her thigh is pressed against Jake's but she doesn't even think about pulling away. In response, he drapes his arm along the back of the sofa, fingertips grazing her neck. "Here," he murmurs, passing her a champagne coupe.

She knows her pupils must be huge, her skin flushed. It's almost unbearable that only their thighs are touching.

"Tell me what you guys have been doing, apart from trying to find the bottom of the brandy bottle," she says to Ed and Joy, hoping her voice sounds normal.

Joy laughs. "Ed found it in a cupboard and said it was very expensive and it's definitely delicious, so we drank it."

"You stole their brandy?" Blythe asks, laughing too.

"They owe us at least that," Ed says darkly. "While you were at dinner, you missed the latest row between them and Jake over a huge puddle of water the cleaners left on the floor that Mom almost slipped in."

"It was very impressive," Joy adds. "It reminded me of what happened the day after Jake introduced Blythe to us."

Jake and Blythe share a glance and quickly look away. There are some things about the night she met the Blacks that are best not recalled in company.

"Yes!" Ed says, laughing. "You thought you were bringing Blythe to dinner to meet just Mom and Dad but Mom invited all of us without telling you. You were actually very restrained. You let Blythe eat her dinner and then came back in the morning and gave Mom a roasting like I'd never heard you give her before. Joy and I were staying there for the weekend and we heard everything."

"Because I wanted Blythe to stick around," Jake says, smiling a little. "Subjecting her to the interrogations of my entire family wasn't something I thought would help."

"I just remembered!" Joy breaks in, having now drained her glass. "At dinner that night, you guys couldn't take your eyes off each other and…" She giggles. "I whispered to Ed when you left that you were probably about to have sex in the elevator."

Blythe's hands cover her flamingly red face and Ed cracks up.

"We do not need to go there," Jake says, eyeballing his brother.

"I need to go to bed, don't I?" Joy says to Ed, words slurred with brandy indulgence.

"Maybe," Ed says, pulling her up from the sofa and kissing her.

"Let's take the elevator," she says to him with a wicked grin.

* * *

As soon as Joy and Ed leave, Blythe stands. It's one thing sitting beside Jake on a sofa with other people around but it's another thing entirely when they're alone. She makes her way over to the fireplace, dizzy and hot from everything except the flames.

She hears him stand too, the chink of his glass as he sets it down.

Feels the slight stirring of air as he takes slow steps toward her, hears the uneven sound of his breath, the scent of cloves and ambergris teasing her nostrils the same way his fingertips had just sent ripples cascading over her skin.

Her shoulders are so tense from holding herself still that she can feel the strain all the way up in her jaw.

Then Jake is right behind her, only the thinness of her dress separating them, and she almost can't stop the carnal moan that sits in her throat from escaping. She wraps one hand around the edge of the mantelpiece.

And then she feels it. The exquisite brush of his lips against her neck. Her head tips to the side, exposing the entire length of her neck, and she hears the sharp inhale of his breath in response, the achingly gentle drift of his mouth a little lower.

"I love you, Blythe," he whispers. "Sweet dreams."

Then he's gone and she knows her dreams will be anything but sweet.

THIRTY-TWO

ASTRID BRICARD AND HAWK JONES

1972 is the year of Astrid and Hawk. Nobody in Manhattan can talk about anyone else's clothes. Hawk's so damn happy—but he's also furious. He knows Fairchild's a shit-stirrer who loves to anoint winners and losers. But still... The week after Hawk failed to accept the check from Candace, her name appeared in Fairchild's "In and Out" column in the "Out" list, and he heard she was demoted from her corporate position to assistant designer for Halston. And the month after *Vogue*, *Cosmo* and *Harper's Bazaar* have covers featuring MIZZA, he sees on the "In and Out" list that Fairchild has listed only two items: *In: Hawk Jones. Out: Astrid Bricard.*

He has to call Alix because otherwise he'll call Fairchild and make things worse.

"They call her a dressmaker whereas Oscar de la Renta's a 'designer.' And Halston's 'at the top of the fashion showbiz heap.' Fairchild might grudgingly admit that designing for working women is as profitable as hell, but last week he said it made for creatively mundane clothes. Do you know how much I wanted every woman in Manhattan to march into Fairchild's office and strangle him with their 'workaday trousers'? And you know how lazy newspaper journalists are and how everyone loves a salacious bit of gossip. His shit gets picked up by them and republished like it's truth."

"My advice," Alix says crisply, "is to not read *Women's Wear Daily*. Working women—God, I hate that term—see Astrid as a godsend. The consumer magazines love her. She herself will be on the cover of *Vogue* next month. And her business is spectacularly profitable. In fact, she's making more money than you are."

He's about to rant into the phone again, say that's the kind of news Fairchild should be printing, but then he laughs. "Your honesty is always so good for my soul, Alix."

She laughs too. "If you want someone to heap praise upon you, go to a nightclub. My job is—"

"To keep me in business." He finishes the oft-repeated sentence for her, then sits down in the chair in his new office, which has no mirrors or conversation pits, and which is in the building next to the original store. His sigh echoes loudly.

"Hawk." Alix says his name in a way that makes dread curl in his stomach. *Astrid's getting married. Astrid hates you.* He hears all the rumors about who she's dating—every eligible bachelor in the darn city, and he hopes those reports are as baseless as the gossip about his liaisons with everyone from Lauren Hutton to Linda Ronstadt.

"Are you ever going to talk to her?" Alix asks.

Even though he and Astrid are invited to all the same parties, they never meet. Somehow, if he's planning to arrive late, she goes early and leaves before he gets there. Or if he goes to one party early because there's another to fit in that night, he'll find she's done the opposite. Their paths don't cross, ever.

The press is fascinated. They rehash Hawk and Astrid's relationship endlessly, reprint old photographs of the two of them, especially the ones from the Cheetah—her in the silver dress, or him kissing her bare stomach while she's sitting on the bar. He can still taste her skin on his lips.

None of it hurts his business—his stores are busier than ever. But his soul—man, that's taken a beating.

"Yes," he says to Alix at last. "I just don't know when."

The confrontation is inevitable, and he braces himself for it every day of his life.

* * *

Astrid's next collection is called "Seven Easy Pieces" and it is, quite literally, just seven pieces. But from those seven pieces, more than twenty outfits—some for the office, some to dance in, some to run the kids to school in—can be made. It's such a shock for everyone—the idea of mixing and matching a handful of separates. It's a concept that years of bouclé suits and shift dresses haven't prepared anyone for. So Astrid starts running workshops in the store in the evenings to help women understand and to—she says laughingly to Velvet—"pry their matching skirts and jackets from their fingertips."

Her clients lounge on the leopard-print sofa drinking champagne and saying things like, "Your clothes are the best thing that's happened to me since the pill." Or, "There's a rule in our office—no pants for women. But I wore your navy pants to work yesterday. What were they going to do? Tell me to take them off and walk around in my panties?"

Astrid goes home smiling every night, and smiles still more when she sees the windows of the downtown department stores displaying an array of items labeled *Six Easy Combinations, Eight Pieces that Go Together* or even *Seven Pieces, Twenty Outfits!*

It's a compliment—being copied is validation she's doing the right thing, especially when each month in all the magazines now there are features about how to wear your bathing suit to a nightclub or your lingerie into the stalwart restaurants that still won't let women in wearing pants.

I would never have done this two years ago, she writes to Mizza. *Until I worked with Dior's and Givenchy's clients, I didn't understand exactly what a woman's day involved and how restrictive the clothes were that they thought they had to wear.*

It's almost like saying, *I'm glad I left Hawk*. Which is both true and heartbreakingly false.

Mizza's reply is, *You need to win an award. That will change things forever and make the trade love you as much as consumers do. When Tian won the Fashion Oscar in 1947, it gave the House of Christian Dior a gravitas it was difficult to argue with.*

She shows Velvet the letter.

"That woman is probably right," Velvet says. "And it's not too late for this year. They moved the Cotys to November, remember? A Coty Award would stop Fairchild writing this shit." She glares at John Fairchild's latest article, labeling the new collection SEVEN LOUSY PIECES.

Astrid knows she should probably quail. But she already tried that. She ran away to Paris, for God's sake. So she grins. "Let's raise some hell."

She calls in not-quite-discovered photographer Deborah Turbeville and poses with her hair pulled back, one hand on her hip, her other arm alongside her face. It's everything she wants it to be—strong and very sexy. In the photo, she doesn't look afraid. She also has Deborah shoot her in a blazer she's made into a mini dress, which thus evades both Fairchild's and Manhattan restaurants' dislike of women in pants. She makes hers very, very short—she'll make the ones she sells in the store a half inch longer—but if she's going to provoke, she might as well dress as provocation.

She has both photographs enlarged and hung in every window of her shop, alongside the words—*If this is what lousy looks like, then call me a louse...*

It turns out half the women in Manhattan are louses too because the shop is full that day, and the next. The blazer mini dress sells out in two days. The Turbeville image of Astrid wearing it is reproduced in newspapers everywhere. She knows Fairchild will be even more brutal to her now and she armors herself in a scarlet tank dress and pretends not to care.

Still, she decides to include a couple of "Trafalgars" in her next collection, a term Mizza told her Dior coined for the showstopping gowns destined for a thousand photographs and very few actual buyers—gowns that dreams, not money, are made of. Trafalgars are the kind of thing that will win her an award, even if her customers might only wear them when the moon is in the seventh house.

She shows Velvet the first sketch. She's drawn a fabric that might not even exist—a metallic, argent blue, like silver flirting with a Norman sea. The dress is totally Astrid—almost unstructured, not black and white, elegantly, sensually beautiful.

Velvet sighs over it. "You don't need me to tell you it's fucking sensational. But you do need me to tell you it'll be expensive."

"But I've called it the Fairchild," Astrid says, grinning. "So I don't really care if it doesn't make me any money."

Velvet tries to be disapproving of the extravagance but she starts to giggle. "Oh, Jesus, we are in trouble."

Astrid wears the Fairchild to the next party she attends. Across the room, she sees Mick Jagger leaning against the bar. He sees her at the same time and she gives him a smile and a shrug. She knows—and he knows—that if he crosses the room to her right now, their photograph will be the only thing anyone talks about tomorrow. If she's going to be publicity fodder, she might as well flavor it with a dash of spice. And Mick is never averse to attention.

Astrid wearing the Fairchild while Mick Jagger kisses her cheek is on the front page of the *New York Times*. Enid Nemy, the fashion writer, calls both the dress and Astrid spectacular. The headline reads: A WOMAN REINVENTING THE SILVER DRESS—AND HERSELF.

Astrid and Velvet go out for dinner to the old Corner Bistro, where Astrid once worked, and they drink two bottles of champagne and laugh like the young, carefree women they could be if only the world cut them some slack. Which maybe it's just started to do, for Astrid at any rate. She still has to hail Velvet's cab for her at the end of the night.

The Fairchild makes the cover of *Vogue* too. Lauren Hutton buys it for her twenty-ninth birthday party. And the best insult Fairchild can come up with is to call Astrid "confused."

Astrid hangs the picture of her and Mick Jagger in the window along with the caption: *If This Is What Confused Looks Like, Then Let Me Be All at Sea.*

After that, two whole issues of *Women's Wear Daily* are published without a single mention of Astrid.

"Do you think he's retreating?" she asks Velvet hopefully. *Do you think I'm winning?* is what she means.

Velvet gives a half shrug. "He's starting to look petty. The *New York Times* says the whole city is happily drowning in MIZZA's sea, and the *New Yorker* says you're one of the twenty most influential people in the city—not just people in fashion, Astrid, but people, period. You, the girl I went to college with."

Astrid grins. That praise isn't an award, but it's close. She crosses to the window of her office and looks down at the city she apparently holds some sway over, which is a thought so outta sight she can barely get her mind to grasp it.

Then Velvet says, "But is he just waiting to pounce?"

There's always that *but*. And the one person Astrid wants to pour out her heart to is the one person she can't go near.

Will she ever speak to Hawk again?

Down below, the city looks just the same as it did back in 1971 when she left it behind. Leaving broke her heart, but eventually repaired her soul. She can't do anything to damage it, not now.

On the sidewalk, she can see women entering her flagship store—one of dozens all over the country—with smiles on their faces. She can see them exiting with shopping bags and heads held high. But what she can't see is a time when she'll be mended so completely that she can withstand having her name paired with Hawk's again.

In quiet moments awake at night, she remembers the taste of the hot chocolate he'd make for her in the evenings, the way he'd hold the cup so her fingers would brush against his when she took it, remembers how he'd exhale at that feather-stroke of skin on skin.

Surely there'll be a future when that love becomes something more enduring than their only legacy now—a silver lamé dress.

THIRTY-THREE

BLYTHE BRICARD

Blythe's dreams would be anything but sweet if only she could get to sleep. But Jake occupies her every thought. Sometimes she thinks she imagined him saying *I love you*. Then she recalls the heat of his lips against her neck.

Jake's well and truly searched his soul. He's told her how he feels about her. And rather than making her turn around in the library and respond to his declaration, he'd left it with her so she could decide what to do.

She rolls onto her side, looks at the empty space in the bed where his body might be if she just texted him right now.

But what her body needs is different from what her heart wants. She should see how both feel in the morning without champagne and blazing fires. The sensible thing to do with sleeplessness is work, so she throws on a sweater and searches for her iPad.

She finds it on top of Astrid's portfolio. And it's only then, at three o'clock in the morning, that she realizes she'd been so caught up in Velvet's fury the day she received the portfolio that she hadn't properly considered two very obvious questions. Who sent it to her? And why send it without a note?

And then the same thought she'd had when Remy told her about the portfolio—who else but Astrid would have Astrid's portfolio?

But that would mean Astrid is sending things to Blythe.

Now her heart is pounding. She's being ridiculous.

What if the next thing that arrives for Blythe isn't a parcel, but her mother?

* * *

Wishes and fears that arrive in the dark are the most unsettling of all and the hardest to ignore. They're large and terrifying and you have to close your eyes against them or drown. Blythe eventually drifts off into an uneasy sleep, rousing when her phone buzzes.

Blythe, I know this is last minute but can you come to Paris today? I'm ready to back you, and I've found another potential investor. But you need to meet them and agree because you kind of know them. I don't want to say too much in case it puts you off, but please come. Marcelline.

The phrases *I'm ready to back you* and *another potential investor* make Blythe beam. But the rest of the text is so cryptic Blythe isn't sure whether to be trepidatious or excited. *You kind of know them.* What does that mean?

In the car, she lets all her ridiculous early-morning fears about Astrid fade with the sunlight and fortifies herself with Joni Mitchell albums while she drives.

Marcelline greets her with kisses on the cheeks and dives right in.

"There's one thing the proposal you sent me doesn't address. How you're going to show a one-off on a runway, a one-off that's made from delicate secondhand fabric, and then make sure that same one-off is in good enough condition to sell to a client. Sure, some things will survive being tugged on and off by dressers at a fashion show, but some won't. And don't tell me you're not going to do any shows—MIZZA's a brand that *demands* a show."

This is why Blythe's always admired Marcelline. She cuts straight to the core of the problem and harries you until you clean up the mess.

"That's the one last thing I need to figure out," Blythe confesses.

"Dammit, Blythe. I was going to give you a check. But now I can't. You need to figure this out."

"I know," Blythe says, sitting as upright as a mannequin, too scared to slouch. "If you'd seen how far away from a proposal I was just a week ago, you'd know I don't need much time to come up with something good. I'm just one all-powerful brainwave away from the answer."

"Then go back to that chateau and, I don't know—talk to Jake," Marcelline says. "You guys always used to come up with the best ideas when you were assigned to a group together. And I'll think about it too. Because you've fired me up with the idea of investing in women-led fashion businesses and I don't want anything dousing that spark."

At the same moment, another woman enters the room. Marcelline stands and says, "This is your other potential investor. We met at a women-in-fashion thing in Paris a few years back and we've kept in touch. She's been working in Paris since 1973, and in New York before that. She saw the article about Nathaniel and got in touch because she knew we were friends. Her name is Candace Winters."

Candace Winters. Blythe stares. She knows that name. Where from?

Then Candace says, "I'm *that* Candace. The one whose blood was on Astrid's dress."

THIRTY-FOUR

ASTRID BRICARD AND HAWK JONES

W hat's Fairchild done now?" Astrid asks on a morning in October when Alix arrives at her office unannounced. She tries to keep her voice light, but even she can hear the fear.

She doesn't know what else she can do, how many more magazine covers she has to be on, how much more money her business can make, what other outlandish ideas she can come up with before he'll leave her alone to be just a great goddamn fashion designer. Before he'll leave a space where she can go and see Hawk and not have it mean anything more than a man and a woman trying to find their way back to one another.

She tells herself to cool it. At the end of the day, it's just clothes. Nobody will live or die by any of this.

But Alix starts to cry.

Astrid stares at her, horrified. *What if she just ran away*, she thinks despairingly. Then she'd never have to find out whatever Alix can't bring herself to say.

"I'm sorry," Alix manages at last. "I just...God, I don't think I've cried like this since my wedding day." Her hands grip the chair arms. "*Élan* is publishing the list of Coty Award nominees next week. I'm not supposed to tell anyone, but, Astrid..." A smile breaks through. "You're on the list."

"What?" The word is so thin, a waft of chiffon.

"You won the battle," Alix says, crossing to Astrid, sinking down beside her and squeezing her hand. "You have a Coty Award nomination. You did it."

"Oh my God. Oh my *God*." She can't stop saying it. Can't stop cry-laughing. Almost can't find a way to believe it, even though Alix would never lie.

Champagne might make it real, so she takes out a bottle, fills two glasses so high that bubbles spill onto the table—as much from the excess as her shaking hand. She says it aloud. "I have a Coty Award nomination!" And now she's spinning, dancing like she did one night on a podium at the Cheetah.

"All I need is to win." Because that will be enough. Then she'll know that she is, at last, just a great goddamn fashion designer.

"You will." But then Alix's smile vanishes and she puts down her glass. "Hawk's been nominated too, Astrid."

Her body stills, euphoria gone. She's competing against Hawk. Is it possible to beat him? And what would it mean if she did?

There's only one thing she knows for sure—there's no way to avoid being in the same room as him at the awards ceremony. Which means it's time for them to face one another at last.

* * *

Astrid waits on the stoop of the building next door to Hawk's new apartment at seven o'clock on the morning the nominations are announced, having no idea what Hawk's habits are now. When they were together, they were never out of bed this early. She'd wake to feel his lips sweeping over her breastbone, her eyes would catch in his and then…Even the memory is searing and she has to close her eyes against it. Which means her only warning is the voice saying, "Astrid?"

Her eyes fly open.

How could he be even more handsome? The confidence she'd always admired simmers more quietly now, ripened. He's filled out too, but with muscle. His jaw is still stubbled the way it was when she first met him—it's something of a trademark now, one that magazines, and women especially, seem to love. A gray cashmere sweater ripples over his chest like her hands want to. He's like an after-midnight tuxedo—the formality long gone, leaving behind a much sexier kind of style.

She clasps her palms together to stop herself from reaching out. "Hi," she says.

"Hi," he replies, very softly. "You look…" He falters, suddenly and delightfully shy. "I was probably going to say something inappropriate."

The wry smile at the end is the most irresistible thing in the world. If she stands up right now, she'll be too close to him to bear it.

She speaks instead. "We'll both be at the Cotys so…I thought it'd be better to have our first meeting without cameras around."

"The cameras won't agree with you." The frustration in his voice tells her he's as exasperated as she is by the scrutiny they attract, even apart. "Come upstairs," he says, stepping back, which means that when she stands, there's enough space between them.

Inside his apartment, she spins slowly around. One large space, whitewashed. But there's still one wall of amber sunset. "It's like the grown-up version of the old place," she says, a smile touching her lips. Then she sees the old leather sofa. "You kept it?"

"I love that thing. No way I was leaving it behind."

She collapses onto it and her eyes close as the scent of the leather sends a thousand memories swirling through her—finding it in a thrift shop and knowing it would be perfect, nights spent curled up beside him, talking and making love.

Her eyes snap open. This is harder than she'd thought.

Hawk is watching her, the expression on his face hard to read. "Champagne?" he asks. "I know it's early, so I'll make it a mimosa if it makes you feel better."

She laughs. "Why strip something of its essence? Straight up, please."

He carries two glasses over, hesitating when he reaches the sofa as if he's deciding where to sit, turning from his initial impulse to sit beside her. He sets her glass down and takes the curved velvet armchair opposite.

They raise their glasses.

"John Fairchild is a jerk," Hawk says fiercely.

"I never thought coming back would be easy."

"But they don't have to make it so fucking hard."

His vehemence makes Astrid's words tumble out. "Do you think we can do it? Talk like acquaintances at the Cotys in a way that means there'll be no breathless reportage, or photos that show something that isn't true?"

He grimaces, stares down at his glass. "Something happens when you and I are in a room, Astrid. I don't know…Maybe I'm an arrogant jerk, but I don't think I'm the only one who feels it. I'm just glad I figured it out here first."

"You're not an arrogant jerk." It's the closest she can come to saying, *I feel it too. But I can't let myself, not yet.* Because she still doesn't know the answer to—*But when?*

She stands. "Thanks for the champagne. And good luck."

"You'll win," he says suddenly. "MIZZA is like nothing the world has ever seen. It's easy to make people gasp over an evening dress. It's almost impossible to make them do the same over an outfit a woman wears to an office every day. But you made them gasp."

She'd wanted to leave without crying. That's impossible now.

She presses a hand to her cheek, catches the tear. When she reaches the door, she looks back at him. Gray cashmere sweater, stubble, jeans.

One elbow resting on his knee. Eyes that match his sweater—soft, smoky, seductive.

It's like the grown-up version of the old place, she'd said when she stepped into the apartment. Now, looking at Hawk, she thinks, *It's the grown-up version of you.*

"Were we just too young?" she asks suddenly, the sound of grief caught in her words.

"I don't know," Hawk says quietly. "I don't know."

* * *

Astrid enters the Alice Tully Hall on the night of the awards ceremony with Velvet on one side and Alix on the other. Her eyes immediately find Hawk's. He's wearing a tuxedo and she just about dies. She's never seen him in a tuxedo before, which is a good thing—otherwise they'd never have made it out of bed.

Velvet rouses her with a well-placed elbow. "If you don't want that expression caught on a camera, don't wear it."

Astrid rearranges her face. Hawk whips his head away.

"You gonna tell me what happened when you saw him?" is Velvet's next question and Alix's attention fixes on Astrid too.

"Nothing and everything," Astrid tells them.

"That bad, huh?" Velvet sympathizes. "Then you go win a Coty and I'll find a way to stick it up John Fairchild's ass."

Alix grins and Astrid convulses into laughter.

Astrid's parents, James and Beth, have come in response to Astrid's invitation and they embrace her and tell her she's done well. Beth's actually wearing a MIZZA dress, and she twirls for Astrid with a smile on her face.

"Wow," is all Astrid can say. "You look ... wow."

"And you look beautiful, sweetheart," her dad tells her and this time, unlike when she turned up on his doorstep after her first *Life* cover, she's the one pushing him away because the sentiment will have mascara running all down her face. She squeezes his hand though and knows he gets it.

After dinner, when the minor awards have been presented and it's time for the big announcement, Velvet makes sure to whisper, "Remember John Fairchild's ass," the moment the envelope is opened so that, no matter what happens, Astrid will be caught on camera smiling.

It takes so long for that small piece of paper to be extracted, for the presenter to say, "Well, folks, it's a Coty first. We have joint winners."

A drawn-out pause. Astrid's nerves feel like rusted zipper teeth being pried apart.

"Give it up for Hawk Jones!" the announcer roars. Then he adds, "And Astrid Bricard!"

Did he just say her name?

Velvet and Alix leap on her, squashing her almost too tight to breathe, and Astrid knows for sure. She just won a Coty Award.

Far out.

"I'm going to cry," she whispers to Alix who says firmly, "You are going to beam with pride. You are going to walk up there knowing you've triumphed."

Velvet whoops, and the sound—proud, euphoric—makes the tears vanish. She's done it. Surmounted the obstacle of her heritage and her relationship with Hawk. And it's not just Velvet and Alix who are cheering—Beth and James are too, looking overjoyed for this child they mightn't have adopted if they'd known how much trouble she was going to be. The rest of the room is applauding too.

Astrid wishes suddenly and achingly that Mizza hadn't been too ill to come.

Only as she walks toward the stage does a flicker of doubt intrude. It's a shrewd move. Hawk winning would have been newswor-thy. Astrid winning would have been newsworthy for different reasons.

But Hawk and Astrid winning together will ensure a publicity maelstrom. Is that the only reason she won?

Then she laughs. She just got what she wanted and she's still questioning herself. No more. Tonight she's going to be the Astrid who danced with abandon on a podium, expecting only good things.

Hawk steps in beside her and they stare at one another. There are so many things she wants to say, things she doesn't want anyone else to hear. She slips her hand into his, hoping he can decipher her thoughts in her touch, and he holds on tightly as if he can.

They cross the stage hand in hand. The flashbulbs are like the midday sun.

They make their acceptance speeches. They don't let go of the other, not until it's time to leave the stage. At the bottom of the steps, he whispers in her ear, "I'm so fucking happy for you."

The sudden separation of her skin from his as they each walk away is excruciating.

For the rest of the night, she and Hawk avoid one another. His it-girl models—Pat Cleveland, Marisa Berenson—keep him busy on one side of the dance floor, while Astrid dances with Velvet, with Graham, who returned from Vietnam a few months ago and now teaches sewing as therapy for returned vets, with the crowd from *Vogue*, spinning beneath the strobe lights. She beams at Alix and says, "Maybe it doesn't take centuries to change things after all."

Alix's answering smile falls away as John Fairchild takes the stage. The music stops. The crowd quiets. Alix takes her hand.

"Eleanor Lambert was going to make this announcement," Fairchild says, referring to the PR doyenne who's done more for fashion over her lifetime than almost anyone. "But she's ill, so I was asked to step in."

Is it Astrid's imagination or is he looking at her?

Her hand twitches, smoothing down her dress, checking for rucks, a missing button, something for Fairchild to laugh at. All the essentials are covered. She hasn't made a single misstep all night.

You need to win an award, Mizza told her. So why does she still feel like a schoolgirl kneeling on the ground having her skirt length measured?

"What is it?" she whispers to Alix.

Velvet steps in on her other side and hisses, "Sons of bitches. I just heard they're having a shindig at the Palace of Versailles. The French versus the Americans. They're billing it as a battle of the American designers versus the French couturiers for fashion supremacy. Bohan from Dior, Givenchy, Pierre Cardin, Yves Saint Laurent and Emanuel Ungaro on the French side. The five Americans are all men too. Like a woman never made anything worth a damn."

In the pit of Astrid's stomach is a painful gnawing. *There has never been another Chanel.* What if there never is?

"Who's representing America?" she asks.

On stage, John Fairchild has just given a more honey-tongued summary and now he says, "The men who'll do battle for America to win the global fashion crown are..."

Everyone's attention is focused on Fairchild. Because this is monumental. After decades of scrapping at the heels of the French and always being considered inferior, America has been invited to share the stage with the most famous designers in the world, to prove that French couture isn't the only way to make beautiful clothes.

"Bill Blass," Fairchild shouts to stupendous applause. Blass looks about as smug as he did when he called Astrid a muse and threw her out of his office.

"Halston," Fairchild goes on. "Oscar de la Renta. Stephen Burrows. And..."

There's a dramatic pause. And Astrid knows what he's about to say because he's looking right at her.

"Hawk Jones."

An eruption of cheers. Hawk's models go berserk, flinging their arms around him. In their midst he looks shocked, surprised—elated.

She catches his eye and mouths, *Congratulations.*

Once she's done that, she can turn away and let it sink unsparingly in—five men have essentially just been named the best designers in the United States of America.

All Astrid can do right now in front of an audience is smile and press a hand to her chest, where she can feel a grinding she knows is jealousy. A successful business and a Coty Award, neither of which she had a year ago, are still not enough.

I've been waiting very impatiently for years for a woman to rise up, Alix had once said.

We try, Astrid thinks as she slips out and goes home to an empty apartment. *We try so damn hard,* she writes in a letter to Mizza, ink stained with tears.

THIRTY-FIVE

BLYTHE BRICARD

T hat," Candace says, opening her phone and pointing to the photograph of Blythe raising her finger at the world, "is what I wanted to do to Halston and everyone else at Versailles in 1973. And it's what I've wanted to do to every man who's come along since."

"You want revenge?" Blythe asks, bewildered. On whom? Her? She shoots a quick glance at Marcelline, who looks worried too.

Candace shakes her head adamantly. "No. What I want is for every woman who comes after Astrid to never have to read a McKinsey report saying that only fourteen percent of major fashion brands have a female executive in charge, that only five percent of Fortune 500 clothing companies have female CEOs. And I never want to read another hand-wringing report about a female designer taking over from a man at a famous fashion house that wonders how she'll live up to the great genius who went before her."

"Wha..." is Blythe's inarticulate reply.

"I was the last person to see Astrid at Versailles that day, but I was definitely not the other woman in Hawk's life—Hawk barely thought of me, let alone had feelings for me. You want to know why there are hardly any photos of the grand battle at Versailles? Why it's an event that's nearly faded from history? The Americans beat the French. It should be the center of every book about late-twentieth-century

American fashion. But it isn't. Because everyone carries the shame of what happened there. Including me. I let Astrid walk away from me and I will regret that for the rest of my life."

"Jesus Christ."

Blythe jumps at Marcelline's exclamation. Her hands are on her hips, eyes glowering. "Nathaniel Champlain just made an announcement that makes me want to stick a stiletto through his heart." She holds out her phone.

And Blythe sees the headline NATHANIEL CHAMPLAIN SEEKS TO SECURE RIGHTS TO MIZZA NAME.

"Can he do that?" Blythe tries desperately to recall what she learned of trademark law at grad school. Who owns the MIZZA trademark? Blythe? Astrid? No one? Can Nathaniel steal it from her?

This is a disaster. Blythe is one woman. Nathaniel owns a conglomerate with tons of cash. He'll win this fight if it goes anywhere near a court of law. And his opening gambit is to put it out there in the media, trying to frighten her into avoiding a legal battle, hoping she'll hand over a name he views as profit potential.

But MIZZA isn't just a name—it's leopard print. Lamé. Love. Loss. Legacy. Legend. It's a name Blythe never wanted for most of her life, but it's a name she'll do just about anything now to hold on to.

* * *

On the way back to Montsoreau, Blythe lets rage fill every heartbeat as she plans her counterattack. She needs to talk to Jake. He's resurrected zombie brands and will know the law. But there are ways beyond the legal to stake her claim to her family name.

She bypasses the main house and goes straight to the theater, finds the silver dress Iris gave her, carries it over to Astrid's Parsons portfolio, and turns to the page where the dress is drawn in liquid, glittering detail. It could only have been drawn by someone who knew not just the lamé, but how the tricot lining underneath would let the dress slide over the hips, the exact places where the fabric had been stiffened to hang just right.

Whoever sent her this portfolio wanted Blythe to see for herself that Astrid has a creator's claim on this dress. And for a split second, a vision settles onto the paper in front of her: Hawk, Astrid and Blythe. Not who they are now, but the ghostlike vision of the family they might have been, but for everything that happened.

People who say history can't be rewritten have never made acquaintance with the media. Online, in a newspaper—histories are rewritten all the time. Google Marilyn Monroe and the words you'll see are *dead, tragic, president, affair.* She's the beautiful dead girl who could make a man pitch a tent in his pants. Not an actress who won awards for her craft. And so, with a silver dress and a phone, Blythe's ready to do a little redrafting.

* * *

She has to wait a few hours because it's Iris's big party, which is being held in two parts—first a dinner with all the children, followed by a wild night where Iris says the fun will really start. It's after the first party and before the second—once Eva and Sebby are ensconced upstairs in Georgia's room, where they're going to watch movies and fall asleep until Blythe takes them back down to their room—that Blythe and Coco return to the theater and Blythe puts on the silver dress.

If Blythe stamps her ownership all over MIZZA, then Nathaniel will have more of a mess to deal with than he anticipates and a much harder time divorcing MIZZA from the Bricards.

"I'm going to sit on this," she says to Coco, pointing to a round table that references the podium her mother danced on.

She sits with her legs crossed and dangling over the edge. She looks straight at the camera—not veiled, not in profile, not with her back turned. Just Blythe, with a hint of a smile on her lips and a look in her eyes that's almost reckless—as if she doesn't care anymore that her name will always come before her. And she doesn't care, because she's going to make that name have a new meaning. Not Mizza Bricard's granddaughter. Not Astrid Bricard's daughter. Not Hawk Jones's daughter either.

She opens her brand-new Instagram account and explains to the world what she's doing with MIZZA, telling her story, her way. She posts the picture, then turns her phone off. This is Iris's night. She'll attend to the media chaos tomorrow.

And she'll try not to think too much about the fact that there's one fragile part of her heart hoping that, if Astrid was the one who sent her the portfolio, she'll see the photo. And maybe she'll come to find Blythe—and she'll explain everything at last. In the meantime, she and Candace have set a time to talk the day after tomorrow when she hopes Candace will explain exactly what she meant about Versailles.

"Go on ahead," she tells Coco. Then Blythe gives herself a final once-over, anticipation coiling in her belly. Because she wants more than one slow kiss on her neck from Jake tonight.

In the mirror, her hair falls in its preferred loose wave to her shoulders, parted low over the top of her brow. Her eyes are smoky and her lipstick pale. She has on her highest heels. Then she smiles, reaches under the hem of her dress and removes one final item from her body.

* * *

Upstairs, the living room has been transformed thanks to David and Anton. Fairy lights glitter all over the ceiling. A tan leather sofa stretches along an entire wall, with sensational purple velvet ottomans opposite. There's a wood-paneled bar in the corner. Blythe remembers an interview where Hawk said the discos of the seventies made you want to simultaneously dance until dawn and make out until morning. The room definitely has that vibe and the minute she has the thought, Jake slips in beside her.

Without a doubt, if there was no one around, she'd make out with him until morning.

"Hi," he says softly. "That dress is so…" He inhales deeply. "Actually, I need to not think about you and that dress for a minute. I'll get drinks. Champagne or brandy?"

"I feel like I'm on dangerous enough ground already. Just champagne."

"I know what you mean," he murmurs.

Iris appears in what Blythe thinks is a late-1970s Oscar de la Renta gown in a glorious goldenrod hue. She sparkles, as if she isn't ill at all and the short future she's been promised is a lie. Then Charlie and Frieda stop to talk to Blythe, surprising her as they're definitely the two Blacks she knows the least. But as they're both doctors, she asks them how Iris really is.

Charlie grimaces. "Worse than she lets me tell anyone. And…" He glances at Frieda, who nods decisively.

"I feel like Jake either doesn't get how near the end it is or he's refusing to think about it," Charlie continues. "And I think Ed's in denial too or else I'd ask him. Jake's the least prepared, but he'll suffer the most when she's gone. I'm hoping you can talk to him—make sure he's ready. I know you think he's been a total dick these last couple of years but he'll listen to you."

"I don't know if he'll listen to anyone when it comes to that." Now Jake's walking back toward them, so Blythe changes the subject. "Where are you working at the moment?"

When Jake joins them, they're discussing the difficulties of working in a war-torn country where Charlie and Frieda do what they can to help large numbers of women and children who are unvaccinated, hungry, and die too often in playground bombing attacks.

Then Charlie claps Jake on the back. "I've been meaning to thank you for your donation. It helped fund a pediatric trauma center, which we desperately needed."

"Tell me what else you need and I'll make it happen," Jake says. "But later. This is Mom's night."

And Blythe knows two things—that Jake's determined to help any child in the world who might be suffering in ways worse than he did, and also that he doesn't want to be thanked for it. And she loves him for that, for his innate and unstoppable kindness.

She jolts at her mind's choice of words: *she loves him for that*.

Before she can grapple with that idea, Iris taps her glass and the party quiets.

"When I decided to have this party, it was only a month ago and I'm very grateful that on such short notice you're all here," Iris says, voice like a decades-old gown trying to keep itself together. "Everyone I love most. But I've done a lot of talking in my seventy years and it's time for someone else to speak. Perhaps tradition dictates that my eldest child should say a few words, but Ed just laughed and said, *We all know Jake would be best at this.* So, Jake, my youngest and definitely most troublesome child"—she smiles here—"please say whatever you wish to."

Jake steps into the center of the room. He stares at the floor and a moment of silence passes before he speaks.

"Iris Black tried to teach me a lot of things in my life, some of which I took on and some of which I ignored. Now that I'm older and wiser"—he gives a brief smile—"I want to reach back into time and take hold of that kid ignoring his mother's wisdom and tell him to listen. Most of the good things in my life have come about because of what Mom said to me, often late at night when I was a little drunk. She'd make me a cup of coffee and listen to me talk and at the end she'd say something like, *I would give you a piece of my mind, but if I have to keep giving you pieces of it, I'll have none left for myself. So I'll let you figure it out. I know you can, better than I will.* I'd get so mad because I thought mothers were meant to solve problems and be your conscience. But it's way too easy to let someone else be your conscience and so much harder to build your own, to hear what it's saying, and to take heed. But that's what she taught me, and hopefully I'll teach it to Sebby and Eva, with less eloquence no doubt, and also less elegance."

Everyone laughs.

"Iris is the beating heart of this family and nobody here would say anything different. If I reach the end of my life being the beating heart of a family, I'll consider I've had the best life possible." Jake stops, eyes flickering briefly to Blythe, and if it was possible for words to make a heart stop and feel all the pain and love in a single moment, that's what Jake's declaration does to her.

"So, to Iris, who's given us her mind and her heart, so much of it that we've…" A long pause now. "We've taken too freely of it. Thankfully, Iris had so much of both to begin with. And we're so damn lucky that we get to keep, for the rest of our lives, the gift of those pieces of herself she's given us. Thank you, Mom." Jake's voice cracks. "I love you."

"Oh, Jake," Iris whispers, reaching out for her son.

And everyone loses it. Herb cries in Ed's arms. Joy rubs Ed's back, giving him the strength he needs to comfort his father even while he's hurting too. Blythe takes Coco's hand because Coco's lips are trembling. With that, Coco breaks down and Blythe embraces her until Ed beckons his daughter over.

Then Jake crosses to Blythe's side. "That was beautiful," she whispers. Then she stands on her tiptoes and grazes her lips over his.

In reply, he slides his hands around her waist and draws her in, but a dozen champagne bottles pop, making them both jump.

"Why are there so many people in my family?" he murmurs.

"That's okay," Blythe says. "We can try that again later, when there isn't anyone around."

The pulse in Jake's throat quivers. He hasn't taken his hands off her. "Blythe," he whispers, but someone is passing them champagne and it's time to toast Iris again.

Soon, half the party is dancing, while others mingle on the ottomans. Blythe finds herself in a corner talking to Joy and Ed and Jake, and there, unobtrusively and in the dark where no one can see, Jake's fingers drift slowly up and down her spine. It takes her all of about one minute to lose the entire thread of the conversation so that when Ed says, "I see you're taking on the media," Blythe has no idea what he's talking about.

He holds out his phone and there she is. Her Instagram post has been picked up and elaborated upon by just about every entertainment and fashion news site. In most there's the photograph Coco took, with the photograph of Astrid beside, both of them wearing the silver dress.

Rather than looking away, Blythe says, "Yes. I am."

And she sees, in some of the articles, quotes that make her startle, then smile. The actress who starred in the movie Blythe just made the costumes for is reported as saying, *"I'll be first in line for MIZZA. I'd wear an apron if Blythe designed it."*

But the pièce de résistance is an article written by the fashion editor of the *New York Times*, who Blythe once met at a party. It says:

If Champlain Holdings keeps backing copycat fast-fashion brands over the uniquely beautiful pieces Blythe Bricard makes, then I suspect nobody will know who Nathaniel Champlain is in ten years' time—but we'll know who Blythe is forever.

"Holy shit," she says.

Coco pounces on her, grinning ecstatically. "Maybe everyone else has been quietly raging too."

THIRTY-SIX

ASTRID BRICARD AND HAWK JONES

I t's the third meeting of the designers chosen to show at the *Grand Divertissement à Versailles*, which will be attended by the likes of Princess Grace of Monaco and the Duchess of Windsor. They're gathered at Oscar de la Renta's apartment, with his exquisite wife pouring drinks, then slipping away. There are chandeliers. Fresh flowers. *Objets*. Things that match. Hawk feels like a five-year-old. He wants to play Carly Simon's "You're So Vain" but maybe de la Renta doesn't own anything as lowbrow as a record player.

He sips his coffee, but even that's too weak. He's pissed off, which isn't really the fault of anyone in the room. Ever since he and Astrid walked onto that stage hand in hand, the scrutiny of them has been like nothing he's experienced before. Someone from the press offered money to his doorman in exchange for Hawk's trash. Fairchild published a report saying Astrid's going to give up the "dressmaking" and return to being his muse. Rumors abound—driven by Fairchild's gossip column—that they had sex on the neighbor's stoop. On the other hand, magazines like *Cosmopolitan* have anointed Astrid on the cover as ASTRID THE GREAT. And *Vogue* said, *Every young woman in America wants to be Astrid Bricard.* But then they'd added, *especially now she looks to be reuniting with heartthrob Hawk.*

He never should have held her hand. But how do you walk calmly onto a stage beside someone you've been more intimate with than your own self? And there's a nagging thought in his head—did he do it because the laws of Hawk–Astrid physics meant he couldn't *not* do it, or because he knew what a sensation it would cause?

He doesn't think it's the latter. But now he questions everything. The only way he and Astrid will be together is if all this shit goes away. She doesn't want this kind of attention, casting her into a role she hasn't auditioned for. So he tries not to do the wrong thing—except everything is wrong for getting him and Astrid back together.

"We'll each show for twenty minutes," de la Renta is saying. "The French think anything worth doing is worth prolonging. But a long show is boring. We don't want to be boring."

Hawk decides he likes de la Renta just a little. "How about ten minutes?" he says. "If it takes just three minutes to play a rock song that gets the whole country dancing, then gorgeous gowns should be able to rouse a crowd in ten minutes."

"Maybe it's hard for you to find enough silver scraps to fill twenty minutes, but Halston can manage," Halston says bitingly.

Halston started referring to himself in the third person at the first meeting. Hawk has to resist a very immature urge to repeat the words *Halston can manage* in a whiny mimicry. Hawk and Halston do not like one another. They've been compared too often and, besides, Halston's an asshole with a vicious temper.

They go round and round and back and forth—too many egos in the one room—then Blass says, "Let's move on to the sets. We can fix the time later."

So de la Renta wants to be the leader, Blass the peacemaker, Halston the shit-stirrer. Burrows is the wide-eyed naif. What's Hawk? The ungrateful bastard, perhaps. He should ignore Halston, stop thinking about Astrid and concentrate on taking on the French in France. Because it's an unbelievable thing to be attempting.

"Perhaps Halston can open the show?" de la Renta says and Hawk's liking for the man goes up another notch. The sneaky bastard wants to go last—they all want the grand finale. Proposing Halston as the show opener is a smart move.

"Halston is going last," Halston says.

And Hawk Jones is going to vomit, he only just stops himself from saying.

The door opens and Eleanor Lambert, the PR doyenne behind this showcase, enters. "The French added another man to their team," she says. "Paco Rabanne. They wanted someone young, given one of our team will still be in his twenties"—she looks at Hawk—"and one will have only just turned thirty." Now she glances at Stephen Burrows.

"Who will we get?" Blass asks. "Geoffrey Beene?"

Hawk yawns exaggeratedly and sees Eleanor press her lips together, holding back a smile. The door opens.

In walks Astrid.

"Fuck off," Halston snarls.

Hawk stands and Eleanor steps between him and Halston, neatly stopping him from punching Halston in the nose.

Astrid slides into a chair. "Lovely to see you too," she says sarcastically. "Save the passion for your designs."

"Halston is leaving." And he actually storms out.

Blass and de la Renta stare after him, dismay writ large on their faces. Halston might be an asshole, but as the one with arguably the most success in Europe, he's a drawcard. Nobody wants to lose him.

But Hawk just looks across at Astrid and smiles. She's been chosen to show at Versailles. That'll shut John Fairchild up.

Wasn't the Coty Award supposed to do that?

Hawk's head starts to pound. What if Fairchild reports that Hawk was the one who walked out, not Halston? And that it was to get Astrid on the team?

In a temper of apprehension, he glares across the table at Candace, Halston's assistant. Candace blabbed untruths to Fairchild the night Hawk won his first Coty. She's probably itching to do it again.

Candace doesn't meet his eyes and his headache sharpens.

Eleanor leaves to deal with Halston. Blass stares at Astrid with obvious dislike. Hawk searches desperately for words.

"What were you doing before I stopped traffic?" Astrid asks coolly.

"Talking about the show order," Hawk jumps in.

"We need everything to be sensational," de la Renta interjects.

Hawk watches Astrid tuck her hair behind her ear. *You can do this*, he urges her. *Beat the dickheads down.*

And she does.

"You might have worked with Balenciaga once upon a time," she says to de la Renta, "but I've holidayed with him. I've also worked with the Houses of Dior and Givenchy. And you"—she turns to Blass—"haven't worked with anyone French. So let's not start comparing résumés. I can tell you exactly what the French will do. Everything will be about their couture bloodlines—the past, in other words. Let them have the past. We have the future. Energy. Excitement."

"Halston asked Liza Minnelli to perform," Hawk says in lieu of cheering her speech.

"That'll work," she says, and it's like they're sitting in his studio throwing ideas into the air, watching them turn into sparkling, alive things like they used to. "Liza is all about energy and excitement. You've been playing music at your shows, Hawk. Let's do that at Versailles. Maybe we can get someone to choreograph the mannequins to dance, or at least move to the music."

"We'll get Kay Thompson," de la Renta says, referring to the legendary choreographer. "Liza can do an opening number. Kay can choreograph the models. We choose our own music. We each get fifteen minutes."

Just like that, Astrid's idea becomes de la Renta's. Hawk is almost shocked at how easily it happens. Astrid's about to tuck her hair behind her ear again when she stops and says to de la Renta, with the sassiest smile Hawk's ever seen her wear, "Maybe I'll get Mick Jagger to play during my segment of the show."

Needless to say, de la Renta can't come up with a reply—nobody's ever written a song about him. Hawk grins.

The meeting wraps up. Burrows jumps in a cab, Blass steps into a town car. And Hawk finds himself walking beside Astrid, the best place in the world to be, hands shoved in his pockets so he doesn't forget himself and reach out to tuck her in at his side. She's wearing a tiger-striped coat with black fur cuffs to ward off the cold. Everyone turns to look at her. De la Renta definitely doesn't have to worry about her being sensational.

"What a pack of jerks," he grouses and she laughs. "I'm glad you're on the team," he adds.

"Thanks."

It sounds like a farewell and he can't let it be. "I'm going to see my folks," he blurts out. "Do you want to come say hello?" He sounds like an eager boy. It's Friday evening. She probably has a party to go to, or a…*date*. No.

But she says, "Sure," and he wants to punch the air, feels as drunk and high on Astrid Bricard as he's ever been.

* * *

"Hey, Mom," Hawk calls when they step inside. "I brought Astrid with me."

The moment he says it, he realizes they're the exact words he used the first time Astrid visited. His eyes flicker toward her and she isn't smiling now, as if she too just felt the shock of the past rushing into the present.

"Astrid!" Meredith embraces her and leads her to his father's room. "Matthias will be so pleased to see you."

Hawk hovers in the doorway and Meredith comes to stand by his side. They watch Astrid sit by Matthias's bed and say, "I missed you."

Tears leak from his father's eyes. The muscles in his hand no longer work, so he can't do anything except blink. Then Astrid wraps one of her hands around Matthias's and takes out a tissue and wipes his eyes.

Fuck. Hawk almost sinks to the floor with his face buried in his hands and sobs like a baby for everything he did to ruin himself and Astrid, for the waste, the goddamn cataclysmic waste of the kind of love he was gifted.

Astrid is the love of his life and he will never meet another woman like her.

But his mother is weeping and he needs to put his arm around her and let her cry before she rights herself and says, "I bet you haven't eaten. I have a pot roast on. Astrid, you'll stay for dinner?"

At Astrid's nod, she bustles off to the kitchen.

"I'll let you get some rest," Astrid says to Matthias. In the hallway, she says to Hawk, "I didn't know he was worse. I'm so sorry."

And then, incredibly, impossibly, Astrid reaches out for him and draws him in.

Hawk's arms move ever so slowly as they wrap around her back, not wanting to screw this up. God, she smells good. And she feels incredible. Slender wrists, curved hips, a waist he wants to span his hands around. But more than that, her compassion is what he clings to—knowing she understands how hurt he still is by the diminishment of Matthias's life to one room makes it hurt just a little bit less.

His head drops down to rest beside hers. And he feels her nestle in closer, can't stop the clench of his hand against her back.

"How have you been?" she whispers.

"I don't even know."

He lifts his head, strokes her cheek. She brings his knuckles to her mouth and he can't breathe from the searing heat of it.

"Hawk, can you get some wine?" his mother calls.

They both jump. "She has terrible timing," Hawk murmurs.

"Remember, we're in her hallway, so maybe her timing is for the best," Astrid says, smiling, and he tightens his grip on her at the same time as she shifts deeper into him, the impossibility of separating themselves the same as cleaving a soul from a body.

"Hawk?" his mother calls again. "Did you hear me?"

"Yes!" he shouts back, his entire body feeling as flushed as Astrid's face. They disentangle, their fingertips the last reluctant things to separate.

"See you in the kitchen," she whispers.

Hawk needs a moment to pull himself together before he gets the champagne. What just happened? And what does it mean?

Back in the kitchen, he tells Meredith, "Astrid's coming to France too, so we're celebrating."

"Really?" Meredith says delightedly. "I bought two pairs of your trousers last week, Astrid, and I had nothing but compliments all day. Don't tell Hawk though." She smiles at her son, who laughs.

"Traitor," he says.

Then he pours champagne and they raise their glasses. "To beating the French," he says with his mouth. With his eyes, he says to Astrid, *To us.*

* * *

After dinner and cognac, Hawk and Astrid walk home and she asks him, smiling a little as if she knows how impossible it is to answer the question, "What have you been up to the past couple of years?"

He nearly gives her an upbeat reply but knows she'll see right through it. "I got too drunk and too high and then I got myself cleaned up. I didn't go to rehab or anything like that—it was bad enough, but not so far out of my control that I couldn't fix it myself. So now I'm a one-glass and no-dope guy."

She's silent for a beat and then says, "I didn't know."

"Now I have Fi and Nancy to keep me on the straight and narrow, and to tell me what makes your clothes so great and mine so bad," he says, smiling now at having got that out of the way.

Astrid laughs. "Fi and Nancy worship you. I miss them."

"They miss you too. They talk about how you used to sit in the store and draw. They loved that." *I did too*, he doesn't say because he knows it will never happen again and that hurts pretty bad.

They're quiet after that and when they reach his apartment building, which is on the way to Astrid's, they pause and she asks, "Do you think we can beat the French?"

"Beat the men who invented couture at a fashion show? Nobody thinks we can."

"And do you think they'll..." She tucks her hands in her pockets. "Do you think Halston and the others will accept working with me?"

He wants to tell her to ignore Halston. But Halston is wealthy and powerful and famous. Hawk is the last of those, and maybe only half of the other two. Astrid is the last also, and Alix says she's wealthy now too, but powerful she definitely isn't.

"Eleanor will make them," he says, which is true, but also not what she wants to hear.

"Eleanor told me she's fought some monumental battles over her decades in fashion but she's never had to fight harder than she did with the Versailles committee to get me on the team," Astrid says quietly. "That half of the board still won't speak to her. Only the ones interested in publicity agreed—publicity is the one thing my involvement guarantees. Apparently I'm carrying Eleanor's reputation, my reputation and the future of women in fashion on my shoulders. So, no pressure." She shrugs. "Velvet says I'll just have to be tougher than I've ever been."

He wants to rage. How much stronger does Astrid need to be? "Velvet's probably right," he says, knowing this conversation is heading into all the reasons why they broke up. "Which won't be fun."

"But that's just it. It *should* be fun. We've been asked to show our clothes at the Palace of Versailles, to compete against the French. It's a designer's dream. It's *my* dream, but all I can think is that I *need* us to win. If we lose, I'll be blamed. But if we win…" She says the words like they're a voluptuous hundred-year-old cognac she wants to roll around on her tongue. "I *need* this, Hawk."

Her raw honesty—and the fact she's right—have him forgetting all the rules that two people like them, who exist as printed images separate to their actual selves, should obey. His hand is on her waist before…*Flash*.

The camera is eye-blindingly bright. Hawk whirls around, anger written all over his face, and he knows he has to get hold of himself. "Come upstairs," he says to Astrid.

Inside his apartment, Astrid hangs up her coat and slides onto the sofa. "They don't give up, do they?"

"We should have caught a cab," Hawk says grimly.

She smiles. "We've always walked. A cab would have been way too grown-up."

He laughs, still standing in the entrance to the room, not able to make himself move into it properly because she's wearing the tank dress that made his whole body ache when he saw the first MIZZA shoot in *Élan*. Her body is outlined beneath the fabric, her arms are tanned and bare, but her face doesn't wear the relaxed expression it had in the magazine picture. She looks wistful as she curls up her legs, stretches one arm along the back of the sofa and rests her head against her hand.

Too much has happened tonight and his strength of will isn't what it needs to be. He lowers himself onto the step and rubs his jaw. "I get so mad because they love you—they literally *love* photographing you—and everyone thinks you're the sexiest woman on the planet. Which is definitely not a lie," he adds, a little ruefully. "But then they call you a dressmaker, whereas Halston's a genius, Bill's a master and Oscar's a couturier."

"And Hawk Jones is the premier fashion designer in all of America," she quotes from a recent and euphoric article in *Life*. "I agree with them, you know."

"Astrid," he says, and he can hear all the pain and love and yearning wound like thread around his heart.

What happens when two people who love one another, and who want one another, are in the same room with a past and a present between them, and no idea of a future?

Then he realizes—he has no idea if she *does* still love him. Hands steepled under his chin, he says pensively, "I love you, Astrid. The first day you came to my parents' apartment and picked up my dad's hand—I remember thinking back then that I'd fallen in love with you and the fall was so fathomless I'd never find my way out. It's still true."

He watches her hand move up to her eyes and wipe away the glimmer of tears. "Why does it always make me cry when you tell me you love me?" she says, voice low, sexy—so damn sexy.

"Maybe because I haven't said it for a long time." His voice is husky too.

She leans forward on the sofa, rests her elbows on her knees, pose matching his. "I thought because I was the one who walked away, I shouldn't say it."

"I get it—MIZZA wouldn't have happened if we'd stayed together. Two years ago, it hurt like hell and I did hate you for about five seconds. But you did the right thing. Wait," he says, smiling. "You didn't tell me whatever it was that you thought you shouldn't say."

"Oh," she begins offhandedly, "it was just that..." Then she stops with the nonchalance, fixes him in her eyes and says, "I love you, Hawk. Endlessly."

What had flickered between them in the hallway of his parents' apartment now feels like a match barely kindled. What exists now is wildfire.

Two years before and they would have run straight into it. Now they both stay where they are. He lets his gaze drop to her neck, which he's dragged his stubble over so many times. Then lower, to the thin strap of the dress around her shoulder. If he stares at it hard enough, will it slide down to the top of her arm, leaving the line from her earlobe to the point of her shoulder bare?

She reaches up and nudges the fabric aside. Watching it fall over her skin is a pleasurable kind of torture.

He lets his eyes wander lower. Her breasts are outlined against the dress, the movement of her chest up and down too rapid for normal breathing.

That's all the looking he can take.

He crosses to the sofa and drops to his knees in front of her, touching one fingertip to her breastbone, feeling the heat and the fire of what him just looking at her does to both of them.

"Astrid," he whispers as she shifts closer into him. "I want to kiss you for a long, long time." He drops his lips onto hers for less than half a second. "Before I even let myself take off your clothes." He brushes his next kiss onto her neck and her hands twist in the fabric of his shirt.

"So long as I can do the same," she whispers back, grazing his jaw with her mouth. "I wonder who has the most willpower?"

He grins. "Probably neither of us."

She laughs as she pulls him onto the sofa where they kiss for a very long time. She's naked more quickly than he'd imagined and so is he. But that's okay because then there's so much more to kiss, so much more to taste—not quite for all night, but this is just the first time. *There's still the second, third, fourth and fifth*, she whispers to him as she lies in his arms much later, making him almost certain that the second time will be the wildfire; the third and fourth the long, slow blaze; and the fifth the inextinguishable fire of the burning stones that sit in the center of the earth, and inside Hawk Jones's love for Astrid Bricard as well.

THIRTY-SEVEN

BLYTHE BRICARD

As the music at Iris's party turns sultry, Blythe takes Jake's hand and leads him onto the landing where the light seeps in from the living room. Jake's arms thread around her waist, drawing her in so they're not really dancing, just holding on, rediscovering how it feels to be this close to one another.

When the song ends, she tips her head back, catching a look of wonder on his face—as if it's almost unreal that his hand is making the bare skin on her back tingle into goosebumps once more.

That's when she knows her earlier thought wasn't a slip, but a truth. "Jake," she says almost shyly.

He tilts his head to the side, his expression shifting from awe to uncertainty. And that makes her even more sure she has to say it, because she wants him to be as confident about the two of them together as he used to be.

"I love you, Jake Black."

And he isn't hesitant anymore.

He slides his hands lower, dragging her hips against his. But he stops abruptly when the thinness of the fabric makes it completely obvious to him that she isn't wearing a single thing under this dress.

"I need some air," he says a little breathlessly.

She smiles. "It's still cold up where your room is, right? So there must be air up there."

"Blythe..."

His voice is so husky it's almost too hard for her to pull away and say, "Give me a minute."

She slips back into the party. The kids will be much better off staying in Georgia's room for the night, but she needs to make sure Ed doesn't mind.

Her face must give her away because he whoops. "Do not come and get them until at least midday. In fact, make it dinnertime. I don't want to see you or Jake until then."

Realization hits Blythe. "You invited Cameron to dinner—"

"And I encouraged him to ask you out. I knew he could handle rejection. And that Jake needed to experience a little jealousy. It was either that or hit him. Now go."

On the landing, Jake's leaning against the far wall. She crosses over to him slowly, his eyes on her the whole time. She's about ten steps away when he strides toward her and slides a hand into her hair, their lips not quite touching, both of them anticipating the moment until it's too much and she pulls his mouth down onto hers.

He kisses her the same way he'd always kissed her—a little rough, like his self-command had slipped, as if, with her, he was a little bit wild.

"Blythe." Her name in his mouth is so close to a groan that she laughs and says in a mock-commanding manner, "Stairs. Now."

At last they're in his room, where the kiss deepens still more. Then Jake's hand slides lower, lifting the hem of her dress, exploring, making certain she really isn't wearing anything at all beneath the silver.

Now she's the one who needs air.

"I wonder what divorced sex is like," she manages to gasp.

Jake shakes his head. "I don't want divorced sex. I want to make love to my wife."

And that's the final moment when she realizes there isn't a chance they'll be using the bed, not this time.

* * *

Later, when they're finally in bed catching their breath, so like the first night they made love thirteen years ago—bodies slick with sweat despite the cold, Blythe's eyeballs still rolling back in her head—Jake props himself up on his elbow and says, "We'll have to get married because nothing can ever be better than that."

She laughs, but then a frown settles onto her face. "This is just very . . . fast."

"I've known you for more than a decade," Jake says. "That's not especially fast."

"I know, but this"—she indicates the bed—"was never a problem. Real life was. I need to know how we work in real life with the kids."

"But we can still have sex while we're figuring that out, right?" he asks teasingly. Then he fixes his eyes on her. "I'm just scared that if I don't marry you now, it'll never happen and the rest of my life will pass by without you. When I said tonight that I wanted to reach back in time and shake myself because of how I was with Iris—I want to do the same with me as your husband. If I hadn't fucked it all up, then you'd be lying beside me smiling, not worrying about me hurting everyone again."

"Jake." She wraps her arms around him. "If there's one thing I've learned since we've been here, it's that regretting the past is futile. We can only fix the present, and you've done that. So ask me that marriage question again when we've been back in New York a month. After we've had reality, not just chocolate soufflés and French chateaux."

He sighs. "How great would it be if life was only chocolate soufflés and French chateaux? And a bed with you in it. And the kids somewhere down the hall where they can't hear us."

His grin is bewitching and she lets herself fall under its spell. "How noisy can you be, Jake Black?" she asks, running her hands down his chest.

Suddenly she's on her back and his kiss is rough against her neck. "Let's find out."

* * *

It's impossible that dusk has rolled around so fast. Blythe curls into him, trying not to succumb to the hand that's tracing tempting circles over her thigh, knowing it's truly tomorrow and she has to deal with this. "I need to talk to you about something."

His hand stills.

She tells him that Nathaniel is coming after the MIZZA name. "There's no way Astrid has renewed the trademark," she says. "I remember enough to know you're supposed to renew it every two years. So does that mean he can just…" She falters. She'd been so brave in her Instagram post, but here in bed with Jake who knows her best, all the fears seep out.

"I'm going to kill him," Jake says darkly.

"This isn't your fight," Blythe tells him. "I need advice, not fisticuffs and testosterone and men putting themselves in the middle of my story."

Jake tugs her closer, both of them lying on their sides, bodies fitted together. "You're right. I'll kill him after you've got MIZZA up and running." He frowns. "He'd have to challenge the validity of the trademark registration, say that the entry currently recorded in the register is wrong because it's in the name of a person who might be dead. But then maybe he'd have to prove Astrid is dead. So it's not easy for him, but…"

"He doesn't need it to be easy," Blythe finishes. "He just needs my investors to fall away because they don't want the risk of a legal battle. To cast enough doubt to put me back in my place of being the Bricard who excels at giving the finger to the world and being a disappointment."

"Blythe." Jake kisses her forehead. "We can—"

"Jake." She cuts him off as lovingly as she can. "Thank you for letting me talk it over. I want to keep doing that, so long as you're okay with it..."

She hesitates, not wanting to dump any more onto him, but he says, "Tell me," like he really wants to know what else is on her mind.

"I need to call Hawk."

"I think that's a good thing."

Maybe it is. Because Hawk can tell her part of the story of what happened to Astrid Bricard—his version. He can also tell her about the silver dress and why it's in Astrid's portfolio. But how will she know if he's telling the truth?

* * *

Blythe and Jake make it downstairs just before dinner to find a grinning Ed doing his best—or worst—not to whoop and clap.

"There you are," Eva says. "You and Daddy must have had lots of work to do."

"Yes, they've been working very hard," Ed says solemnly.

Jake balls up a napkin and tosses it at him. Then he says, "Seb, Eva—how about you guys come downstairs? Your mom and I need to talk to you."

"Why don't you talk to them here, Jake?" Ed says, obviously having decided to be as devilish as possible.

Jake stops and mouths, *Fuck off* to his brother, which only makes Ed throw the napkin back at Jake.

The last thing they hear is Joy saying, "Ed, behave yourself," in a barely admonishing manner and Blythe knows that everyone is enjoying themselves very much at her and Jake's expense.

"Maybe we skip dinner and stay in bed," Jake mutters to Blythe, not quietly enough.

"I'm hungry, Daddy," Eva says. "And it's way too early for bed."

"Do not say it," Blythe hisses at Jake.

"Spoilsport," he whispers and she smiles through the jittery nerves in her stomach at somehow explaining this to the kids.

Jake sits on the bed and beckons for Sebby and Eva to sit beside him. He'd asked if he could be the one to tell them, and while Blythe has reservations, if they're going to make this work, she needs to let him tackle the tricky stuff too.

She expects some preamble, a warm-up, but Jake just says, "Your mom and I talked last night..."

Blythe doesn't dare look at him for fear of bursting into laughter at this outrageous euphemism.

"And because I love her and she loves me, we decided to try out being together again," he continues. "Hopefully we'll get married again soon. What do you think?"

Blythe's mouth is hanging open at this rapid-fire summation of events but Sebby jumps off the bed, says, "Yay!" then yawns. "Can we have dinner soon? I'm starving."

"Sure thing, buddy," Jake says, ruffling his hair. "You get started in the bathroom and I'll come in a minute and run the shower."

Eva has a few more questions. "Does that mean you're going to stay down here with us?" she demands.

"Do you mind if I sleep in your mom's room though?" Jake says. "You snore so loudly I'll never get any sleep." He reaches over and tickles her stomach.

"Daddy!" she shrieks, laughing hysterically. Then she starfishes on the bed and says, "This is the best holiday ever."

* * *

Later that night, after the kids are tucked up in bed with assurances that when they climb into Blythe's bed tomorrow, Daddy will be there too, Blythe and Jake curl up next to one another on the sofa in the library. Ed and Joy, and David and Charlie are there too, mostly behaving themselves, although Jake has a pile of napkins beside him just in case. His hand has slipped under her sweater, his thumb retracing the same delicious circles on her back as the night before. Blythe's torn between overwhelming tiredness and dragging Jake downstairs, where they'll have to achieve a much lower noise level than the night before.

The door opens and Iris comes in, held up by Herb and Coco as if her bones are liquid. Fear passes though Jake's eyes.

"That's the best thing I've seen in a very long time," Iris says, gesturing to Blythe and Jake. "It's all I needed, in fact."

Blythe shivers at the words.

As soon as his mom's gone, Jake pulls Blythe to her feet. She waits until they're in her room before she slips her arms around him and says, "Your mom's going to be in the hospital soon. You know that, right?"

She thinks he's going to find a pile of napkins to throw at her but she keeps her hands on him, her eyes too. The thing with having the kind of deeply felt emotional bond that she has with Jake is that a face is a conversation. He doesn't have to speak for her to know what he's thinking, and he gives in to it, rather than turning away or pretending he feels nothing.

He leans his forehead against hers. "I think maybe if you..."

He hesitates and she continues to hold on to him, letting her presence tell him she'll do whatever she can.

"If you're with me, I can handle going to the hospital. And I'll handle whatever comes after that because, like I said in my speech, she gave me a hell of a lot and it's her turn to receive."

"Go up and see her," Blythe says. "I'm healthy and happy and have years left on this earth. I can wait for you for an hour or so."

He kisses her, then leaves.

After he's gone, Blythe discovers a package on the table. In her bones, she knows it will be from whoever sent Astrid's portfolio. She tears open the envelope and a book falls out.

Tell Me About the Silver Dress, it's called. The subtitle is: *What Happened to Astrid Bricard*.

The same question Blythe has been asking. Except it isn't phrased as a question, but as a statement—as if the author knows the answer. And Blythe remembers Remy telling her that the Met was restoring Astrid's portfolio so it could be photographed for a new book about her.

Then Blythe sees the author's name.

Hawk Jones.

Her legs actually refuse to keep her upright. She drops onto the bed. *Hawk* was the one who sent Blythe the portfolio. Not Astrid.

That tiny sequin of hope that had started to glow inside her a couple of days ago loses all its light. Astrid isn't about to appear on Blythe's doorstep. Her mother is never coming back from wherever she's gone.

And now Hawk has taken it upon himself to write her story.

THIRTY-EIGHT

ASTRID BRICARD AND HAWK JONES

Astrid wakes first in the morning and for about three seconds she feels happier than she's ever been. But then fear catches hold. From the moment she stepped into Hawk's parents' apartment last night, her common sense had hung itself up at the door. It was like when they were first together and she had no idea that loving this man would be her undoing.

Not this time, she vows, smiling at Hawk asleep, one arm flung above his head, the other around her. Even his fingers haven't relaxed with sleep but hold her fiercely against his body.

The phone rings, rousing him, and she watches him stretch the same way he does everything, with a casual nonchalance that's so damn hot. He gives her a sleepy smile before he reaches for the phone with one hand and tugs her closer to him with the other. She presses her lips to his chest, letting her hand trail over his stomach, and he tugs her mouth up to his, kissing her as soundlessly as possible. She smiles as she hears the person on the phone say, "Hawk? Are you there?" and he pulls away from her with obvious reluctance to say, "Yeah. See you soon."

He hangs up and kisses her properly, hands in her hair and then on her back and then around her hips as if he wants to touch her everywhere all at once, which would be her idea of heaven.

"That was Eleanor," he murmurs. "There's a Versailles meeting at ten."

"Then we'd better be quick," she says with a grin, but something in his expression makes her smile fall away. "What?"

"John Fairchild wants to write about the American team, so she's invited him to the meeting."

Astrid feels like she's crawled out of a nightclub three drinks too late. "I'll need to get ready with armor and ammunition," she says faux-lightly.

"You were great yesterday," Hawk says, cupping her jaw in his hands. "We've been meeting for a month and hadn't settled on anything. Then you walk in and we have the future, theater and music. You've got this," he vows and she tries to believe him.

Back at her apartment, ready to armor herself with MIZZA, she finds a telegram from Mizza Bricard.

I TRIED TO CALL YOU. YOU MIGHT LIKE TO KNOW THAT THE FRENCH TEAM ARE SPENDING ONE HUNDRED THOUSAND DOLLARS ON EACH OF THEIR SEGMENTS——MORE THAN HALF A MILLION DOLLARS IN TOTAL. THEY WILL HAVE A FULL ORCHESTRA. RUDOLF NUREYEV WILL DANCE. THEY'RE NOT USING BACKDROPS BUT ENTIRE SETS——A DIFFERENT ONE IS BEING MADE FOR EACH DESIGNER. FOREWARNED IS FOREARMED, I HOPE. LOVE, MIZZA.

Shit. Eleanor told Astrid only that their budget is small. But how small? Enough to compete with famous ballet dancers, orchestras and a hell of a lot of money?

They need to figure out a way to not lose before the show even begins. Because she *cannot* lose. Especially not after last night—not after every inch of her has given in to the necessity of not just loving Hawk, but of being with him too.

* * *

When she arrives at the meeting, she and Hawk don't dare look at one another, not with Fairchild watching. He sits at the end of the table, benign, bucktoothed and smiling just like he did when he sat in her office and let her think he was listening.

"Eleanor," Astrid asks. "What's our budget?"

"Fifty thousand dollars," Eleanor replies.

"Per designer?"

"No. For the whole show."

Astrid had tried to set her expectations low, but this is below the nadir. "I hate to be the harbinger of doom," she begins.

Halston curls his lip. "You arriving yesterday made certain we're doomed."

Screw you, she thinks, but doesn't dare say it in front of Fairchild. "Halston, how many *Vogue* covers did you have last year?" she asks coolly, knowing MIZZA's had two, Hawk and Halston one each. She doesn't let him reply, just tells them everything she knows about the French team's infinite resources.

The subsequent silence is deadly.

"Where did you hear that?" Blass asks.

"From Mizza Bricard."

Halston slams his fist on the table. "A Frenchwoman. Whose side is she on? She's lying. Or you are."

Excellent. Astrid's whole future is riding on a team who hates her, and a budget one-tenth the size of the French. *Give up*, that vicious voice inside her snarls.

"Why would she lie?" Hawk breaks in. "If anyone here wants to win, it's Astrid."

Fairchild smiles at the cold, hard truth of that and Eleanor cuts in. "Let's discuss this later. John, over to you."

Halston glares at Astrid. Hawk glares at Halston. And Fairchild smiles a little more. Then he pushes over a photograph of Astrid and Hawk outside Hawk's apartment building last night. Fairchild's chosen a shot where Hawk's head is turning back toward Astrid so it looks as though *she* is the source of his exasperation, not the photographer.

"I just wanted to confirm there's been a reunion," Fairchild says. "And that my headline is accurate."

He proffers a piece of paper headlined, THE MUSE BEGS HER MAKER TO LET HER GO TO FRANCE. Underneath are the words, *Who really designs MIZZA?*

Hawk jumps to his feet. "You fucking—"

"Hawk!" Eleanor snaps. "You can leave. In fact, everyone can leave. I need to speak to John."

"Can you ever attract the right kind of publicity?" Halston hisses at Astrid.

"No, Halston," Astrid says furiously, on the verge of losing it in public for the first time ever. "It doesn't seem like I can."

She exits onto the street and feels someone catch her hand. She yanks it away. *What if this is all there is?* Her always scrabbling at the base of a mountain, knocked back by an avalanche of misogyny.

"Eleanor will tell everyone it's bullshit," Hawk says. "*I'll* tell them it's bullshit."

She's so furious at all the people she can't afford to scream at that she erupts at him. "I don't want you to have to fix it! Didn't you tell the press after your first Coty win that the dress I wore was one of my designs, not yours?"

He nods.

"And what did they say? *Oops, sorry, the story's already run.*"

"Astrid—"

"Goddammit." She turns and presses both of her hands against her forehead because she knows what she has to say, can't believe she has to say it again—and on a Manhattan street, of all places. Can't believe that it isn't Hawk's fault or her fault but they're the ones who'll suffer for it.

"Every time we're together, the world takes something from me, Hawk. *You* don't take anything from me, but the way it's photographed and written about does. I become less than you, an object you use to fuel your genius."

Hawk swears, then says ferociously, "I want it all to stop. God, how I want everything except you and me together at last to stop."

The traffic lights change and a pedestrian horde charges toward them, pushing them back against the wall of a building. After the flood has passed, Astrid speaks the truth, anger gone, only sadness left. "It won't stop." And she sees on his face the moment he understands where this conversation is going.

"No," he says sharply. "You are not just a muse. They'll see that."

But if she weakens now, then she might as well just walk outside in a silver lamé dress, wearing a model's smile, and let them strip her completely bare. A car horn blares. Someone shouts. And one little hidden seam of stubbornness makes her say, "Tell me about the silver dress."

"The one I made for you? It's still hanging in my wardrobe."

There are tears all over her cheeks. *The one I made.* She turns her back on him but now everyone walking past—strangers—can see that she's crying.

"Astrid," Hawk says, voice raw. "I love you."

"I know you do," she says, spinning back around to face him. "But Versailles is my last chance to take center stage with you and Halston and the others. If Versailles doesn't change everyone's minds, then nothing will. And . . ." She knows her voice is going to break on these next words, and it does. "I'll have to accept it."

How strong do I have to be, Mizza?

She leans her back against the wall and closes her eyes, Mizza's words echoing in her mind: *we can't have two generations of women who might have.* Which means she just has to say it, crying in the middle of a goddamn street.

"I love you, Hawk, but until Versailles, I can only see you in meetings." She makes herself open her eyes and look at him—it's the least she can do when she's breaking their hearts all over again. "The day after the show it won't matter if we're together—I'll either have the respect I want. Or I'll have given up on the idea of it."

"Astrid." Hawk tugs her into his arms and holds her, both having forgotten that all of Madison Avenue can see them. Two sets of tears land on her face. His, and hers.

One long but too-short moment of holding him passes by, then he cups her jaw in his hands and says vehemently, "I'll wait forever if I have to. Nine months is nothing when set beside the chance of us finally being together. The only thing that matters is that I don't lose you forever. We'll win at Versailles, and then we'll be together. I promise."

She nods. She can do this. She just has to make the best clothes she's ever made in her life. Clothes that will outshine orchestras and half a million dollars and Fairchild's power. This time, she and Hawk will win. They have to.

* * *

For the next few weeks, Astrid gets up at five in the morning. She goes to work and sits at her desk and draws as if her life depends on it. Because it does. She draws just lines and ideas for now, seeing dresses that are tall and strong—powerful—but at the same time fluid and female. The powerfulness she's always craved is nothing like Fairchild's power, a viciousness that makes people cower. What she imagines is everything she was that night on the podium at the Cheetah, dressed in silver and music and light.

But can a woman be sexy *and* strong in this world? Or does being the first make everyone treat you with contempt? The Equal Rights Amendment still hasn't been ratified by the necessary thirty-eight states, and Astrid can't make herself contemplate a world where it won't ever be. So she has to find a way to say in this collection that they all have to keep fighting. She has to stand on a stage at Versailles with clothes that show not just women but men too that the world is only half of what it could be when power is defined as someone losing something—and when women are merely the beautiful and the damned.

This collection isn't just about winning. It's about every woman who's ever had a man make her into someone less than she truly is.

It's a sentiment that keeps her working from before dark to after dark, chasing that elusive idea. She's getting closer, she thinks, until the day she finds herself sitting in a room protesting, "But I'm on the pill."

"You said you had food poisoning," the doctor harrumphs. "Did you have intercourse in the two weeks after that?" He says it like it's a certainty, and Astrid hates him for it.

She thinks back to her night with Hawk. It was about five days after she'd been ill. She'd been terrified she'd have to miss the first Versailles meeting, but had been fine in the end. And she's been feeling off since sometime after the night she spent with Hawk. She'd thought it was a lingering effect from the food poisoning.

"If you have any vomiting for more than a day, then you must use additional methods of contraception," the doctor pronounces.

This can't be happening, Astrid thinks as she pees in a jar.

But the doctor disagrees. He telephones her later and tells her in a pompous voice, "You're pregnant."

* * *

Someone from the doctor's practice leaks the news and there it is in *W*, Fairchild's magazine for the masses—Astrid's Having Hawk's Love Child.

Nausea makes her flee to the bathroom. She hasn't even told Hawk, has been trying for the last week to work out what to say to him. But now everyone knows.

She isn't surprised when the doorbell buzzes. She lets in Hawk, who stares at her, a tear leaking from his eye.

Then he reaches out and places a hand on her belly. "Hey, little one," he says. "I'm..." A smile breaks through. "I'm your dad."

"You're happy?" she asks, voice a whisper.

"I'm over the fucking moon," he says. "Did you think I wouldn't be?"

"I don't know. What about Versailles? God." She shakes her head, presses away from him and shoves the heels of her hands against her eyes. "There's an actual human inside me and I'm thinking about work. What if that means..." There are so many things she could drown in right now, it's almost like she just has to pick which ocean to engulf her. "I don't know how to be a mother, Hawk," she says. "My biological mother gave me away and...I don't know how to do this."

Those last words are low and ashamed. Motherhood is instinctual, natural, everyone says. But all her instincts are telling her that she'll be no good at this. She has literally turned this tiny baby inside her into a headline in its first weeks of existence. It's no bigger than a peanut, but it's already taking up column inches.

"Astrid." Hawk puts both hands on her stomach now, his eyes a blazing, passionate silver. "You do. Just be you and you'll be the best mom in the world. And I'm going to be the best dad. We're going to rock the word *parents* in a way that makes a Led Zeppelin song sound like a nursery rhyme."

He's smiling at her now and she hears herself give one small laugh. Hawk *will* be the best dad. And maybe, with him, she can do this. Her hand drops to rest on his and she lets herself start to fall in love with what they've made.

"We'll figure it out," he says, clasping his fingers around hers. "Maybe it sounds like I'm being cavalier, but we're having a baby. I can't... I can't even..." He swipes at his eyes. "I'm crying like a baby at even the thought of it."

We're having a baby. Astrid's smile is extravagant now. What matters is loving this baby and making sure it knows how loved it is. So,

"Hawk," she says, a little shyly. "What if, the day after Versailles, I made myself a white tuxedo jacket? What—"

She doesn't get to finish her sentence because Hawk is kissing her more fiercely than he's ever kissed her before. "Then I would find the nearest church," he says, voice raw with emotion, "and get the priest to marry us on the spot. Then I'd take off your wedding jacket and make love to you for an entire week."

"Hawk," she whispers, her insides burning. "We'll have a baby. We can't just—"

He cuts her off. "My mom will look after the baby while we're in France. You're going to send your clothes out onto that stage at Versailles and the applause will smash every mirror in the damn hall. Nobody will ever call you a muse again. Then we're getting married. And Astrid?"

She's bewitched by the belief shining in his eyes.

"We'll spend the rest of our lives together," he tells her. "I promise."

* * *

Astrid refuses to be interviewed by the press. The baby is her business and Hawk's. But the press take her silence as hauteur and, in the absence of words, theirs flood in. HAWK TO TAKE OVER DESIGNING MIZZA and THE BABY SHE PLANS TO GIVE AWAY are just some of the headlines that follow her around.

The last one hurts worse than the rest. She stares at it for an entire night, not sleeping. When she'd spoken to Hawk, her goal had seemed simple—to love the baby so much that it knew, the same way it knew how to breathe, how loved it was. Now she worries it will hate her for making it into a headline before it even has a name.

Nauseatingly, the publicity sends her sales through the roof. Suddenly she has so much money it's ridiculous. It should be easy for her to believe that the Americans will win and everything Hawk promised will happen. But she doesn't have a single finished design to show. She needs to draw something. Otherwise she'll prove everyone right—that she's talentless, except in bed.

"Peppermint tea." Velvet interrupts her thoughts one day in July when Astrid is staring at the ideas and concepts she'd drawn before she found out she was pregnant.

"And granola." Velvet deposits both on the desk. "The baby needs it. You need it."

"Coffee with cognac might be more inspiring," Astrid says ruefully.

"I'm not bringing you either," Velvet says. "But I might break a bottle of cognac over Fairchild's head the next time I see him. How's it coming along?" She indicates the sketchbook.

"I see the press's words in my head, not dresses."

"I'm canceling our subscriptions. No more reading this shit."

Velvet dumps the papers in the trash, then picks up the sketchbook and flips back to a drawing of a sculpted white gown Astrid made before the first Versailles meeting, when she was riding high on the thrill of being chosen.

"This," Velvet says. "It's like one of those columns you see in pictures of Ancient Greece—everything in ruins, but the column still standing tall."

Astrid stares at her drawing. And she remembers when she was in Europe with Mizza and they went to Athens for a few days and visited the Temple of Athena Nike. The goddess of victory, her columns standing proud above a city, outlasting everything. Out of the ashes, out of the ruins, out of the taunts and barbs and oppression, come the women, marching.

She smiles at Velvet, picks up her pencils. "I think you just gave me my collection."

* * *

But the baby comes too quickly in a rush of blood and confusion in the middle of the night. There's no time to call Hawk and he isn't there when his daughter comes into the world almost six weeks early and weighing only four and a half pounds. Astrid is barely there either, lost in darkness, waking to an empty room.

She rings the bell and a nurse whose forehead is riven with lines arrives and tells her, "You had a girl. She's in the neonatal unit and will be there for at least a few days."

"I have to see her," Astrid says. She tries to stand but whatever they gave her has made her woozy. "I need to call Hawk."

The nurse doesn't even ask who that is. Of course she knows who Hawk is, who Astrid is. "We'll call him periodically," she says. "Get some rest."

Rest? How can anyone rest when their baby is gone?

She starts to shake all over.

The doctor finds her curled up in bed holding on to her knees, and he calls for the nurse to give her a sedative. But first he tells her that the baby has something called hyaline membrane disease. "It's relatively common in babies born too early," he says. "It's also very dangerous. Right now, a machine is breathing for the baby until its lungs can function properly, or until..." He clears his throat.

"Until what?" Astrid asks, even more frightened now.

The doctor looks at the nurse. The nurse looks at the doctor.

Suddenly and horrifyingly, Astrid understands. "That's... It's what Jacqueline Kennedy's son had."

The doctor nods. "Her son was born at around the same number of weeks as your infant. He had hyaline membrane disease too. But that was ten years ago. We're now able to treat the infants with ventilation. It saves some."

It saves some.

The Kennedys' son had died.

No.

"I want to see her," Astrid cries.

"Get her a sedative," the doctor tells the nurse again. To Astrid he says, "The neonatal unit will permit you to visit in the morning."

Permit her. She needs permission to see her child. But how will her baby know she loves her if she can't even see her? *Please,* she begs, not knowing who this desperate plea is aimed at. *Please don't let me fail at this too.*

All she can do is curl up into a ball again and stare at the clock, praying for it to be morning because then she'll see her daughter. She starts shaking again, and then someone slides onto the bed and pulls the back of her body against the front of his, folding her in his arms and pressing his face, wet with tears, into her hair.

And Astrid finally lets herself cry. She cries in Hawk's arms, cries and holds on, cries and holds on, and that's how the night passes— the two of them weeping for a daughter they haven't met, but love all the same.

THIRTY-NINE

BLYTHE BRICARD

Blythe's hand darts out to open the cover of Hawk's book about Astrid even as her eyelids want to shutter it from view. The first line reads:

You think you know Astrid Bricard? But did you know this woman?

Below is a picture of Astrid on a surfboard, a longboard, wearing a bikini, eyes narrowed in concentration, riding the face of a wave that's trying to swallow her up. A second picture shows her coasting the foam into shore, arms by her sides, grinning at the person behind the camera as if she'd beaten the wave, not the other way around.

Astrid surfed? Blythe drops onto the bed. Her mother looks happy in a way Blythe's never seen, not in any newspaper or magazine photograph—like a completely different person from the one who's usually portrayed. She just glows.

Blythe turns the page.

Or this woman? reads the next line, followed by a photograph that makes Blythe gasp. Astrid is nursing a baby. That baby can only be Blythe.

In the image, Astrid is looking down at her daughter wearing the kind of desperate expression—*Am I feeding her properly? Will she thrive?*—that holds so much love Blythe has to close the cover and cradle the book against her chest.

A man who steals designs from his lover doesn't then publish a book with pictures as beautiful as these.

Before she even knows what she's doing, she picks up her phone and dials. The same assistant she spoke to a few days ago answers.

"Can I talk to him?" Blythe asks.

The reply is a shocked, "Just a minute. I need to pull him out of a meeting."

Not long after, she hears her father say, "Blythe?" in a voice that sounds like he's known this day was coming, and it's a reckoning Hawk is simultaneously longing for and afraid of.

"I got the book," Blythe says. Then she hears herself blurt, "I thought she was coming back."

"Sweetheart." He says it just like he used to when she was maybe five years old. Back then it made her feel like he loved her more than a father usually did—as if he loved her enough for two.

She slides onto the floor and leans her back against the wall, knees propped in front of her, the same way she'd always sit and speak to him when he called her from work on the nights she stayed with Meredith. *Daddy*, the five-year-old Blythe would say. *I miss you.*

She presses one hand against her eyes.

"I…" Hawk's exhale is shaky. "I thought the same. But now…" A long pause. "Sweetheart," he says again, "I don't think she is."

And Blythe cries in a way she's never cried before. In a pathetic, pleading way—as though if she just sheds enough tears, then the ending she wants is the one she'll be given.

Her dad stays on the phone and when she quiets a little, he says, "I'm coming to France."

* * *

By the time Jake climbs back into bed after seeing Iris, Blythe is asleep, exhausted from the emotion. And the next day, everyone's up early, heading out on an excursion Blythe begs out of because there's too much going on. Hawk is coming to see her at the end of the week. Nathaniel is chasing her brand. She has to solve her sample problem so Marcelline will invest in her.

There's a bleakness in the back of Jake's eyes—maybe talking to his mom last night had made him see how close the inevitable is. So Blythe kisses him and doesn't dump all her troubles on him.

He and the kids have just left the room when she hears his phone ringing and discovers it hiding under one of Eva's sweaters. She answers it while hurrying to the door, hoping to catch Jake.

"Hey, Blythe. It's Anna," Jake's assistant says.

"Just a sec," Blythe says. "He's about to drive off."

"Can you just pass on a message? Another call's coming in. Tell him he needs to decide on a date for the MIZZA launch. I've got venues on hold and they want confirmations. Thanks!"

The phone beeps as Blythe reaches Jake's car.

"You left this behind," she says, surprised at how normal her voice sounds.

Why is Jake planning a launch for MIZZA?

She watches his hand take his phone, hears him say, "I love you." Then his car pulls away but her frown remains. He'd promised to stay out of it. And yet...

Is he expecting her to screw it up? Or for her to not be able to fight Nathaniel and then he'll swoop in, save the day and tuck MIZZA into his portfolio of brands and Blythe into his bed?

No. If she's learned anything from her divorce, it's that things aren't always what they seem. Rather than stew on it, she needs to ask him about it. In the meantime, she has work to do.

But the first task she tackles isn't related to MIZZA—or maybe it is. There's no way Hawk would have sent her Astrid's portfolio if he really had stolen her designs. So Blythe logs into the newspaper and magazine archives Coco's been using all week and searches. An overwhelming number of pages comes up because the subject—Astrid and Hawk—is biblical. It takes hours to sift through, but she starts to find new facts. A tiny article from the *New York Times* in 1971 titled CORRECTION:

> *The dress worn by Astrid Bricard in yesterday's edition of the paper was incorrectly attributed to Hawk Jones. He informs us it was designed by Astrid Bricard.*

A video of a speech Hawk gave when he won his first Coty where he tells the world that Astrid is a better designer than anyone he knows. One photograph—just one—of the Hawk Jones segment at the Versailles show. And rather than his name, the words *Astrid Bricard* are spotlit on the back of the stage and the dress the model is wearing bears those words too.

Which makes no sense at all.

It's midafternoon when Blythe's phone rouses her and Jake's words have her forgetting all about Hawk and Astrid. "I lost Eva," he says.

"Shit. Don't panic," she tells him, trying to take her own advice. But her stomach is a lead weight dropping to the floor. "Eva sometimes wanders off. It doesn't make you a terrible dad."

"It doesn't make me an especially great one either." In Jake's words is the sound of everything that makes one a parent—guilt, apprehension and sheer blind terror. "I thought she was with Georgia and Nick, and while I don't trust Nick as far as I could throw him, I trust Georgia. But Nick told the girls I wanted them to meet me and Sebby in the café. So the girls went to the café, and of course I wasn't there. Nick was planning to go after them and laugh at them, but he got distracted and by the time he arrived the girls were gone."

"So she's with Georgia. That's good. I might kill Nick though," Blythe says darkly.

"I've already given him a roasting so fierce he'll never grow whiskers," Jake says, equally darkly.

"How long have they been missing?"

"Maybe a half hour. That's a long time for a seven-year-old. I just—" Jake stops, exhales furiously, then says, "Wait." A little hope is back in his voice. "What if they were just in the toilet at the café? Eva was keen for ice cream and I said she could have one later. With the promise of ice cream . . ."

"She might stay put. See, you don't need me. Go find them and call me back."

After he hangs up, all Blythe can do is pace and stare at her phone and pray for Jake to call with good news. The phone does ring, but it's a number she doesn't recognize.

"Blythe, it's Charlie. I stayed upstairs to keep an eye on Mom and she's just lapsed into unconsciousness. I've called an ambulance and I'm going with her to the hospital in Paris. Can you tell Jake and Diana? I'll ring Ed and Hugh."

God. Iris. Jake will be shattered.

Blythe's eyes are damp as she calls Diana. That done, she brings up Jake's number, wishing he was there and she could hold him. She's just about to dial when her phone rings again and she's so distracted she doesn't look to see who it is.

"Blythe." Nathaniel Champlain's voice.

Her overwrought nerves twang. "I don't have time—"

He cuts her off. "For this, you do. Your mother is standing here in my office."

"Who?"

"Astrid is here," Nathaniel replies. "She's alive."

* * *

Nathaniel has only just hung up when a text pings from Jake. *I found her!*

How has Jake found Astrid too? is Blythe's first thought. Then she remembers. Eva. Eva was lost but now she's found. Astrid was missing and now she's standing in Nathaniel's office in Paris. It's not possible.

Where are the car keys? She has to go to Paris. Has to see this person who's pretending to be Astrid, has to tell them how cruel they are.

But... Iris. She's supposed to tell Jake. She can't even think, let alone speak the way Jake will need her to at this moment. Her fingers take charge, texting Ed. *You need to tell Jake.*

What if it really is Astrid in Nathaniel's office? The thought keeps pressing in.

Her keys aren't on the dresser or in her purse. She pushes aside fabric and clothes and Astrid's portfolio and still she can't find them. She needs to go right now, has to get to Paris before this Astrid-person leaves. Into the kids' room she flies, hands searching every surface before she darts back to the bathroom and finally sees them sitting unperturbed on the counter.

Thirty seconds later, she's in the car and driving. She has no coat, no hat, no gloves, no presence of mind to turn the heating up, and she's more than halfway to the city before the chill sets in so acutely that actual thoughts filter through the overwhelming paralysis of the impossible.

She's cold.

Iris is unconscious.

She's left it to Ed to tell Jake, which is a lousy thing to do.

She glances down to see if Jake's texted her again about Eva, or if Ed has about Iris. Her phone's not in the console.

Her hands scrabble around the car the same way they'd rifled through her room for her keys and that's when she realizes. She put her phone down to look for the keys. And she didn't pick it back up before she ran out the door.

Shit.

Jake must be on his way to the hospital. With Sebby and Eva.

Blythe needs to make sure Eva's really okay. But she can't. She's done the most irresponsible thing—jumped in a car with no thought for anyone and her phone is lying on the bed in the chateau.

Jake will have to sit with his mother without Blythe by his side and he'll have to care for his children at the same time. She's broken her promise to be with him. What if...? She shudders.

What if breaking that promise means she ruins them all over again? But... Astrid. Is alive.

Is standing in Nathaniel Champlain's office.

It's everything she wanted, but none of it can be true.

* * *

Someone shows her into the boardroom. Through the window, the Eiffel Tower poses—another muse.

Nathaniel says her name. He says it again because Blythe's breath is loud and fast and out of control. It's all hitting her now, pounding her body in a relentless, driving rhythm. Her mother has been alive all this time and she's never once called Blythe. Never tried to see her. Had really and truly abandoned her. The reality is so much more unendurable than the suspicion.

What kind of mother hates their child so very much?

"She read the articles," Nathaniel is saying. "About MIZZA. She didn't know where you were staying, so she came here because she knew I'd be able to get in touch with you. She's in the next room."

Blythe wilts into a chair. She's falling apart in front of Nathaniel, who wants MIZZA for himself. But the more she tries to level out her breathing, the more it refuses to cooperate.

"Where's Jake?" he asks, as if what's required is a man to take charge.

Jake's mother is dying and he lost one of the kids, she tries to make her mouth say.

Get hold of yourself. And she does, for two minutes. "I need to use your phone," Blythe tells Nathaniel.

She calls Jake but of course he doesn't answer because why would he pick up Nathaniel Champlain's call at a time like this? So she texts him.

Is Eva okay? And your mom?

Jake's text comes back like cannon fire.

Eva's fine. Why are you with Champlain?

She drops the phone on the table. Astrid is in the next room. Her mother. The one thing she's been missing all her life.

"Tell her..." she says to Nathaniel, voice quavering. "Tell her..." *What?*

Nathaniel walks toward a door, opens it and stands aside to let Astrid in.

FORTY

ASTRID BRICARD AND HAWK JONES

Astrid's first visit to the neonatal unit is hyperreal. So many tiny babies tucked away behind glass rather than tucked into their mothers' arms. And one glass case holding her daughter—a wraith, a shadow, the finest thing she's ever seen. Too small to be swallowing so many tubes. The hiss and moan of the machines is infernal and Astrid wants to touch her fingers over the too-small ears, wants to scoop her daughter up and never let her go.

The shock of love pouring in is so great Astrid has to brace her palms on the glass so she doesn't fall down. Her daughter's fingers are like delicate thread, her skin like chiffon. Magnificent lashes embroider her eyes.

"My God," she whispers. She will never be the same person if she loses her daughter. She will give up anything to keep her alive.

Like Versailles. It's eight weeks away and her baby can't breathe on her own.

"You need to express some milk," the nurse tells her.

Astrid tries so hard to do this, but it doesn't work. Nothing comes out beyond the tiniest trickle. She's about to throw the suction pump across the room when Hawk appears with his mom.

Meredith takes one look at Astrid and the pump and tells Hawk to go and sit with his daughter.

"You're sad right now but that doesn't matter," Meredith tells her firmly. "The baby matters. That's all. It's like with Matthias—if I ever let myself feel how sad I am, he would never be fed or bathed. Only think about getting some milk into this bottle. Nothing else."

It makes a brutal kind of sense. So Astrid pours her whole focus into her breast and the bottle and within half an hour, she's pumping milk. The joy is so great she starts crying again. That her own milk will be fed into the tube for her daughter feels like the finest achievement of her life. And there are only twenty-four hours to go before she'll be out of the greatest danger. The doctor said that if she made it through forty-eight hours, her chances of surviving were immeasurably improved.

So that afternoon, with Hawk by her side, Astrid says, "She needs a name." But before he can reply, it comes out. "I can't go to Versailles."

Her words are followed by a huge, gasping sob. She wraps an arm around her middle and presses a hand to her mouth to stop her stupid, selfish crying over a fashion show when her daughter can't breathe on her own.

"Astrid." Hawk's voice is an anguished cry for . . . what? What would they change? What would they reach into the past and erase or alter—where would they turn left or right? Would they make the same choices? Would they choose their daughter?

Hawk places all the difficulties to one side and draws her back to the present, arms tight around her, lips pressed to her temple. "My two favorite women in the world and only one of you has a name. What shall we call her?"

Astrid huddles into Hawk, into his love. She wants their daughter to have a joyous name, to possess one euphoric word that will mean she's never sitting in a chair in a hospital, weeping while her heart breaks.

"Blythe," she says, remembering a rhyme Beth taught her. "And may her life be blithesome."

* * *

Forty-eight hours pass and Blythe is still alive.

"She still has a long way to go," the doctor says. "But it's a good sign."

Thank Christ. Hawk's face almost splits in two with how happy he is. And Astrid smiles at him for the first time since that terrible night when he'd been out at the factory trying to solve a production issue at all hours of the morning and had missed all the phone calls, had missed being with Astrid while she, alone and most likely scared beyond anything, had given birth to Blythe.

He tugs Astrid against his body and he kisses her. He kisses her as if every single emotion he's felt since Blythe was conceived is exploding into that kiss.

The doctor leaves the room.

A moment later, Hawk sinks into a chair, elbows on his knees, head in his hands, crying the same way Astrid had cried yesterday, as if pain was the only thing left in the world. He feels her drop to her knees beside him, wrapping him in her arms, saying his name over and over and he knows he needs to get it together, needs to be there for Astrid, needs to be the one gathering Astrid and the baby as close as he can so that none of them will ever hurt like this again.

He swipes angrily at his eyes, takes one deep breath, sees how much worry her eyes hold—they're a murky Verona green, the khaki color of war. "I'm okay," he tells her. "I'm okay."

Because he has to be. Astrid was strong enough to give birth all by herself, strong enough to say she'll cast aside her dreams and hopes and thus her entire self for their daughter. But he can't let her do that. So he says, tone almost savage, "I love you, Astrid. But you're going to Versailles. Mom will look after Blythe. It's four nights—four nights out of the thousands she'll have. If you don't go, then that's the same as giving yourself up. And if you do that, our daughter will never know the inspiring, incredible woman you are. Blythe deserves that woman, not one who hollowed herself out for love."

"Hawk . . ." All of a sudden, Astrid is in his lap, her arms around his neck and they're both crying again—so many fucking tears—but this time it feels like maybe it's catharsis and redemption—that Astrid is letting herself be filled up by the things she has, rather than emptied out by the things she wants.

* * *

Velvet leaves Astrid in peace for another week and then comes to see her with a worried frown.

"There are so many things . . . I don't know what you want. I don't know . . ."

Her face crumples and Astrid understands that the world is still turning. A little of what Hawk said penetrates—if she vanishes, everything she's worked for will vanish too. Then what kind of an inspiration will she be for her daughter?

So she hugs Velvet. Lets her friend cry out all the stress of having had to fend off the insatiable press. "I'm being discharged tomorrow," she says. "I need to spend each day here with Blythe, so I'll work at night because I'm not allowed to visit the hospital then."

She needs to work at night, she realizes. It's the only thing that will distract her from thinking about Blythe, still lying here without her.

From then on, Astrid spends each day at the hospital with her daughter. And she works at night, sitting on the floor of the studio, re-pinning hems, recutting sleeves. Hospital. Work. Hospital. Work. It's the rhythm of her days and nights. Other things get lost—eating. Smiling. Thinking. Sleeping. Anything outside that steady, relentless beat.

She catches herself by Blythe's bedside one day, wondering why her stomach is so sore. Beth, who comes most days to sit with her, says, "When did you last eat? You look pale."

Astrid trawls through her memories for an answer to that question but can't find it. She remembers Velvet bringing her granola one night in the studio but maybe that was on Monday. It's now Wednesday. Yesterday, two nurses had whispered together and Astrid had stared at them, convinced they were talking about Blythe and some new and deadly complication and she'd said to them, "What is it?"

They'd giggled and told her they were wondering when Hawk was coming in and Astrid had said, "Who?" as if she didn't know who Hawk was. And in that moment, convinced they were about to tell her Blythe's heart or lungs were too weak, she'd honestly not known who he was.

For the next few days, Blythe wriggles every time Astrid picks her up—wriggles like she's trying to get away, like she just wants to be put back in the crib she knows better than she knows Astrid. As if she too isn't convinced Astrid knows what she's doing and doesn't want to risk being held by someone who might well drop her or hurt her or make her cry.

After that, there are more and more nights when Astrid finds herself in the studio in a void of nothing, arms empty where her child should be. Every time she rouses from that state, a viscous wave of hate rolls over her. That she's drawing dresses while Blythe is being weaned off tubes and breathing machines. That her daughter is alone after six o'clock each night. That Astrid hasn't broken down doors and insisted on being allowed to stay, even though it's absolutely not permitted.

Fear crescendos. How will her daughter ever trust her? Blythe trusts tubes, the smell of the hospital, the nurses' voices.

Then the shame hits Astrid—the terrible, awful shame of abandoning her daughter to go to Paris. She puts down her pins, pushes the fabrics away.

She can't go to Versailles.

She can't.

* * *

Hawk starts bringing her dinner each night, which she pushes around her plate. He says things like, "Are you okay?" or "You're not yourself."

"I'm fine," she tells him. "I ate at the hospital."

Velvet and Hawk are the only people she sees. Even Meredith and Beth are too demanding, wanting to know how much Blythe has grown. Astrid doesn't want to say, *Not enough*, because then they'll know she's failing at something that's supposed to be so natural—motherhood.

At last they send Blythe home with Astrid and it's the best day of her life. She refuses to let Hawk stay over because, just yesterday, a copy of *Women's Wear Daily* slipped past Velvet's vigilance. Astrid saw Fairchild's article speculating that Hawk was designing her Versailles collection because she was busy with the baby.

If Hawk stays with them, it will only make everyone believe Fairchild's words, even though Astrid has no intention of leaving Blythe to go to Versailles. But still her hands make clothes to be shown there and she wonders if this is madness—this furious and almost obsessive making of something nobody will ever see.

Soon, the days and nights blur together. Blythe cries for long passages of time. In between, she needs to be fed and washed and changed and burped and soothed, and Astrid needs to do all of this as well as it was done in the hospital. In the minutes and moments when Blythe sleeps, there are tears and nothingness and hate and fear and shame and no sleep and no food either because food makes her vomit and thank goodness she called her baby Blythe because there's no joy anywhere.

"Come for a walk to the shop. Or go to yours," Hawk says to her one morning before work. He brings coffee as usual—which she tips into the sink after he's gone—as well as croissants she picks at, food from Meredith for dinner that she forgets to put away. "Blythe might settle in the stroller," he tells her. "I'll come with you."

"No," Astrid says, the only word she speaks while he's there.

"Please?" he says. "Just get some sun."

She tries. She wraps Blythe in a blanket and Blythe smiles at her all of a sudden and Astrid gasps with the wonder of that beautiful little expression, all the trust and delight that lives inside her child.

She calls Hawk and when he answers, all she can do is cry until he says, voice more worried than she's ever heard it, "I'm coming over right now."

Astrid manages to get a grip and say, "She smiled. Blythe smiled."

Hawk laughs and the sound is just as good as witnessing her daughter's joy.

"I'll come to the shop," she tells him, because she wants to show him that their daughter is happy—give him this proof that Astrid must be doing things right.

She puts Blythe in the stroller and goes down to the lobby and out onto the street. Suddenly she's surrounded by people and lights. By shouting and questions. A pack of photographers. She pushes the stroller away from them but they follow her, still shouting. They call out things that Astrid tries not to hear but she isn't deaf and the words penetrate and what if she cries right there on the sidewalk?

Then Blythe begins to howl. Astrid has hurt her child simply by the fact of being Astrid Bricard.

She doesn't go out again. She doesn't go to the studio. She doesn't go to the doctor. She and Blythe stay where they are, inside, safe.

Hawk stands in her apartment at some time—day or night, it's impossible to know—telling her he's worried about her. Then somehow, Mizza is on the phone. Hawk has tracked her down, has asked her to speak to Astrid.

"*Ma chérie*," Mizza begins, voice throaty. "*Ma chérie.*"

Astrid looks at her baby. My dear. My *dear*.

"Come to France," Mizza says. "To Versailles. Four nights is very different than a lifetime. I had only my own counsel in 1945. I see now that I needed some other. So let me give you that counsel. Be Astrid Bricard, fashion designer, for four short nights. Then return to your child and see her and your situation as if it were a new vista. It is no small thing to regret something for the entirety of every moment of the rest of your life, Astrid."

She hears what Mizza is telling her—*I regret giving you up*—and she weeps.

* * *

That night, Astrid catches a photographer with his lens pressed to the window, having climbed the fire escape to spy on her. Chaos ensues—police, arrests, flashbulbs. Blythe cries and cries. Astrid does too.

Hawk calls Meredith to come over while he's talking to the police, and Meredith tells Astrid, "You know, if you go to France, Blythe will have some peace from the press."

With Astrid away, Blythe will be at peace. That's what she hears.

She *is* hurting Blythe. To make it stop, she has to leave.

So Astrid agrees. Versailles is truly before them. It's make or break. But who will break?

FORTY-ONE

MIZZA BRICARD

PARIS, 1942–1944

M izza felt a presence behind her as she walked to a restaurant to meet Jeanne. She turned her head several times and yes, there were Nazis behind her, but not the one who'd waited outside her apartment building.

She said nothing to Jeanne when she arrived, sighing with pleasure as the door closed. Restaurants had coal and warmth—ordinary Parisians had just one bag of coal per person to last the entire winter. Prewar, a bag of coal might last only a week.

"It's almost impossible to imagine when pearls were treasured more than coal, isn't it?" Mizza mused as they shrugged off their coats for the first time in days.

Jeanne laughed, then frowned when she saw the menu. "How to choose between meatless pâté and omelet made from egg and water."

"I had nothing but a ration sandwich for dinner last night, so I'll happily accept meatless pâté," Mizza said with a smile.

Jeanne raised an eyebrow. "Ration sandwich?"

"A ration card for ham tucked between two ration cards for bread."

Perhaps it was incongruous that they wore precious jewels but were starving and freezing. But to let go of those jewels would be like letting go of their spirits.

"We're probably better off eating the ration cards." Jeanne sighed, touching a hand to the bird-in-a-cage brooch she wore, a design that had resulted in her spending a night in prison, as the Nazis thought it was a political statement—which it was. "No more misery," she proclaimed. "Let's talk about the fact that you must get married."

Mizza was the one who laughed now. "Never again."

Jeanne held on to Mizza's hands. "I've been inside a Nazi prison. It changed me deeply, and I was only there for a night. If I can be arrested, then so can you, especially if you keep doing whatever has put the weight of a thousand souls in your eyes."

Mizza tried to straighten her veil to hide the soul of the girl she hoped was safe now, but Jeanne continued. "A husband is a shield you need. And a friend of Pierre's needs protection too." Pierre was Jeanne's lover now that Cartier was gone.

Protection. Mizza recalled the presence she'd sworn was lurking behind her earlier. She had so many reasons for needing a shield. Bernard Dior, a so-called madman. The children creeping along the secret paths under Paris.

"He works with Pierre," Jeanne said as if it were final. "An industrialist making materials the Nazis need. It will keep him safe. And you too."

"Collaborating?"

"Surviving."

* * *

Hubert Bricard kissed her hand. *"Enchanté."* Then he laughed. "Is it like selecting bread at the boulangerie, or the best wine to have with dinner? I have no questions prepared, nor do I have a statement of my strengths and weaknesses."

Mizza smiled. "Perhaps it's better not to know those things in advance."

"I haven't been married before, so I don't know." He proffered a gift—a Helleu portrait of a woman sitting in her corset beside a fire, her back turned to the viewer. "I know as much about you now as I know about this woman," he said, indicating the sketch, "but perhaps one day you'll turn around to face me and I'll know more."

Unaccountable tears pricked Mizza's eyes. He must have asked Jeanne about her tastes, and then had the wherewithal to find a Helleu portrait in a few days, one that he'd made a story around. It was a gesture so thoughtful it hurt.

"You have some secrets, and you want a marriage to hide them," she said—there could be no other reason for him needing a *mariage blanc*. "Are they honorable?"

He looked suddenly and deeply serious, as only a lover can look when contemplating their beloved, all of his heart in his words. "I believe they are," he said, and she guessed he was in love with someone forbidden to him by either family or society or the Nazis.

"My secrets are honorable too," she told him.

They met two more times and Mizza discovered a man who would make the perfect name-only husband. He was kind, which was more than she'd expected. And he laughingly told her that marrying her would make him out to be something of a rake—convincing the mysterious and extremely beautiful Madame Biano to commit—which wouldn't do his reputation any harm in the circles of men he worked with.

She smiled and raised her glass. "Then let's get married."

* * *

One month after taking the children over the bones, and with Jeanne as her witness, Mizza married Hubert. Afterward, she went to work, and when she returned home, Hubert was in the kitchen preparing food.

"How is Balenciaga?" he asked her so naturally it felt as if he'd always been there.

"Despondent about Germany," she said, collapsing into a chair.

Unexpectedly, Hubert kneeled down at her side, took off her shoes, placed one of her feet on his leg and began to rub it with gentle fingers. Mizza closed her eyes and exhaled. Then she opened her eyes and tried to move, uncertain what this gesture meant.

"Your feet are sore?" he asked.

She nodded.

"Then why not have them rubbed."

So simple. And so delightful.

Her husband placed the first foot on the floor, took up the second and began to press his knuckles against the sole.

"War will ruin so many things," she said, needing to say some of it even if she couldn't say all of it. "The buses, the ones that drive into the Marais at night. There are stories of children hidden so they won't be discovered. Where will the children go if the families don't come back?"

Hubert said, very gently, "The families won't ever come back."

God.

That night, the faces of the children Mizza had smuggled through Paris sat like accusations on the inside of her eyelids. The chance of their parents still being alive at the end of the war, whenever that might be, was as improbable as discovering a tiny stirrup bone hiding in the ossuaries. So why continue to endanger herself for lives that were already ruined?

She opened her eyes and took in the four walls around her. The bed she lay in. The room along the hall where her new husband slept. He would protect her, he'd said—and he hadn't even asked, *From what?* He'd simply trusted that she would protect him too.

She had so much more than those children did.

Which meant she had to keep showing them the white heart on the wall of Paris's netherworld. Even a small light could get you through the bleakest darkness.

* * *

The marriage allowed Mizza to work for Balenciaga during the day, and accompany children underneath the city to freedom at nights, untroubled by visits from Nazis. But as the Allies invaded North Africa, and 1943 brought with it huge losses to the Germans in Russia, their demands for successes became greater. Failures in war meant the Nazis no longer had time to plan how to move an entire industry to Germany, but they had other ways of making the couturiers suffer. They came back to see Balenciaga, to make certain he wasn't exceeding his quota.

Of course he was—everyone was. He'd made more dresses than he was permitted to. How else was he supposed to support such a large staff?

While one German officer shouted at Monsieur Balenciaga that they were shuttering his business, another came looking for Madame Bricard.

It was the same Nazi who'd singled her out before. "You're quite famous in Paris, you know," he said. "The woman who's had jewels bestowed on her by Egyptian princes."

What garbage. Before she could protest, the Nazi hissed, "You'll have to find other employment now, Madame Bricard."

And she did have to. Balenciaga told her, almost savagely, the gentlemanly façade torn down by men in brown boots, "I'll return from Spain in a few months. They'll soon forget about the quota—or will remember that their wives want beautiful clothes."

As she walked home from another mission at Sainte-Anne, Mizza was thinking about what employment she might find and wasn't paying attention to her surroundings.

"Madame Bricard," a voice sharp as pins said.

The Nazi. And Mizza had just been under the city, smuggling Jewish children to safety.

"What is it you do at the hospital?" he asked.

"I assist with repairs for the patients' clothing," she replied, the lie smooth on her tongue. "One must always help those who are in need."

The officer eyed her speculatively. "They must. Which is why you will come to the Ritz tomorrow evening. I need help and you will provide it."

Mizza could feel her integrity slide away, a coat made of too-shiny silk. Because she would have to go. She had too many secrets to hide. Children with strong, white hearts. And a map of an underground city of bones.

* * *

Mizza dressed impeccably for her meeting at the Ritz, donning a black worsted Balenciaga suit with two long rows of buttons reaching up to the collar. She filled the space between the collar and her neck with ropes of pearls—too many for taste, but the right amount to show a Nazi she still had spirit left despite the cold, despite the ration sandwiches, despite the closure of Balenciaga.

As she walked through the Place Vendome entrance—reserved for Nazis and their guests—she knew her visit was being marked by many Parisians. Some would shrug. Others would spit. She would spit on herself too.

"Madame Bricard," the Nazi said. "Have some champagne."

"I prefer Perrier," Mizza replied.

Anger flashed in his eyes, a dark stain spreading through the pale blue. "You visit a lunatic."

Her eyes flew up to meet his. "I don't know your name," she said, as if that was the extent of his rudeness.

"Herr Didier." Another dangerous smile.

Think of Lev, she told herself and, suddenly, there was his face, his precious face, just as it had looked that first morning when he'd woken with her limbs draped over his body and his draped over hers as if they each possessed the other as well as themselves. And behind his face, the face of the girl who'd taken Mizza's ruby ring into the dark night of Paris.

"A pleasure," she lied, able to breathe now and sip her water.

"You visit a lunatic," Herr Didier repeated. "What will you do to protect him? You must know your occupiers have no time for lunatics."

It had come to this. Perhaps a sensible person would have given up Tian's brother the day the Nazis arrived in Paris. But one's friends were one's life—its texture, its grace—and she found, suddenly and achingly, that she would prefer what she was suffering right now with Herr Didier to a lonely, graceless life without the blessing of the people she loved. Tian. Jeanne. Hubert now too.

Pretend. Be the woman with too many pearls, a fabulous leopard-print coat, and a remarkable face. "What are you proposing?" she asked.

And she almost inelegantly spat her water everywhere when he replied, "Dresses."

FORTY-TWO

MIZZA BRICARD

The next day Mizza rented two small rooms in a building on the Left Bank. That night, she drew a pattern for a dress. Balenciaga's version was black silk satin with two elegant white strips from shoulder to hem, but she'd make this one in blue and leave out the contrasting stripes so it would look different enough to have come from a copy house.

The thought made her crush the fabric Didier had provided—requisitioned? Stolen? From whom?—in her fist. What was she doing? Stealing designs. Helping a Nazi. Even in her worst moments in 1918, sobbing over Lev's death while four Germans tied her wrists with rope and held a knife at her neck, she had never hated herself. But, right now, she hated Mizza Bricard more than she hated Herr Didier.

But she would just have to hate herself. All Didier had discovered so far was Bernard's illness. She had to keep him away from Sainte-Anne before he discovered any more, before children who were unlucky enough to be Jewish were found to be hiding at the asylum. Those children—and the pilots too—who scurried beneath the city like tiny and defenseless ants, would die at Mizza's hands if she said no to Didier because he would take her and torture her and all her secrets would spill out along with her blood.

Her scissors sliced into the silk.

Didier came the following day with a Frenchwoman who didn't look as if she'd been forced to come. "Where's the mannequin?" the woman pouted. "I thought the dresses would be shown to me, like at the real salons."

Her pout lengthened into petulance and Mizza had to push the scissors out of reach lest her anger tempt her to act foolishly. She pulled her threads tight, keeping herself together. "We're just setting up," she said. "You're lucky to come before the crowds."

Even if she bathed thrice daily, Mizza would still feel filthy. Before today, the word *war* had meant men shooting other men in fields far away. But war, she now understood, meant women thrown into a churning black sea, grasping for any life raft they could find—even if that life raft was full of holes and captained by sharks.

Tears pressed shockingly into her eyes.

The woman pushed Mizza out of the way and put on the sample dress. "It's wonderful!" she squealed. "I want it ready by next weekend."

Mizza nodded.

While his paramour changed back into her clothes, Didier said to Mizza, "I have more people to send to you. You'll make dresses for them too. It must be impressive."

Ah. He wanted to impress. Perhaps he wasn't of the upper echelon of Nazis who could command any woman and any position he wanted and this was his way to gain a little power. Which meant she just had to hold on. If she kept him happy, he mightn't look into Sainte-Anne any further. And it was January 1944. The Nazis had been in Paris for three and a half years. Surely this wouldn't go on for three and a half years more.

* * *

Thus one gown turned into five copied from Balenciaga patterns as Mizza became a dressmaker for Nazi middle officers who couldn't afford couture for the women they wished to impress, but were happy with something close enough and at half the price.

Not that it eased her conscience at all, but Mizza chose the designs that were mostly hers, never ones the master himself had designed. But she still wanted to stitch each dress with red thread, the color of her shame. The only small rebellion she could make was to say no to the Nazis who, despite having brought a woman with them to look at the gowns, asked Mizza if they could take her to dinner.

"Alas, I'm married," she said. "My husband is making things your armies need. I could never betray him."

It was enough to get her out of any further filth. *Thank God for my marriage*, she thought each night.

But it wasn't long before the people in the apartments beside the studio averted their eyes if they passed Mizza on the stairs. They saw Nazis visiting for who knew what purpose and they didn't want to be contaminated by this woman who consorted with the enemy. Somehow rumors snaked from the Left Bank to the Right and a neighbor in her own apartment building hissed, *"Collabo,"* at her.

"Courage, my friend," the building supervisor, who'd been passing on her notes to the Allies since the early months of the war, told her.

Courage. But the only time she felt brave anymore was for a few hours every month when she ferried children underneath the city to freedom.

* * *

The few bright spots in the long winter and glacial spring of 1944 were Mizza's outings with Jeanne, Tian, and her visits to Bernard Dior. Christian had relieved her of the responsibility once he'd returned to Paris after his discharge from the French army, but Mizza continued to go to Sainte-Anne because how bleak was a life where you had but one visitor?

On this day, she found Bernard digging in the gardens. She sat in a chair and watched as he pulled something out of the ground and held it aloft—a tulip, planted in winter, blooming now in spring, a metaphor that didn't relate to life in Paris.

"That one's pretty," the gardener told him. "We leave the pretty ones in the ground."

"It's not pretty," Bernard muttered. "It's weak."

He shook it gently and the tulip's petals tumbled to the ground. Then he lifted a bunch of weeds from a pile, their yellow flowers bright against vivid green leaves, and gave them a vigorous shake. The flowers remained affixed to their stems, the petals to their centers. "These are strong."

Bittersweet tears bloomed in Mizza's eyes. She'd become accustomed to thinking of beauty as what one saw, not the qualities that lay beneath. To be strong was beautiful. How curious that it took a person deemed a madman to make her see that.

She left Sainte-Anne with the curve of a smile on her face. She wouldn't look at her life and see the ugliness everywhere. Instead, she would cling like the yellow flower to her stem until it withered at last.

FORTY-THREE

MIZZA BRICARD

Mizza clung to that stem until, after days of gunshots and artillery fire, the liberation of Paris finally came. As the French and American forces entered the city, she realized the people she most wanted to mark this moment with were the children. But she would never see them again. And now she was going to cry on a day meant for happiness.

She couldn't celebrate with Hubert. As soon as the Allies had landed in Normandy, Hubert had been sent to Germany—as an industrial chemist with explosives expertise, the Nazis wanted to keep a close eye on him. He was safe enough, she understood from his letters, albeit under a kind of house arrest—but what if the Allies' progress enraged the Nazis still more? Surely they wouldn't do anything to a gentle man like Hubert?

Every muscle tight with tension, she went to Cartier to see Jeanne. Jeanne would make her smile—make her see that Hubert would be back soon, that Mizza's sins would be forgotten and everything would be all right.

But Jeanne wept the same way Mizza had done in her arms in 1924. This time, Mizza held her while she cried, tears pricking her eyes like pins, scratching her soul.

"Mon Dieu," Jeanne said at last, giving herself a little shake. Then

she picked up a brooch and pinned it to Mizza's turban. A bird in a cage with the door flung open. "It's over," she said.

"We survived."

Jeanne nodded bleakly, as if she too knew that survival wasn't the same as winning.

Mizza touched the bird. *This one is strong*, Bernard had said. Strong outside, but wrecked within. "I'm going to walk," she told Jeanne. She had to see for herself what liberation was.

There on the Champs-Élysées were people singing "La Marseillaise." Brasseries spilled clientele and wine onto the sidewalk. Allied soldiers kissed every Frenchwoman who passed. Around the Arc de Triomphe, where a battalion of Allied soldiers was encamped, servicemen and Frenchwomen satisfied themselves with one another out in the open. It was as if release from the Occupation was still too abstract to comprehend and it needed to be made physical to be believed.

Mizza understood. Her mind knew liberation had come but her body was heavy with foreboding. Her hand strayed to the brooch Jeanne had given her. The bird was still in its cage, even though it could see freedom through the open door.

"Ma'am?" An American voice by her shoulder, elongating the *a* sound as awkwardly as an askew hat, made her start.

"It is you!" a serviceman said and she shook her head, thinking her veil had made him mistake her for someone else.

"James!" he called and another man jogged over. "It's our guardian angel," he said.

The man, James, agreed with an ebullient smile and Mizza recalled the two men from her first descent into the subterranean world of bones—the one who'd admired her, and the one who'd carried the girl.

And suddenly she felt it. Liberation. Her feet had crunched over skulls with these men and here they both were, alive. "You're safe," she cried.

"Thanks to you," both men said at the same time.

Mizza laughed. She asked the second man, James, "Your fiancée? Are you married?"

He shook his head. "She's in Paris with the Red Cross but we're getting married the minute we get home."

"*Bien*. I'm so glad for you."

"Me too," he said fervently. "Let me introduce us both properly. I'm Flight Sergeant James Davenport and this is my buddy, Flight Sergeant David Paris."

"You have a wonderful surname," Mizza said, grinning like a girl.

David laughed. "I've been ragged about it for the whole war, ma'am."

"Please don't *ma'am* me," she chided. "I'm Mizza. Mizza Bricard."

"That's some name," David said admiringly. "As unforgettable as its owner."

And Mizza actually blushed beneath this man's innocent and eager regard.

"It sure was good to see you, Mrs. Bricard," James said, shaking her hand in a very American way. "I hope you don't mind if I take off. My fiancée, Beth, is waiting for me."

"Good luck to you both," Mizza said before he ran off into the night, leaving her with David, who said shyly, "Would you like to walk with me? I never thanked you properly."

"I'll walk with you only on the condition you don't thank me again," Mizza said. "I did very little compared to what a pilot must have done."

She slipped her arm into his, as one did when walking. David looked still more abashed. "You're very French, aren't you?"

"I hope so." Mizza chuckled.

They set off, moving toward the end of the street where it was quieter, then David asked her, "Has it been hard?"

Hard to steal Balenciaga's designs? To make them into clothes

for Nazis? Hard to help at least two men survive by showing them
through Paris's bones?

"No harder than for anyone else," she said, but there was a sadness
in her voice she couldn't quite hide, which caused the boy at her side
to say, "I'm sorry."

Now she was crying. *Mon Dieu.* That a young man from a foreign
country could make her weep when she'd been able to hold her tears
inside her in front of Nazis. She patted her gloved hand under her
eyes. "What a sentimental night."

That was when he leaned in and kissed her. He didn't kiss her like
Lev had, or like Hubert might if they had that kind of relationship.
He didn't kiss her like the men who'd dotted the months and years
between her marriages, men who'd kissed a thousand women and
who would kiss a thousand more. David kissed her like an ingénue,
uncorrupted by the world.

It almost broke her heart.

* * *

Mizza looked back on that night with David with wistfulness, or even
a kind of homesickness—a longing not just for the man, but for the
moment when all that mattered was tenderness and a larger feeling of
grace, one that touched all of humanity.

But now…there was so little grace and no humanity left in
the world.

The *épuration sauvage*—the shaving and stripping of women
believed to have collaborated with Nazis, the marching of them down
streets to be spat on, their reputations ruined forever—was as swift
and appalling as the Reign of Terror one hundred and fifty years ago.
This time, the victims were all women—women who'd made deci-
sions and trade-offs and compromises and sacrifices. Women who'd
kept themselves and their children and mothers and families alive,

and who were now being told they should have sacrificed themselves and their children and their mothers and families too.

"A dead woman is more noble than one who did whatever she could to feed her sons and daughters," Jeanne said soberly to Mizza as they gripped one another's hands and stared with grim faces at the spectacle outside.

One of the women being paraded through the street tripped and fell and a man placed his booted foot on her back. Mizza had seen a Nazi do the same thing to a woman not six months ago.

The spectators laughed.

"Don't they care that half the men out there only joined the Resistance in the last month when it was certain the French would win?" Mizza said savagely. "Don't they care that so many of those women resisted every single day in some way since June 1940? Don't they care that in order to stay alive and keep resisting you *had* to collaborate sometimes? If we'd all given up our lives rather than resist, would France be free now?"

The crowd thickened into a mob, each face like a wrecked sheet of white cotton, ripped holes for eyes, one large, open gash for a mouth. A man holding the crudest of razors lifted his arm and brought it down, ripping off a weft of a woman's hair. People cheered like they had in this very place just days ago at the victory parade. But today's shouts were not of pride and joy. They were animal, of savagery and spleen, the kind of screams you had to be making too or else they would frighten the skin from your bones.

One by one, twenty women were pushed onto a platform. Their hair was hacked away by the French Forces of the Interior, that group of men lauded as heroes of the French Resistance.

Two of the women on the platform clutched underclothes against their skin, another shielded her naked breasts with useless arms. Swastikas were inked onto the foreheads of others. A sign proclaiming them *Collabos*—Nazi collaborators—hung around their necks. They each nursed babies—Nazi babies, the crowd jeered.

Mizza turned away, pressing a hand to her mouth. They were not *collabos*—they were Parisiennes who'd done what they could to survive. Just like she had.

"Twenty women won't be enough," she whispered.

"Nothing will be enough to satisfy them," Jeanne said bleakly.

Because how was it possible to return all the missing, to resurrect all the dead, to wipe clean the shame of making Hitler a gift of Paris and much of France? That was the kind of shame that left one's bones filthy.

Another woman with a shaved head and a baby in her arms trudged past. The crowd spat. The baby howled.

"Cursed before it can even speak," Jeanne murmured. "That poor child. What kind of life will it have here in a city that already despises it?"

THE PENULTIMATE ACT

THE LEGEND'S STORY...

FORTY-FOUR

ASTRID BRICARD AND HAWK JONES

NEW YORK CITY, NOVEMBER 1973

Velvet packs everything they need from the studio. But Astrid only realizes she needs to pack herself a suitcase when Hawk arrives to take Blythe to his mother's, and Astrid to the airport.

"Let me take your case down to the cab," he says.

She looks at the pile of Blythe's things waiting by the door—diapers, blankets, colic remedies, rattles—and then at herself, still wearing the tank dress from yesterday that she thinks maybe she slept in. Of course she can't go to France in a day-old tank dress and with only a passport, the one thing she's got ready.

"Just a minute." She hurries into her room, hoping he doesn't follow and see that she can't even look after herself, let alone their child. She reappears fifteen minutes later in clean clothes and with a bag in hand.

It isn't until she steps on board Olympic Airways Flight 401 that she starts to emerge from something she hadn't realized she'd been buried in. It's funny how, only when a little light comes in do you understand you've become so used to darkness that you've forgotten stars exist.

The first star is unexpected—like the instant when dusk turns to night and suddenly the sky is constellated with diamonds. A young girl calls Astrid's name in the airport and Astrid cringes, expecting a taunt, but the girl says, "I came to get your autograph." Her smile is golden and it makes the corners of Astrid's mouth lift too.

Then she sees another girl, and another. A line of smiles and optimism. They want to talk to her—to tell her how inspiring she is.

"Me?" she asks the first girl, who nods as if to say, *Yes, of course* you.

"After that interview you did in *Cosmo* where you talked about how the teachers would measure your skirt and how unfair it was to judge our character by the length of our skirts, we organized a petition," another says. "And now our teachers don't measure our skirts anymore because so many people signed it."

"Really?" Astrid still expects John Fairchild to jump out and tell her he's staged this to embarrass her. But the expressions on the girls' faces are so heartfelt—they remind Astrid of herself at that age, passionate, determined.

"Hawk," she says. "Have you got your camera?"

He takes a snap of Astrid with the girls' arms around her—one Polaroid for them, another for her. She tucks it into her pocket and hugs them. "You made my day," she tells them and they beam as if she's made theirs too.

She rests her hand against that picture as she walks down the aisle of the plane, smiling in a way that's sweet with the memory of the power those girls had, and sad at the realization that she doesn't smile much anymore. Up ahead, she sees Candace and her smile dims. She's not as strong right now as she was in college and Candace's barbs are likely to land in her most tender places.

"Hawk," Candace says, and it's impossible to miss—the yearning, Astrid realizes. Not lust or spite but a sore heart. Hawk is Candace's tender place and that's not something to press upon. She'll offer kindness instead, and it's up to Candace if she takes it. She smiles as gently as she can.

Candace turns away.

Which is her right. Just as it's Astrid's right, she suddenly thinks, to be here on this plane. For the sake of those girls, there has to be one woman taking the stage at Versailles. Otherwise how will they ever keep dreaming of a world where women sometimes have the chance to make a difference?

As she and Hawk sit down, she says, not sure if this makes her a traitor-ous mother or a woman who's still just trying to make powerful clothes, "Maybe you were right. I need to do this. I have thousands of other nights to be with Blythe. But I owe the next four nights to those girls at the airport—and to the ones who weren't allowed or were too scared to come."

He slides his hand around to the back of her neck, drawing her in. "I love you," he says fiercely. "There's nobody else in the world I want to do all of this with."

She knows they're both one sentence away from watery eyes and they can't let everyone on the plane see that. Hawk must recognize it too because he grins and points to the seats behind. The designers are in business class. The designers' assistants—Nancy, Velvet, Candace—and the models are in coach. There are passengers unrelated to Versailles too but they're outnumbered, as are the flight attendants, and it's already the Cheetah at thirty thousand feet. The air is tobacco- and grass-scented. Models are dancing in the aisles. Whiskey and champagne slosh into mouths. The ass of at least one model is visible when she bends to talk to a passenger, charming him with not just her smile, but her pert derriere.

"Look at us sitting here while the party goes on three feet away," Hawk says. "A year ago and that would have been us."

A year ago and Blythe didn't exist. The thought is shocking. "I miss her, Hawk."

"I know," he says, resting his forehead against hers. "I do too. It actually hurts how much I miss her."

Hearing him say that makes her realize she's been so caught up in her own pain she's forgotten Hawk feels these things too. "I'm sorry," she says. "I've been, I don't know..."

"Hey. You don't need to apologize. We miss Blythe, and we're both going to feel like we've done the wrong thing leaving her behind. So we might as well work hard and show the French what fashion is. We'll feel just as guilty doing that as if we sit in our hotel room being miserable."

A smile stretches tentatively over her face. He's right. And for the first time she finds the strength to push down the feeling that, since she gave birth to Blythe earlier than she was meant to, she's on trial and failing at motherhood in the eyes of the entire world.

"Okay," Astrid says. "Let's miss Blythe and show the French what fashion is too."

Hawk's answering smile is something she's missed so much.

"I wanted Blythe to have one joyous word of her own," she says, touching a finger to his lips, "but I've forgotten how to be happy. And you have too. But Blythe needs us to be happy, otherwise *she* won't be. I guess maybe…" She hesitates, hopes it doesn't sound selfish. But Mizza was right. By winning at Versailles, she'll find the Astrid who can be both Queen of Fashion, mother to Blythe, and wife of Hawk. Why can't that person exist? "I guess maybe we both needed this."

"In four days' time, we'll go back to Manhattan so happy Blythe will never stop smiling," Hawk says, which sounds like the only future Astrid wants.

And why can't that future start right now? She grins. "Maybe I'll stay in your hotel room. And the rules of that room are that nobody wears clothes, ever."

"Astrid." They haven't made love since the night they conceived Blythe and now Hawk's voice is as low and private and husky as it's ever been. "If we weren't on a plane right now with a hundred other people…"

She arches an eyebrow at him. "But I thought having sex with me in public places was your favorite activity? Don't tell me it's not true."

He laughs and picks up a tendril of her hair. "Blythe has your hair," he says softly. "I love that she has your hair."

"I love that she has your eyes."

Hawk's eyes are shiny now. "Her smile is perfect. It's the best thing we've ever made."

"Versailles will be the second best thing," Astrid vows and Hawk nods, as if to say, *Yes. It will be.*

FORTY-FIVE

BLYTHE BRICARD

It isn't Astrid who enters the room. It isn't a girl in a silver dress with abandon in her eyes.

It's a woman who has long silver hair and eyes full of untold tales.

Astrid is sixty-seven, Blythe realizes with a shock. She's only a little younger than Iris, who's dying.

She hauls herself out of the chair and flees to the window, bracing her palms on the sill, staring at the grand lady in iron outside who never changes, but who is something different for everyone. Like Astrid.

What is Astrid to Blythe?

The woman who didn't teach her to walk. The woman who didn't come to her at night when she cried. The woman who never made anything better—not a cut, nor a hurt, nor a fear, nor a fight.

The woman who showed Blythe what loneliness was.

There are a dozen droplets on the windowsill, and Blythe can feel their genesis on her face. God, she's going to cry like she's never cried before. This is the moment she's always felt coming for her, the moment the world is waiting for—when Blythe Bricard finally breaks.

She pushes away from the sill, ready to run like Astrid did—away from the pain of every absent second, minute, hour and year.

But it's too late—the pain has been unleashed and the memories blind her: being sent to the library to read while the other kids made Mother's Day presents; writing letters to herself that she pretended were from Astrid, who was simply traveling the world on a grand adventure; engaging in a lifetime battle to be different from the icon in the silver dress, but keeping that photo of Astrid wearing the dress tucked in her bedroom drawer. Somewhere at home is a box with the photo nestled inside it, as well as childish letters full of imaginary love, and the imperfect remnants of a macaroni-shell photo frame she tried to make at home one time—just like the other kids had made for their mothers.

* * *

Who knows how long it takes before Blythe's grief eases enough to understand that her mother—Astrid Bricard—is stroking her back. She blinks and shakes her head, stumbles backward.

This is the first time ever in her memory that she's looked at her mother. *God.* She's going to start crying again.

Love is not supposed to make you shed tears like blood.

Her mother's eyes are soaked with tears too. But Astrid is no Niobe, sworn to lament her children forever. Astrid Bricard is the woman who crafted the awful fairytale from which Blythe emerged as a young woman who hid behind sunglasses, finger raised in the air.

"Why are you here?" Blythe rasps out. Only days ago, she'd wanted this—her mother returned. In the abstract, it was a beautiful thing. In reality, it's raw and ugly.

"I thought you might need me," Astrid says shakily.

This is her mother's voice, heard for the first time. It's as double-faced as shantung—smoothness lingering underneath the kind of texture you only earn from a life lived too fully. Where was this full life lived? Certainly not at her daughter's side.

"I needed you when I was two months old and hungry," Blythe cries. "When I was eight years old and Hawk just fucking vanished. When I was thirteen years old and had to learn about you from a freaking movie. I don't—"

Need you now. But that's a lie too.

"You need me to say this." Astrid turns to Nathaniel. "MIZZA is my trademark. You won't win against me in a court of law. So back off."

Nathaniel makes an exasperated sound. "I wish I'd never heard the name Bricard." He turns to Blythe. "You know it was Jake who gave me the idea of resurrecting MIZZA. He told me he could never do it with you because you hated him. Now I wonder if he gave me the idea because he wanted that brand and the only way for him to get it was to have me put the idea in your head." He moves toward the door. "I'd like you both gone in ten minutes, please."

Then it's just Blythe and her mother in the room. And the echo of Nathaniel's insinuation that Jake's been playing her all along.

She can't think about that. Her heart, her whole self, is being pummeled by relentless, unsparing emotion.

She tries to find the easiest of all the shocking things she's grappling with to cling onto. Iris is dying. Blythe is standing in a room with a woman who's never been a mother to her and all the while the mother-in-law who welcomed Blythe into her family is lying in a hospital bed, or worse. And her children are probably scared and sad and confused and want her by their sides.

This is not where Blythe should be.

"You were never there," she croaks at Astrid, who flinches.

"I know," Astrid says in response.

Blythe is already turning toward the door. Her children need her. Astrid never did.

She isn't prepared for the speed at which Astrid moves. They reach the door at the same time.

"I wasn't there," Astrid says. "But I'm here now. And I'm staying."

She presses a piece of paper with a scribbled number on it into Blythe's hand.

Blythe shakes her head. "Staying? You don't know how."

And just as her mother ran away from her almost forty years ago, Blythe runs away now from her mother.

FORTY-SIX

ASTRID BRICARD AND HAWK JONES

The next morning in Hawk's room at the Hôtel Plaza Athénée, Astrid and Hawk climb out of bed and do all the things they used to do. They shower together, clean their teeth together, laugh and talk and it's like old times—*the best of times*, Hawk thinks.

When they arrive at Versailles, they're conducted through the Hall of Mirrors and Hawk can't resist resting his hand on Astrid's ass just to see the gesture repeated a thousand times. She laughs, which is the best sound of all, and he feels himself fall more in love with her than ever. So in love that he wants to marry her right there at Versailles— the penultimate act of their incredible romance. And then will come the epilogue—a true spectacular—because as well as the love they have for one another, there's the love they have for Blythe. So much goddamn love.

Astrid is holding his hand in front of everyone, and while her face is thinner than it used to be and there are darker-than-usual semicircles under her eyes, her expression when she looks at him is as wondrous as when he first saw her staring at a dress in an archive. He slips his arm around her waist because holding her hand isn't enough.

They're ushered into the Théâtre Gabriel where the show will be held. Even Halston's jaw drops at the magnificence of it.

But Hawk's smile falls away. "It's a stage made for a play," he says, almost to himself. "Nobody's going to be able to see how a silk dress moves from up there."

He gestures to the balconies above, understanding now why the French have sets and orchestras and ballerinas. They're putting on a performance in a space made for theater—whereas the Americans thought they were just coming to show off their dresses. He's going to have to redo some of his own pieces to make them bolder than they already are. There's no way the brilliance of Astrid's technique will be noticed. It's an extravagant ballgown space and Astrid has—what? He doesn't actually know what Astrid has. *Shit.*

"Halston's cold," Halston complains and Hawk realizes he's shivering too. As is Astrid. There's no heating. And it's November.

Hawk's frown deepens.

"*On y va,*" a crisp young Frenchman says, ushering them backstage. Hawk has to let go of Astrid as she and Velvet are shown one way and he and Nancy the other. They're assigned cupboard-sized rooms that are apparently supposed to house a designer, their assistant, a fit model, the clothes, the hair and makeup team, plus the other mannequins.

"Hope everyone's wearing deodorant," Nancy says.

Five minutes later, Hawk's making changes to a couple of gowns— okay, he's rethinking them entirely—when Nancy marches over.

"There's no paper in the powder room."

Hawk, whose mind is wrestling with silk satin, says, "What do you mean?"

"Women don't shake, Hawk—they wipe. There's no paper. No water to drink either. Nothing comes out of the taps."

He doesn't have time to deal with toilet paper shortages, but nor does he have time for Nancy to be mad. Especially not as he's about to ask her to re-sew a dress she only made two days ago. "I'll fix it."

But he's prevented from going on the stage to find the person in charge of toilet paper by the crisp young Frenchman. "The French are rehearsing," he tells Hawk, as if God himself is parading across the stage.

Blass just raises an eyebrow when Hawk runs into him. "You think that's our biggest problem? They have orchestras—our set fits in a duffel bag."

Joe Eula, who's made the backdrop for the Americans, is pulling lengths of fabric out of a bag the size of a generous hot dog. He says, "I measured the fabric in feet but I just found out the measurements they gave us were in meters. It's too short."

Now they don't even have a backdrop.

Half a million dollars. Astrid told them the French had spent at least that much. No one believed her or bothered to ask why. They should have. They should have tried to understand what kind of fashion show needed that much money to make it work.

Halston rounds the corner, shouting at Candace. "Buy me a fucking scarf. Or give me yours." He yanks the black wool from her neck.

Candace flees.

It's nearly midnight when the French leave the stage and the Americans are allowed to rehearse, which they desperately need to do. They've hardly agreed on anything in meetings and they've never put it all together to see how—or if—it works. Hawk has no clue what Blass's models will do, what Stephen Burrows is showing, what Liza Minnelli will sing. But just as they're about to start, the French stagehands and lighting operators depart, apparently forbidden from breaking their union rules for anyone but the French.

Darkness descends over the theater, making it impossible to see, let alone rehearse.

There's a crashing noise, followed by Halston screaming, "Fuck!" and Hawk hopes Halston's hit his head so hard it's rendered him speechless. But two seconds later, he hears Halston again. "Candace, get the fucking lights turned back on!"

Hopelessness is waiting behind Hawk to smother him. It's like being back at the hospital and watching his little girl struggle to breathe. So he tries to do what he did then—focus on Astrid. *Everything* is riding

NATASHA LESTER

on this. If he doesn't turn this around, he and Astrid will never be together.

He starts with the easiest problem, feeling his way out of the theater and running as fast as he can to the caretaker's cottage and getting the damn lights turned back on.

"Okay," he says to Nancy when he and the lights return. "Turn the music up." Music always helps, although he tries not to wince at the sight of a tape player plugged in at the side of the stage where just an hour ago, the French had an entire orchestra.

Kay Thompson, their choreographer, starts working with the models on the opening number. "Walk like you have ice in your bras," she tells the girls.

Which would almost be funny except she takes two hours to choreograph the show opener, which is just Liza's song. They still have six individual designer sections to block and they've run out of time. It's already two in the morning.

Hawk goes looking for Astrid, who hadn't been up onstage. He checks all the rooms backstage. Finally, he takes the stairs to the basement. It's so cold down there it's like a new Ice Age is upon them.

"Tell me you chose for some ridiculous reason to be in the basement," he says when he finds her.

"I could tell you that," she says, "but I'd be lying. We were in the room next to Bill Blass and my sewing machine was affecting his concentration. He had me moved. I prefer being away from everyone anyway."

Hawk's head is about to explode. This is supposed to be the experience of a lifetime. Right now, it's too much for anyone's lifetime. "I'll speak to someone."

"Hawk," she says, looking up from her sewing machine, her expression concentrated on the sensational white column dress she's making. She's bundled up in a coat, hat, scarf, and he's sure she'd be wearing mittens too if only she could sew in them.

"I have dresses to finish," she tells him. "I didn't have time before we left and right now I don't care if there's no toilet paper or food. I don't have time to pee or eat. And I don't care if Kay doesn't have time to choreograph my section because I won't need choreography if I have no clothes to put on my models. I love you, but I don't have time for the luxury of histrionics."

"Okay," he says and when he looks around, he can see that so many of her pieces aren't finished. Velvet, head down and wrapped in a goddamn blanket, has barely even acknowledged him. Worry kicks his guts. It's normal to be finishing things right before a show. But this is a lot.

"Can I give you a hand?" he asks.

"Hawk." Astrid's voice is gentle, but determined. "I need you to stay far away from my clothes, otherwise the press will make them yours."

"Right," he says, rubbing his jaw. "I get it. I love you."

He doesn't want to leave but it's clear that's what Astrid wants. So he goes back to the hotel, unable to forget all the unsewn hems. But Astrid is stubborn and indefatigable. He shouldn't doubt her.

She arrives much later, slips into bed beside him, and he wraps his sleepy body all around hers, kissing her hair. She's so cold and, he realizes, thinner than she's ever been. He hadn't quite noticed that last night in the fast hot rush of Astrid back in his bed.

"Are you okay?" he whispers and she doesn't answer, just holds on to him and he holds on to her, and now he feels the hopelessness creep inside him because undersized backdrops and no rehearsals and minuscule budgets and egos are so far out of his control that he can feel the outcome they want receding into fantasy.

"One knockout dress and nobody will care that we have a mixtape and they have violins," Astrid whispers to him and the amount of love in that sentiment—that she's trying to make him feel better when she must be stressed out of her mind too—makes him feel like the luckiest man alive.

* * *

The following day, Astrid walks past Stephen Burrows, who's doing battle with a bright yellow dress while Bethann Hardison, his fit model, is being revived from a faint. Next door, Halston is losing his shit—again. In the next room, Oscar de la Renta is fuming over Halston's behavior.

"Thank God we're in the basement," Velvet says as they hurry downstairs.

By midday, the white column dress is finished. Astrid lets out a breath of immense relief as she slips it on and all the fear and the worry slide away because she suddenly sees not just stitches and seams, but what matters.

She catches Velvet's eye and says, "You know how there are some days when you put on a dress and you look in the mirror, and something about that outfit and the way the sunlight hits your hair and the song playing on the turntable makes you think, *I look fucking great*? And then you smile and you win and you glow all day long. There's no booze, no dope, no sex making you feel like that—you don't need it, because you and that dress are enough. And every time you wear the dress, a little bit of the power of that day fills you up."

Velvet nods. "Yeah, I do."

Astrid spins around to face her. "Imagine the stage in darkness. 'Touch Me in the Morning' by Diana Ross starts playing. Then one spotlight comes up and hits Pat Cleveland wearing this dress. She doesn't move. She just stands there—one tall proud unbreakable column feeling the power of every great outfit she's ever worn. One by one, lights come up on the other models wearing magenta, turquoise, emerald, ruby, sunflower and indigo silk jersey. By the time we get to that fabulous chorus about being strong, they all start dancing. And it'll be like the way you can only see all the colors in a ray of sunlight when raindrops bend that light to make a rainbow.

"Somewhere in the last few months I forgot I'm not just making clothes—I'm making days. I'm making girls in airports tell their teachers that enough is enough. This is everything I ever wanted to

THE DISAPPEARANCE OF ASTRID BRICARD 391

do since we went to that rent party and danced underneath pink balloons. And I'm calling this dress *Blythe* because I want Blythe to be the column of white that makes the whole world beautiful."

Velvet wraps her in a ferocious hug and they stand there, remembering the vows they made at that long-ago party, the time they held hands and marched down streets and asked for more, the *Life* covers and the Rolling Stones song and the columns of lies and the glossy pages of gowns. All of it lives in Astrid's designs. The beauty of the world, and its spleen. The romance, and the loss.

And that's why girls look at a picture of a dress and go out and tell their teachers, *No more*. Loss drives beauty. Vulnerability drives power. The second without the first is unearned and it's ignorant and it's why people hurt.

"The Americans will win," Velvet says fiercely. "Because of you."

* * *

The day of the show dawns and the Americans finally get the stage for rehearsals at around noon. Kay Thompson takes her time with Liza Minnelli, who's performing "Cabaret" for the finale. Astrid stands in the wings beside Hawk, watching. Something about it feels wrong—as if the finale should be more than what it is right now.

"What if all the models came back out at the end too," she says to Hawk. "Didn't Kay say she'd written another song, something like 'Bonjour Paris,' but didn't know where to work it in? What if the final number of a fashion show isn't a celebrity singing on the stage by herself, but all the models in our gorgeous dresses waving goodbye to Paris?"

Nancy, who's on the other side of Hawk, says, "Yeah, I was just thinking—why does Liza get the final spot when the dresses we've been working our asses off on are meant to be the stars of the show?"

Hawk is frowning, but in that way he does when he's thinking, and Astrid reaches up to smooth her fingertips over his brow. "Tell me what genius is happening in there," she says teasingly and Nancy rolls her eyes.

"You two are…" She shakes her head. "I'm not gonna say perfect for each other, because you're not. You know how everyone says people are perfectly matched when they finish each other's sentences? Like if one person starts something, the other should know how to finish it? You two…" She considers. "You two don't even have to start the sentence."

Almost as if Nancy's made it happen, Hawk and Astrid say at the same time, "Black dresses."

And Nancy just about pees herself laughing. "What are you talking about?"

Hawk says exactly what Astrid was thinking. "We get Liza singing that song and all the mannequins come out and they're all wearing black dresses. It's the only color we all have enough of except…" He frowns again. "Except Astrid." Then he grins. "Your white dress comes back out. The one I saw you making yesterday. It's the centerpiece. You're always going to stand out. Be the star against the night."

He bends down to kiss her and she understands exactly what Nancy was saying. She and Hawk—one isn't the start and the other the end. They are the span of measureless time.

* * *

Astrid gets Hawk to tell the others about the finale idea. The designers actually agree, then Kay tells Astrid she's ready for her.

Astrid explains what she wants for her segment.

"Perfect," Kay enthuses as the spotlights beam down, first on Pat, then on the others.

It looks fantastic, just how she imagined, until Halston snipes, "Some people's clothes need spotlights, otherwise nobody would look at them."

Astrid ignores him, sees Hawk holding his fist in his hand as if he's trying to stop it from acquainting itself with Halston's face. She shakes her head and he grimaces.

"Then I want the girls to dance," Astrid tells Kay.

"On podiums and without any underwear?" Halston asks bitingly. "Hurry the fuck up, Astrid. Or get the fuck out."

"Fuck off," Kay shouts at Halston.

Then Candace steps in. Astrid feels her body brace for another attack but Candace says to Halston, "I need you for a moment," and it's almost like she's drawing him away from Astrid.

Halston swears at her too and Astrid sees Candace take it without even flinching. How much must a person have suffered to not flinch at an assault?

Why didn't anyone at Parsons teach us that this was the world of fashion? Astrid thinks.

Candace's eyes flick to Astrid and a strange kind of communion passes between them. She somehow hears Candace's silent reply. *Because they didn't want us to know how to fight.*

Candace isn't fighting, not anymore. But Halston knows how to fight—and nobody ever calls him anything other than a fashion god. If Astrid let one single expletive fall in front of a journalist, she'd be crucified. But Halston can rain down obscenities like a biblical flood.

Then Blass interjects. "You're taking up too much of Kay's time, Astrid. You got on the ticket last, and only because the French added someone else. Your choreography can wait."

"Besides, nobody gives a fuck about third-rate choreography for a fourth-rate dressmaker whose boyfriend designs her clothes," Halston hisses. "Halston is the only one everyone is here for."

Ignore them, Astrid tells herself, because there are reporters in the seats by the stage. But, "Go to hell," her mouth says.

"Knowing you're about to let down the entire American fashion industry in front of the whole fucking world is my idea of hell," Halston screams at her. "I'm leaving!" He storms out, but stops in front of Enid Nemy from the *New York Times* and snarls, "If you report that, I'll never invite you to another show."

"Halston," Enid replies coolly, "you never invite me to your shows as it is."

Maybe it'll be okay, Astrid tells herself as she goes to the bathroom to brace her shaking hands on the countertop. Maybe Enid will be scared enough of Halston too that she won't tell the world that Astrid, the sexed-up, half-naked, podium-dancing muse, provoked Halston into quitting, thus ruining any chance the Americans had. Maybe the whole American team won't hate her, the fourth-rate dressmaker, for being the one who made Halston quit.

And maybe Astrid will find a way of blocking out his words— *. . . you're about to let down the entire American fashion industry in front of the whole fucking world.*

* * *

Hawk tries to go after Astrid but Velvet stops him. She indicates the reporters. "You're the last thing she needs right now."

He's just recovering from that when Bill Blass tells him the show order they'd agreed on has changed. De la Renta, who'd been given the task of sending the show order to the French, has put himself in the coveted final position. Now Hawk wants to swear like Halston. It had been agreed after countless arguments that Hawk would show last. But the programs are printed. There's nothing he can do.

A whole lot more swearing ensues and everyone storms out.

Hawk sits in the theater with his head in his hands. Above him, unlit crystal chandeliers hang heavily, unsparkling. The stage feels like a massive black hole that Astrid's garments will get lost in. Nobody will see the skill and the detail, even with a spotlight and a fabulous model and a knockout dance track.

The day after the show it won't matter if we're together—I'll either

have the respect I want. Or I'll have given up on the idea of it. That's
what she'd told him, months ago.

But he can't imagine an Astrid who's given up. Through all of it,
every untruth and lie, every barb and cruelty, every barrier and obstacle, she's come back stronger than ever. But how much strength does
she have left? And how long before it runs out?

Crossing back over the stage, he almost stands on a length of pink
chiffon, so fragile. It's been left behind by Astrid and he scoops it up
because otherwise it will tear. It reminds him of the Astrid of last
month, the one who'd been so easy to put out of his mind over the last
two nights because the Astrid in his arms then had been happy. So
he'd concentrated on that, not on how thin she's become.

He remembers the dark circles under her eyes, knows it means
Astrid hasn't slept properly for weeks. And for her to be so thin—she
mustn't have been eating properly either. Before getting on the plane
two days ago, she hadn't smiled for a long time. In fact, over the last
month, she'd hardly been able to keep her mind in the same room
as Hawk. He'd say her name, then he'd say it again and again until
finally she'd blink at him, not even realizing she'd been someplace
else. She'd say, "I don't think I'm doing it right," like she thought
motherhood was a subject she needed to pass, but was in danger of
failing. It had all happened so gradually that, while he'd known she
wasn't herself, he hadn't realized the magnitude of it until this shift in
Paris over the last two days to being more herself.

She's so fragile, he thinks. Tonight will decide her future. It
shouldn't, but that's how she sees it.

Then his head shoots up. When she'd left the stage after telling
Halston to go to hell—he's never seen her look so scared. And he
doesn't wonder what she's frightened of. Instead he wonders, *What
isn't she frightened of?*

She's ready to tear more easily than the chiffon. And he needs to
somehow stop it from happening.

FORTY-SEVEN

BLYTHE BRICARD

Blythe stops at reception to use the phone before she leaves Champlain Holdings, calling Ed because she knows Jake won't pick up. "Which hospital are you in?" she asks.

"What the fuck is going on, Blythe? Jake's like a migrainous lion and nobody knows where you are."

"I'm coming."

The drive is only twenty minutes but it might as well be in another time zone. Blythe can barely recall the road rules.

Astrid is alive.

And Jake...

What did he do? He spoke to Nathaniel before they came to France. He's planning a launch despite Blythe telling him she's doing MIZZA on her own. He told Blythe he loved her after she said he couldn't have MIZZA. What if it's just a ruse to get MIZZA under his belt, after which he'll abandon the kids and Blythe too?

These are ridiculous thoughts. Jake would *never* do that. Except he did abandon them once before.

And what is she supposed to do about Astrid?

Fuck.

The only thing she can do is collect her children and keep it together until they can go somewhere out of the way. Nathaniel will tell the world Astrid is back—will dish out interviews about the two crazy women in his office. Blythe's job right now is to be there for her children and protect them from the fallout.

She arrives at the hospital at almost nine o'clock and is directed to a private waiting room. Eva and Sebby fling themselves on her and the relief of holding them close is almost staggering.

"I didn't mean to be lost," Eva wails.

A solemn-faced Sebby tugs on her jacket. "They said Grandma's dying." His little face crumples.

Blythe sits on a chair that's been hastily vacated by Frieda. She puts Eva on one knee and Sebby on the other and lets both of them cry on her shoulders while she rubs their backs in gentle circles like Astrid had just done to her.

What's going on? Ed mouths at her from across the room.

Blythe shrugs. The Blacks have enough to deal with.

"Where's your dad?" she asks Eva, who shakes her head and wails some more.

"I don't know! He found me in the café and yelled at me to get moving and then he didn't speak to us in the car and we came here and then he went somewhere and I don't know!"

Eva's sobbing intensifies and Blythe cannot believe the fates have decided to resurrect her mother and steal Iris all on the same day.

"Do you want to see your grandma?" she asks, keeping herself fixed on the things that need to be done. "She probably won't be awake. If you don't see her now, you might not have the chance again, and that's okay—you saw her this morning and you can remember her like that."

Eva's eyes are enormous, Sebby's the same. "She kissed me goodbye this morning," Eva whispers. "Told me she'd always look out for me and Sebby."

"Then I think you're good."

Blythe motions to Ed and he comes over, frowning. "Can you sit with Eva and Sebby? I want to see Iris, if that's okay. Then we'll go."

"What about Jake?" he asks, clearly riled that she's intending to leave Jake to deal with his mother's impending death on his own.

"After I've gone, take a look at the news."

Ed's frown deepens. "It's through there. Only two people allowed in at a time, but getting either Dad or Jake out is like trying to move concrete."

She turns into the hall. A door slides open. She embraces Herb, who holds on to her for a long moment before he leaves the room.

In bed, Iris is small and fragile, like a baby bird tucked into a too-large nest. Sitting in a chair, his mother's hand gripped in his, head pillowed on one bent arm, is Jake.

It's impossible not to stroke his hair. As she does, fear grips her. What if he can't explain exactly what he's up to with MIZZA, just like he could never explain his behavior over the last couple of years? What if this is the real life without soufflés and chateaux that she feared would be too much for them?

But everything is too much right now.

Jake jumps at her touch and the moment his eyes land on her, he looks desperately relieved. But sleep is still clouding his thoughts. As consciousness returns, he stands, indicates that Blythe should take the chair and then walks out without a word.

Blythe blinks. She can't cry yet. The kids are waiting for her. They need her. So she picks up Iris's hand.

"I can't be there for him," she says, swallowing hard. "He's losing a mother and I've somehow gained one, and if I could swap it around, maybe I'd go back to being motherless in an instant if it brought you back. If you have any words of wisdom about Astrid..."

Of course Iris can't give her any advice. It's up to Blythe to figure out what to do. But she has no idea.

Jake's waiting outside. They stare at one another. Blythe has no idea what to say. It all hurts so much. The silence lengthens into something she just wants to get away from before she loses it completely. Her eyes drop to the floor.

And Jake exhales like she's hit him. Then he walks right past her, intent on his mother—and on being angry at Blythe for breaking her promise to be there for him.

* * *

Blythe drives back to the chateau and collects their things. She's found a cottage about half an hour away that costs too much, so she's had to, with utmost reluctance, use some of Jake's maintenance money.

They arrive around two in the morning and fall into bed. Blythe goes straight to sleep but, while the emotion was a temporary sedative, it's also the thing that wakes her an hour later, dreaming of a woman sitting on her bed, smiling at her. Blythe turns on a lamp and searches through her luggage for the book Hawk wrote about Astrid.

Hawk. *Shit.* Does he know?

She pulls out her phone, sees she has a few missed calls from him and one message. *You should talk to Astrid before you talk to me,* it says. *She never got the chance to be listened to.*

She opens the book, turning to a picture of her mother wearing a sapphire blazer and trousers, feet bare, hands shoved in pockets, staring straight at the camera. This was Astrid's moment of bravura confidence when MIZZA was launched, just like Blythe's moment of bravura confidence in the silver dress two nights before.

What happened? The photograph can't answer. Only Astrid can tell the story of how she went from this strikingly self-assured creature to a ghost in a bloodstained dress in the Hall of Mirrors at Versailles.

"Mommy."

Blythe jumps and sees Eva at the door. Her cheeks are sprinkled with tears and her brow is furrowed with complex emotion.

"Come here, darling." Blythe opens her arms and Eva scampers over, snuggling into the bed beside her.

"I'm so glad I have you, Mommy," Eva says. "I woke up and I was scared, but I feel better now."

I'm so glad I have you, Mommy.

I wanted you, Astrid, Blythe thinks now, a silent plea that sits behind all the anger. But if Blythe has wanted her mother all her life, then why is she turning her away now?

It's so hard to put yourself deliberately in the line of hurt. But—*she never got the chance to be listened to,* Hawk had said. Blythe doesn't want to be yet another person who accepts the story and doesn't bother to go looking for the facts.

She takes out her phone and the piece of paper Astrid gave her and texts Astrid her address.

The reply is brief: *I'm coming.*

Two hours later, Blythe opens the door to her mother.

* * *

Blythe and Astrid stand in the living room. Blythe is mute with nausea and doubt and, also, hope. But what is she hoping for?

"Are you here with Eva and Sebby?" Astrid asks.

Blythe blinks. "How do you know their names?"

"I read the news. Your life is a book as open as mine was."

Of course. The names of Blythe's children were widely reported when they were born, golden futures in fashion predicted for both Eva and Sebastian Bricard, who carried their mother's surname and not their father's, a fact that's always been much pondered over in the press.

"They're asleep," Blythe says, not quite able to believe how banal their conversation is. "Coffee?"

Astrid nods. "With a finger of cognac, if you have it."

Blythe decides to acquaint her own coffee with cognac too.

When they sit down, there's a shift in the room, like a red curtain unfurled, the hush of anticipation before the show begins.

"It's in the news—my reappearance," Astrid begins. "I was always there for the finding, but people assumed there was nothing to look for. A dead girl is a much better story." She smiles sadly. "I called Hawk a few hours ago. He was..."

She shakes her head. "He was angry. Of course he was. He cried. I...I did too. He said to me, *Nancy once told us that most people call it love if one person can finish the start of the other's sentence. But that we were more than that.* He told me he'd thought at the time how right she was—that one of us wasn't the start and the other the end. But that after I left, he realized he was always going to be the end of me."

Astrid's eyes glisten with tears and pain. She takes a deep breath. "I thought that if I took myself out of the story, it would end by itself. But stories never end—the tellers just find another girl to ruin with words."

How many girls ruined with words are strewn across the world? How many women caught in the line of a song? In a dress? In a painting? In black type on white paper? Frozen in oil, in thread, in a C-major chord?

But nobody, no woman, is one note, one color—one fine strand of silk.

In front of her, Blythe can see the cheekbones of Astrid Bricard. The height. The effortless style. The gentle fretting of years. A person who is more than a silver dress and a photograph. A person who is not yet a mother. That word is still an empty space. *Fill it*, her mind begs. *And then let me decide if I want it.*

Then Astrid says, "The world was, and perhaps still is—I don't know. I'm waiting for you to prove things one way or the other." She stops and tries again. "The world is designed for the Ophelias to die and the Hamlets to rule. I made sure to fit that preordained pattern. I didn't have the strength at the time to do otherwise."

It's a statement Blythe wants to refute. But she can't, not based on the evidence of her life so far. It makes her ask, "What happened to Astrid Bricard?"

FORTY-EIGHT

ASTRID BRICARD

It isn't until Astrid walks back toward the stage that she sees John Fairchild. "I had some labels made up for your frocks," he says, passing her a sheet of stickers with *Hawk Jones* printed on them. Then he adds, "Spectacular performance."

He must have been standing in the wings while she screamed at Halston. And he'll publish everything he heard. She will forever after be known not just as a dressmaker, but as a fourth-rate dressmaker whose boyfriend designs her clothes. The woman who let down the whole American team.

The woman who let down her daughter by doing something—what was it? What was the wrong thing Astrid did?—that caused her to be born too early and too small and too fragile. The woman who's let her daughter down again by leaving her in New York, by being fourth-rate at motherhood too, by turning Blythe into an object of scrutiny and making her cry and cry and cry.

And now Astrid is crying and she can't go back out onto the stage like this because then she'll be the hysterical fourth-rate dressmaker. She needs to leave. She'll go back to the hotel and lie down in a dark room and weep and nobody will know. Nobody will care either. They all think—Blass and de la Renta and Halston and Fairchild—that she should be the one leaving, not Halston.

So she does. She walks out onto the street, not feeling the bitter November air or the sleeting rain on her face, isn't even aware of it drenching her clothes.

Part way to Paris, she realizes how far it is. How long has she been walking for? It was light when she left and now it's nearly dark.

When a cab passes, she rouses just enough to hail it.

Back in Paris, she crosses through the foyer of the Plaza Athénée and it isn't until the busboy calls, "Mademoiselle! Can I help?" that she catches sight of herself in the mirror. She looks like a vagrant or a madwoman.

There, staring at a reflection of a woman who is somehow Astrid, she knows she will never win. The stories win—they go on and on forever. Stories where Astrid is a thing made up by everyone else.

Except Hawk. Or... She stumbles, nearly falls.

Maybe Hawk too.

* * *

"Astrid?"

Hawk's already in the hotel room. How did he get back faster than her?

"What happened? I've been going out of my mind wondering where you were..." He stares at her and repeats, "What happened?"

She looks down. There's a puddle of rainwater under her feet. Her teeth are chattering. Even her legs are shaking. But why can't she feel the cold?

Hawk approaches, arms open as if he's going to hug her, but she raises a hand to ward him off.

"Tell me about the silver dress," she manages to say, voice shaking with cold too.

"You're frozen. You need a shower—"

She interrupts, tries to steady her voice so he'll listen. "Do you remember making it?"

"I guess it was all credit to Nancy who actually made it," he says while he grabs towels and offers them to her. "You're scaring me, Astrid."

She's used the wrong words. She needs to take hold of her concentration for just a few more minutes and then she can let her mind lose itself. "Do you remember designing the dress? That's what I mean."

"I could never forget it," he says urgently, hands on her shoulders as if he's trying to gather the scattered threads of Astrid and knot them all back together. "You were all I thought of when I designed that dress."

No.

Hawk believes the story too. That the silver dress is a Hawk Jones design.

She's the only one who doesn't. Perhaps *she's* wrong. Or perhaps she's mad.

That would explain everything.

FORTY-NINE

ASTRID BRICARD

Astrid tells Hawk she's going to use her own room to get ready. That tonight she has to stand alone.

"But you're frozen and I can tell something's wrong. Astrid!" he calls as she leaves.

She worries that he'll follow her, but he must remember how John Fairchild will make it look if Hawk's seen trying to cajole his drenched and benumbed muse back into his room. He lets her go.

Bypassing her own room, Astrid catches a taxi back to Versailles, still soaked with rain, actually feeling the cold now.

She goes down to her basement workroom because that's where the fabric is, where the clothes are—the only things she loves that don't hurt her.

She startles at finding Candace in the basement, holding Astrid's white column dress against her body, studying herself in the mirror as if trying to make her reflection into something else.

When Candace sees her, she jumps so much that she stumbles, flinging out a hand to steady herself. But it catches on Astrid's newly sharpened scissors, which have been left on the worktable with the blades open. They slice into Candace's hand.

"Ow!" she cries, curling her hand into a fist, wrapping her other hand around it and bringing it up to her chest where drops of her blood spill onto the white dress.

Another ruined thing.

"Shit! I'm sorry." Candace stares at her. "Are you all right?"

Astrid should be asking Candace that because she has just cut herself. But her eyes are arrested by the white dress stained with blood. Just like the many ways Astrid is staining her daughter's life with words and pictures and scrutiny, with gossip and lies and blood. That dress is a parable of her daughter's future. Astrid makes things—and then she somehow makes them bleed.

She drops into a chair, thinking, *This is my life.* She gets dressed in the morning and she worries about how it will look in the press. She gets abused by Halston and she worries how it will look in the press. She considers every word before she speaks because she worries how it will look in the press. She wakes up every day and agonizes about all the many ways she's hurting her daughter.

"This is my life." The words come out of her mouth.

"It is," Candace says. Then she adds, bleakly, "So many people think the things they want to happen are their life. But this, right here, is life. One of only two good things my mom ever taught me."

For the first time today, someone has said something that makes sense. Because Astrid has believed for all of the last nine months that her life would begin once she stepped off the stage at Versailles as a victor. She would be celebrated as a designer. She would marry Hawk. And she, Hawk and Blythe would live happily forever after. Those are the things she wanted to happen. But they are not life. They were just dreams.

"What was the second thing?" she asks.

"The second thing?" Candace repeats.

"You said your mom taught you two good things."

Candace shakes her head and pulls off her sweater. "Put this on. I'm not telling you the second one."

"Please."

She's aware of how desperate she sounds, as if she's pinning everything onto Candace's mom's advice. And she is. She has no idea what to do about Halston and Fairchild and Hawk and the silver dress, and maybe it's crazy to think that Candace's mom's advice might help but she's sitting in a chair beside a bloodstained white dress, shivering with cold, and her life is something she doesn't want it to be and in her head are so many words. Hawk's words—*You were all I thought of when I designed that dress.* Halston's words and Bill Blass's words and John Fairchild's words. Why not throw some more words in?

Candace exhales slowly. "I once told you, that day at the Women's March, that my dad was a drunk who used to beat up my mom. She kept bringing him back into our house, chasing after the thing that broke her until I was the one who shattered. So I learned never to believe in something so much that all you do is hurt someone else with that stupid, blind belief. Except..." She shrugs. "I don't know."

She kept chasing after the thing that broke her until I was the one who shattered.

Just like Astrid keeps chasing after a life of abuse and lies and heartache. A life in which she's the girl in the silver dress and Hawk is the one who made both the dress and Astrid too.

If she keeps choosing that life, Blythe will be the one who shatters.

She bends over in the chair, not able to stay upright beneath the sheer, terrible force of the image. Blythe was born nearly broken. And now that she's healed, what kind of mother would let her break all over again?

Astrid's body trembles all the more forcefully and she doesn't know if it's from cold or fear. She can hear Candace saying her name. But her thoughts are louder, screaming at her to stop being so selfish—to hurt herself more than the people she loves.

For a minute, Astrid pictures Hawk, just Hawk, taking Blythe out in the stroller. People stop him and ask for his autograph like they always do. The press takes photos, but from a respectful distance, because this is Hawk Jones, the premier fashion designer in all of America. Those pictures would run with the headline, HAWK THE MASTER DESIGNER TAKING HIS DAUGHTER FOR A WALK. And Blythe wouldn't howl, ever.

Loving isn't possession, Mizza had told her two years ago when Astrid had been crying over how cruel she'd felt leaving Hawk. *Sometimes loving means accepting the greatest hurt of all so that the one you love doesn't have to suffer.* Mizza had meant Hawk would have to accept the hurt so Astrid could heal. But now, those words have taken on a different meaning.

Astrid stands. "Can you please leave," she says to Candace, who stares at her for a beat too long. "I want you to leave," Astrid repeats, surprised at how clear and strong her words sound. Then she adds, "Thank you," which makes Candace pause in the doorway and look back at her.

What will she do if Candace tries to stop her? And worse... what will she do if Hawk arrives and tries to stop her?

She turns her back on Candace until she hears the sound of footsteps retreating.

She has to focus for perhaps half an hour more. Her concentration narrows so much that she's no longer shivering, even though her skin is very, very cold. All she's conscious of is the need to do this—how necessary it is for Blythe.

If she just jumps in a taxi, they'll find her. Hawk's too determined. So it seems perfectly logical that she needs to create a buffer of a few days. Something to draw everyone's focus along a path she hasn't taken. A few days for her to vanish instead down a different track.

The idea lodges itself in her mind as if it's been embroidered onto the inside of her skull.

She gathers up the bloodied white dress and takes it with her to the Hall of Mirrors. She drops it on the floor—this dress that is both the ghost of everything that's happened to her, and the ghost of everything that didn't happen because she fell in love with Hawk.

She hopes it's enough to redirect attention—a dress stained with blood and reflected in a thousand mirrors. It will make a good story.

Then Astrid walks away from the white dress, from her life, from herself. After today, there will be nothing left at all of the legend of Astrid Bricard.

And Blythe will never shatter.

FIFTY

HAWK JONES

PALACE OF VERSAILLES, FRANCE, NOVEMBER 28, 1973

In the Hall of Mirrors, Hawk picks up the empty dress—all that's left of Astrid Bricard.

Remember the silver dress?

He spins around. It's as if Astrid's in the room. But she isn't anywhere.

Except here she is in front of him. They're at Parsons, standing beside a mannequin, a width of silver lamé in their hands.

"Silver lamé doesn't need any encouragement to be flashy," he's saying. "So you make the dress long, and suddenly it's more mood lighting than neon billboard."

Astrid is narrowing her eyes at him. "Or you make it so short that somehow, despite its tendency to exhibitionism, the lamé isn't the first thing you see." She re-pins the fabric into a dress that's all about the woman, not just what she's wearing.

That dress danced on a podium. It had both beating heart and beautiful soul.

Because he and Astrid made it together.

His palms press against the mirrored walls, holding his body up.

Her portfolio from Parsons flips open in his mind. He sees the white tank top with the Hawk Jones logo in medieval script. The white tuxedo jacket. He could go on and on. Through piece after piece. So many of them should have borne Astrid's name.

His label is sexy and spirited because that's what Astrid is. All the things that make his designs celebrated are all the things that make her Astrid.

Hawk Jones is Astrid, not the other way around.

* * *

The world dresses for the occasion of the Battle of Versailles in a black sky sequined with white snow and a full and golden moon. The guests walk past guards wearing blood-red uniforms with sabers at their belts. Princess Grace of Monaco sports a tiara, the Duchess of Windsor an excess of sapphires. Simone Levitt is so draped in Van Cleef & Arpels diamonds that she's accompanied by a bodyguard.

Amongst the glamorous crowd is one man in a gray sweater and jeans trying with his whole heart to fix what he broke. His apology starts here, and maybe if she sees it, she'll come back. She has to come back.

But first he's forced to sit in a box. The designers aren't allowed backstage. They're meant to be in the audience to applaud their peers. The assistants will make sure everything happens onstage and Hawk hopes to God that Nancy and Velvet and Candace too—Candace, who's defected from Halston to help—will be able to pull it off.

So he waits, ignoring every impulse to scour the streets for Astrid because he knows he'll never find her that way. That she doesn't want him to find her. So he has to show her that he understands he was just another man who let her be less than she is.

He will *never* do that again. If she just comes back.

Violins cry out, the overture from *Cinderella* drifting into the theater. Cinderella's pumpkin coach rolls onto the stage beside the House of Dior's designs, so muted he's certain Mizza would be shocked—perhaps that's why she's chosen not to come. The pumpkin outshines the gowns.

Next a rocket ship and Pierre Cardin. It's a graceless leap from fairytale to future-tale. The vinyl jockstraps and space-age aesthetic are like lost children against the backdrop of a Versailles forest.

Ungaro's clothes are ushered in by a wooden cart and a man wearing animal ears—but what animal is he supposed to be? Nobody knows. The mannequins stand stiffly on a stage meant for theater.

Now an antique car for Yves Saint Laurent, and at least the dresses trimmed with feathers are amusing, but it's impossible not to wonder how this show has gone from pumpkin to rocket ship to unidentified animal, to a cardboard cut-out of a car.

Then Givenchy, set against a basket of flowers that outperform a rose-colored gown. The penultimate act of the French set is a drawn-out *pas de deux* with dancers Rudolf Nureyev and Merle Park. The audience naps, waking only for the finale at near on midnight—Josephine Baker singing about her love for Paris. The applause that follows is for her rather than for French couture.

Could it be, Hawk wonders from beneath the sharp, spasming ache of his heart, *that everyone is bored?* Could it be that the Americans have a fighting chance?

His hands clasp together in front of him like he's praying—and he is. Because if they win, Astrid *will* come back. She'll take her place as one of the greatest designers America has ever known.

Then Liza Minnelli races out, singing "Bonjour Paris." It's stark, but somehow beautiful onstage, dressed with only the hasty backdrop Joe Eula made by using a broom to draw an Eiffel Tower onto white paper with black paint. The models stream out, energy radiating from them, and Hawk watches the audience take in something about these models—almost half of them are Black. It's a stark contrast to the French half of the show, which was whiter than the snow outside. It's impossible not to be drawn in by the way these women move. They're the spotlights, and all eyes turn their way.

They exit the stage, ready for the first designer. It was to be Astrid.

There's a minute's silence instead. And all Hawk can think in that dark and silent minute is that it *has* to work. Because without Astrid, there is no forever.

The Stephen Burrows section begins. His butterfly-colored gowns are made even more magnificent by the models who don't just stand around, waiting to be admired. They're fluid where the French models were static, alive where the French models were dead. Pat Cleveland spins across the stage in a dress with a whirling train in every color and just when everyone thinks she'll spill off the end, she stops, poised on the very edge.

The crowd throw their programs into the air and cheer.

Blass, de la Renta and Halston do what they do superbly. For the French, unused to seeing models move to music, the vigor is stupendous. They can't get enough.

Then it's time for the finale. The Hawk Jones segment. He's played every card he possesses to reclaim the climax, has all but manhandled de la Renta into returning it to him. Because this is the most important thing Hawk has ever done in his life.

Everyone waits, breaths held.

The words *Astrid Bricard* are spotlit on the curtains instead of his name.

Then they sweep open to reveal a stage dotted with podiums. On top of each is a model dancing, losing herself in the music. The pieces onstage are Astrid's pieces and Hawk's pieces, labels torn from all of them. They each bear one name—Astrid Bricard—written at the back of the neck where the label should be. Because it's all hers, everything he's ever made and more. Everything he is, is Astrid's.

If only he'd understood it the day he was led by her into making a silver dress that is its own legend.

The crowd goes wild.

The Americans have won.

But Astrid remains gone, missing, vanished or dead. Hawk doesn't know.

Knows only that he is dead inside too.

* * *

The police investigate, but there is no body. They eventually close the case. People are allowed to leave—it isn't a crime. But the question remains: is Astrid gone, missing, vanished or dead? Everyone speculates, and they never stop.

When Hawk returns to New York and to Blythe, the doctors and social workers are scandalized at the very idea of him raising a child. It's not something men do, not in 1973. When his mother tells him he must register the child's name as Blythe Jones, he's adamant. She will bear Astrid's name. She's the one work of art Astrid will own forever.

Meredith looks after Blythe during the day and sometimes Beth takes her for a couple of days while Hawk buries himself in work, and in the success that overflows from Versailles. Blythe stays with him most nights, except when the work goes on too long, or the parties do—and gradually there are more and more of those. As the years pass, his worst instincts get the better of him and soon they're not instincts anymore, but necessities. Until the day Matthias calls him in and confronts him about what a shitty dad he is and Hawk yells at him and that afternoon Matthias dies and Hawk nearly does too— and then he goes to rehab.

But he can never take Blythe back because, while apparently he's better, he still hears his dad's voice telling him he's a terrible father. Matthias had spoken the truth—Hawk *had* been the worst. He has no confidence at all in his ability to be the kind of parent who can raise their kid to be the superlative adult Blythe deserves to be. What if he relapses? He can't even look at that seductive red-gold color of a finger of cognac without wanting to bathe in it. Red, gold and brown are banned from his collections, and if his hold on sobriety is nearly unloosed by fall leaves and sunsets, then he has to leave Blythe with Meredith, who can stop after just one Tom Collins.

It makes him feel still more of the truth of why Astrid left—to be drowning in shame at your own apparent incompetence at parenting, which is something so simple even animals can do it.

He throws himself with a fury into telling every interviewer the true genesis of the silver dress, Bianca's tuxedo jacket and all the rest. But they interrupt and ask who's inspiring him now, or they don't print it—in fact, each time he mentions Astrid, he makes it worse. Defending Astrid only seems to give more air to the rumors that he designed MIZZA, as if the press think he's still so seduced by the muse he propped up in life that he's continuing to buttress her, even now.

He starts to write a book no one can ignore or edit or overdub. But when he sits down to do it, he finds himself back at the Cheetah with booze and grass and dope all around and he shoves the paper away, knowing he needs to wait until sobriety is a certainty, rather than a new habit he's still trying to form.

And so the stories keep unfurling for decades on into the future. It isn't long before, in words on paper, Astrid becomes only the muse the world wanted her to be—the one who inspired Hawk's genius, the one who had her heart broken by him.

Ophelia, drowning offstage while Hamlet rules.

FIFTY-ONE

MIZZA BRICARD

I t was impossible to sleep after having witnessed the craven hunger of her countrymen trying to purge their own sins by hurling the blame for what had happened over the past four years onto the women of Paris. Huddled under a blanket in her salon, Mizza tried desperately to remember the faces of the children she'd helped save. What if she just told everyone about that? Would it save her, the Nazi dressmaker, from *l'épuration sauvage*?

They would come for her, she knew they would.

The telephone rang and when she answered it, she heard someone weeping. "On my way home, I saw..." Jeanne's voice trembled as if she'd never been more afraid.

Could there be anything worse than what they'd already seen? But Mizza could sense that it was and she closed her eyes as if that would help her not to hear this new and terrible thing.

"I saw them kick a woman until she died," Jeanne said brokenly. "She'd slept with Nazis, they said. But I knew her. She used to beg for money near my boulangerie. Her husband was a prisoner of war and she had five children, plus her own mother and her husband's mother to care for. She needed food and there was no other way, and now her children have no father and no mother either."

And Mizza knew in her bones that no matter what she said,

nobody would believe her. No one waited for explanations before they kicked. Out there on the streets, people believed that the *résistants* who'd fought bravely and almost hopelessly for years for France's liberation were men, not women who lived in fine apartments with jewelry and couture gowns.

The following days proved that fact. Even the untouchable were snared. So many fine scalps—actress Arletty was in prison. Coco Chanel was held by the FFI for a day until the British arranged her release. But Coco was friends with the British prime minister. Mizza was not.

To think that so many women had bargained with whatever they had left in order to keep their children alive for a world that no longer deserved their courage.

She crossed to the window, staring out at the darkness. Paris was still blacked out—the war continued all around, the Germans fighting on across Europe. *Imagine how shocking light would be*, she thought. *The headache you would get from all that brilliance.*

And there it was. The sensation of the German soldiers' hands around Mizza's neck back in 1918, the blade of a knife pressing against her cheek, the ropes gouging into her wrists. It was happening again—and she would once more lose almost everything to men and violence and war.

FIFTY-TWO

MIZZA BRICARD

Mizza stayed home. She hid. If they didn't see her, they might forget about her. And she avoided mirrors—she couldn't look at herself. Until she understood something that the dread and fear of the last few weeks had caused her to overlook, something that made her leave the apartment and walk to the American Army Headquarters.

She asked where she could find David Paris. The receptionist directed her to another building. Waiting out front was James Davenport. His eyes fell to the ground and she knew David was dead. Perhaps killed in the fighting going on in Belgium.

Mizza tilted her head up to the sky and blinked. When would the tears stop?

David was a young man owed decades by the world. Instead it had given him twenty years. Why grant him life just so he could die before he'd loved? Before he'd learned about a brand-new life Mizza hoped—the most towering hope of her life—would know decades and love and so much more than wreckage and ruin?

"I'm sorry," she said, her voice raw. "I know you were friends."

Then he looked at her properly and saw why she'd come.

"Shit," he said softly.

"I didn't want to force any promises from David," Mizza said, touching her stomach. "Just to tell him. I ... I didn't know him well, but I think he was the kind of man who would have liked to know he was..." Her voice cracked. "To be a father."

James looked up at the sky too, eyes shining.

She waited a moment before asking, "Is there someone I should tell? His parents..." She faltered as James shook his head.

"They're proper, churchgoing folk. They're in pieces over what happened to him. I don't think hearing..."

"That he's fathered a child with a forty-four-year-old married Frenchwoman will make them feel better?" Mizza finished softly. "I understand."

David's parents were in America, far from war. They didn't know what it could do to people. And they shouldn't think less of their son. "I'll write *Father unknown* on the birth certificate."

James studied her, compassion in his eyes. "What will you do?"

I did things during the war that people whisper about. Is it fair to give that burden to a child? She shrugged. "I'm sorry. I was expecting to see David, and now..." Her hand wiped away the dampness beneath her eyes. "I'm somewhat adrift."

She started to walk away. But James called out, desperately, "Wait!"

* * *

When Mizza reentered her apartment building, the same neighbor who'd hissed *collabo* at her a few months ago was on her way out. She took one look at Mizza's gently rounded stomach and said it again— *collabo*—but with more authority now. "I haven't seen your husband since June," was her parting shot. "The baby cannot be his."

It was pointless hiding now. She'd been seen. That she'd consorted with Nazis during the war, was now pregnant and had not seen her husband for months were facts Mizza must live with. It was time to resume life, to brace for her turn. Would she be questioned? Arrested? Beaten? Shaved? Shunned?

"Lucien Lelong will give you a job," Tian told her. "Any couturier will give you a job. You did nothing wrong during the war."

But she couldn't ask Lelong to make her his assistant. *L'épuration sauvage* had not yet come for her but whispers about collaborationists and Nazi lovers floated around like the fragrance of horse chestnuts—potent and sticky. It was best to be invisible, especially as the loudest whispers came from those with the most need to protect themselves—wealthy women with powerful husbands who'd done business with the Nazis and who were trying to re-dress themselves in patriotism. Those women patronized Lelong's couture house and might see Mizza and talk about her the way everyone now talked about Coco Chanel and her Nazi lover.

Coco had run away to Switzerland. But running was akin to giving up entirely on oneself. Mizza couldn't do that, not if she wanted this child to become everything she herself hadn't been able to. She just needed to wait until Hubert returned and everyone forgot—and she needed to hope that nobody turned their attention toward her child.

So Mizza donned a white coat, and took a discreet, anonymous position as a seamstress for the Théâtre de la Mode, an exhibition to be held at the Palais du Louvre—a fashion show with doll-mannequins one-third human size. The dolls would wear micro-scale haute couture and jewels, set against backdrops designed by Cocteau—like the Rue de la Paix, where exquisitely dressed mini-mannequins paraded in tiny Charles Worth gowns. Or L'Opéra, where petite diamond bracelets adorned wrists lifting Schiaparelli skirts from the floor. The exhibition was supposed to resurrect the couture industry and Paris—a city that lay on the other side of occupation and shame.

Mizza tried to just make tiny beautiful clothes for tiny beautiful dolls. But the rounder her stomach grew, the more people shunned her. Nobody wanted to sit near a pregnant woman already much gossiped about, not so soon after the war, when badges of innocence were worth more than coal and even the rumor of a dishonorable association could stain a name forever.

Mizza had long known that being beautiful, and owning jewels so stunning they made you gasp, did not endear her to everyone. And how people loved to see the supposedly mighty fall.

Mizza did not just fall. She tumbled.

The rumors swirled the way rumors always did—small and close to the truth.

Mizza had entertained Nazis.

Mizza's husband had been away in Germany for months and couldn't possibly have fathered her child.

Then a little embellishment was added and soon the *on dit* was more extravagant than the court of the Sun King.

Mizza had tried to kill herself rather than live with the shame of her Nazi baby.

No, the scar on her arm was caused by a jealous Nazi wife throwing vitriol at her.

Mizza seduced young maquisards and tried to turn their heads from the Allied cause while they were in her bed.

Mizza had been the lover of everyone, from Hitler himself to the King of Egypt.

The baby kicked at her insides. And Mizza knew it was time to bring down the curtain on what had been set in motion on that day in 1937 when a man called Christian Dior had walked into the studio at Molyneux and a friendship was kindled that had led her to the grounds of the Centre Psychiatrique Sainte-Anne—and thus to this place where her reputation now meant that her child would not be allowed to become everything Mizza had not been able to. Unless she did something truly, painfully unselfish.

She went back to see James, after having previously told him no— she would never give up her child.

FIFTY-THREE

MIZZA BRICARD

The night after Mizza made the arrangements with James, she sat at her desk, running her fingers over her belly. Scattered moments from the past four years framed themselves in her mind. Walking over bones. The pearls around her neck that had made Herr Didier stop and look. Bernard shaking the petals from tulips, leaving their pistils bare. Meeting the same two pilots on two different evenings. The bald heads of women blamed for a nation's shame.

And—conceiving a child on the night of the liberation of Paris. A child conceived on such a night could be nothing other than spectacular.

But Jeanne's words echoed in the dark. *Cursed before it can even speak. That poor child.*

Mizza would not let that happen. Her child would not pay for her sins. It would live in a faraway land where people had never heard the word *collabo*, where nobody would ever curse a child or believe rumors about Nazi fathers—where it could be as bold and spectacular and brilliant as its conception promised.

She picked up a pen and wrote:

Chérie, some might look back on everything that happened over the past four years and say I should never have done any of it.

Except—but for those things, you wouldn't be here. And you are the one thing I can never regret. Know that you are made up of bones and of weeds, of pearls and of tears. You are made up of a small girl who was saved beneath a darkened city. A child made of those things is like a star exploding against the night, forever and always.

I know you are a girl. So I'll ask them to name you Astride—the divine beauty.

The last words blurred with the fall of her tears.

* * *

Mizza woke near midnight with pain clenching her belly. She wished Hubert was there. He'd finally been freed from house arrest in Berlin now the war had ended and he was making his way back to France through the ruins. He would never meet the baby. But she would tell him about her and she knew he would understand. Someone who'd been in Germany would know better than Mizza why a child should be allowed to grow up in a continent far from war and rumor and shame.

At the hospital, she lost herself in the pain, emerging from it sometime later when a child cried.

Her child.

Would she have dark hair like Mizza's, or fair like David's? Mizza's green eyes, or David's blue?

All at once a face began to form, and Mizza wanted desperately to press her lips upon that tiny forehead. It blurred into the face of the girl with the white heart, the face of all the other girls Mizza had carried and cajoled and cared for over hours underground in the near dark, girls she'd had to say goodbye to, their hands slipping from hers as they cried out that they didn't want to go, that they wanted to stay with her.

Her tears came in a huge, gulping, endless rush.

She telephoned James and told him he needed to come now. If she held Astride, she would never be strong enough for this last letting go.

* * *

There were so many stories she could ask them to tell the baby, Mizza thought as she placed Astride in James's arms. That she was the child of a nameless French seamstress. That she was the child of Mizza Bricard. And even though that was the reason she was giving the child to someone else to raise, that's what she asked them to tell Astride later, never imagining her stain would reach shores so far away as America.

"We will," James promised. "And her last name will be Bricard. In honor of you. You saved my life."

The young woman at his side, Beth, smiled at the baby as if she were the most precious thing in the world.

Which was why Mizza turned away, keeping only a note she'd meant to send but could no longer bear to part with.

As James and Beth left with the baby, she felt herself gripped by a sudden terror that perhaps it would have been better for Astride to have been born to a nameless French seamstress. Because what if Mizza's name alone was a burden nobody could bear?

If only she could have seen, in that moment, what would happen in just a few years' time. How a man called Christian Dior would rise up, how the name of the woman who worked alongside him would weave itself into legend too.

THE BEGINNING...
OF A NEW LEGEND

FIFTY-FOUR

BLYTHE BRICARD

Blythe lies on her bed, unable to rest. Astrid is asleep in the spare room. Sebby and Eva are napping too, having stared at this woman, this grandmother who suddenly exists, all through lunch.

What Blythe has now is Ophelia's story. The story of the drowned woman. What of the story of the person who made her drown?

Blythe shuts her eyes and remembers Hawk trying to talk to her about Astrid, remembers telling him to shut up because hearing him say that Astrid loved her hurt so much. She remembers rejecting him as a thirteen-year-old, and then again as an eighteen-year-old after Meredith's funeral. She recalls the way she's avoided his calls since, has fixated on the truths about him that he was too ashamed to tell her. And look how she's judged him—he was right to be afraid to confide in her.

There are so many other memories she could have dwelled on— those journeys to beaches where maybe he was looking for Astrid, and where he taught Blythe to swim. Blythe had held on to his arms, trusting him to never let her go under.

Was she so scared of losing another parent that she pushed him away before he could run?

The self-examination goes deeper still. Her divorce from Jake— was it just Jake who screwed up? Instead of talking to him, had

Blythe run away because her whole life has been spent anticipating the moment when someone would leave her? Maybe, just as she'd done with Hawk, she has a habit of accumulating evidence and jumping to the conclusion that Jake doesn't love her—just look at her suspicions after the phone call from Jake's assistant, and her suspicions about why Jake had spoken to Nathaniel about MIZZA. She'd thought it meant he had ulterior motives. But why didn't she just ask him? He'd been at the bedside of his dying mother and had she told him she loved him? Had she said, *Astrid's back and I'm really scared?*

No. She hadn't. And another uncomfortable question asks itself. What if it wasn't Jake who was intent on being angry yesterday? What if it was Blythe who'd run away—again—without explanation? She hadn't even tried to comfort him. What kind of person did that make her?

How many things in Blythe's past, things she's mourned, are all her fault?

She hears herself laugh. She laughs and she laughs and she can't stop. It is ironically, stupidly funny that she's ruined every relationship she ought to have treasured. The strange cry-laughter is a bit like a blood-letting—crazy and wild, hand pressed to mouth, eyes damp, an outpouring of resentments she no longer wants to hold on to.

At last she pulls herself together and texts Jake the address of the cottage. *This time, I owe* you *an apology*, she says. *Please come when you can.* And she tries to quash the thought, *What if he's had enough of her lack of trust?*

There's yet another person she hopes hasn't given up on her. She texts Hawk.

I spoke to Astrid. And I want to talk to you. Are you still coming?

His reply is immediate and brief.

I'm just getting on the plane now.

* * *

That evening, after Eva and Sebby have had dinner and gone back to bed, Blythe checks her phone. Nothing from Jake. *I love you*, she texts him. Words she should have said to him yesterday. Words she wants to say to him every day of the future. If they still have one.

She stares at her phone. No reply.

"Blythe?"

She gasps and turns around to see Astrid, who smiles at her and turns the kettle on, taking out two mugs. "Can you bear to listen to the rest?"

Blythe exhales, knowing the revisioning of history isn't finished. There are still some parts of the story—what happened after Astrid left Versailles?—that she wants to know. She opens a drawer and shoves her phone inside so she can't torture herself with Jake's silence.

Astrid makes her a cup of tea and sits by her side as if they're an ordinary mother and daughter sharing a late-night confidence.

Like Jake and Iris used to.

Blythe stares fiercely at her mug because this is nothing like Jake and Iris. Jake always knew his mother loved him. Whereas Blythe is only now starting to think that perhaps her mother loved her too, but it still hurts more than it heals.

"Did you have postnatal depression?" Blythe's been thinking about Remy, who, after her baby, Xavier, was born, suffered panic attacks, was obsessed with not leaving her apartment in case something happened to the baby, withdrew from everyone. She remembered Remy telling her that traumatic birth experiences, which Remy had had, were a risk factor. Astrid had given birth to Blythe early and Blythe hadn't been able to breathe on her own, which would have been horribly traumatic.

Astrid nods. "It was the seventies though. It wasn't even a recognized diagnosis back then. If things got really extreme, you might be given a Valium. So I had no idea. And no treatment. I actually thought, back at Versailles, that I'd gone mad. And I think back to how I was—nearly hypothermic with cold and convinced that the rational thing was to leave a white dress as a prop in the Hall of Mirrors to buy

me some time. It seems so obvious now that I was behaving absurdly.
But I'm grateful to Candace for saying what she did—that her mom
kept chasing after the thing that broke her until Candace was the one
who shattered. If she hadn't, maybe I'd have gone back to Manhattan
after Versailles and then I don't know what would have happened to
you." Her voice trembles. "Untreated PND is…It's very dangerous."

Astrid sips her tea, taking a moment to compose herself. "I wasn't ever
running away," she continues. "I didn't know what I was doing. I'd heard
the term nervous breakdown before but it wasn't my nerves that were
broken—it was myself, the real Astrid, overpowered by the one in the
newspapers. Luckily a part of my brain sent me to Mizza's apartment.
She wasn't well herself by then but she packed a suitcase and we caught
the train to Venice. She looked after me for months. She tried a couple of
doctors but, like I said, PND didn't exist medically, not in 1973."

Astrid shrugs, as if she'd rather not go into the way she was treated
by the doctors back then who just wanted to give her Valium.

Blythe feels her heart unpleat and something like empathy finds
its way in. Both her kids had been born on time and healthy and she
hadn't had the press screaming that her work was someone else's and
she hadn't had people shouting abuse at her either but still she'd felt
useless and alone and frightened from time to time. She can't imagine
how awful it must have been for Astrid—to have had people climbing
the fire escapes to photograph her and her child. If someone had tried
to do that to Eva or Sebby, Blythe isn't sure what she would have done,
but she knows it wouldn't have been rational either.

"Mizza looked after you?" she asks.

Astrid nods. "It took me nearly a year to recover. And then…"
She pauses.

Blythe watches her press a hand to her mouth and then blink and
swallow, swallow and blink. How can she not reach out and slip her
hand inside her mother's?

Shockingly, Astrid says, "I went back for you, Blythe."

Blythe's response is a whisper. "What?"

"I sent a note to Meredith. She was looking after you during the day and I was too scared to go to Hawk first. I told her when I was coming, that I was planning to spend a couple of quiet weeks with you and then I'd make it known that I was alive. I asked her not to tell Hawk—but that I'd call him once I'd had a couple of days with you. I needed to tackle one thing at a time. I was terrified of losing my grip on reality again by opening myself up to too many emotions at once."

Astrid pauses, studies her hand wrapped in Blythe's. She has true *doigts de fée,* Blythe sees—the fairy fingers French seamstresses are reckoned to have. Precious.

"There's a small park you have to pass on the way to Meredith's apartment," she continues, very quietly. "As I was walking past, I saw a lady pushing a little blond girl in a swing. The lady turned her head and saw me—it was Meredith. She picked up the girl, whispered something in her ear, and the girl wrapped her arms around Meredith's neck and said, so loudly I could hear it, 'Momma.' The girl was you, and you clearly loved Meredith. You thought she was your mother. Meredith turned back to me, and she didn't speak, but I know what she was telling me. That if I was to take you, I'd be hurting you all over again. You had no memory of me."

A long, aching moment passes before Astrid goes on. "She left the park, and I almost left too. But I...I wanted you so much. So I went after her. But it was as if she knew..."

So many tears in Astrid's eyes now that they fall down her cheeks and Blythe tightens her grip, telling Astrid that she's here for her in this moment, even if she still isn't sure, is still afraid.

Astrid takes a shaky breath and repeats, "It was as if she knew I wouldn't give in so easily. There was a folded note on the swing. I shouldn't have picked it up. If I hadn't..."

Another pause. A bleak smile. "Maybe it wouldn't have turned out the way it did," Astrid finishes.

"What did the note say?" Blythe asks with trepidation.

"That if I was to take you, I'd be proving everyone right," Astrid says flatly. "I'd show everyone I really was mad. Because only mad mothers run away from their children. I had never, *never* considered until that moment that I'd abandoned you. I was getting better so I *could* be your mother. But reading Meredith's words, I realized there was a new story coming for me. One in which I would be the mad mother. And you would suffer all over again as the mad mother's daughter. So I killed that story by leaving—leaving you with someone I thought was better for you than who I believed I was, back then. Believing you're capable of raising a child when the whole world's told you that you're mediocre, fourth-rate, and only good at letting people down..."

Astrid exhales shakily, then swipes her fingers under her eyes. "That's pretty hard to do. Maybe with proper treatment, I'd have known it was normal for someone with PND to think they're failing their child. Maybe I would have had more self-belief...I don't know. Watching Meredith walk away with you, all I believed were her words, the press's words—the evidence."

She laughs bitterly. "I'd been told by doctors I was hysterical. When your mind is beaten, those words are hard to shake. And then...I thought leaving the first time was the hardest thing. Leaving the second time was..."

Astrid's voice cracks wide open, cracking Blythe open too, and she stares into the vast chasm of what might have been. But who's to say that chasm would have been better than what Blythe had had? Who's to say that if Astrid had raised her, Blythe wouldn't still have worn a uniform for the wrong school and hidden behind sunglasses?

Her mind grapples with what to say. "Did Meredith...Was she..."

Astrid is silent for a long time. "I don't blame Meredith," she says at last. "She was protecting Hawk, her son, who I'd hurt badly. And she thought she was protecting you. And look at you."

The smile she gives Blythe is full of pride. "You're such an impressive woman. You've raised two kids largely by yourself. You're starting a business. Mizza and I polished the stone and the diamond finally emerged. I can't be angry at Meredith. By the time I understood what PND was—which was around the nineties, when it finally became a diagnosis—and I realized my behavior back in 1973 was normal for someone with untreated PND, it was too late to change the fact I'd abandoned you and you most likely hated me. Can you imagine how strong you need to be to confront a child who hates you? You love your children more than anything, and for them to hate you—even if you deserve it...Let's just say it redefines pain. So I thought it was better to stay hidden. I was a coward, Blythe, scared of what it would mean to return. I'm so sorry."

"But you're here now," Blythe whispers.

"I am. And it hurts even more than I thought it would."

Blythe's head drops to her mother's shoulder and Astrid's arms close around her. It's the first time in her living memory that her mother has embraced her and now Blythe knows exactly why Eva and Sebby hold on so tight when she hugs them.

* * *

An hour later, Blythe has tucked Astrid into bed. While she's exhausted from everything she's learned, her mind is still busily contemplating what it all means.

At the end of their conversation, Astrid had explained that, from her seaside home in Spain and via Mizza's—and Dior's—very discreet lawyer, she's been funding five scholarships at FIT and Parsons for female students every year since she disappeared. That Blythe's trip to Peru, which had been financed by a grant supporting a recent graduate to work in sustainable fashion, had also been funded by Astrid's foundation, set up to try to make fashion a more ethical and inclusive industry. That Marcelline's similar grant that same year to explore marketing strategies that didn't rely on fast fashion was awarded by Astrid too. That she and Marcelline are two women who've been supported, unbeknownst to them, by another woman who's seen how easily women lose out to men in the strange world of fashion, where the customers are largely women but the people in charge are men.

Astrid said that the world was designed for the Ophelias to die and the Hamlets to rule—but Blythe can't let that be true. She takes out Hawk's book about Astrid and there in the last pages are Astrid's dresses on the stage of a theater in a palace. An idea stirs. She picks up her phone and searches for pictures of the 1945 Théâtre de la Mode that Coco told her Mizza Bricard had once worked in.

"Oh," she says in wonder. Tiny, beautiful dolls in tiny, beautiful dresses. Theatrical. Fabulous.

Before she can consider her fledgling idea further, she hears a car pull up. Maybe it's Jake?

She hurries to the door and sees a man climb out of a sedan. A man who'd held on to her calves while she sat on his shoulders as an eight-year-old girl and watched the Rolling Stones play Madison Square Garden, the two of them singing their hearts out, completely out of tune with the music but in perfect harmony together. Afterward, he'd taken her backstage to have her *Tattoo You* album signed by Mick Jagger, then they'd gone out for burgers and milkshakes even though it was midnight, and she'd thought she was so happy her heart might burst its seams, coloring the whole world red with her joy.

And she feels her feet do what they'd done at the start of that same night—run toward her father, expecting only wonderful things rather than sadness. The look on his face when he sees her really does split her heart right open—and love spills out.

Hawk wraps her up in a hug and she realizes she doesn't need to speak to him. She's been speaking to him in her head for all of the past week, chasing down the story of their past. But the past is gone and her dad is here and he's saying, "Hi, sweetheart," against her ear.

She pulls back and smiles at him. "Hi, Dad."

* * *

It must be the hour for arrivals. Hawk and Blythe have just opened the door to go inside when another car pulls in. Jake.

"I get the feeling you need to talk to him right now more than you need to talk to me," Hawk says to her with the kind of perception only a parent possesses.

She nods. "There's a spare bedroom just to the left of the kitchen. It's yours." Then her face crumples a little. "I might have messed it all up. With Jake."

Hawk kisses her cheek. "It's impossible not to love you, sweetheart. I bet he feels the same." Then he disappears inside.

And Blythe turns to her husband, who appears on the doorstep looking as emotionally bedraggled as she feels.

"That was your dad," Jake says gently. "And your mom's back too."

Blythe's heart leaps a little that this is the first thing he says—that maybe he's been thinking of her and what she's been going through, just like she's been thinking of him.

"Come in," she tells him.

He stands in front of the fire, tall and unshaven, dressed in a dark navy turtleneck sweater and jeans, almost too tall for this low-ceilinged, centuries-old room, wrecked. They stare at one another, on opposite sides of the room, and this silence isn't quite like the one at the hospital, but nor is it comfortable.

"How's Iris?" she asks.

His jaw tightens. "Still hanging in there."

"Shit. I don't know if that's worse or better. That you have an extra day, or that she doesn't have peace. And why are you here if she's still—"

"This is where my mom would want me to be," he cuts in. "I've said goodbye, and she has twenty-four other people to sit with her. You were right to refuse my stupid offer of marriage. I thought one blissful reunion really did mean everything would be chateaux and soufflés. But the very first crisis and I think you've run off with Champlain and I leave the kids in the waiting room even though they're scared, and I'm back to being the same jerk I've been for the last few years."

"Jake..." She shakes her head and a terrified look crosses his face.

"You've been facing your own battles by yourself again because I wasn't here," he says, voice vehement. "And as well as that, you probably think I'm interfering in your business. I know you spoke to Anna and she told you about the party, but it was just meant to be a surprise to celebrate your launch. I should have asked you about it though. Otherwise it's like me taking over. And Nathaniel told you I spoke to him about MIZZA first, but it was just because I wanted you to do it. If I gave you the idea, you never would have. So I dropped it on him. I'm sorry. I might tattoo that onto my hand so I can remember that if I don't behave like a dick, then I won't need to keep apologizing."

"Tattoo it on your hand?" she says, unable to resist teasing him, touched by how thoughtful he'd been, wanting to throw her a party—and wanting her to start up MIZZA so much that he'd given the idea to his competitor. "You're more likely to have someone make you a fabulous T-shirt with the words printed on it in your favorite shade of blue."

His answering smile is half-hopeful, half-afraid.

"I'm sorry too," she tells him. "Before we divorced, I didn't just tell you I wanted both you and my dream, no matter how long it took. I left you instead. And at the hospital...I walked away again. I'm expert at leaving."

She pauses—excavating the things she's clung to since she was a baby who thought her mother didn't love her suddenly makes her so very sad at all the moments she's missed because of her own stubbornness.

"Hey," Jake says. "Look at us now though. Talking like grown-ups. Like two people who love one another, maybe."

He says this uncertainly, as if he still isn't sure how she feels.

She takes a step toward him. "Exactly like two people who love one another. What do you say we keep doing that?"

"Talking or loving?" he says, quirking a smile at her and pulling her into his arms. His lips brush over her neck. "Because I know which one I prefer..."

She laughs and tugs him into her room.

* * *

They don't unwind their limbs from one another when they've finished. They don't sleep either. They talk about so many things. Iris. Astrid. Hawk. Their own life together. And Blythe's business.

"I think I've solved my last problem," she tells Jake excitedly and his hand on her back draws her in closer as if he's as eager to know as she is to speak.

"I'll show the ready-to-wear—the clothes inspired by the one-offs— on a catwalk," she explains. "And I can make tiny samples of the one-offs from the fabric left over from the vintage pieces. Miniature dresses adorning pint-sized dolls in my own Théâtre de la Mode." She beams and watches his eyes flash with the same buzz that she feels.

"That is actually genius," he says and she laughs. Because it is.

Her customers will love the idea of buying their unique, refashioned vintage after seeing it modeled on a tiny, beautiful doll.

"And I have one more brilliant idea," she says, wriggling in even closer to Jake. "I'm going to show my first collection at Versailles. If I have to use Hawk's name or even your name to get in there, I will. I need to finish that story properly, not with a bloodied dress and a question mark."

FIFTY-FIVE

MIZZA BRICARD

PARIS, NOVEMBER 1946

The way to do it was the way she'd done everything since 1945—to be a character. Mizza Bricard: brazen, scandalous, renowned. A couture house demanded style and Mizza had an excess of that. It demanded lashings of gossip, to be always at the tip of the world's tongue—and Mizza would guarantee that. And it demanded a way of seeing things that were unseen—the weakness in the flower and the strength in the weed.

At eleven in the morning she began to prepare. Eyeliner was the first element of her mask, kicking up at the corners like the arm of a dancer. Lipstick in a soft red offsetting creamy skin that looked as if it had hardly aged at all. Occasionally women would ask what her secret was and, rather than admit she didn't know, she would smile and say, "The pillows I sleep on at the Ritz."

She didn't even live at the Ritz, but that was just one of the many lies that would later be told about her.

A black dress with a low neckline. Three strands of pearls, each looped once so they formed six strands. A leopard-print turban, a veil carefully affixed to create a haze behind which the real Mizza could never be discovered. A leopard-print scarf tied over the scars on her wrist. Solid gold earrings the size of twenty-franc coins.

Then it was time to get herself to 30 Avenue Montaigne—to the House of Christian Dior.

* * *

Tian, or *le patron* as he was to be called at work, gathered Mizza into a room with four other women: the *directrices* of the studio, the ateliers, the fitting rooms and publicity. This last was a much younger woman named Alix St. Pierre, an American, the only one who appeared to know nothing of Mizza because her eyes were fixed equally on each of them, as if trying to read the words printed on their souls.

What does mine say, Mizza had a peculiar impulse to ask, and her eyes locked with Alix's and she knew Alix had had a hard war too.

Suffering wasn't a thing to bond over. Whoever said that a pain shared was a pain halved had never truly hurt. A pain shared was a pain multiplied. Mizza withdrew her eyes from Alix St. Pierre because, if her pain was to multiply, it would surely fell her.

She turned her attention to the dress in the middle of the room that Tian was frowning over. "It needs a belt," she said decidedly.

She advanced on the dress while simultaneously selecting three belts, discarding two into the hands of Madame Raymonde and affixing one around the mannequin's waist, cinching it tightly. A subtle transformation. Tian nodded approvingly.

But it wasn't enough.

"Walk," Mizza commanded. "And turn." Then Mizza saw it.

"A disaster," she pronounced, indicating the back of the neckline, which hovered uncertainly in the space between the base of the neck and the shoulders. "The collar should elongate the neck, as if it's beckoning a fingertip to drift over it."

Alix exclaimed, "Oh, yes!" and Mizza almost smiled at her exuberance. Instead she took up pins and then draped and twisted and tucked the black silk taffeta into a new shape.

Everyone sighed when she'd finished. What had been as dowdy as a Victory Suit was now transformed.

And so it began again. Not just the prompting of brilliance, but the making of it. But few people would ever see the soul of Mizza that lived inside every Dior gown.

So be it.

FIFTY-SIX

BLYTHE BRICARD, ASTRID BRICARD AND HAWK JONES

Blythe looks around the Hall of Mirrors in the Palace of Versailles, seeing not the fifty-seven mirrors, the seventeen glass doors or the more than eight thousand square feet of parquetry. She sees her tiny dolls wearing spectacular—no, fearless—MIZZA designs.

Then she plunges into the chaos backstage where she checks over every outfit that will stride down the hall and be redoubled in the magical mirrors. Finally, she and the mannequins stand in a circle, hands joined.

"To Mizza and Astrid Bricard," she says.

Someone adds, "And to Blythe Bricard," and everyone cheers.

The show begins.

Out walk the mannequins wearing slinky jewel-toned tank dresses paired with leopard-print boots. Tuxedo jackets atop organza dresses with deluges of delicate ruffles. In the background, one of the Théâtre de la Mode sets shows a miniature shop with posters of a brave woman hanging in the windows. In the middle of the shop stands a micro-scale model wearing one of a dozen incredible vintage blazers Blythe's remodeled into mini dresses. Another set is a nightclub where a light show flashes over canvas-draped walls. Two dolls gaze up at a third one dancing on a podium in a silver dress, a look of abandon on her face.

The eyes of everyone in the room swivel back and forth. They don't know whether to look at the theater or the catwalk—they want to look at it all. And Blythe can't stop the excitement building, thinks maybe they love the clothes as much as she does—that they're dying to wear these remade and reclaimed stories from history, beautiful now, the stains and tears of time not simply cut away, but part of the fabric.

Soon, it's time for the finale. Blythe makes her way deeper into the backstage area and knocks on the door of the one private dressing room. She hears Astrid laugh and Hawk's voice call, "We're coming."

Hawk Jones and Astrid Bricard step out. They take their daughter's hands and the three of them walk through the Hall of Mirrors together.

Astrid is wearing a white tuxedo jacket. Blythe is wearing a white column dress that is tall and proud and unbreakable. It's a showstopper of a dress and it's finally being allowed its rightful finale.

The hall erupts. And Blythe leans in to kiss her mother's cheek, and then her father's.

The cheers crescendo, so loud now that Blythe sees Sebby, held tight in Jake's arms, clap his hands over his ears and then wave at her. Beside Jake are all the Blacks: Ed and Joy, Coco, even Charlie and Frieda. Remy and her partner, Adam, stand a little farther along, applauding wildly. Marcelline and Candace whoop and whistle alongside her mom's friends Velvet and Graham. Right at the back, Blythe glimpses a dark-haired woman in a white coat and ropes of pearls, as if Mizza has been let out of heaven for a day to bring her blessings here too.

Then her eyes skip back around to her husband and children. Jake's crouched at the same level as Sebby and Eva now, his arms around both his children. Photographers are urging him to step onto the runway and have his photo taken with his wife.

Jake shakes his head firmly. "This is Blythe's show." He turns his back on the media and stays where he is, on the sidelines with his children while Blythe takes center stage.

Blythe, Hawk and Astrid stop at the end of the runway and Hawk and Astrid lean in at the same time to kiss her cheeks. The cameras are like fireworks, seizing a moment nobody ever thought would happen.

Then some instinct tells Blythe to take a step backward. As the disco lights turn on and the music starts to play and everyone begins to dance, Blythe walks over to her family. She slides one arm around Jake's waist and holds on to Eva and Sebby's hands and the four of them dance, laughing, to the music, surrounded by Blythe's dream come true at last.

* * *

As her daughter steps into her own happy ever after, Astrid turns to Hawk. They've done a lot of talking. A fair amount of crying. But right now, he says to her, "I remember the silver dress."

And even though he might be wearing shoes now and forty years have passed since she first met him, there's more than a hint of the Hawk Jones who once told her she looked like she was planning to put the devil into hell with a dress. And she wonders—if they'd known how much it would hurt, would they still have done it? Did the way they loved leave more in their hearts than just the scars of what they lost?

He says, without her needing to start the sentence, "It was the best thing I ever did, loving you. It's still the best."

Of course her eyes flood with tears.

Hawk slips his arms around her waist. "You still cry when I tell you I love you. I'll just have to tell you so many times that you'll eventually start smiling."

His grin is as sexy as ever. She lays her palms against his chest and says, "I'm wearing a white tuxedo jacket. So that means, I do."

"About damn time."

While she's laughing, he kisses her and she has no idea how many more chapters will be written in the Legend of Astrid Bricard and what they will say and nor does she care. Because the story she's writing now with Hawk, and with the daughter she can see just over Hawk's shoulder, is the only one that matters. The true story. The one that hurts the most because it's so damn real. The one that only they will know and that they will never share with anyone. They'll take it with them, to their graves—all the unspoken sentences they never needed to say because some legends are wordless and written only on hearts.

And that's the way it should be.

AUTHOR'S NOTE

Open a newspaper, a magazine, or scroll the internet and you'll discover that Britney Spears is ruining all young girls. Angelina Jolie's a home-wrecker and Jennifer Aniston's the woman who couldn't keep her husband—but Brad Pitt's a heartthrob. The *Evening Standard* puts Amy Winehouse on the front page with cocaine residue under her nose and cares nothing for the consequences. Amber Heard makes millions for the media exploiting her trial. Justin Timberlake rips Janet Jackson's top at the Super Bowl but Jackson's the one who gets trashed in the press and banned from the Super Bowl. Kurt Cobain wrote Courtney Love's album. Anna Wintour ran off with Bob Marley for two weeks. Cher had ribs removed to slim down. Lady Gaga's a hermaphrodite.

Find a famous woman—and find a stream of falsehoods and cruelties in her wake.

My book is a work of fiction. In trying to tell some parts of a true story, I've made up a hell of a lot, which perhaps means I'm as much to blame as anyone who's ever published untruths about a woman. But I hope this explanation shows you what my motivations were—and then you can judge.

Germaine Louise Neustadt (or Neustadtl as it's misspelled in the Paris Archives), also known as Madame Biano, Mizza Bricard, Mitzah Bricard, and Christian Dior's muse, was a real person. And then she became a made-up real person.

Anecdotes such as this abound in books, newspapers and magazines: "She never wore briefs and was only ever found in one of three places—at home, at the Ritz, or at Dior. It was said that she had once performed in a nude revue..." That's from Marie-France Pochna's oft-quoted 2008 biography of Dior. Or John Galliano, who said upon launching his Dior collection inspired by Mizza, "Have you gotten to the bit where Mr. Dior says she never wore any knickers? She was the last of the demi-horizontale. She was fabulous!" Celebrity milliner Stephen Jones writes in the *Financial Times Weekend* in 2016, "Then there's Mitzah Bricard, who was Christian Dior's muse... a hooker who had made good." And in Nigel Cawthorne's 1996 book, *The New Look: The Dior Revolution*, he asserts Mizza "had once been a demimondaine—that is, an expensive prostitute..." I could go on and on with quotes that turn Mizza into a knicker-less whore.

So what's the truth? Only Mizza knows. I believe the truth is more likely to be found in the accounts of those who knew her, rather than men reporting on her thirty or forty years after her death who've decided that the racier the anecdote, the more chance they have of being published.

For example, as quoted in my novel, fashion writer Elene Foster in a 1950 article says of Mizza, "She is a most important person on the Dior staff, second only to the great man himself... she is first assistant designer to Christian Dior." Or Cecil Beaton, renowned fashion photographer, who says, "There are in the world of fashion those whose names have become almost household words merely through the good offices of their Personal Relations Officer. There are others who remain unsung, yet who are held in the highest respect by the brightest talents: Mizza Bricard is such a one.... The greatest dressmakers know her worth."

The questions in all of this are: How does a woman, who was always seated at Dior's right hand while all other employees were asked to sit behind him, a woman who influenced and designed for arguably two of the greatest talents in fashion—Balenciaga and Dior—become a courtesan, a whore? How and why are women constantly reshaped by the media into something they aren't? And why can women only be the inspiration in the creative process, rather than the creator? Those questions drove the writing of this book, and thus required me to invent Mizza's daughter, Astrid Bricard, and Astrid's lover, Hawthorne "Hawk" Jones, as well as their daughter, Blythe Bricard. But around the invention is a great deal of fact.

Let's start with Astrid and Hawk and the 1970s fashion scene. I've based Hawk's ascent on Halston's rise to fame at around the same time—from one buzzing, theatrical store where disco queens and society madams were dressed, to a fashion empire. Just as Halston was offered sixteen million dollars by Norton Simon Inc., Hawk is offered money for his business by a conglomerate. Just as Halston was named the "premier designer of all America" by *Newsweek*, so is Hawk similarly crowned. The energy of the discos (the Electric Circus and the Cheetah were real nightclubs), as well as the protest marches around Vietnam, equality and gay rights, fueled society at the time, including the fashions. Diana Vreeland coined the term "youthquake," but at a slightly earlier time than I have referred to it in the book—in 1965—to describe the way music and culture were changing fashion and the world. Other breaches of the truth include having Hawk make Bianca's infamous wedding tuxedo, which was actually made by Yves Saint Laurent. John Fairchild, editor of *Women's Wear Daily*, was a real person who's been described as "tyrannical" and the "onetime terror of the fashion industry" by *Vanity Fair,* and by other sources as mean, intimidating, and a man who loved to anoint winners and losers, especially in his infamous "In and Out" column, but I've obviously invented his animosity to Astrid. It's based in truth; as Diane von Furstenberg says of Fairchild in *Vanity Fair,* he "made people, and destroyed people," and the quotes Hawk recalls Fairchild saying about everyone from Jackie O to his attitude to women in pants are real.

The Phaidon publication *Halston* and the Rizzoli publication of the same name were useful sources for the Astrid and Hawk part of the book, as was Bill Blass's memoir *Bare Blass*, where he recounts the excess of the Charles Revson parties (the bingo prizes did include Gucci luggage and toilet seats embedded with hundred-dollar bills). Robin Givhan's excellent book *The Battle of Versailles* contextualizes the shift from the Jackie Kennedy suit to the anything goes disco style of the late 1960s and early '70s, as well as the social and cultural eco-system that fed fashion and shaped the mood of the times.

Speaking of Versailles...there was a battle at Versailles between the French and Americans for fashion supremacy in November 1973. One female was chosen out of ten designers: Anne Klein. It's my biggest regret that I had to cast Anne aside—as is so often done to women—to make room for Astrid.

Like Anne Klein, Astrid revolutionizes fashion for "working women," introducing the concept of separates, and the idea of mixing and matching pieces of clothing. Anne Klein was looked down on by the (male) fashion establishment because her customers wore her clothes to work. She made a lot of money—was arguably more suc-cessful than her peers, in fact—but garnered little praise from those peers. Her treatment at Versailles by the male designers was nothing short of execrable, according to Robin Givhan, who recounts, "None of the other designers—not the French, not the Americans—wanted her there. Their scorn for her was obvious. She was shunted aside.... She was belittled. She was forced into a workspace in the basement..."

Donna Karan, Klein's assistant, supports this, saying, "They did not like Anne. She knew the others were totally against her. It was horrible." And one of the models said, "People thought they could push her around and walk all over her."

Was it because she was the only woman? Was it because her sports-wear, her clothes for "working women," were seen as couture's lowly tenth cousin, thrice removed?

Eventually the atmosphere at Versailles, where there was no heating, no toilet paper, no water, and too many male egos trapped in one small space (Givhan says that Oscar de la Renta really did change the show order to put himself in the coveted final place) erupted. The target of that eruption was Anne Klein. Givhan describes "a major screaming shout-down" by Halston that was "so vicious that Kay Thompson quit," as did Halston, screaming "Halston is leaving" (he did refer to himself in the third person). Halston threatened Enid Nemy of the *New York Times* that she'd never be invited to his shows if she reported his behavior. As in my book, Nemy's response was classic. Her 1973 *New York Times* article "Fashion at Versailles: French Were Good, Americans Were Great" was also an important source for my book.

Blass, in his memoir, also says that at Versailles, Halston "behaved like a monster," and that although they'd won, "it was impossible to feel completely proud of it" because "we were so terrible to one another." He also comments that Anne Klein had "no talent." Apparently she fired Blass when he was just starting out.

When writing about what happens to Astrid at the show, I took this history of "tears, screaming matches and backbiting" as Givhan relates it and imagined what it might do to a woman already bullied and hounded to her very edge.

In spite of all of that, the Americans won the night. You'd think that would go down in history. But it's surprising how little is known about the event, how few photographs exist. Perhaps the atmosphere was so sullied that, afterward, people only wanted to forget. For more on this event, make sure you watch the 2016 documentary *Battle at Versailles*.

To include Astrid and Hawk in the numbers at Versailles, I invented the fact that Paco Rabanne was added to the French team. He was not. Clare Hunter's book *Threads of Life* gave me the statistics about the number of men, etc., in the *Bayeux Tapestry*.

Moving into the present—Blythe and Candace present some shocking statistics about gender bias in fashion, and gender bias in equity funding for women-led businesses. Most of the workers and the consumers in the fashion industry are women. But the men rule. If you want to know more about this, there are dozens of articles including *Vogue's* 2021 "Fashion has a gender problem, so what can we do about it?" and the *Business of Fashion*'s "Fashion Is Marketing Feminism, But Its Progress to Gender Equality Is Slow."

Blythe's first collection riffs off the Théâtre de la Mode, that show of miniature mannequins, gowns and jewels—they even wore tiny knickers!—designed to revive Paris couture postwar. It really happened, opening on March 28, 1945.

Back to Mizza. She's a true mystery—as many names as she has histories. She was born Germaine Louise Neustadt in 1900. Her father died when she was young, her mother remarried and Mizza was sent to a convent school. She told Lady Jane Abdy, who wrote her obituary in *Harpers & Queen,* that she married a Russian prince, a Romanian and a Frenchman. The records at the Paris Archives show a marriage to Romanian Alexandre Bianu in 1923, and a marriage to Hubert Henri Bricard in 1941. No Russian.

But that detail recurs in a naggingly truthful way in other sources, such as Cecil Beaton's pen portrait of Mizza, kept in the archives at St. John's College, Cambridge. It wasn't until I stumbled across a letter from Diana Vreeland in the archives at the Metropolitan Museum of Art that I decided to flesh out that part of Mizza's history. Vreeland writes to *New Yorker* fashion writer Kennedy Fraser that she knew Mizza Bricard when she worked with Molyneux, and that Mizza told her she lived in the house of Ida Rubenstein for eleven years. Rubenstein was a Russian ballerina who lived in France for much of her life. Did Mizza live with her for eleven years? It's a remarkably specific detail. If making it up, why not choose a round number—ten years, or five?

So I decided to let Mizza be brought up by Ida Rubenstein, thus providing her with a way of meeting her Russian prince, who—if he did exist—she clearly loved dearly, as she was still talking about him decades later. As there are no official records of a marriage, I've written about an intense love affair that felt like a marriage. It's not such a great leap to imagine this happening, or to imagine this is how she began to acquire her astonishing collection of jewelry (which was partly furnished by Jeanne Toussaint from Cartier, rather than Mizza's supposed lovers). Russian exiles often brought their family jewels with them when they fled to Paris. Mizza also had a scar on her wrist that she covered with a scarf, usually in leopard print, tied around it like a bracelet. The rumors about how she got the scar are as elaborate as all the other stories told about her. I have imagined a different origin for the scar. My inventions in the book have grown out of what's on the record, asking the question *What is possible?*

Mizza was photographed by all the famous fashion photographers. The Dahl-Wolfe image of Mizza wearing a fur coat pulled low in the front, strands of pearls around her neck, leaning provocatively forward, gets the most airplay because it supports the legend of Mizza Bricard. Maybe part of the fuss is because she dared to have such a sexy picture taken when she was fifty-five years old—aren't women supposed to be shriveled up and asexual by then?! It reminds me of the controversy surrounding Nicole Kidman's photograph on the cover of *Vanity Fair* in 2022.

Mizza did work as a designer at the Houses of Mirande, Molyneux, Balenciaga and at Dior. She did travel by herself to New York in 1924 representing a Paris-based fashion company. I have the passenger records. I also have articles published in the late 1920s and early 1930s about Madame Biano, designer at the House of Mirande, whose clothes the Queen of Spain wore. Pierre Balmain's autobiography, *My Years and Seasons*, describes designer Madame B, as he calls her, working at Molyneux. Balmain seems to be utterly mesmerized by her, saying, "She intimidated, but also fascinated me. I could see her playing the role of a central European spy." It's an idea that's repeated by others, notably Justine Picardie in her book *Miss Dior*, where she says, "Balmain was not alone in speculating that Mizza could have been a spy…"

What's an author to do with an idea like that? Especially when you couple it with other facts. Many of Mizza's dear friends were connected to the Resistance, including John Cavanagh and FFE Yeo-Thomas (Tommy), with whom she worked at Molyneux. She lived in the same building as the commander for all the resistance troops in her arrondissement. Her closest friend, Jeanne Toussaint, protested her feelings about the Nazis in her jewelry and was arrested for it. Mizza's letters show she made hats for Martine de Courcel, who was married to Charles de Gaulle's right-hand man. Mizza's ex-husband Alexandre Bianu liaised with SOE, the British intelligence organization. Christian Dior's sister Catherine nearly lost her life for her work with the Resistance. I have absolutely no evidence that Mizza worked with the Resistance—I have made up that part of the story based on her having so many connections to wartime resistance fighters.

Mizza and Christian Dior's friendship has always puzzled me in terms of its origins. They were extremely close. Dior calls Mizza his dear friend in his memoirs. Justine Picardie notes that Dior never referred to Mizza as a muse, but always as his assistant. Natasha Fraser-Cavassoni in her book *Monsieur Dior: Once Upon a Time* says that Dior and Mizza met through mutual artistic friends at the Hôtel Nollet. Lourdes Font, professor in the Fashion and Textile Studies Department at the renowned FIT in New York, says that Mizza and Dior probably met at Molyneux. I've extrapolated from Font's explanation, as her article "Dior Before Dior" is well-researched and includes much detail from people who met Mizza.

I knew Dior's brother Bernard was incarcerated (but not at Sainte-Anne)—in what was then referred to as an asylum—for mental health issues. So I created a deeper link between Dior and Mizza to explain their abiding friendship—they shared the bond of caring for someone society had cast off. This also allowed me to let Mizza be a kind of spy, helping Jewish children escape Paris. Again, this is based on what is possible, not fact. In an article entitled "The fate of Jews hospitalized in mental hospitals in France during World War II," authors Yoram Mouchenik and Véronique Fau-Vincenti discuss records from Sainte-Anne that indicate after each round-up of Jewish people by the Nazis, several children were admitted to Sainte-Anne. They suggest the children were taken to the hospital for protection after losing their parents. I coupled this with the extraordinary map created by Sainte-Anne neurosurgeon Jean Talairach of the ossuaries beneath Paris.

According to Pierre Bourdillon, Marc Lévêque and Caroline Apra in their article "Second World War: Paris neurosurgeon's map outwitted Nazis," Talairach stumbled upon a secret entrance to the underground tunnels while working at Sainte-Anne in 1938. He and a colleague mapped the network of tunnels, delivering a detailed map to French Resistance commander Colonel Henri Rol-Tanguy, who used it to establish the underground headquarters from where he coordinated the Battle for Paris in late August 1944. There are stories about people using the tunnels to escape or hide in during the war, none well-documented, but I conjoined facts with my imagination to create a secret mission for Mizza.

What she really did during the war is a complete unknown. It is absolutely undocumented, besides brief mentions of her working at Balenciaga. Based on everything I've researched over many years about what Frenchwomen don't speak about from their time during the war, I think it's as plausible to suggest that Mizza may have worked unselfishly helping others as it is for everyone else to call her a vulgar whore.

As Mizza discovers, the repercussions for women after the war were catastrophic. I've written about *les femmes tondues*, the women stripped and shamed and paraded, in a few of my books. As Hanna Diamond explains in *Women and the Second World War in France, 1939–1948,* "Young men, often last minute additions to the ranks of the Resistance… wandered around towns… brandishing rifles, anxious to find victims to help prove their allegiance to the cause of the Resistance." According to Diamond, the collective shame and anger was often directed at women who had little contact with the Germans, and that "women who were well dressed… were easy targets… Jealousies and rivalries played an important part." Needless to say, men's heads were not shaved and many commentators make the diabolical point that, without the shaving of women's heads, many more would have died as the crowds' hunger for a way to ease their collective guilt was not easily satisfied. All it took was a whisper, and reputations were ruined forever.

It's clear that someone, at some time, decided to ruin Mizza's. It's hard to say exactly when that happened or why it happened. But take this description of Mizza from famous mannequin Praline, who says in her 1951 memoir, *"Dior est protégé de Dieu. Des déesses aussi. C'en est une que cette exquise Madame Bricard, au teint pâle et yeux verts, femme du monde s'il en est (connue par moi chez Lelong où elle était révérée cliente) qui s'intéresse tant à la firme qu'elle sert…"* Roughly translated, this means, "Dior is protected by God. Goddesses too. One such is the exquisite Madame Bricard, with a pale complexion and green eyes, a woman of the world if there ever was one (known to me at Lelong where she was a revered client) who is absorbed in the business she serves [the House of Dior]."

Revered and a *goddess.* I don't think anyone has to look too far to think of a woman who's been remolded by the media, by gossip, and by spite into something less than she actually was. It's been happening for centuries, and it happens still. I hope historical novelists in one hundred years' time aren't still writing notes like this.

READING GROUP GUIDE

BOOK CLUB QUESTIONS

1. The book is narrated from four different points of view: Astrid, Blythe, Mizza, and Hawk. Which of the three women did you prefer and why? Was it because you could relate to their predicament or because you enjoyed the era in which their story was set, or was there some other reason?

2. Why do you think the author included Hawk's point of view? How would the story have been different if his point of view wasn't included? Did you forgive him for what he did to Astrid? And did you forgive Astrid for what she did to herself and to others? Do you think there's any truth to the idea that we tend to forgive male characters more readily than female characters?

3. Had you heard of Mizza Bricard before you began reading the book? Why do you think women such as Mizza, Camille Claudel, Dora Maar, and others who worked alongside male creators have been cast in the role of muse rather than given their rightful due as artists in their own right? Do you think this is changing in contemporary times or not?

4. The author hopes that the story will make us all think twice about what headlines we click on in the media. In clicking on headlines that diminish women or distort their narratives, we're telling the media that we want more of those stories. What are your thoughts on this? Are you willing to reconsider the types of articles you

consume in the media? Do you believe that doing so will make any difference?

5. Which character did you dislike the most? Why?

6. What did you think of the author's decision to invent a daughter and granddaughter for Mizza Bricard? Should authors play with the truth in historical novels or stick to the facts?

7. What did you think of 1970s fashion before you read the book? Did your opinion and ideas change after finishing it? What other aspects of the 1970s storyline did you enjoy reading about? If you could have attended the Battle of Versailles, what would you have worn?

8. Were you surprised to learn that the fashion industry is so heavily dominated by men? How can we, as consumers of fashion, change that?

COURTESAN AND MUSE, OR A GREATER DESIGNER THAN COCO CHANEL?

BY NATASHA LESTER

This is the story of a research journey that led me around the world, a story of paying attention to the smallest clues, of finding a trail of evidence that's somehow been ignored by almost every person who's ever written Christian Dior's so-called muse Mizza Bricard into a book or an article. Or perhaps the evidence wasn't ignored—perhaps those writers didn't bother to look for it. After all, the story of the male creative and his female muse is so well-known that it seems to have been accepted as truth in this case, and thus another female artist has had her genius stolen and given to the man whose name hangs on the awning outside the shop. Let's take a look at the tragedy of what history has done to Mizza Bricard.

Let's start with some quotes from nonfiction books about Christian Dior that include a few paragraphs about Mizza Bricard to titillate the reader. From Marie-France Pochna's oft-quoted 2008 biography of Dior: "She never wore briefs and was only ever found in one of three places—at home, at the Ritz, or at Dior. It was said that she had once performed in a nude revue…she was feminine seduction incarnate."

Now let's turn to John Galliano and what he said about Mizza Bricard when he launched his Mizza-inspired collection for Dior: "Have you gotten to the bit where Mr. Dior says she never wore any knickers? She was the last of the demi-horizontale. She was fabulous!"

And on to an earlier book about Dior, one written before the deluge that has been published over the past five years or so: "Mizza had once been a demimondaine—that is, an expensive prostitute…She was his muse" (Nigel Cawthorne, *The New Look: The Dior Revolution* [Wellfleet Press, 1996]).

I could list dozens more similar quotes. Needless to say, all these writers go on to declare, unequivocally, that Mizza was Christian Dior's muse. I want to reiterate that these quotes come from nonfiction sources, so they're meant to be true. Based on that, you'd be forgiven for thinking Mizza was a panty-less whore who existed only to stimulate Monsieur Dior to design beautiful dresses. That's certainly what I believed when I began researching her a few years ago. What made me change my mind?

The Lily of the Valley Clue

When I started writing *The Disappearance of Astrid Bricard*, I didn't intend to write a raging alternative portrayal of Mizza. I wanted to look into the female muse / male creator story and pull it apart a bit.

But then I stumbled across this line in an article by Lourdes Font, a professor in the Fashion and Textiles Studies department at New York's renowned FIT. She describes how Dior met Mizza, or Mitzah, as it's often Anglicized: "At Molyneux's couture house, located in the rue Royale steps away from Dior's apartment, he probably first made the acquaintance of Mitzah Bricard... She decorated the couturier's [Molyneux's] spring 1938 collection with one of his favorite flowers— the lily of the valley—placing 'knots of them on every other dress' and on the simple hats..."

It's a seemingly unimportant piece of information, except that lily of the valley is one of the House of Dior's "codes"—motifs that appear in most collections every year. Everyone says Dior began using it in his designs because he grew up surrounded by flowers in the garden of his family home in Granville. But here's a renowned fashion professor saying that Mizza Bricard was using lily of the valley back in 1938 at Molyneux, nine years before the House of Dior even existed.

Coincidence?

I didn't think so. Add to that the fact that most of the nonfiction books and articles I've referred to above never even mention that Mizza worked at Molyneux prior to Dior, and I knew I had to find out more. What was Mizza doing at Molyneux? Was she his muse too? Or something more?

The first thing I did was look at photographs of the hats at Molyneux's spring 1938 collection. And yes, they're adorned with lilies of the valley. So it seemed that the professor's assertion was at least partly true. Then I began wondering—did lily of the valley become a House of Dior code because Christian grew up surrounded by flowers or because Mizza Bricard introduced it to him as a design idea? Was Mizza's role at Dior bigger than we'd been led to believe?

To Know Someone, You Need to Know Their Names

Thus began a research journey that took me to archives across the world, into obscure corners of the internet, and on a thrilling quest to prove that Mizza Bricard was so much more than what history had allowed her to be. My first port of call was the Paris archives. If you want to find out about someone, you need to know the names they used in their lifetime. A couple of books and articles conjectured that Mizza's real name was Germaine Louise Neustadt and that she was born in Paris in 1900. So I tracked down her birth certificate.

The great thing about French birth certificates from that era is that every time a person had a civil event in their life, it was recorded on the birth certificate. Any marriage or divorce was handwritten onto the original birth certificate. On Mizza's, there's a record of a 1923 marriage to a Romanian man named Alexandra Bianu, which gave her the surname Biano. There's also a record of a 1942 marriage to Hubert Henri Bricard. The other thing I knew from researching French women in the past was that they didn't always use their first name. So I'd need to look into Madame Biano and Madame Bricard, as well as Mizza Bricard and Germaine Biano.

A New York Adventure

The next place I headed was Ancestry.com. Lots of people use the site for family tree research, but it's also a historical novelist's friend. Because, once again, it contains the records of people's lives. Census records will give you the address where a person lived; shipping records will tell you where they traveled.

The first thing I found that made me sit up and pay attention was a shipping record from 1924 that showed Mizza (or Germaine Biano) had, at just twenty-four years of age, traveled from Paris to New York. Back in 1924, most twenty-four-year-old women rarely left the village they were born in, let alone voyaged across the world to another country. What was she doing in New York?

Luckily, the shipping manifests also record the address of where the traveler plans to spend most of their time. Mizza stated that she would be at the Harry Angelo Company on Fifth Avenue in New York City. So the next thing I did was investigate exactly what the Harry Angelo Company was.

In the 1920s, French couturiers hadn't yet set up boutiques in Manhattan. Instead, they sent their most trusted representative from Paris to New York once or twice a year to show the large garment manufacturers their designs. These garment manufacturers in New York would then purchase the right to make those designs for their American customers. Harry Angelo was one of those garment manufacturers.

It seems to me that the only possible explanation for why Mizza was traveling as a twenty-four-year-old woman from Paris to New York to spend time at the Harry Angelo Company was because she was the trusted representative of a French couturier, given the job of showing designs to Harry Angelo. That's a pretty big responsibility. You don't send a knickerless demimondaine to do something like that, do you? You send someone who's intelligent, who knows the designs well, who's persuasive enough to be able to convince Harry Angelo to purchase those designs. You send a woman who is nothing like the description of Mizza that's been recorded in all those quotes I started this article with.

This led me down another research rabbit hole. Which couturier was Mizza working for in the 1920s? How did she get from there to Molyneux in the 1930s? What exactly was her role in these couture houses?

European Spy, Cocotte, or Just an Excellent Designer?

I spent a lot more time inputting various combinations of Mizza's names into different newspaper and magazine databases. The *Vogue* database. The Newspapers.com database. And what I found was that Mizza began working for Paris couturier Doucet sometime in the early 1920s. From there, she moved to a Doucet-owned brand named Mirande, where, according to a 1930 *Vogue* article, she designed "a great many models." (Remember that in this era "model" is the word for a design, whereas "mannequin" is the word for the woman who shows or parades the design.) But the key word here is that she *designs*. No mention of muse-dom. She was someone who did the creative work.

Then, around 1933, Mizza left Mirande and went to Molyneux. Pierre Balmain, who began his career as an assistant designer at Molyneux, confirms this in his autobiography *My Years and Seasons*. He refers to Mizza as Madame B, and he seems equal parts fascinated by and frightened of her, taking pains to describe the diamond star brooches she wore (stars are another House of Dior code!) and the scarf she tied around her wrist to cover a scar that he conjectured was from vitriol burns.

This seems to be from where another story about Mizza grew—that one of her lovers' wives threw acid on Mizza in a jealous rage. But let's look at another tale of Mizza's supposed retinue of lovers. Nonfiction writers claim that her magnificent jewelry collection was furnished by her lovers. But on Mizza's birth certificate, it says that the witness at her 1942 wedding was Jeanne Toussaint. Jeanne was Cartier's jewelry designer. I found much more evidence to suggest that Mizza's jewels were provided by her good friend Jeanne (and perhaps from a White Russian prince she fell in love with in around 1917–1818) than that they were payoffs from lovers for services rendered. But of course the latter makes a much better headline, doesn't it?

Balmain also makes the throwaway claim that he could see Mizza "playing the role of a central European spy, or as one of the cocottes who revolutionized Maxim's in 1900." Unfortunately, it seems later writers took the second part of this offhand and fantastical remark and turned it into solid fact. But it's interesting to look at Balmain's motivations here. He admits to being envious of Mizza's ability to speak fluent English to the Briton Molyneux and his two English deputies (Mizza spoke at least four languages) and of how she "electrified the atmosphere of the studio," and he was also jealous of the fact that Molyneux generally picked many more of Mizza's designs to be a part of each collection than he chose of Balmain's designs.

Yes, that's right—Mizza was designing for Molyneux. It was common practice in those days for the man whose name hung on the awning outside the boutique to employ assistant designers who would create designs that the couturier would then use in his collection. The assistant designers were never named, hardly acknowledged, but always an integral part of each collection, as Mizza was at Molyneux.

So far, we've gathered evidence that Mizza was a fashion designer, with a definite je ne sais quoi when it came to enlivening the couture houses she worked at. No evidence that she couldn't keep her panties on. What about after Molyneux left France when the Germans moved in?

One of Balenciaga's Closest Friends

Mizza worked at Balenciaga during the war. It's unclear how long she was there, and it's also unclear what else she did between 1940 and 1944, although I have a few theories based on the number of résistant friends she had. What is clear is that she was one of Balenciaga's very good friends. In her letters to fashion photographer Cecil Beaton and Princess Marthe Bibesco, which I discovered in two different archives, one in Cambridge in the UK and the other in Austin, Texas, she talks about spending much time in Balenciaga's home in Spain. She vacationed with the great couturier. And in 1968, *Paris Match* photographed Balenciaga at his home in what is one of the very last photo shoots before he died. He chose four friends to be in that photo shoot. One of those friends was Mizza Bricard.

Balenciaga is arguably one of the greatest couturiers of all time. It seems unlikely that he'd choose a knickerless whore to share his final photo shoot for *Paris Match*. Isn't it much more likely that he'd choose his most intimate friends, people whose minds and talents he also admired?

How Dare They?

Let's take a look at those letters to Cecil Beaton I mentioned above. Beaton is one of the most renowned fashion photographers of the 1930s–1950s. He had a long correspondence with Mizza, and he kept all her letters. With those letters, Cecil also kept what he called a pen portrait of Mizza. He used to write descriptions of famous and interesting people, and he published some of these in a book called *The Glass of Fashion*.

As I read through Cecil's portrait of Mizza, I once again found a very different woman. I could quote many paragraphs as evidence of the grave injustice done to Mizza, but I'll settle for this:

> There are in the world of fashion those whose names have become almost household words merely through the good offices of their Personal Relations Officer. There are others who remain unsung, yet who are held in the highest respect by the brightest talents: Mizza Bricard is such a one... The greatest dressmakers know her worth... the great Balenciaga himself, as well as everyone in Paris who knows fashion, concedes that there are few women who are as knowledgeable on the subject as she.

And let's back up that assertion with a statement made by Lady Jane Abdy in the obituary she wrote for Mizza, which was published in *Harper's and Queen* in 1978:

> In her modesty she submerged herself in the shadows of these great names, and never sought any personal recognition, though many considered her to be a greater designer than Coco Chanel.

A greater designer than Coco Chanel? That's almost like anointing Mizza as the most talented fashion designer who's ever lived.

You can see why I was raging when I wrote *The Disappearance of Astrid Bricard*. How dare the people who wrote history steal so much from her?

The Legendary Mizza

The last piece of evidence I'm going to present in my case that Mizza was a couturier in her own right, although she didn't own a boutique or a fashion brand, is an article published in the *Sydney Morning Herald* in 1950 titled "Dior's Assistant: A Woman of Chic." Among other things, it says:

> On the opening day of a new collection at the Maison Christian Dior, you will find, seated at the back of the main salon, a charming, ultra-smart, brown-haired woman in her early forties, whose keen green eyes are focused on every detail of the passing models . . . She is, in fact, a most important person on the Dior staff, second only to the great man himself, for she is Madame Germaine Biano-Bricard, *first assistant designer* to Christian Dior. She works with him in the creation of every model. (emphasis mine)

So there it is, in black and white. Mizza was not just a muse. Yet, somehow, Mizza has been demoted from her true role as Dior's first assistant designer to an expensive prostitute.

A Gown with the Name Christian Dior Stamped in the Back

It's interesting how, once you know the facts, you can look back over everything else that's been written and see it in a new light. Let's return to that quote from John Galliano that I presented at the start.

When he says, "Have you gotten to the bit where Mr. Dior says she never wore any knickers?," Galliano is referring to Dior's memoirs. Dior published two; I have copies of both. Once I had this new version of Mizza my head, I realized I couldn't recall ever seeing in one of Dior's memoirs any paragraph that referred to Mizza not wearing knickers. So I went back through both books to see if there was any mention of Mizza undressing herself or being unclothed in any way. This is the paragraph I found:

Madame Bricard comes in dressed in her work smock, jewelry, hat, and a little veil. She looks over the dress I am working on. She likes it or doesn't. She undresses, puts it on herself, twists the sleeves, puts the front at the back, drapes the skirt into a pouf and opens the neckline. The effect is divine. A touch of fur trim and I have another dress.

What is this paragraph actually describing? It's describing the process of Mizza Bricard designing a Dior gown. It's describing her taking apart something that Christian Dior designed and then making it better. Making it new. Making it something that Dior would then show in his latest collection with the name Christian Dior stamped in the back of it.

Doesn't It Make You Mad?

There should have been two names hanging over the awning outside that first Dior store. The brand should have been called Christian Dior and Mizza Bricard. In every book and article written about Dior since he became one of the most famous couturiers in the world, there should be at least a chapter on first assistant designer Mizza Bricard, who contributed so much to Dior's success and to the couture house's enduring success. But there isn't. Doesn't it make you mad?

As I said in the author's note at the end of *The Disappearance of Astrid Bricard*:

> I don't think anyone has to look too far to think of a woman who's been remolded by the media, by gossip, and by spite into something less than she actually was. It's been happening for centuries, and it happens still. I hope historical novelists in one hundred years' time aren't still writing notes like this.

But unfortunately, common sense and history tell me they probably will be.

ABOUT THE AUTHOR

Natasha Lester is the *New York Times* bestselling author of *The Three Lives of Alix St. Pierre*, *The Paris Seamstress*, *The Paris Orphan*, *The Paris Secret*, and *The Riviera House*, and a former marketing executive for L'Oréal. When she's not writing, she loves collecting vintage fashion (Dior is a favorite), practicing the art of fashion illustration, learning about fashion history, and traveling to Paris. Natasha lives with her husband and three children in Perth, Western Australia.

You can learn more at:
NatashaLester.com.au
Facebook.com/NatashaLesterAuthor
Instagram @NatashaLesterAuthor

GRAND CENTRAL

Your next great read is only a click away.

 GrandCentralPublishing.com

 Read-Forever.com

 TwelveBooks.com

 LegacyLitBooks.com

 GCP-Balance.com

A BOOK FOR EVERY READER.